Folks Called Her Sadie

By

Barbara Neveau

Barbara Neveau
12/24/07

PublishAmerica
Baltimore

First printing

ISBN: 1-4137-3171-6
PUBLISHED BY PUBLISHAMERICA, LLLP
www.publishamerica.com
Baltimore

Printed in the United States of America

*When you are a parent you
are never again a single entity.
Your children and grandchildren
are extensions to your life.
This book is dedicated to my
wonderful, loving,
extensions.*

Table of Contents

Folks Called Her Sadie

Chapter One
The Betrayal

The sobbing child stamped her bare foot on the cold wooden floor and whispered to the silent, nearly empty room, "I'm not a harlot!"

Smells of bread toasting on the hot stove had drifted up and waken Sadie; the heavenly aroma of cornmeal mush filled her nostrils. Her ravenous appetite had forced her from her bed. Mama always made a delicious breakfast. Peeling off the cotton nightdress from her shivering body, she wished that the horrible episode of last night was simply a dream, but it wasn't.

With tear filled eyes she glanced around her bedroom, drinking in every detail, from the block quilt Momma pieced together from scraps, to the three-legged stool Papa made just for her when it was still fun to help milk the cows.

A cold dread crept through her body and settled in her gut as she remembered the previous night. She replayed that awful scene in her head, the horror of Papa catching her and Thomas down by the creek making love. Her cheeks flushed with embarrassment even though there was no one to see. How could she have been such a fool? What seemed so right at the time now seemed foolish and tawdry!

The stillness of the crisp fall night had been shattered by shouts of rage, Papa's vow to kill Thomas if he ever caught him near his daughter again.

Thomas' arrogant laugh had infuriated her father. She could still hear Papa yelling, "Get off of my land, you little bastard," as she gathered up her undies and her skirts and ran toward the house. Thomas taunted Papa by spitting over his shoulder, "Your not hurting me old man, they're plenty of other farmers looking for help and I'm a good enough hand to find work anyplace in the Saginaw Valley."

The girl never felt so alone. Why hadn't Thomas defended her? She had heard him say, "I'll go anywhere I please, old man," but, he hadn't said,

"And I'm taking Sadie with me." Her father's angry words had echoed off the barn as he had shouted, "As for you Sadie, you think you're the only one that he's been sniffing 'round. Well, you ain't! He's got two other bitches with bellies full over Saginaw way and him already married. You and your highfluuting ways, yer nothing but a trollop." His voice trembling in rage, he shouted, "You carry the, 'Mark of Cain' and everybody will see it. You can get the hell out of my house, you little trollop. You probably got a belly full too and I ain't raising no bastards. Pack up and leave tonight! I never want to see you again!"

Racing up the stairs, Sadie had flung her shaking body on her bed. "What have I done? Does Papa hate me now? Have I been so bad that he can't love me anymore?" Questioned the sobbing child.

She could hear Momma pleading with Father hoping to soothe his hardheaded German temper.

"Please Gerhardt, the child is only fourteen. She made a foolish mistake, but you can't punish her by throwing her out."

"Like hell I can't! I won't have a fallen women in my house."

After much persuasion, Sadie heard Papa say, "Let the baggage stay till morning and then out she goes!"

Thank God Mama finally convinced him to let her stay the night, what will I do if he doesn't change his mind?

When the house was still and her husband was fast asleep, Sadie's mother crept into Sadie's room with a small pitcher and basin. Motioning for the child to lie down and spread her legs, she then proceeded to flush the girl's inner parts with a fluid that burned as it went into her womanliness. The horror of what she had permitted Thomas to do to her shook Sadie's very soul.

"Mama, is there something wrong with me, why didn't I refuse Thomas? Am I as bad as Papa say's I am?"

"No child, you're not bad, just foolish," answered the heartbroken mother.

The enormity of their misdeed had finally hit home and Sadie realized what damage would be done to her reputation.

"Oh dear God, Mama, what will my dear friend Phoebe say if she hears the scandal? I just know she will understand. She will remain loyal to our friendship I know she will!"

They had giggled often enough when the gossip was about someone else, now it was about her.

"My foolish child, If Phoebe doesn't already know, she would most certainly hear it from the ladies at the next church meeting. That kind of news always leaks out."

Shame and fear tormented Sadie most of the night. She was surprised she had slept at all.

Her fear was so great she didn't feel the chill of the frigid room. She longed to climb back into the rumpled bed, cover her head and make this disgrace go away forever.

As she dressed, the mirror reflected the image of a lovely young woman, tall and slim like her father, but with her mother's large gray eyes. Her long dark hair covered the white collar, frayed from years of laundering.

The scuffed black work shoes she always wore did nothing to improve her self-image. Brushing her hair and noticing the dark circles under her eyes, she prayed that they would draw some sympathy. Wiping the dust from the top of the mirror, she added it to the dark smudges beneath her eyes. With one last look in the mirror to see if her face reflected the humiliation she was suffering and with terror in her heart, she slowly dragged herself down to the kitchen below.

Sadie and her brother, David, had always raced each other to the breakfast table. She usually let him win, for after all he was only ten and just a child. Breakfast was their favorite time of the day. Mama loved singing hymns in the warm, cozy kitchen and took pleasure in the playful interchange between brother and sister with Mama finally saying, "You younguns behave."

This morning Mama wasn't singing. It was too quiet.

Poor little David. I wonder if he heard what was said last night. I hope not. He is awfully young to hear the names Father called me.

David was sitting at the wooden table pretending to eat, but Sadie could tell by his hunched shoulders and bowed head that he wished to be anywhere else but here.

The pot-bellied stove in the corner was throwing enough heat to warm the kitchen and the small room leading to the back yard. The family always hung their work coats on pegs behind the back door. The boots were placed on the rug below, so's not to get Mama's spotless floor dirty.

Sadie saw all the room as if seeing it for the first time. The feeling of impending doom frightened her. As she stood at the bottom of the stairs absorbing all this, she heard her father's footsteps coming in from the milking. Going quickly to the table, she slid onto the bench next to David and sat with head bowed.

Oh God, she thought, *maybe if I pray really hard a miracle will happen.*

13

The strange look on her father's face gave Sadie some hope. She had never seen him look so close to tears, maybe now was the time to beg his forgiveness.

She pushed away from the table and ran to him. Kneeling at his feet and clasping his legs, she pleaded, "Papa, please forgive me, I'll be good, I'll never do that again, I promise." Sobs stealing her breath, she cried out "Please, Please let me stay! I love you, I love my family, if you make me leave, I'll have nowhere to go, I'll be all alone."

When she looked up and saw her father's tight colorless lips and his black eyes hardened with disgust, she knew that no amount of begging or pleading would change his mind. Gerhardt Schmitt never changed his mind. She was doomed!

He grabbed her arm, pulled her to her feet, jerked her up the stairs to her bedroom and pointed to the floor. There lay two empty grain sacks. She knew immediately why they were there. Why hadn't she noticed the bags earlier? She picked them up and began the task of packing her belongings as neatly as possible in the clean white sacks. She was lucky that her father let her take her clothes. He could have made her leave last night with just the clothes on her back, and not be blamed at all by. Friends, neighbors, and relatives would surely agree with Papa's treatment of her for being a shameless hussy.

As Sadie packed, she wondered what would happen to Thomas. Would father go and kill him for what had taken place? He had let him go last night, but he was even angrier this morning.

What if he did change his mind and went hunting for Thomas; then everyone would know what they had done.

When she finished the heart-rending task of putting her life into two small bags, and placing her favorite hairbrush in last, she closed the bag on her innocence. Taking her best cloak, and pulling it over her everyday dress, she was as ready as she ever would be to leave the security of her birthplace.

"All my dreams are shattered because of one foolish mistake," she lamented.

With downcast eyes and dragging feet, she came down the stairs and headed toward the kitchen. She wanted to say good-bye to her mother and to a shame faced David, who had returned to the kitchen in her absence, and was kicking the leg of the scarred wooden table.

As she entered the room, all talk stopped and the silence was a condemnation. She knew at that moment that there was no use in going on with her farewells as they no longer considered her part of the family. She was as good as dead to them!

Sadie frantically searched her mind. Where would she go? What would she do? She knew nothing of the outside world.

At the front door she paused for a moment hoping that someone would come from the kitchen and tell her it was all right, all was forgiven.

No one came.

She went through the open door and into a totally different world.

The path to town was rough, muddy, and filled with twisted tree roots. The beauty of the trees turning from green to gold was lost on the frantic young woman. It was going to be difficult to carry the bags and walk the seven miles, but she had no other choice.

She had walked this path often when visiting her best friend Phobe who lived down the road, but never with such anguish as she felt now.

As she walked, she wondered if that frenzied groping in the barn had been worth all the trouble. If only she had stopped Thomas then, when it first started, instead of pretending that it was wonderful and what she wanted.

It wasn't as if she had even enjoyed it, that final act. It had hurt and she wondered if the other things Thomas said were true. He had promised her that the more they did that, the more she would like it. The shame once more filled her being and she touched her burning face with an ice-cold hand. She had only done it to please Thomas. Besides, he said he loved her and would ask her father for her hand in marriage. How was she to know he was already married and a regular bounder at that?

She remembered hearing her father shout, "That damn fool Thomas has got a wife and two other women in 'The Family Way' over in upper Saginaw County."

Damn Thomas and his lies; she would never have allowed him to touch her at all had she known what a liar he was. *Fool,* she thought, *stop crying and figure out what you're going to do next, where you will sleep and where your next meal will come from.*

Sadie couldn't believe how heavy her bags were getting. She leaned heavily against a tree limb that hung close to the path.

Looking back, she felt the tears fill her eyes and spill down her cheeks. The empty feeling was growing in her heart, flooding it with loneliness and despair.

The only encouragement Sadie had right now was the thought that Phoebe's house was just over the ridge. As she trudged the long empty trail to town, she hoped Phoebe would be able to persuade her father to let Sadie to stay with them until she could make permanent arrangements. Phoebe's parents had always liked her, and she prayed that would work in her favor.

The sound of a buggy coming along the trail caught her attention and for a moment she hoped it would be her father saying all was forgiven. Could it be Father? Her heart beat faster, but as the buggy came into view, her despair came flooding back. She should have known better. Father never changed his mind. Maybe whoever was in the buggy would give her a ride to Phoebe's place. When the buggy pulled along side of her Sadie recognized the driver as Mr. Fredrick Duso, one of the farmers who lived in the valley beyond her father's farm.

"Good Morning, Miss Sadie," he said as he doffed his battered cap in deference to her gender. "Can I give you a ride somewhere or are you just out for a stroll?" As he said this, a malicious grin split his usually friendly face.

Sadie felt a sick feeling start in her chest and slowly drain into her stomach. She replied, "I'm doing just fine, sir."

"You sure, little Miss Prissy? Ain't farmers good enough for you? Can't handle real men, can ya? Need ta get boys ta keep ya happy."

This made Sadie angry and frightened, but she stood her ground.

She blurted, "Go away, old man, I've done you no harm" and waved her hand in the direction of town. She was looking for a good strong stick to thump him with if it came to that.

But he snapped the whip over the plow horse's heads and they jumped as though bitten and headed in the direction of town. As the wagon passed, she heard him mutter, "I will meet up with that persnickety little trollop again. Then I'll give her what she's looking for!"

Sadie had to face the fact that the news of her indiscretion had traveled far and wide thanks to that wretch Thomas. He probably stopped at the saloon on his way out of town and told everyone there why he was leaving. She would be lucky if anyone would have anything to do with her. Curse this double standard that allowed a man to philander at will, yet held the woman responsible for what happened. After all, she was only human. Besides if what happened between her and Thomas is all there is to this sex thing, they could keep it! She muttered under her breath, "I want nothing more to do with it. Dear God, why didn't I know all this before I became involved with Thomas? Although, I must admit he is a handsome devil."

Just looking at him had made her heart skip a beat. Just thinking of him right now made her stomach feel all mushy and her blood race through her veins like she had run a mile. The perspiration drenched her body like a spring rain, leaving her shaking and hungry for something she had never tasted or even recognized. The vague yearnings tormented her even now, but she must put aside those feelings, for as far as she was concerned all men were liars, bounders, and philanderers, and she no longer trusted any of them.

Sadie's feet hurt, her shoulders ached and she had never been so tired in her whole life. Helping mother with the housework, putting up the preserves, and feeding the chickens didn't prepare a girl to work this hard.

At last she could see Phoebe's house in the distance. The old weathered gray house looked welcoming to the exhausted young girl. Spotting Phoebe hanging clothes on the line that was strung from the house to the great oak that stood in the side yard, she waved and shouted a greeting. A gentle breeze was whipping Phoebe's red hair, and teasing the gray cotton dress and white apron she wore.

Sadie waved again as she drew near, but there was no return wave.

Phoebe pinned a faded plaid shirt to the line and tried to ignore her friend's waves and shouts.

Sadie waved one last time, heart pounding violently, running closer to the fence she shouted, "Phobe, may I talk to you and your parents, I'm all alone and need your help."

Phobe shouted back, "We're not allowed to speak to you. Papa says you're a harlot."

Using Phoebe's nickname, Sadie pleaded, "But Phebs, I was sure I could count on you, how could you abandon me like this?" the heart broken Sadie replied. She couldn't believe the friendship that she had shared with Phoebe was over. As she neared the gate, Mrs. Sobzack came to stand at the kitchen door, watching. Her hair was the same color as her daughter's, but it was dull by comparison because of the gray that threaded its way through her twisted bun.

Sadie passed the gate and looked back, Phoebe and her mother were still watching. A few hundred yards around the bend stood Schectors General Store, the first building you saw as you entered Bay City.

"I'll just rest for a minute," she told herself as she sat down on the bench in front of the store. She had no more than laid down her heavy burden, when Mr. Schector came bursting out shouting, "I don't allow tarts to hang around my store. Decent people don't want to rub elbows with loose women!"

The despair came crowding into her very soul as great gulping sobs shook her whole body. She fought hard to contain herself. Shattered, she picked up her bags. They had become burdens to her now, but she would need them later. She dragged both the bags and herself farther down the buggy rutted street to a rotted stump standing between two buildings. Shoulders drooping, head bowed, she knelt and placed her clasped hands on the tree trunk. If God was in his heaven He seemed to be busy elsewhere. Was He too busy to hear the prayers of a frightened young lady in an alley praying for guidance?

Without warning she felt a hand on her shoulder, she flinched and tried to pull away, but a pleasant male voice said, "Don't be afraid, I'm not going to hurt you. It looks like you have been hurt quite enough!"

Looking up at the stranger, she whispered, "Thank you."

He debated walking away from this girl with the wonderful eyes. He changed his mind when he looked into dove gray eyes that were deep enough to drown in. I must find out more about this young lady. I wonder if she is as innocent as she appears.

"Child, what are you doing bag and baggage out on the street?" He watched closely as she explained that her father was upset by her behavior and had thrown her out.

"That doesn't sound like any father I've ever met. There must be more to it then that."

"Well, he did have good reason," Sadie said as she defended her father's action.

"Tell me all about these good reasons he had to abandon his daughter." Gently taking her elbow with his left hand and toting her bags with his other, he steered her toward the Imperal hotel. Her feeble protest stopped as he guided her into the dining room. Choosing a table in the back, away from the staring eyes of the other diners, he waved to the waiter and asked him to bring them some wine.

"I have never had wine before," she told the stranger, "And I don't think I should drink any now. My father never permitted me to drink wine. He said I was too young for strong drink."

The stranger looked at her with surprised amusement, "You mean to tell me your father thinks you are too young to drink wine, but not too young to throw out of the house for one misdeed, and you're still worried about what he thinks?" he questioned.

Now that she had time to think about it, Sadie realized the stranger was right. Papa had thrown her out to the evils of this world without a second chance; well she'd show him!

She leaned forward saying eagerly, "Yes, yes, I would like a glass of wine." When Sadie had finished the glass of wine, they ordered lunch and another bottle of wine. By the time they had finished eating, her eyes had become heavy and her tongue was numb causing her to slur words. She couldn't remember, did he say his name was Harrison or Hiram, oh well, whatever his name was, he promised to get her a room at the hotel for the night, no strings attached. She might be a little woozy, but she was smart enough for that!

He had escorted her to the room, unlocked the door, threw the bags on the settee, planted a kiss on her forehead, told her to lock the door and left. Was everything she had heard from Phoebe wrong? Were there men out there that didn't take advantage of young innocent girls?

"Oops, I forgot, I'm no longer an innocent," she giggled. Maybe it was as her father had said; she did carry the mark of Cain. Well, she was just too tired to worry about her heartless father or thwarting the advances of a stranger. *I'll worry about that tomorrow,* she thought as she bolted the door.

While stumbling around the room getting her clothes off and hanging them up on the peg on the back of the door, she vaguely wondered why What's-His-Name was doing all this. It wasn't as though she didn't need all the help she could get. She staggered to the bed, fell across it, and was instantly asleep.

Sadie opened her eyes to a blazing pain that seared through her skull. Her head was pounding, eyes burning, and her stomach felt as though it were lava burning its way up and out her throat. She swallowed hard to keep from making a mess in the bed. Mama would be very upset if she soiled the bed. Then she remembered where she was, the stranger and the wine she had drunk last night. That would be the last time she would drink wine. She sat up aching in every part of her body. Just a few more minutes, she promised herself as she snuggled back down into the warm comforting cotton sheet. She promptly went back to sleep.

When she awoke again, she heard someone pounding on her door and a voice asking if she planned on sleeping the day away. She jumped up and ran to her dress. She didn't remember hanging it up, but then she didn't remember much of anything about last night. Quickly donning her clothes, she opened the door.

Holding the door half open, she faced the stranger from last night. What was his name? Harrison, Harry, Hiram? How could she find out without hurting his feelings? After all, he certainly has been a great help to her. She saw a smile steal across his face when she said, "Come in, sir. " *Oh, oh, she*

19

was caught; he knew the game she was playing.

"You don't remember my name, do you?" The handsome stranger asked.

"No," she answered and nearly fainted when he burst out laughing.

"I'm not surprised," he mused.

Even though she was embarrassed, she did notice how she felt when she heard his deep rumbling laugh. The unsettled feeling in her stomach the chuckle gave her or was it just from the wine she had drunk?

"First things first. My name is Harrison. Second, I have no designs on you other than to see that you are presentable when I introduce you to someone. She may be able to help you out of this mess in which you found yourself. Now that we understand each other, I will be waiting in the dining room."

What did he mean? It sounded so strange. What had she gotten herself into?

Pulling off her shabby dress and laying it on the bed, she bathed herself with the cool water she had poured into the bowl. When her birdbath was finished, she carefully dressed and combing her long dark hair, she felt almost unsullied. She was anxious to find out what this was all about. Harrison had promised her breakfast, so the questions could wait until after she'd eaten.

Harrison sat at the same table they had shared last night. He stood, held her chair, saying, "My dear I have taken the liberty of ordering for you." *Well,* she thought, *she'd show him.* She wouldn't eat.

How dare he presume to know her so well that he knew what she wanted for breakfast! The heavenly aromas of the food chased away any ideas of not eating. Sadie's mouth was watering from the smell alone.

When she had eaten her fill, she pushed back and stared at Harrison, slowly evaluating what she saw. A handsome man in his mid-twenties well dressed with tan trousers, a chocolate brown waistcoat, a fawn colored vest and a striped cravat to finish his attire. His attitude was a bit arrogant, but not unpleasant. His sandy hair and goatee gave him the look of a country gentleman. She had seen a few boys at the barn dances that were better looking, but he held a fascination for her. He was so worldly. She couldn't let Harrison know how inexperienced she was. He might try to take advantage of the situation, not that he couldn't have done that last night. She felt a wave of self-pity engulf her mind for an instant. She was in a bad situation and there was no one except Harrison to offer aid.

Why was she putting herself in the hands of a stranger? She leaned forward to whisper, "What happens next?"

He smiled. "We visit a friend of mine and see if she agrees with me."

Standing, he held her chair and waited while she gathered her two bags. Harrison reached out, took the bags, and led the way out to the street. As a man brought the carriage; Harrison took her arm and guided her to the part of the porch that was closest to the street, so she could avoid the looks of the townspeople.

The driver helped them into the carriage, and when they were settled, he asked, "Where to Sir?"

"Take us to Madam Kate's House over Saginaw way. Do you know the place?"

Nodding, he answered, "Yes, Sir, I know just where it's at," and with a knowing smile on his craggy face the driver turned the rig around to face the noonday sun. This trip was going to pay for the two days he didn't have any riders. Not many folks wanted to go to Saginaw in the middle of the week. That Madam Kate's whorehouse must be some ritzy titsy place for her pimp to be dressed so fancy. The driver couldn't wait to get back from his trip to inform his cronies at "The Frog Town Inn," how he transported another whore to Madam Kate's house of ill repute, what they said, and how they acted. He was a little disappointed when the woman fell asleep and nothing happened, but he decided he could always come up with some interesting tid bits. Nobody in town would ever know he had made them up.

Sadie tried to remember where she had heard that name before, but the ample breakfast and the hectic night had lulled her into a stupor. Clutching both bags on her lap, protecting what little property she owned, she felt her head nodding. She tried to fight, but it proved too powerful. Shifting the bags to the seat beside her, she allowed her eyes to close for a moment. Lowering her head onto the bags that now served as a pillow, she was soon dozing.

Sadie awoke with a start. She was still in the buggy, but Harrison was nowhere to be seen. She looked all around but didn't recognize the place. Where was Harrison?

Dared she pound on that magnificent door and rouse the ire of the owners or should she wait? She had to know right now! She couldn't just sit here and wonder. She jumped down and proceeded to the front door.

It opened and Harrison stood talking with the most beautiful woman that Sadie had ever seen. She stared opened mouthed at the smiling woman. A gold braided halo of hair, which was wrapped around the woman's head, and wide blue eyes, convinced Sadie that the lady must be an angel.

Harrison laughed softly and introduced Sadie to the women he called

Kate. They shook hands and entered the waiting room. He asked the woman what she thought of his latest acquisition. Kate walked around Sadie looking from top to bottom as Sadie followed her in the circle wondering why she was being judged like a lamb at the fair.

Nodding her head, the woman said, "So far, so good!"

Sadie said nothing.

The house was grand inside as well as out. Sadie couldn't help herself; she gaped at everything from the gigantic pictures on the walls to the velvet swags that hung from every window. As she continued to stare, both Harrison and Kate stared at her as though they were judging an animal they were about to purchase.

Sadie felt their eyes on her and turned to stare back. She straightened her back, lifted her head, and dared them to continue their evaluation. Kate was the first to speak, "If she has as much spirit as she seems to have, she may work out very well. If she decides to stay, she will need a few lessons. Do you think you want to handle that job for me?"

Harrison smiled, "I will be delighted to handle that assignment."

Chapter Two
The invitation

Sadie knew something important had just happened, but she was darned if she knew what!

Kate led her into the parlor, sat her on a red brocade sofa and began to explain exactly what they did in this house, how they entertained the men who visited and what was expected of the ladies who lived there.

"That's disgusting, I can't do that," Sadie burst out, "I'd rather die first!"

The woman was no longer beautiful; her face was a cold mask.

She looked Sadie straight in the eye and said, "You have one week to change your mind or out you go, back on the street where you came from." She stood and left the room.

Sadie found Harrison watching her with amusement. She felt a rage take over her senses. "Why," she screamed, "did you bring me here to this house of ill repute, this den of iniquity? Why, oh, why?"

"You foolish girl," Harrison explained, "my job is to find young ladies down on their luck, who are willing to change their lifestyle. Kate pays me very well to do my job, and it permits me to live like a gentleman with little effort on my part."

Sadie couldn't believe her ears; all the time she thought Harrison was helping her out of the goodness of his heart! Never again would she trust a stranger. First Thomas, then Papa and now Harrison. Dear God, what a fool I've been! Now she thought, *I must find a way out of this mess, should I run, but where would I run to?* Resignation washed over her face, and she surrendered to temptation. *I will, by God I will stay at least for this night maybe tomorrow will bring an answer. That Kate woman said I have a week in which to make up my mind, well that will give me time to find something else. I only have a week to plan.*

Harrison picked up the bags and headed for the stairs, motioning for her to follow. Sadie followed him with some reluctance. She knew she didn't have any choice. He stopped at the third door on the left, pushed it open with his shoulder, entered, and dropped the bags on the bed.

Sadie came into the room just as he was tossing her belongings on the bed. Anger again spewed into her throat and out her mouth before she had time to think. She accused him of tossing her, as well as her belongings, to the dogs. She knew she was being unreasonable. He owed her nothing. She knew she was behaving badly, but she couldn't stop herself.

Harrison stood patiently waiting for Sadie to finish her outburst, and then he told her, "Because we have missed the noon meal I will send someone up with some tea and toast." He turned on his heel and left her to her frustrations. The furious outburst left Sadie contrite and exhausted. Yawning, Sadie lay down on the huge bed waiting for the tea and contemplating her uncertain situation.

She awoke with a start looking wildly around, she saw a pretty young girl entering the room with a tray in her hands and a washcloth and towel slung over her shoulder. She was simply dressed and wore a friendly smile. When she saw that Sadie was awake she said, "Greetings. They told us there was a new girl here, but I didn't expect anyone so young and lovely." She sat the tray on the table near the window and left.

She said I was lovely, Sadie thought. No one has ever said that to me before. She went to the mirror, looked at her reflection, and spoke, "Why, I don't look any different than I always have. These people are crazy or something." Well, she hoped they didn't come to their senses until after she found a place to work. In the meantime she would play along with their little game.

She looked at the tray. There was tea and toast just as Harrison had promised and she was starving. She tore into it. When she had drunk the tea and had eaten two slices of the thickly sliced bread, she suddenly felt eyes watching. Looking up from her feast, she saw Harrison, standing in the doorway, wearing his lazy smile, and watching her.

Well, let him watch, she thought, *I don't care what he thinks.* But suddenly she did care.

"Sadie, I'm not here to hurt or to judge you. I'll help you, but only if you choose. You know what happens here in this house, in these bedrooms, but only by choice. We do not hold these young ladies against their will. They are here because they had nowhere else to go. Their families turned them out just as yours did or they left for reasons only they know. All of them need a place to stay until something else comes along. When you're finished with your food I'll introduce you to some of the young ladies who are working here. I think you will be surprised." With a wave of his hand, Harrison left the doorway and waited at the top of the stairs.

Sadie couldn't swallow another morsel. Closing her door to prying eyes, she went to the mirror and straightened her clothing. "I look like a ragbag, like I slept in my clothes," she muttered. "Just can't let them know how slovenly I feel." She would pretend she was a queen. That had always worked at home. She straightened her shoulders, sucked in her gut, opened the door and went into the hall prepared to meet a house full of tarts and wicked women.

She noticed for the first time the magnificent staircase. The wood shone red against the forest green carpet that graced each step. The paintings that hung on the wall seemed to stare down at her, asking, "What's an urchin like you doing here?"

Harrison took her arm as they descended the stairs. Soon other doors began opening and young ladies of all sizes and shapes emerged and headed for the staircase.

When they reached the bottom, Kate met them and ushered them into a room as large as her father's entire house. Sadie could only stand and stare. The ceiling glowed as though it were painted with gold, and the sidewalls were the palest green with paintings in gold frames hung in every available space.

Kate sat down on one of the many brocade sofas and settees that were placed about the room and asked that the others please be seated.

"Ladies, I would like you to meet Sadie. While she is here, please be kind enough to help if she asks for it, but please do not influence her decision either way. If and when she decides to come to work with us it must be her choice, just as it was with each of you."

"Will each of you stand and give your name and if you wish, you may want to tell us what brought you here. We'll start with you, Maybelle."

A pretty young woman stood and announced, "My name is Maybelle. I was married at fifteen. My husband decided because I had not given him any sons after five years of marriage, that I was a slut and that I was preventing children by witchcraft. He said I enjoyed the act too much. Decent women didn't enjoy it, so I must be a fallen woman. He threw me out in the middle of the night. I was lost until I met Harrison and Kate."

A very young red haired girl stood up next, "My name is Penny," she whispered, "short for Penelope. I come from a family of twelve. My father was killed in a logging accident. My brothers tried to feed and keep the family together, but it soon got too much for them and they are so very young to be saddled with a ready made family to support. With a blush, she added, "I struck out on my own. I really ran into some hard times until I met Harrison." Looking at him with unashamed admiration, she sat down.

The next young lady looked at Sadie with a look of pure hate. "My name is Margaret. My friends call me Maggie. I come from a family, if you can call it that, of all men. My mother died in childbirth, so when I got old enough they decided it was easier to use me. I was free, and it saved them a trip to town. I decided if that was the kind of life I was going to have, then it was going to be because I chose it. I ran away. I like my work, my life is better than it has ever been, and nobody better look down their nose at me!"

The fourth girl who stood was a tiny, very blonde young woman. Shyly she said, "My name is Loraine, but they call me Lorrie. I'm here because I like men, all men. I think this is the best job in the whole wide world. Here I can do what I like doing best and get paid for it. You can't ask for more."

As each of the others stood and gave their names and told their stories, Sadie realized that they all were in the same boat. Sadie quietly counted the ladies in the room. There are eighteen girls who have made the same mistakes I made. I should feel at home with the rest of these fallen women.

When everyone had given her name and story, Kate stood and announced that dinner would be in an hour.

"Please use this time to become better acquainted. It will make this coming week more pleasant." Kate left the room with Harrison at her heels.

Sadie didn't know what to do; she had never been in a room full of strangers before and had no idea where to start.

Lorrie stood up and came over to where Sadie was sitting and began asking her questions about her life and what her plans for the future were. She did it in such a way that Sadie knew she really was interested, not just nosy. She instantly liked this friendly, happy girl and told her all about her life up until the incident when she was caught in that unfortunate situation. Her face burned scarlet and she began to cry, first tears welled up into her eyes, then great gulping sobs that racked her whole body.

Lorrie took her in her arms and gently rocked her, patting her hair and crooning low until the sobs became sniffles and Sadie was in control again.

"You needed that," said Lorrie, "We can't go through life carrying all the pain, hurt, and disappointments the world dumps on us and expect to survive without an tear or two. Every so often a woman needs to sit down and bawl her eyes out! Damn, it makes you feel better. Why, after I do that, I feel like I could whip the world!"

Penny walked up as they were talking and towering over them, she looked directly at Sadie and said, "If you're going to be in this business, you have to have better control of yourself and get used to disappointments. You can make money, but the outside world looks down on us like we are pieces of garbage, so get used to it."

"She's right, but we don't have to see the townsfolk very often, and the men who visit treat us well when they are here. Course, when we see them in town, they shun us. That's to be expected, isn't it?" Lorrie's smile softened the words.

Sadie really liked this girl. Too bad they wouldn't have time to get to know each other better. As soon as she was rested, she would find something else.

A bell tinkled softly and everyone stood and headed toward the sound. Lorrie said, "Come with me," as she steered Sadie toward the main hall.

She was led into another room that was dominated by a long table. The table was covered with a white tablecloth, and in the exact middle stood a centerpiece of wildflowers. They filled the room with the scent of a spring. Sadie enjoyed the feeling of being accepted.

The meal was an adventure for Sadie. Some of the foods were strange, and with Harrison's urging she tasted everything. It was a delicious meal. *Too bad it's the kind of house it is,* she thought, *I would love to live like this.*

The room was alive with the gentle rumble of friends talking. Sadie was lulled into a sense of security. The thought of her family crossed her mind and tears formed. *Stop that!* She thought, *I can't sit around feeling sorry for myself, and I have to get on with my life. Darnit, I will be a success at whatever I do. I will go back and make them sorry. I'll show them all!*

When the meal was over, the girls stood and headed toward the stairs to go up and get ready for the evening. At first Sadie didn't understand why they were leaving, but then it dawned on her that these were working girls. They had to make themselves desirable for the men who would be coming later.

My God, I forgot that they were ladies of the night. Sadie was amazed at her failure to remember their profession. "They seem just like everyone else," Sadie whispered as she headed for the stairs, planning to spend the rest of the evening in her room.

"Would you like to stay downstairs and see how the gentlemen behave, and get a true picture of the job?" Harrison asked.

Sadie was consumed with curiosity. *Darn right I want to see what happens in a house such as this. Was it as sordid as it seemed? Well, maybe I will find out tonight!*

Harrison kept her entertained until the ladies began to filter down to the sitting room. He then moved to the Spinet piano at the far end of the room, dropped down easily on the bench, and began to play a gay little ditty on the beautiful instrument.

In her homespun cotton dress, she felt like a hen house chicken in a room full of swans. The music lifted her spirits and she longed to be a part of this lovely, friendly, place.

The first gentlemen started arriving. There were three of them in one buggy, laughing and patting the youngest one on the back. The young man smiled with red-faced confusion. It was obvious that this was his first time to visit the house and he clearly did not know what to expect.

Sadie felt a surge of sympathy for the young man. She knew exactly how he felt.

Kate came to the young man's rescue and led him to the place where Lorrie was sitting. She introduced them; Lorrie reached up and took the young man's hand, coaxed him down on the sofa beside her, and began to chatter happily to him.

Sadie could see the tension go out of his body as he leaned forward hanging on Lorrie's every word.

It seemed so easy to become acquainted here in this pleasant atmosphere. Sadie wondered if the rest would come as easily. Stop those foolish thoughts. *You weren't brought up that way! But, then neither was the others.*

Looking up she found Kate standing next to her accompanied by a very handsome young man whom she introduced as Henry. "Sadie is just visiting us, but we want to make her feel at home so please feel free to spend time with her, but in this room only," she cautioned and wandered away.

The stranger sat beside Sadie and told her his name really was Henry and that she was very lovely. It was too bad that she didn't work here because he would most assuredly come here more often if she were waiting for him.

Sadie didn't know what to say. She sat red faced and head bowed. In her heart of hearts she wished that she did work here. It would be nice to get to know this man better. *If I worked here, I certainly would get to know him better*, she thought and had to stifle a giggle.

Henry noticed the twinkle in her eye, took her hand and pulled her to her feet,

"No," she protested, but he led her to the piano where Harrison was playing a sprightly tune. He took her into his arms and began to dance. She'd never danced while being held, and found it strange, but thrilling. This was a lot different than dancing at the barn dances. She liked being held by a man. *Maybe Lorrie has the right idea. Maybe this isn't so bad after all!*

All these thoughts were whirling about in her head as she was guided around the floor to the gayest of tunes. She was both dizzy and confused, dizzy from the dancing, confused by the thoughts that flashed into her mind. She couldn't stop the flood of ideas that filled her head. Maybe I could do this for a while. Would it be any worse than the mess she was in with Thomas? Pleading a sudden headache, she asked Henry to please seat her somewhere and bring her a glass of water.

When Henry left to get her water, the thoughts came rushing back, have you gone mad? You can't just jump into something like this. You still have six more days to decide.

She wasn't going to rush into anything, but she was pretty sure what her answer would be at the end of the week. She questioned, *where would you go if you left here and who would associate with you if you were to leave. Sadie girl, it's not as though you have something to lose, your virginity is gone. Thomas took that.*

She hadn't noticed but while she and Henry were dancing, the room had filled with men. Some were dancing, playing cards, and a few were smoking their cigars and listening to the music. What a pleasant evening this was turning out to be.

Henry came back with the water, handed it to her, bowed and excused himself saying "Maybe next time" with a hint of disappointment in his voice.

His leaving dismayed Sadie. She wanted this man to stay and share the evening with her, but she realized that he was here for more then just a pleasant night of dancing, so she swallowed her protest, smiled sweetly and nodded her head discreetly.

Harrison walked toward her with two glasses of wine in his hands and sat besides her, handing her one of the glasses. He asked, "How do you like the evening so far?"

Hiding her disappointment, she told Harrison, "I'm having a lovely time, but I am feeling tired and I think I will retire for the night."

Sadie's eyes wandered around the room and stopped when she saw Henry

29

talking to Maggie. They left the room. *Darn, darn, darn,* she thought, *it could have been me with him right now.* A strange excitement took hold of her and she gulped the wine. She began to choke and sputter from the strong drink, while Harrison soundly patted her back. When she regained control, he said, "Ladies always sip their wine."

Kate came back into the room and walked directly to where Harrison and Sadie were sitting. "You have made quite an impression on Henry. He asked if you would be here next week when he comes, and if so, would I keep your whole evening open for him."

Sadie was both embarrassed and pleased. She didn't realize how quickly the evening had passed until she saw the last gentleman put on his Homburg, grab his cane, and head for the door.

"Come on, ladies, it's been a long night and we all need our rest. Tomorrow is our biggest night." Kate said as she ushered them out of the room. Some of the girls looked a little worse for the wear, a little less lovely, but still able to impress Sadie with their beauty. She hoped that someday she would be half as pretty and popular.

The next two days were carbon copies of the first and Sadie settled into the routine of the household.

On the fourth evening, after the gentlemen had left or retired for the night, Sadie sat on the huge bed and faced the fact that she was not going to leave this house of comfort, she belonged here and here she would stay.

Clad in slippers and robe, she padded down the hallway to Kate's room, knocked and when Harrison opened the door she announced, "I'm staying if you still want me."

Kate, who had joined Harrison at the door, gave Sadie an odd look and said, "Harrison my dear, start the lessons tomorrow and to make sure she is ready by the next weekend." Kate closed the door and hugged herself. "That is one fine young lady I have added to my house."

Sadie had a million questions for Harrison.

"Now is not the time to answer your questions," replied Harrison. "Wait until tomorrow. My dear girl, tomorrow I will show you."

Sadie's head was churning. She padded back to her room and lay down waiting for sleep to come; she just knew she wouldn't be able to sleep a wink. However, she was startled awake by the knocking on her door and was shocked to find out that she had slept through the whole night.

Lorrie, grinning from ear to ear, announced breakfast in a cheery voice.

"What are you so happy about?" Sadie asked.

"We just heard the news that you have decided to stay. I'm happy because I just know we are going to be the best of friends! I hope you haven't changed your mind, after all it was a rather hasty decision."

"No, my dear, I haven't changed my mind. Where else could I go where I'm accepted just as I am?"

"Well don't just lay there, you ninny. Get out of that bed. We've got a big day ahead of us." Lorrie reminded Sadie of a puppy she'd once had, all warm, wiggly, and completely loveable. How could they not be friends?"

Sadie rolled out of bed and hit the floor running. She made short work of getting ready for breakfast. She was hungry and they did serve good food. She hopped and skipped down the stairs just as everyone was sitting down to a table.

Kate waved her to a chair next to her's and said, "Good morning ladies, meet the newest member of our household, Sadie."

The breakfast hour would prove to be the best time of day for Sadie, a time of friendly chatter and a chance to get to know the other girls better. This morning turned into a shopping spree with Harrison and Kate helping her choose a wardrobe. They left right after the morning meal. The ride to town was interesting to Sadie as she had slept on the way to Kate's house. Just outside town, Harrison pulled the coach over to the side of the road.

Turning to Sadie, he said, "First and foremost, you must ignore whatever is said. You must always act like a lady. Second, you must not let on that you recognize anyone. And, lastly, remember that you don't owe them a thing. It was their kind that turned you out in the first place."

Harrison gave her a few minutes to think. "Are you ready?" he asked.

"Ready."

"Good girl!"

The rest of the way into town an uneasy silence prevailed.

It was Saturday morning and the town was bustling with shoppers. Women buying yard goods for their gowns, farmers buying supplies, cowboys renting baths and buying new clothes, and a few men in the land office buying or selling property.

Sadie glanced across the street and her heart skipped a beat. That looked like cousin Marcus in the land office. It had to be him; no one else had those wonderfully wide shoulders and that same springy way of walking. He was taller than most men, but to Sadie, he had always been head and shoulders above the rest. Maybe it was just that crop of dark curly hair that made him seem more handsome. She seemed to drown when she looked into the pool of his gentle brown eyes.

Her face flushed red just thinking of the time they had kissed when he was seventeen and she was twelve. They had been playing hide and seek and Marcus had found her in the barn. Her uncle, Marcus' father, had been furious when he found out about the kiss. Damned that cousin Jeffery for telling on them. She remembered the very real pain she felt when Marcus was forced to marry the girl from the next farm that following year. Sadie had heard Papa telling Mama that it was just as well that he had a wife now because cousins can't marry. Idiot bastards are all that would come out of that kind of union. He said what Marcus and I did in the barn was against Gods law. If a kiss is a sin then God is a tyrant.

Sadie ducked her head praying Marcus wouldn't see her in the carriage with a pimp and a Madam.

Harrison noticed her attempt to hide and asked from whom she was hiding.

"No one," she replied, but she wasn't very convincing. He didn't press the matter, but made up his mind to find out what that was all about.

The rest of the day was like a dream. She had never seen so many beautiful gowns. The three of them had narrowed it down to six dresses; Sadie didn't get a vote even though they would be her gowns. Six dresses, that's more then I had ever hoped to own at one time, she thought. Their next task was to select the under garments. Even though Sadie felt uncomfortable, Harrison always helped the ladies choose the things that they would wear for their gentlemen visitors. After all he was a male and knew what the clients would expect. When they finished shopping, they had a late lunch at the hotel.

Wearing one of the newly purchased outfits, Sadie received many admiring glances.

Kate smiled and said, "This is good advertising."

Harrison frowned, "Sadie isn't ready to begin work yet. She hasn't been properly introduced to the work."

"I know," Kate replied, "but the men will come anyway.

Harrison," she scolded, "You know I never start a new girl until she is properly trained!"

Sadie sat feeling like an object being bartered, but the feeling wasn't as displeasing as it had been the first time.

The male patrons sneaked looks at their table, but none spoke, nodded, or stopped by the table. It was obvious that no one wanted to admit they knew the three diners.

She didn't know any of these men anyway, so she didn't care. Just as they finished their tea and were about to leave, a fat, jovial little man came to their table and shook hands with Harrison, all the while staring at Sadie with a grin on his face. Sadie could almost see the drool on his lips and it sent a shiver down her spine. She had forgotten that not all the men who came to the house were young and handsome.

When they were safely in the buggy, Kate explained to Sadie, "It's men like him who are willing to pay the most to visit with my young ladies. Most of them are kind and lonely. They make the best clients, believe it or not, and they are to be treated with respect. Besides, I will be able to charge him double to spend a few hours with you. The longer he has to wait, the more he will be willing to pay!"

Chapter Three
The Promise

The ride home went quickly. She was anxious to get to her room and get settled. *It is my room,* she thought, *I have a permanent place to live again. I didn't know what I had before, and I carelessly threw it away. I won't do that again. I will work hard and save; maybe someday I can have a place of my own, and then no one can make me leave.* She made herself promises that only a woman, child of fourteen can do with such sincerity. It was nearly dinnertime and Sadie's stomach was making small rumbling noises.

"Take your things to your room and come down for dinner," instructed Kate as she headed for the stairs. "I need to record the money I've spent on you today."

Sadie looked askance at Harrison and he nodded, "You didn't expect Kate to buy all these clothes for you for nothing, did you?"

"No," she answered, but she lost her sense of excitement and realized that she was preparing to go into a career that was both demanding and costly. She would learn that in this business no one did anything for free. Well, she would become just as heartless as they were! Sadie ran quickly up to her room, slammed the door, and threw herself on the bed.

Harrison was right behind her and he was furious! "Who in the hell do you think you are? We have been more than patient with you and this is the thanks we get. You might as well get your things and leave if this is how you're going to behave! This is a business. We don't have the time or the inclination to put up with your childish behavior."

She was immediately both sorry and ashamed for the way she had carried on. Sadie realized she was behaving like a spoiled child, and she'd be lucky if they didn't throw her out!

"Do you still want to be part of this household?" asked Harrison. "If you do, you must understand that these temper tantrums will not be tolerated!"

"Yes, I do want to stay and I promise it will never happen again," she answered.

"Good! We will begin your training immediately. I think you have too much time on your hands.

"You must remember always to make the gentleman you are with feel as though he is the most important man in your life. You can't wait to see him again. You're yearning for his return. Are you a good enough actress for that?"

"Yes, I think I am."

"We'll see." The lessons began.

The rest of the day was spent balancing a book on her head as she strolled around the room to improve her poise.

"Why must I change the way I walk," asked Sadie.

"Can't have you entering a room like a plough horse now can we?" teased Harrison.

Sadie was tired of this game but was too embarrassed to complain about it. After all she had done nothing but behave like a spoiled brat since she got here and she was sure they would toss her out if she complained one more time.

When she complained to Lorrie of her aches and pains from walking around with a weight on her head. Lorrie laughed and said, "We all went through the course, did you think we learned refinement and social graces all by ourselves? You must remember we all are farm girls at heart."

Switching her hips and feigning aloofness, Sadie ambled around the room until Lorrie doubled over with laughter. The lessons became a game for the child inside Sadie, a game she must win.

Teaching Sadie the etiquette of proper dining was easy for Harrison, as Mrs. Schmidt had taught Sadie and David good manners from birth.

Sadie was happy with all the training she was getting, but her heart ached. She needed to be loved by people that she had known all her life, Mama, Papa, and David, and yes even Marcus.

"Kate, Sadie and I have finished the social graces part of the instructions and will be starting instructions on how to please the client today. She learns very quickly, but this lesson will be the deciding factor.

" I have no qualms about Sadie's aptitude for this work, she is one sensible young lady. Enjoy the lessons, my friend," Kate waved as she started toward the kitchen, then turned and said, "I know she will."

Harrison made his way up the stairs to Sadie's room and knocking, announced, "We are having our lesson on the many enticing ways of disrobing." Harrison began removing his clothes. He spent the rest of the day teaching Sadie how to seductively remove her clothing. The next afternoon was spent in erotic touching and fondling. The final lesson came on Monday and it was the combination of all the lessons Sadie had learned. She hadn't expected the exam so soon.

But she was anxious to show him what she had learned.

She went to him and slowly began to help him disrobe. Leisurely removing his clothing, and making soft whimpering sounds while caressing him. Slowly folding his garments, she placed them on a chair. When he was completely naked, she just as slowly began to remove her own clothing. Caressing her own body, just as he had taught her, she moved toward the bed where Harrison sat waiting. Letting out a low moan she gently pushed him down on the bed and spreading her slender legs, she mounted him, slowly lowering herself down to engulf his ready male member. With her hot wet tongue, she explored every crevice that she could reach while rotating on him. Her sexual prowess went beyond anything Harrison had ever experienced.

He became a helpless captive to her every move. Harrison felt himself giving in to lust. He could not control himself for very long and exploded in her quickly. His movements were frenzied and not at all as he had planned. He hadn't felt like this for a long time. In fact, he had thought the thrill was gone.

When he was calmed he asked, "Sadie, do you always get this excited when you're with a man?"

Sadie just smiled and began touching him again, softly at first, then a little more firmly, softly moaning, tongue flicking his flesh and her body moving to the beat of Harrison's heart. He couldn't believe what was happening. He hadn't been aroused twice in one day in years. Passion burned like a flame and nearly consumed him. When they both were at rest again, he asked her the same question.

"Either you are the most ardent women I have ever met or the best damn actress in the world! Which is it?"

Still, she only smiled.

As Harrison dressed himself, Sadie lay watching him with knowing eyes. Harrison knew he would be back soon for another lesson, but he was no longer sure who was the teacher.

Sadie secretly congratulated herself. She had done it and she had convinced Harrison that she was indeed as passionate as he. All she had to do is pretend she was someone else, and it all fell into place. It really did work!

Harrison went to Kate's rooms and flung himself on the chaise. He was completely exhausted and confused. Kate had never seen him this way and she grew curious about him. They had been friends, lovers, and business partners for years.

"How are you coming with Sadie? Have you started the training yet?" she asked.

"You won't believe this, but she is either a natural born whore or the best damn actress I have ever met!" He proceeded to tell Kate everything that had happened to him when he was with Sadie.

Kate threw back her head, laughed raucously, "I would give anything to have seen that. Did you use protection?"

"Good God, Kate, using a shield was the last thing on my mind!"

"No matter. If she needs help at the end of the month our old friend Dr. Chessman's little comfort pills will take care of everything. Now what about this man she was trying to hide from when we were in town?"

"Oh, that was just a farmer boy from her hometown, one of her cousins I believe. A handsome boy, but nothing to worry about."

"Well, my friend, break her in sparingly, I want some left for our clients. I think we are going to have some interesting times ahead," Kate said with a chuckle.

Back in her room, Sadie lay on the bed wishing she had been as satisfied as Harrison. She had never experienced it, but she just knew there had to be more. The hunger was always with her day and night. Even when she touched herself down there in her hot spot, the yearning didn't go away, she just didn't feel as empty.

Choosing a royal blue gown for her first night as one of the ladies of the house, she hoped Kate would let her begin to work tonight. She felt ready, and she was sure Harrison would agree.

"Come in, Sadie. "

"How did you know it was me?" questioned Sadie

"Harrison was here earlier and told me of his experience with you. By the way, he was very impressed, so I knew you would be here to ask to work tonight. Normally I don't let a new girl start for a couple of weeks, but Harrison tells me you are a natural. I will let you start tomorrow. Tonight we dangle you before the visitors as bait. Besides, each night they have to wait, the price goes up."

Sadie was disappointed, but she could see the reasoning behind Kate's decision.

"You do understand, don't you?" Kate asked.

"Yes, I do and I will try to be patient," answered Sadie.

"You know, Sadie, I think I'm going to like you and I can't say that to many of my girls. Most of them are just a means to an end. Treat'em decent, but don't get too close!"

Sadie flushed with pleasure, left the room. As she closed the door, she saw Maggie watching.

"What were you doing kissing Kate's ass?" she asked with a sneer. "We know all about bitches like you. You think yer better than anybody else, but yer not. Yer just as big a slut as I am, so don't get on yer high horse with me!" Maggie ran into her room and slammed the door.

Papa had been the only one who had spoken to her in such a rude manner until now and Sadie was shocked. Have I made a grave mistake in choosing this life; is this the way I must always expect to be treated? Will it change me into someone I can't respect? Going to the mirror she stared at the naive child staring back. No, she vowed she could not let this life change what is in her heart. Checking her hair and makeup, straightening her dress, and making sure she was presentable, Sadie closed her door and started toward the stairs. When she reached the top, she sensed something at her back. Just as she was about to turn and see what or who it was, she lost her balance and went plunging down the flight of stairs.

Hurtling toward the bottom, the last thing she saw was the carved newel post coming at her. Hitting the bottom, she felt her head connect with the post and she lost consciousness. The next thing she knew she was on her bed, surrounded by the residents of the house.

Kate asked, "Where is Maggie? That's really odd. We all ran to see what had happened, except Maggie. Do you remember what happened?" Kate asked.

"I don't remember much, but I did think I felt something touch my back, then falling, that's all."

Kate gave Sadie an opiate and a glass of water, saying, "Take this and get some rest, I will be back later to see if you remember anything." As Kate closed the door the frown on her face deepened and she looked at Harrison with a look that he recognized as hell for someone. She headed toward Maggie's room, and barged in without knocking.

"Who the hell is coming in my room with out a 'by-your-leave'?" Maggie shouted. Seeing Kate, she turned white and sat down.

Kate stared at her with such venom that she didn't dare open her mouth again. "If I find out you had anything to do with Sadie's so-called accident, you will be out of here so fast you won't know what hit you. Do you understand?"

Maggie gave her a smug look and answered, "Sure, I understand. I knew she was going to be one of your favorites."

As Kate left the room, she replied, "You're right about one thing, she is special and nothing better happen to her or I might do something drastic."

"Bitch," Maggie mumbled under her breath, "You will pay for the treatment you give me. I'll see to that." She finished her makeup and slipped into a gown that was lovely but slightly soiled. Noticing the stains she muttered, "Oh, well, the men who come here don't notice little spots like this, they only have one thing on their mind. I need all new clothes like that bitch Sadie.

Sadie lay on the bed trying to sleep, hoping the headache would be gone when she woke. Her mind wandered back to her family and the farm. She missed them and wondered if they missed her too. Her thoughts traveled back to the times her family had visited uncle Toby's farm and her joy at seeing Cousin Marcus. Her heart began beating faster, and she felt warm and sweaty. Dammit, why do I always get this way when I think of Marcus? It is so wrong? Everybody says so. Papa told me it's wrong and Phoebe agreed with him. She told me I'm not supposed to feel this way about my cousin. But then she told me a lot of other things too, like friends forever, and when I needed her most where was she?

I can't remember when I didn't yearn for Marcus' touch. I wonder if he saw me when we were in town. Lord, I hope not! Of course, if he came here as a customer I wouldn't have a choice, I would have to entertain him. She fell asleep with a smile on her face and dreamed she was floating in his warm brown eyes.

When she woke up her headache was gone and except for being a little stiff, Sadie felt fine. Rolling out of bed and grabbing a robe, Sadie went into the hall and down to where everyone was having breakfast. The girls surrounded her, all talking at once, asking questions and chattering at the top of their voices.

Kate stood up and shouted, "Sit down and be quiet!" The room grew silent; they went back to their places, sat down, and waited.

"Now," said Kate, "tell us how you feel and what you remember about your fall."

"I feel fine, just a bit stiff, but that's all. I don't really remember anything, but something is bothering me, I can't quite place it, maybe later it will come to me."

Sadie filled her plate with all the good things she saw within her reach. The others resumed eating and soon they were laughing and talking as though nothing had ever happened, which was all right with Sadie. She didn't want all that attention.

Half way through her meal Sadie felt someone's eyes on her. She looked around the table. Everyone seemed busy eating or carrying on a conversation, except Maggie. She was looking off into space and smiling to herself.

Sadie felt a chill go down her spine; she couldn't help but feel as though someone had walked over her grave.

I think I had better watch my step with that lady. She no longer felt hungry and rose to leave the table.

"Wait," Kate called out, "I want everyone to be very careful the next few days. We don't want any more accidents, so we go everywhere in twos. Lorrie, I want you to stay with Sadie. You others pick a friend to share time with." Staring directly at Maggie she said, "I can't afford to have even one girl laid up for accidental reasons!"

Sadie and Lorrie left the dining room together. As they ascended the stairs, Sadie looked back and Maggie was watching from the doorway. The icy smile she wore told Sadie that this woman hated her with a passion.

"Hurry," she said to Lorrie, "I feel a chill!"

The two girls hurried to Sadie's room, sat on the bed and all of a sudden feeling foolish for the fright they both felt.

"Do you think you're in danger from Maggie?"

"I don't know, but something is bothering me. When I see her it slips away into the back of my mind," Sadie answered. "I do know one thing for sure, I don't like or trust her." The girls spent the next hour talking and rearranging Sadie's room to suit her.

"You're very fussy," Lorrie told her.

"Yes, I know," she answered, "I don't feel clean in a messy room."

"That's strange," Lorrie, commented, "it doesn't bother me one way or the other but then we're all strange in some ways."

Sadie agreed and began to quietly hum.

"What is that you're humming?"

" Listen to the words and then you tell me," with that Sadie sang in a lilting voice, a ditty that she had learned from her mother. When she had finished the song, Lorrie sat with tears streaming down her face.

"What is it, what have I done that you should cry so?"

"Nothing," Lorrie said still sobbing, "it was just so beautiful. I felt my heart fill with the sound of your voice. It is a pleasant ache," she added.

"What a lovely thing to say. No one has ever said anything as nice about my singing, thank you."

"No, it is I that should thank you. The world seems right when you sing."

"Why, I thought the world always seemed right with you. You're always so good-natured and happy," Sadie told the girl.

"Only an idiot would be happy all the time," she whispered. "I try to make the best of my situation, but I miss my home and family sometimes. I know I could never live there being the way I am, but I like to think I have a choice, even when I know I don't." Lorrie smiled a big smile and said, "You just gave me a big taste of home with your song and it was a pleasant taste, not the way home really is."

Sadie gave Lorrie a big hug.

Suddenly the door burst open and there stood Maggie with a leer on her face. "What the hell is going on here?" she demanded.

Sadie didn't understand what she meant, but she did know that Maggie had no business in her room without knocking. Lorrie sat red faced and shaking with fear. Her heart was beating so hard she thought it would burst.

Sadie rushed to the door, pushed Maggie out, slammed the door in her face, and turned to Lorrie saying, "That takes care of her. Who does she think she is? I bet she won't try that again!" Sadie felt better than she had in days. At last she had taken charge of her life.

Chapter Four
The Accusation

A knock came at the door, and opening it she found Kate looking angry and very upset. "What is going on around here? Every time I turn around there is another crisis!"

Lorrie stood up and in a shaky voice told Kate what had just happened.

"Well, I've had it with Miss Maggie. She causes trouble all the time and I don't have the patience to put up with her little games! Out she goes!"

"No!" shouted Sadie. "Not on my account. Please give her another chance."

"You want me to give her another chance. You know she had something to do with your fall, don't you?"

"I suspect her, but I can't prove it. I don't want to be to blame for her being thrown out with nowhere to go. I know how that feels and I don't want to be responsible."

"Well, I guess I can give her one more chance, but there had better not be any more accidents.

"By the way when Maggie came to my room a few moments ago, she told me that you two were lovers and that she had seen you making love here in Sadie's room. If that is true, please be more discreet and don't let it interfere with your job. What you do on your own time is up to you." Kate quietly closed door, leaving the young ladies shocked and speechless.

The silence was deafening. Finally, Lorrie found her tongue and began to sputter so fast that Sadie could not understand a word.

"Slow down, I can't make out a word you're saying and I suspect I really don't want to know."

They stared at each other for a long time and suddenly they both began to giggle, laugh, and then roar until they were in tears. When they finally stopped, they were gasping for air but both felt better. An unspoken bond had been forged between them.

The clock striking the hour reminded them that they must get ready for the evening's work. It was very important to Sadie to look her best tonight. Not only was it her first night of work, but also she hoped to see Henry again.

When Sadie was ready to go downstairs, Lorrie came quickly out of her room and ran to where Sadie was standing. Breathlessly she said, "Now we can go down together."

Many of the others had gone on ahead and were sitting, standing, or dancing with each other. Harrison was playing a perky little tune that made both Sadie and Lorrie long to dance, but the accusation was too fresh in their minds to take the risk of dancing together. They stood near the doorway and swayed to the music.

That is the picture Henry saw when he entered the room. The girl called Sadie enchanted him.

He went to where Kate sat and began to talk to her about Sadie, telling Kate of his deep yearnings for the girl. Kate threw back her head and laughed a loud unladylike laugh that filled the room.

"Henry, if I let you have Sadie tonight you would have to stand in line behind ten others, and my other girls would have nothing to do for the evening except dance with each other. You spend tonight with Maggie and I will see to it that you have time with Sadie tomorrow night."

Henry looked Sadie's way and answered, "I don't want Maggie. I'll wait for Sadie. Tonight I'll just join the card game. Maybe I can win at cards since I'm not lucky in affairs of the heart." Maggie, seeing Henry talking to Kate and looking her way, walked toward him smiling and took his arm, ready to spend another evening with him. Henry gently shook off her hand and walked into the game room.

Maggie turned to look at Kate with a question in her eyes. Kate just shrugged her shoulders and turned away.

Looking very old and rejected, Maggie stood perfectly still for a moment, then she made her way to the stairs and climbed slowly holding the banister to steady herself.

Sadie had seen what was happening and felt a tremendous sadness. Please, God, don't ever let that happen to me. She ached to go and tell Maggie that she was still lovely and desirable, but she knew that whatever she said or did would be wrong as far as Maggie was concerned. Maggie hated her and there was nothing that Sadie could do to change that!

After a few moments, Sadie saw Kate and the man from the hotel coming toward her. Sadie thought she could still see the drool on his lips. He was wearing the same foolish smile. He began to stutter hello, but it sounded more like gurgling to her and she gave him a wide smile to keep from bursting out laughing. His face turned red and he stuttered even more. Sadie felt compassion for this funny little man; taking his arm, she led him to the dance floor. Putting her arms around him, her head on his shoulder, she began to move to the beat of the music.

Kate smiled and motioned one dance with her finger and wandered to the piano to watch the dancers moving around the room to the sounds of the, "Blue Danube Waltz."

Holding Sadie, he told her his name was Otto. He was from Germany and he had come to this country to get a new start. All of his people were back in the old country, and that he was lonely. He hadn't made many friends here. Near the end of the set, he was talking without stuttering. She found herself liking this funny little man. A week ago, I wouldn't have given this man a second thought. Otto led her to the piano where Harrison was playing for the next set of dancers.

"I will leave you here und see you tomorrow night."

He proudly walked into the card room where he sat down and began to play.

Kate came over to Sadie, took her hand, and said, "You've just performed a miracle. He has never been at ease enough to dance or go into the game room."

"I like him and hope we can be friends."

"Do you think you can go to bed with him and still be friends?" asked Kate

"I'll do my best to make that happen, after all this is just a job," Sadie replied

"Good, and now I want to introduce you to your partner for the evening. Be nice to him. He has paid a handsome price for the privilege of your company." Smiling she waved her hand to a tall, good-looking man standing on the other side of the room. He, in turn, set down his empty glass, walking with long strides; he made his way across the crowded dance floor. When he reached the place where Kate and Sadie were standing, he took Sadie's hand, kissed it in gentlemanly fashion, saying "I have waited forever it seems for this honor."

"Sadie, meet Robert. He is the most striking man you will ever meet," Kate said, smiling, but her eyes were guarded.

Sadie felt her flesh crawl as he touched her hand; she had never felt dirty until this moment. All that she could think of was a chance to escape his piercing eyes.

Her brain instructed her: *come on, don't panic, he is your first client; treat him as though he were your own true love. Welcome him and prove yourself to Kate and Harrison.*

"How do you do? My name is Sadie and I will be your companion for the evening."

"So, that is what you call it. Well, so be it. We will call it that from now on; it will be our little secret. Come, my dear, I paid for the whole night and I'm anxious to get this night started. If you are as good as you look I will be a steady client."

Sadie felt a moment of panic, but she shrugged it off and gave him her arm, all the while cringing inside. She turned and smiled at Robert to ease her pent up feelings. He merely frowned and kept walking.

When they reached the top of the stairs, she led him to her room and opened the door; the room looked as though a cyclone had hit it. Pieces of clothing, makeup, and furniture were thrown everywhere; the only thing that was where it belonged was the bed, only because it was too heavy to move.

"Dear God, what has happened here? My beautiful room is a shambles."

"Never mind that, I'm ready to begin the evening I paid for." Grabbing Sadie, Robert threw her on the bed and began tearing at her clothes.

"Stop! Stop! She screamed. "I'll take them off. You're tearing my gown!"

"Yes, he said, "I will tear your gown and a lot more than that before I'm done! You're a bad girl and I must punish you." He didn't even bother to remove his clothes. Bending over her, he began slapping her with his open hand, leaving angry red welts on her inflamed buttocks. The night became a living hell for Sadie with Robert standing over her tearing and slapping; it seemed to go on forever. Finally, he reached the pinnacle of passion, gave a grunt of satisfaction, rolled onto the bed, shuddering and groaning to himself. He lay on the bed, a satisfied smile on his face as a wet stain spread across the front of his trousers.

Sadie lay perfectly still, hoping he wouldn't want to repeat that horrible act. *If I don't move, maybe he will forget I'm here,* she thought. Time stood still. At length she decided she could move and get out of there. Picking up a torn robe as she made her way to the door, she looked back and saw Robert watching her.

"Tell Kate I've enjoyed myself very much. In fact, I've decided to reserve you the first Friday of every month. I like the way you whimper and groan. You accept your punishment very well." He smiled again, rolled over on his stomach and began to snore.

Going to Kate's room and tapping gently, Sadie told Kate that she was sorry for disturbing her, but she needed to tell her what had happened.

"Come in." Kate sat at the desk in the center of the room, writing in a very large book. "This is where I keep my records," she said pointing at it, and critically eyeing Sadie's appearance, "so I will know to the penny what each of my girls bring in and how much I spend on them. I have a feeling you will do very well."

"Thank you, but this is what I want to talk to you about. My new clothes have been torn to rags and my room is a terrible mess, things thrown everywhere. It was like that when Robert and I got to the room."

"Sounds like that bitch Maggie must have been up to her old tricks, I'll take care of her in a moment, but how did you manage your first night with Robert?

Kate had been watching Sadie closely when she said this and then she asked, "Aren't you going to complain about your first night on the job? I know I promised you a more enjoyable first time, but the money he offered was too good to say no."

"Yes, I was surprised by Robert's bizarre lovemaking, if that's what he calls it. He finished the mess in my room by tearing the gown I was wearing to shreds. Now I have nothing to wear. I only hope that he is not the way all your clients are.

"I was surprised by his obsession with brute force, he enjoyed slapping me over and over and seemed to get his satisfaction from making me cower. But you must be aware of his methods, since he's no stranger here. He tells me he pays very well for the privilege. In fact he said that he was thinking of booking me every month, he was that pleased. I will need some new clothes. What Maggie didn't destroy, he did. I hope he paid enough to replace the one he tore at least."

"Yes, my dear, he paid enough to replace five new gowns and I'm sure he will be glad to buy a couple more, now that you have not rejected him. He will be putty in those soft little hands. Just be sure he doesn't go too far!

"You are going to be an asset to my business. Two conquests in one day, I can't believe my luck!" Kate smiled and continued; "I guess that I should have expected something like this from Maggie. I just didn't think it would come so soon. Well, so much for giving her another chance. She's a troublemaker and it's time to get rid of her. That bitch has pushed me too far. She's getting out right now with what she has on her back." Turning to Sadie, she asked "What, no pleading for her this time?"

"No," replied Sadie, "not this time. She needs to pay for what she has done."

When she got back to her room, Robert was gone but there was a pile of money on the dresser. The girl picked it up, and looked at it. She had never held money before.

Father had always paid for everything. She had no need for money until now; she put it back on the dresser until Kate came to tell her what to do with it.

She began to straighten the room. Even the rugs were stained with makeup and perfumes. The walls would need washing and the draperies were splattered as well.

Kate didn't bother to knock. She simply walked in.

"You can take Maggie's room for tonight. She won't need it. We can get this mess cleaned up in the morning."

"No, I'll sleep here. I don't even want to sleep in her old room. I've had enough of that woman to last me a life time!"

"Suit yourself. Good thing you don't have to change the bed linens or worry about getting with child from Robert, isn't it?" Kate asked.

"Yes, I dislike the idea of flushing myself with vinegar and lye soap. It burns so much. Mother made me do that after father caught Thomas and me, and it hurt."

"My dear Sadie, we don't use that crap. We now have the most up to date methods known to medical science. We have many new things to teach you. The Pessarie, the shield, if you can convince the client to use it, and of course, coitus interuptus, you know, withdrawal. That is what they have to do at home, so it is usually out of the question here. If all else fails we have old dependable Dr. Chessman's menstruation pills," she said with a twinkle in her eye.

"By the way, I see Robert left you some extra money, how much did he leave?"

"I don't know, I didn't count it, I guess I'm not very good at counting money. I've never had any before." Sadie felt stupid saying that, but it was the truth.

"Will wonders never cease? An honest girl and she works for me. I have been blessed!

"Sadie, this is your money. Robert paid me for the evening with you when he came in my office, anything he leaves in this room is in appreciation for your services. I could put it into an account for you if you wish."

Sadie said, "Yes, please do."

Kate counted the money and whistled, "Girl, you must have really been good to Robert. What in hell did you do?"

"I only laid there and reacted to his rage, I have never been beaten before and it was a shock. I guess I only got what a bad girl can expect."

"Like hell you did!" Kate exploded, "You're not a bad girl, bad girls don't get caught. They are way too smart for that. Honey, if you don't want to entertain Robert again just say the word."

"Well, the money is important to me and I guess I can quit anytime I want to," Sadie said as she continued straightening the room.

The days seemed to fly for Sadie. They grew into weeks and then months. Soon she realized that she had been there for six months and she was just as much in demand as when she had first started. Her only regret was the empty feeling she still carried with her.

She didn't voice her need, but if anyone looked deep into her eyes they would find a woman waiting to be released. She wished just once she could honestly feel what she pretended. She felt lucky to be able to support herself; she could be in the same fix as Maggie, selling her wares on the corner.

Kate said, "Maggie's charging five cents and no one wants to buy." Sadie's mind went back to the stories she had been hearing about Maggie, the desperate circumstances that had befallen her. Just the other day Lorrie saw her digging in the hotel's garbage for food.

"I had better get ready for tonight," she said to herself, "or I could end up like Maggie."

As she prepared herself for the evening to come, she wondered what had happened to her little brother David. Had he grown any? Was he still playing in the barn now that she was no longer there to share those times with him? She did miss him and Mother. I think I will always hate Papa a little for not giving me another chance. Her thoughts lingered with her parents and the farm until Lorrie rapped softly on her door. Lorrie always seemed to know when she was lonesome or depressed.

As she put the finishing touches to her toilet, they exchanged confidences about the coming evening.

Lorrie told Sadie she hoped that the young man with the handlebar mustache would ask for her again tonight.

48

"He's so gentle and takes his time reaching a climax. Some times I think he really visits here for the conversation. His wife never lets him get in a word when he is at home. I'm more than willing to spend some time with him, he makes me feel good and I get paid for it."

"You get the best of both worlds," giggled Sadie. And then on a sadder note she gazed out the window and grieved silently for her absent love. She didn't remember when she first realized that she had special feelings for Marcus, but she also knew it was wrong to care about him the way she did. She'd heard Mama gossip about the Henry girl and her cousin, fooling around in the barn. The neighbor, Mrs. Lars VanIdior, whispered behind her hand, "The hired hand at the Henry farm caught them two or three times and that old reprobate took pleasure in watching them carry on.

"Lars told me to watch our daughters close, cause he didn't want to be the father of such trollops that cavort with family members. He said 'Why, woman if you could see those fools gather around him at the tavern when he told of the antics that Henry girl and Joseph performed. Makes a man ashamed to be seen with such women.' "

What must dear sweet Mama think of her now? Mama most surely had heard from the town gossip's how she made her living.

Sadie had read enough books to know that the kings, queens, and royalty in Europe married first and second cousins so why was it so wrong here? Oh, well, she wasn't even sure Marcus felt the same as she, although she did catch him glancing her way when they visited, but that didn't mean he loved her. When her folks had taken her to his wedding to the girl from the next farm, Aunt Polly said she was glad to have him settled down and not day dreaming all the time. Did he daydream about her?

Chapter Five
Awakening

To boost her spirits, Sadie put on her favorite blue dress, piled her hair into an elaborate style on top of her head with ringlets framing her face, put extra rouge on her cheeks, and suddenly felt as giddy as a young filly in spring. When she was finished she was very pleased with the results and in a much better mood. A feeling of anticipation was coursing through her body. *What is going on with me?* She wondered. *Have I lost my mind? This is just another day, and not a busy one at that! Oh well, I'll just have to wait and see what the night will bring.*

She and Lorrie made their way down the stairs and into the sitting room. A few of the steady clientele had already arrived and were playing cards, drinking their usual beverage or just sitting and waiting for the ladies to come down. Sadie and Lorrie sat on the sofa and began chatting with one of the men who was waiting for his favorite lady to join him.

Suddenly the room went strangely quiet, even though when Sadie looked around people were talking. Harrison was still playing the piano and the gamblers were still arguing over cards. She was aware of someone near. She could sense, smell, and almost taste him. She knew he was there and it frightened her. She abruptly stood and turned; there stood her beloved Marcus.

She nearly fainted. She wanted to run away and yet she never wanted to be out of his sight, ever again.

Marcus took her hand, softly whispering her name.

She had no will of her own; he guided her to the stairs. She couldn't resist if she wanted to, and she sure as hell didn't want to. She had dreamed of this. When they were in her room, Sadie touched his face with her index finger, tracing his features as though to memorize them forever. His liquid brown eyes sent a quiver down her spine.

"If I die right now, I will die happy," she whispered.

He began to undress her in slow fluid movements, building her passion like a sculptor creating a masterpiece of love. He gathered her into his arms and laid her naked body on the bed, and he began to disrobe.

Sadie watched with anticipation, her body generating heat as though the volcano burning within was about to erupt in her private parts. When he joined her, she went quickly into his arms. They lay for a while kissing, holding, and touching each other. She ran her fingers through the thick mat of hair on his chest, nibbled on his nipple and nuzzled his neck. She could wait no longer. He responded with the same torrid passion as she, and the night lost all time and dimension.

When their passion had cooled for the moment, they began to talk; she wanted to know all about him, his innermost hopes, and dreams.

"Are we sinning? If so, why do we love? Do you believe in God? What will become of us?" All of these questions tumbled off her lips.

"Whoa, slow down, we have all night. Let's make the most of the time we have together. My darling, you know we can't be together anywhere but here. But I can visit here on my weekly visits to Saginaw. You know I'm married and my family is important to me. Any man worth his salt must do whatever he needs to do to protect them.

"I have tried to stay away. I fought my yearnings for you, but I can no longer fight. Sadie, I have loved you for as long as I can remember."

"Me too," sobbed Sadie, "I thought I was evil for loving you!" The tears made a path down her cheeks and Marcus bent and kissed them away. Rushes of love filled her soul and she cried out in pleasure. "No one has ever loved as we love."

Marcus took her in his arms and soothed her until the sobbing stopped.

When Sadie awoke in the morning, Marcus was gone.

She rolled over and buried her face in the pillow where the scent of him lingered. Stretching leisurely, she buried her face deeper into the pillow and daydreamed of Marcus. She was complete.

When she finally did get up the breakfast hour was over, but some food had been left on the table for her.

Kate came in while she was eating and sat across from her. "Sadie, it has come to my attention that you really care for this Marcus and I can understand that. That won't be a problem as long as your feelings don't interfere with my business, is that understood?"

Sadie swallowed the food she had in her mouth, and replied, "Marcus and I talked about this and decided that there was nothing we could do about the situation except continue seeing each other. He will live his life and I will live mine."

Kate stood and said, "Good girl. I knew I could count on you.

True to her word, Sadie lived her life the way she wanted for the next joyous two years, working, saving and once a week being with Marcus. She would have been content to go on forever, but when Marcus showed up this time for his regular appointment, Sadie sensed there was something wrong. Marcus took her in his arms, caressing her as he talked.

"It seems there has been talk going around about my leaving town every week, and it has gotten back to my wife and child. The talk is also affecting my job. I was in line for a promotion, and if they hear the talk and believe it, they will give the promotion to someone else."

"If there were any other way," he said, "I would try it, but the only solution I can come up with is not to see you anymore. It's breaking my heart to have to tell you this. I don't know if I can make it without you!"

"We can survive, we've had these last two years and that's more than we ever thought we would have, so let's be grateful. I know I'm never alone with you in my heart. We will have this night to remember."

"No," Marcus said, "we won't have this night, I must go home immediately. We're having guests for dinner, your parents, and it's going to be hell being so close to them and so far from you."

"My parents! Have they ever mentioned me?" she asked, hoping against hope.

Marcus slowly shook his head; his eyes reflected the pain they both felt.

"No, my darling, but I have seen your mother glance in my direction a few times as though she wanted to ask me something, but she never has. She no doubt heard the gossip about us. Your father would probably throw her out too, if she asked."

They held each other silently for a long time; abruptly Sadie broke away and left the room not looking back.

"It's done," she said through tears, "all over, the end!"

Making her way to Kate's rooms, she banged on the door not caring how much noise she made.

Kate answered almost immediately, "What is all this racket all about. Goodness, child, what has happened? Has the world come to an end?"

"My world has," said Sadie. "Oh, Kate, I don't know what to do! I tried to be brave for Marcus, but I can't fool myself. I need him in my world!"

When she stopped crying so she could be understood, she explained what had happened, how Marcus wouldn't be coming to see her again and why.

"This works out to my advantage." Kate paused, took a deep breath, and asked, "How would you like to move to New York with me? I've been thinking of moving for the last couple of months. There are so many more opportunities in larger cities. Now that women are being hired as workers in many other jobs besides prostitution, this means the better class of young ladies will be going into other fields to support themselves. You have heard about that new machine they invented that writes, haven't you? Anyway, I don't want to end up with a bunch of low class whores.

"If you say yes, you can go with me. Lorrie will be going and Harrison of course. You don't have to answer right now. Sleep on it and let me know in the morning."

"What about the rest of the girls? What's going to happen to them? We won't just leave them will we?"

"No, Sadie, we won't just leave them. Jenny, my oldest girl, has saved enough to buy the place from me and most of the girls want to stay.

"A couple of the younger ones are retiring to other parts, as widows, so they can marry, be respectable, and have children. After all, this is the 1900's. Women are gaining new freedoms."

"Harrison doesn't mind moving?" Sadie questioned. "I thought he was content here."

"He will be content wherever we go. He has no other means of support. He's the second son of a wealthy family in England and his older brother inherited everything. The brother got tired of supporting Harrison, so he gave him enough money to get to this country in hopes that he would make his own fortune. Harrison doesn't know how to do anything except be a gentleman and play the piano, so here he stays with us."

"When will you be leaving?" Sadie asked.

"As soon as we can pack and arrange transportation," Kate answered exuberantly. You've worked hard, and you were smart enough to save. If you decide not to go, you will be able to support yourself for quite a while. Think it over and let me know tomorrow."

"I've thought it over and there is nothing here for me. I'm going. This is going to be an adventure and I'm ready for a change, too." Sadie felt suddenly lighter, a sense of unreality settled over her. It was as though she was watching events from a distance and didn't really know these two women who could pick up and leave a life they had made for themselves.

"Are you sure you don't want to think it over? It was a pretty hasty decision.

You still have till morning to change your mind."

"No, I've made up my mind and although Robert's spankings kept my body and bankbook in good condition, I sure won't miss either him or his perverted lovemaking!"

Harrison came into the room and asked Kate if she had told Sadie what was going on. Kate nodded.

"She's going with us." A smile lit his face and he gave Sadie a big hug. "Welcome aboard. We are going to have a grand time."

It took them three days to get ready for the move. Sadie packed and unpacked, changing her clothes every time she unpacked, but it kept her busy and out of the way. She needed that time alone.

There was a chill around her heart that she knew would never go away.

Harrison had gone into town to buy one of those new horseless carriages, such a modern convenience it was. She was really moving in a very up-to-date crowd. *Imagine me,* she thought, *coming from a small farm near Bay City, and then to Saginaw, and now on to the big city of New York.* Her mind was filled with fear and anticipation, what else did the future hold in store?

When he arrived with the Jalopy, as he called it, the weather had grown so cold that the adventurers needed blankets to cover themselves from the waist down.

"Ladies, I have hit it lucky with our transportation. A local fellow in town ordered this for his mistress, and then died before it arrived. He'd ordered it from Germany and when it finally arrived, the widow refused to accept it. Can't blame the old girl! She said she would rot in hell before she'd accept that vehicle of a harlot. It was left on the docks for the price of shipping." Harrison laughed when he told them how much he had paid for the machine.

Everything that would take up a lot of room had been sent ahead to a warehouse in New York to be held until they arrived. The four nomads took only the clothes they had selected for the trip. Two trunks were in the rear compartment, which Harrison called the spare seat, and two more were tied on top of that compartment. The Jalopy looked like a giant ant hauling its food home in its hind legs. Sadie stared at the funny looking transportation, and she began to giggle, then Lorrie joined her, and before long they all were doubled over with laughter. At last, when they could hardly move, the spasms stopped. Meekly they got into the Jalopy and began their adventure.

It became a contest among the four of them to see which one would become motion sick first. The roads were filled with holes, wagon ruts, tree roots, and it did, indeed, seem as though they were sailing on choppy seas. Sadie was the first to feel queasy, then Harrison, and finally Lorrie. Kate teased them, saying, "It takes a tough old duck to weather the storms in life."

They took turns driving when they were in open country, but when they came to a town, Harrison drove the Jalopy, saying, "We can't have people staring at us now can we?" That set the women off again. They laughed until their stomachs ached. Every time they thought about what he had said they started laughing again. When they were too weak to even giggle, they settled into a comfortable silence.

Well, Sadie thought, *the die has been cast and she would just have to make the best of her decision right or wrong.*

After Kate had driven for several hours, Harrison tapped her shoulder motioning for her to stop the machine. The noise from the engine made it almost impossible to carry on a conversation. The Jalopy needed its usual addition of water to the steaming radiator and the travelers needed a rest from the bumpy unpaved roads

"We have to find a place for the night," Harrison commented. "We don't want to spend the night on the road. I hear it can be dangerous after dark."

"Otto told me he was almost robbed on the way home from his trip to Ohio last month. He thought they were going to kill him. He said if the horses hadn't reared when they did, he was sure they would have shot him. It scares me just talking about it. Imagine poor Otto. I bet he stuttered all over the place. He said he is thinking of moving to a larger city where it is safer to travel."

"Sadie, Sadie," said Kate, "Don't you know that Otto would follow you to the ends of the earth and back? He will be in New York before the end of the year. You mark my words. If he didn't own that hotel, he would have followed right behind this Jalopy. I would bet my life on that!"

Sadie's face turned a bright crimson, but she also wore a tiny pleased smile. "I think maybe you're right, and I'm glad that I will have another friend in such a big town."

Weary from traveling, they searched for a place to spend the night. In the distance they saw a house and large barn. A dog was guarding a flock of sheep in the field.

"Harrison, maybe we can rest here."

"That looks like it might be the owner coming up the path from the woods," said Lorrie. "a stern old cuss from the looks of him."

"Sir, we are in need of a place to rest for the night. Are you able to help us in that manner?" Harrison asked the farmer.

"I have plenty of room for good Christian folks, but not for the likes of you. Pack up your loose baggage and git off my land." Raising his gun he aimed it at Harrison's head.

Kate, with disdain dripping from her words, told the irritable old codger, "We would rather take our chances with highway men, than stay here with good Christian folks like you. At least they don't pretend to believe in helping their neighbor." With that they piled back into the Jalopy and headed for the road.

Sadie had grown used to the town's folk shunning them when they went into town. She had ignored them and told herself that everyone wasn't that way. Some people understood that this was the only way a girl could support herself when she was on her own. Besides, who were their best customers? The men from town, married or not, that's who!

The farmer had stolen their sense of adventure with his vicious attack; the time hung heavy on them for the next couple of hours.

"Blast him," Kate burst out, "Who does he think he is anyway?" she raged. She was silent for the next few minutes, and then she started to hum a song that Sadie knew. Sadie joined in the song; soon the feeling of despair left them, a sense of belonging settled in. They were a family and they could take on the world!

The next farm they came to Harrison went alone to ask if they could accommodate the travelers. A woman, who looked as though she were in her mid-forties, welcomed them and told them they could stay in her barn.

"It's clean and there is plenty of hay for sleeping." She seemed hungry for company; someone to talk to, after all, the farm was miles from town and their nearest neighbor. When she heard their story about the farmer and his rude manners, she smiled and said, "I know how you feel. Not too many years ago I was in the same fix and nobody would help me. I worked for a woman down Ohia way. I decided I'd had enough of that life, so I drifted around for a while looking for a place to put down roots. I met my husband in a small town that I was drifting through.

He ain't much to look at, but he's a good man and I'm willing to settle for that. I got me two children now, and that's something I never thought I'd have. All in all this life is purty darn good.

"By the way, we don't talk about what I was before I met my Efrem. He don't like to think about it."

She led them into the barn, and she was right; the barn was clean and the hay was sweet smelling. It would be a good place to spend the night.

Sadie wondered aloud, "Why do people want children? The girls back at your old house, that's all they talked about when they weren't talking about men."

Kate got a faraway look in her eye and murmured, "Someday you will understand." She busied herself making a bed in the straw.

The woman came back with quilts for them. "Here ya go, they're not much, but I made them myself. Not much to do around here in the evenings when the mending is done."

Sadie had never seen such beautiful quilts. Her mother had made quilts too, but she never made them pretty. Mother always said, "After all who ever sees them?"

The woman said, "I like to try brightening our lives as much as I can. Efrem says that I'd make the whole world a picture if I could," she blushed as she said this. Her tired face became lovely at that moment. Sadie felt a warm glow begin in her. This woman is loved. They all settled down for the night. Sadie was just dozing off when she felt movement. She lay still and pretended to be asleep, hoping that whatever it was it would go away.

The fragrance of lily of the valley came to Sadie and she knew it was Lorrie. Quietly she whispered, "What is it? What's wrong?"

"Nothing," came a small voice. "I just felt so alone. I needed to be close to someone."

Sadie rolled over and gave Lorrie a kiss on the forehead. "Well, you have me as your friend so rest easy. Good night, everyone, sweet dreams." There was no answer. Even if there had been, she would not have heard it, for she, too, was asleep.

When they awoke in the morning, a basin of clean water and a couple of towels were waiting.

On a stool set up in the barn was a fresh loaf of bread, warm cow's milk, and home made butter. It brought back good memories to Sadie, but to Kate it only reminded her of her life of misery and rejection.

"I can't wait to get to a town and away from these country hicks," Kate told the others as they ate the food provided by the farmer and his wife. "Harrison, I want you to leave them a five dollar gold piece for their trouble, then let's get going."

Harrison was silent for a moment and then he casually said, "You know if I leave them any money it will insult them. Their kindness was freely given. It was given as a gift and that is the way we need to accept it! I have said my last word on this subject," with that said, he stalked away.

"He's right," Kate, said, "I'm forgetting my manners. I will see if there is some other way I can reimburse them for their generosity without insulting them."

"I would like to buy one of her beautiful quilts," Sadie piped up.

Lorrie chimed in, "They are beautiful, aren't they?"

"Well, that's it then," said Sadie jubilantly, "We will all buy quilts, if she has enough to spare, and pay handsomely for them. That should make us all feel better."

"Not this gal," scolded Kate. "I have enough quilts already, and in my business I really don't need them. You girls can do whatever you want about the quilts and even old stick-in-the-mud Harrison can't find fault with your plan."

When they finished their toilet, they went to the house and knocked. Annie answered with one child tucked on her hip and the other wrapped around her leg, hanging on for dear life.

"Did you have a good rest?" she asked. "I didn't think you would be up this early, but Efrem took some bread out to you anyway. He said you might wake up hungry and hesitate to impose. I told him you knew you were among friends, but he did it anyway. He's hard headed that way." Again she smiled the shy little smile they had seen the night before.

Annie is in love with Efrem, concluded Sadie. I wonder if she even knows it. She's a lucky woman. Memories of Marcus flooded her mind and heart. The bittersweet beauty of the moments spent with him was indelibly printed in her heart.

"Annie, I was wondering if you had any spare quilts that you would sell us for the journey."

"I sure do have extras, but I couldn't take money for them. That's just the way I pass the long evenings on the farm. They ain't worth much. I'd feel like I cheated you!"

"Annie, these quilts are worth a lot of money. I won't take no for an answer. Besides, they are so lovely, I would be proud to have everyone see them." With that, Sadie called Harrison and asked him to pay one dollar for each quilt that Annie wanted to sell. She had twelve in all, each one a work of art.

"Well, a dollar is too much to pay for these quilts, but Efrem could use a new set of work clothes," Annie whispered.

"The price has already been set, Miss Annie. We don't hold with backing out on our word," Harrison teased. He was enjoying this little episode

58

immensely.

It was the first time Sadie had seen Harrison with all his defenses down. She liked seeing him that way.

A tearful Annie thanked her so many times that Sadie was getting embarrassed just hearing it. To break the flow of thanks, Sadie asked if Annie would mind making a lunch for them to take with them on the road.

Annie was only too willing to fix a basket; she hustled to the kitchen to prepare the food for their trip.

When she was out of hearing distance, "Pretty clever," quipped Harrison. "Buy something from her and save her dignity. You know you are paying her more than a year's wages for those quilts, don't you? Efrem could never make that much money in one year on this small farm."

"Yes, I do, but they are so lovely. I couldn't pick just one, I had to have them all. I hope Lorrie doesn't mind paying a dollar for her quilt. If she does I will take that one too. We have to make room for them on the automobile. I just can't bear to leave even one of them behind!"

When everything had been shifted around to make room for the quilts, there was one valise left over. It belonged to Kate and inside was a blue velvet gown with pristine white lace at the neck. The dress had obviously never been worn.

"Humph," grunted Kate, "That old thing, just toss it in the ditch, I won't miss it at all."

Her eyes wandered to the others standing there and she spoke with such vehemence that they knew she meant it. "I mean it, get it out of my sight!"

Harrison handed the bag to Annie asking her to please dispose of it any way she wished, knowing full well if it didn't fit her she would restyle it or have a good start on another quilt, for these industrious people wasted nothing.

When they had gotten a short way down the bumpy road, Sadie looked back. Efrem, Annie, and the two children were waving through a cloud of dust at the shrinking automobile.

Chapter Six
The Detour

They didn't take chances with their sleeping arrangements from there on out. If it was early and they were near a town, they stopped for the night. Hotels were not as hypercritical as the farmers along the way. When they left Saginaw, they headed in a southeasterly direction toward Sarnia where some of the riverboat captains had told Harrison they could cross on barges that forded the St. Clair River most of the season.

When they reached the border of New York State, Kate piped up; "I want to visit someone in Buffalo before we hit New York City. There's a man I want to talk to and I have to do it face to face."

Harrison, Lorrie, and Sadie all looked at each other questioningly, but nobody spoke a word.

Sadie was beginning to feel a little upset to her stomach and she couldn't figure out why. The roads were so much better, hardly a bump in this new stuff called concrete.

When they reached the building where Kate's friend lived, it proved to be a saloon. Inside the place was plain, but clean, a huge mirror hung across the back bar and there were stairs leading to the second floor. Giant wooden columns stood at each end of the back bar and on the front of the serving bar were carved cupids with bow and arrow pointing at the sky.

Ignoring the women completely, the man behind the bar asked what Harrison would have.

Kate stepped forward and asked where Andrew Johns was and did he still own this establishment.

The giant of a man behind the bar, with tears streaming down his face, told them, "Andy was killed three nights ago by a cheating gambler. We buried him that next day in the local cemetery with lots of friends, but no kith, nor kin to see him off."

Kate's face went white. Her hand shook as she raised it to her mouth as though to stifle a scream and she slowly slid to the floor like a broken doll.

Harrison was the first to reach her. He picked her up and looked at the bartender for direction. The man nodded his head toward the stairs and reached them just ahead of the little group. He led the way up to an apartment that was fully furnished with the latest in furniture and whatnots. Clearly, this was the home of someone with excellent taste. On the mantle was a tintype of Kate, obviously taken in another time, under other circumstances. The gentleness around her eyes told the whole story.

Harrison laid Kate on the sofa that was in the alcove near the window, raising the window a crack to let fresh air blow over the inert woman. She stirred and let out a low moan. She sat upright and visibly pulled herself together.

Sadie watched wide-eyed as Kate transformed herself back into that hard, defiant woman that she had first met. It was a moment, Sadie never forgot. She hadn't realized how much Kate had changed since she had first met her. But, after seeing this transformation, she knew she liked the other Kate better.

Glancing around she became aware of the lovely things that were arranged in specific areas in the room. Under the gilt mirror that hung over the fireplace was a small ivory elephant with an upraised trunk. Sadie couldn't take her eyes off it.

She had never used the word exquisite before, but the word popped into her mind and stayed there, as though the word had been created for the carving.

"Who are you," Kate asked, "What gives you the right to be running Andrew's saloon?"

The huge bear of a man spoke in a soothing, singsong Irish brogue.

"Dear lady, I'm not sure who you be, but it's apparent that you cared for Andy and that's good enough for me. I loved the man like he was my brother. We were partners in the place and soon I was going to buy him out. He had some secret plan in mind that he wouldn't even tell me."

With a nod toward Kate, Harrison introduced Kate and the others to the now concerned man and a smile lit his amiable face.

"Now that I see you, Miss Kate, I think I know what he had planned. If I am right, you are entitled to half the place. No doubt about that."

Kate looked through the man and then she announced, "I don't want this place, just put a decent head stone on Andrew's grave."

"Mam, that is already being taken care of. I told you, I loved him like a brother."

"You're an honorable man, Sir," Kate replied, "And just what is your name?"

"Me name is Evan O' Brian, and I am at your service, Madams and Sir."

"Well, Evan O'Brian, if you don't mind, we will rest here for the night and be on our way tomorrow." Kate took charge of the situation as though nothing had happened.

Evan led them down a hall to bedrooms that were just as tastefully done as the main room. In the largest bedroom was another Ivory Elephant just as exquisite as the smaller one in the living room. It, too, was on the mantle, and it, too, was the first thing Sadie noticed.

She wanted to ask about the elephants, but she didn't know the man well enough to delve into his business. Besides she had a feeling Kate had more answers than Evan?

The morning came all too soon for Sadie. She had not slept well and her stomach was still upset from the ride. When she did get up, it was a wet dreary day and her spirits felt the same way. *Heavens,* she thought, *I have to stop moping around like this. Kate is the one that had the shock, not I. Maybe I will feel better after I have had something to eat. Lately food makes me feel better. I am going to have to watch that or my gowns won't fit.*

She found a basin of water and began her morning ritual of bathing first her face then the upper part of her body.

As she prepared to bath the lower part of her body, she saw spots of blood on her undergarments. *My curse has come too soon,* she thought, *I'm two weeks early, no, come to think of it, I don't remember having one last month or the month before or even the month before that. Oh, my God! I am with child! But that can't be. I took every precaution with my regulars.*

It's Marcus's child! It has to be! I can't lose it; it will be all I ever have of him. She quickly went back to bed and propped her legs high on the pillows, saying a silent prayer, tears welling in her eyes, heart beating wildly. Frantically she begged, promised, and even threatened her God to keep this child safe.

When she hadn't come out for breakfast, Kate came looking for her. The moment she saw Sadie she knew what was happening. Grabbing the basin filled with the bloody water, dumping it into the commode at the end of the bed, she hastened out to get fresh water and linens. Meeting Harrison in the hall, she hastily told him what was happening. She talked while she worked, not wanting to lose a second

The large pitcher of water in the hall was fresh, clear and slightly chilled.

This ought to be refreshing to Sadie. The poor child's going to need all the strength she can muster. Harrison didn't know what to do with his hands that kept reaching out to help Kate even though she didn't want nor need his help.

"For God's sake, Harrison, make yourself useful. Get me a bottle of brandy."

Perfect, thought Kate, *just what we need. I wanted to get out of here today.*

Evan, hearing footsteps above, came up the stairs two at a time, to see what the commotion was all about. He and Harrison passed each other on the stairs, shouting to each other as they passed, "What's going on?"

"One of the girls is ill," answered Harrison. "Where is the brandy?"

"On the middle back bar," Evan shouted over his shoulder, "Bring the good stuff!"

In the few moments that had passed, Kate made her way back to Sadie's room laden with sheets and the basin of water.

"We are in for a long day," she muttered to herself as she bathed the pale, helpless Sadie lying in a small heap in the large bed.

When Harrison arrived with the brandy, Kate took the top off, took a huge gulp straight from the bottle. She replaced the top and went back to bathing the brow of the suffering Sadie.

All of a sudden Sadie felt a wave of pain begin in the pit of her stomach. Then another, then like a gusher, the blood began to pump out of her. Every time her heart beat, the gusher increased. The pain subsided, but a sense of emptiness began to ebb into the place where the child had been. Sadie had a feeling of great loss that could never be filled. The tears flowed unheeded, washing her anguished face.

There was nothing Kate could say or do that would take away the great pain and hollowness that blanketed this small girl in this bed of misery. Holding her hand, rubbing her arms, and bathing her sweat-filled brow was the only comfort that she could provide for the desolate Sadie. She crooned as she cared for the bodily needs of the girl she had grown to love like a sister. She knew what it was like to lose a child. The pain is with out description. Hers was a different kind of loss, but a loss never the less.

In an unusual moment, Kate decided to confide in Sadie hoping it would keep her mind off the pain that Kate knew would follow. Kate went back in time to a happier life in her hometown.

"I was sixteen and in love. The man was a traveler who came to town selling pots and pans. I had loved him at first sight. He had a charming way, a ready wit, and the most beautiful smile. He stole my heart when he turned his smiling face my way. I felt his love engulf my whole being. I even shook from sheer ecstasy. I must get to know this traveling man, I vowed. Well, I did, and later found out that not only me got to know him intimately, but so did all the available women and girls in the county. Damn, what a fool I was.

" I remember the day I found out that I was with child. When I told my lover that I was with child he left town.

"I wanted to keep that baby, but I knew Pa was right. I had to give it up to be able to keep my head up in that town. Only bad girls had babies and no husband! What a laugh now!"

The memories came pouring back.

"That very day I packed to go visit Aunt Abby in Detroit, supposedly to help her as she had fallen and broken an ankle. That was what upright Christian families did when a girl was in trouble, send her away and give the baby to whoever would take it.

"Time dragged while I waited for the birth of the child. Aunt Abby kept me busy learning to tat, play the piano, and to sew a fine seam. I made gowns for the child and tatted lace on the collars to pass the long boring days.

"When the time came for the child to be born, Aunt Abby sent for the midwife to help with the birthing. She came into the room and examining me and announced, "Get ready for one hellava hard time. You are carrying twins and they are both big babies!"

"I knew I was huge, but I didn't expect or even think about two babies. Did I have enough gowns, how would I manage to take care of them? Then I had to stop and think; I couldn't keep them anyway. But how can I bear to give them up?" Kate's face reflected the pain even after all these years.

"I remember the midwife mumbling something about two more females to spend their lives in servitude to a man. I can still feel the wrenching pain when the midwife took the two tiny bundles, left the room without even showing me the infants. Sadie, the effort had drained my body, but never seeing the little girls has drained my soul."

Sadie's face reflected her sympathy for her tortured friend.

Kate sat with tears running down her face, crying for herself as well as Sadie. *Damn it,* she thought, *first Andrew dead, then Sadie's loss and now me sitting here digging up old memories.*

"I don't need these memories for me to remember all the pain. I carry it with me everywhere I go. Every time I take a breath they are in my thoughts.

I thank God for my cousin Dorrie. Being a widow she was able to take the girls and raise them as her own. She came along when I needed her. She was a blessing. She was right about my not seeing the girls too, even though it has hurt all these years. I would have liked to see them once at least. They must be ten years old by now. What I wouldn't give to get one peek at them."

What foolishness are you thinking, she questioned her heart, *you gave your word you wouldn't try to see them so stop all this foolish daydreaming and get down to the task at hand!*

Sadie began to stir and moan, like the mournful baying of a lonely wolf complaining to the moon.

Such anguish Kate had heard only once before, and then it had poured from her own soul.

Harrison softly knocked on the half-closed door and whispered, "Sorry to disturb you but Kate you need to keep up your strength, too, and lunch is ready when you are."

"Please go eat something. I will be fine. The pain is going away and I will probably sleep for a while," Sadie rolled over and drifted off to sleep.

Kate entered the hall leaned against the wall feeling rather shaky, and spoke to Harrison, "Good thing I'm going to eat something. I'm feeling a bit strange. It must be the long night, the strange place, and the stress of Sadie's illness."

Harrison took her arm, gently guiding her to the parlor where a sumptuous meal awaited. Lorrie and Evan were already eating ham, eggs, huge biscuits dripping with butter, and the best coffee Lorrie had ever tasted.

"I'm starved and I didn't even realize it until now," Kate burst forth. "No wonder I felt weak."

A concerned look passed over Harrison's face as he held the chair for her.

The three of them sat and talked for hours about the events that led them to be here at this time. Evan warmed their coffee several times, explaining that the extra flavor in the coffee was from eggshells and salt, which also took care of the bitter taste that usually comes with the chickery coffee.

Evan explained that Andrew had been near death when he and his partner had found him beaten and starving in an alleyway.

"We took him home, fed him, and patched his wounds and soon became friends. We told Andrew that he could stay with us as long as he needed to. Andrew worked every job that came his way and saved enough to buy out my partner. He vowed he would become the kind of man that a woman and child would be proud to call husband and father. Andrew had bought the carved ivory elephants in memory of the love he had lost and her child. He had hoped to return to that woman and make her his wife. "

Kate sat stunned. "I was that woman. I stopped to tell Andrew about the twins that he had fathered. I expected to find that footloose and fancy-free young rogue. Instead I have found a caring, sensitive human being, someone I would have been proud to call friend and lover. Life dishes out bitter fruit more often then it gives the sweet morsels of pleasure," Kate whispered.

They heard a muffled sound in the hall and turned to see Sadie leaning against the doorway.

"Please don't get up. I'm fine, just a bit weak. I would like a cup of that delicious smelling coffee and maybe a scone or two."

Everyone jumped up and began scurry around fetching food, coffee, and a chair for her.

Kate told her about their plans to stay a few days to look over the city, check on a few friends, and then be on their way.

Sadie was much relieved that she wasn't the cause of their delay in getting to New York City.

Kate had much to think about when she finally did retire for the night. The stories about Andrew were whirling around in her head. She rolled and tossed till the early dawn, at which time she fell soundly asleep.

Sadie woke with a start and realized that she felt weak, but at peace with the world. She had come to the conclusion that if God had wanted her to have Marcus's child this would not have happened. Sadie believed that God had a plan for everyone and it was not in his plans for her to have this child. Her body felt empty and her heart was a desolate place, which God would fill with the birth of another child someday. She rose slowly, bathed and dressed for the day. She went down to the tavern and watched the patrons who came to enjoy the ale and conversation. She sat quietly in a secluded corner just enjoying the warmth and friendliness of this refuge for the lonely.

Harrison woke early, but stayed in his room so as not to disturb the others.

He thought about all the things that had happened in the last few days and wondered if this was a wise move. He had such pleasant memories of his home in England, he wondered if he should think about a visit home. But no, he had given his word to Kate that he would be there to help get the new house up and running. "Well," he told the empty room, "enough of this daydreaming. Better get up and busy."

When he had bathed and dressed, he knocked on Sadie's door to see how she was feeling. There was no answer on the first knock, so he tapped a little harder. He became concerned and pushed the door open. The bed was empty, the bedclothes were draped across the end of the bed, and the soiled sheets were in a neat pile near the door.

Seeing all this, he knew she was all right, just needing time alone. He also knew he would not be satisfied until he located her. He could stay close and yet not disturb her.

Coming down the stairs, he spotted her sitting in the corner looking small and fragile. He smiled and tipped his hat to her, waiting to see if she would motion him over.

Sadie smiled back, a wan little smile, and continued to watch the men who came and went through the swinging doors of the tavern.

Harrison went to where Evan was wiping the already clean bar with a rag, making wet circles on the wood.

"How long has she been here?" asked Harrison.

"About two hours."

"Did she want anything to drink?"

"No, I asked when she first came down and she said no, she would let me know when she wanted something. My other patrons seem to enjoy her presence. They like looking at her. She is lovely. Sad looking, but lovely."

"She's had a hard time the last few weeks. She needs some quiet time to sort out her problems and put them in their proper place in her life. That is not easy for a young girl, yet it must be done if she is going to survive in this world. Hard times come to us all. They are no respecter of age, beauty, or gender."

Evan nodded his head in agreement with Harrison and kept polishing the spotless bar.

"Harrison, don't look now, but Lorrie just came in and she is headed toward Sadie's table. Lorrie is sitting down with her, that's a good thing, isn't it?"

Evan wasn't sure about what he was saying, he only talked to keep his mind busy, and he really didn't know these people well enough to decide what was good or bad for them. While he liked these new friends, he was anxious to have things back the way they were.

Besides, he had lost his best friend and really hadn't had time to mourn him. Maybe after they left he would be able to get his thoughts together. He felt like he was being disloyal to Andrew wanting these people to leave, but his life had been torn to shreds by the events of the last few days and he needed closure too. *Sure, I'm a selfish bastard,* he thought, *but my mum was right. Life does go on and I need to clear my decks and get on with the business of living.*

Harrison watched the two women out of the corner of his eye and was relieved to see a momentary smile spread across Sadie's face. It was gone as quickly as it started, but it gave Harrison a sense of relief. Things were going to be okay!

The men stood silent and watchful while Lorrie worked her magic on Sadie. If anyone could ease the grief that the girl was suffering, it was Lorrie with her gentle, happy nature. She was just what Sadie needed to help her to mend the shattered soul.

As they watched, the women rose, went to the stairs, and began the assent to the rooms upstairs. Harrison turned to Evan with a wide grin and patted his shoulder.

"If I'm not mistaken, we are on our way to recovery. She's a strong lass."

Again Evan nodded.

Harrison felt a sense of relief. Until now he hadn't realized how much he had come to like the girl. Now he knew what people meant when they said, a weight had been lifted off their shoulders.

Upstairs the women went to Sadie's room and Lorrie helped the exhausted girl onto the bed.

"I will just lie here for a little while. I'll be fine," Sadie whispered. "I wish I had one of my quilts to cover me. Will we be leaving for New York City tomorrow?"

Lorrie covered the tired young woman with a coverlet that was on the bed and left the room saying, "You rest for a while and then we will worry about what tomorrow will bring."

She went quickly down to where Harrison was standing and asked if it would be too much trouble to get one of Sadie's quilts for her.

Harrison immediately went to the barn where the Jalopy was stored and came back with quilt in hand.

It was a lovely thing with many bright colors patterned to look like the ocean with mountains in the background. Tiny scraps had been fashioned to look like flowers around the edge of the water. It was a restful, calming creation that resembled a splendid painting by an old master.

Taking the quilt, Lorrie went back to the room where Sadie lay deep in sleep. She gently removed the coverlet that was thrown aside by the sleeping girl. Lorrie gently arranged the quilt over Sadie, tucking the edges under the ticking of the feather filled mattress. Sadie snuggled deeper into the warm little nest that Lorrie had made for her.

Lorrie knew that somehow this quilt would have special meaning for Sadie when she awoke. *I'm glad that Harrison cared enough to select such a beautiful quilt,* Lorrie thought. *He is a good and caring man. Too bad he has this thing about Kate. I wonder if Kate knows he loves her. Oh, well, not my business.*

Now that Evan is a handsome lad. I wonder if he is interested in seeing a lady of the night, who is more than willing. We could be very good friends for the time that we are here. God, he has such a huge body and such large muscles, I wonder how he would be at lovemaking. Well, enough of that, you're getting yourself all worked up at the wrong time. Think about something else.

Kate had awakened and was preparing herself mentally to face the ordeal of visiting the grave of her dead lover. *Why does God give us the right person at the wrong time in life,* she pondered, *and then when you do meet again, one is taken away? Oh blast! It probably wouldn't have worked out anyway, so quit your feeling sorry for yourself.*

"Ladies," said Harrison, "this would be a fine time to go shopping for some new gowns, since your's are packed away and the excursion might help to take our minds off the visit to the grave."

Lorrie accepted right away, but Kate wasn't sure they should leave Sadie.

"Run along," volunteered Evan, "I'll watch over the girl. Besides, she'll probably sleep all day."

Kate agreed with him and the three of them set out to see the town. "This is what I need. To see his town and the people in it, before I visit Andrew's last resting place."

They saw black and Chinese people for the first time and decided that the dark skinned people were the more handsome of the two nationalities.

Lorrie and Kate had never seen a black person before and were fascinated with the handsome young black boys working in the hotel dining room. Lorrie's blatant staring at the handsome bronze waiter that brought them their meal was both funny and embarrassing to Kate and Harrison.

"Behave yourself," Kate chided her. "That is one man you can't have. It is not permitted, even in our society." Harrison nodded his head in agreement.

They finished their meal, and found a small shop where the gowns were not only lovely but also priced well within their budget. While the girls tried on the many selections, Harrison kept the proprietor busy asking questions about the town.

The woman was more than willing to give him as much information as she possessed. After all, they had picked out the best gowns from her stock and that would be enough money to pay her mortgage for the next three months. She told Harrison, "My name is Millicent Thayer, but my friends call me Millie. I'm a widow with three children to support. My husband was killed in Canada in 1884; he was in a gunfight over a claim he found. Durn fool went off looking for gold and found it, but before he could stake his claim some men came and drove him off. An old friend of my husband brought back the news. He was working the gold fields in Canada with my Fredrick. A band of rowdies rode in and run them off at gunpoint. Well, it seems my Fredrick, stubborn old cuss that he was, weren't about to give up what he worked so hard for. He waited till they were asleep and tried to take it back. It was a gamble and he lost. We would have much rather had a husband and father than any amount of gold, but it's too late now.

"My oldest boy works at the livery stable and my daughter keeps house for us all. My young one was just two years old when he left us to strike it rich, but with all of us doing our share we manage pretty well."

Millie suggested the travelers attend the many church picnics in the area, and of course the opera house in the center of town.

Harrison replied, "I doubt we would be welcome to the church doings, but the opera house sounds like a good bet for entertainment.

"What are the chances of finding a buggy for rent while we are here?"

"There is a fine one for rent at the livery where my boy works."

"What's your boy's name," inquired Harrison, "I will walk over and make arrangements for the buggy. Will your boy be able to drive us where we want to go? I will pay him extra to show us the town. Later we want to visit the cemetery on the outskirts of town. Does he know where that is?"

"He should. His grampa and gramma are buried there. Just wished his pa was there so I could visit him sometimes and tell him how we are doing. Suppose he knows, anyhow, if he went where I think he went. Sometimes I feel like he is looking down and saying, 'You got to watch those younguns better Ma, they need a man's strong hand to guide them.' I thought about trying to find a husband to help with the raising of them, but I've just been so busy and it didn't seem worth the effort. Sides, they're almost growed. Baby is old enough to feed the chickens and slop the hogs."

When Harrison came back from the livery stable, the ladies had changed back into their gowns and the packages were stacked beside the door. The boy with Harrison stood at attention waiting for instructions from the man who had hired him for the day.

"Come on, boy, help me load these packages. The ladies bought out the store!" With eyes twinkling, he began to pick up the carefully wrapped bonanza of gowns.

"Sir, my name's James, not boy, and I will be honored to help you load the stuff in the buggy, but I think you might want to have the ladies get in first. That buggy ain't that big. Course, I could always deliver these packages later, after you've seen the town."

"James, you stop yer sass. If Mr. Harrison wants you to load the buggy, that's what you better do," Millie shouted at the boy.

"Millie, I think the boy, er, James is right. I wasn't thinking about our comfort and I should. We've all had trying times lately and we need all the niceties we can get. You are raising a thinking lad. He will be a credit to both you and his father's memory."

James stood silently by while this discussion was going on, his face was red, his eyes were shining his chest expanded, and he looked as though he was about to burst.

When he turned toward Harrison, the hero worship was perceptible. Harrison had made a friend.

"Ladies, let us follow this young gentleman to our buggy and begin our afternoon jaunt. First, we will drive by the opera house, then to the museum to see some art. I hear they have some famous paintings from France hung in their exhibit hall. You ladies haven't seen anything until you have seen how those crazy Frenchmen put paint on canvas.

The opera house was impressively grand and would be open the following evening with a presentation by Miss Jenny Lind. They all agreed that they must see Miss Lind while she was in town.

As excited as children at their first circus, they ran to the back entrance of the Opera House and pounded on the door until the caretaker came.

"We're from out of town and we wondered if we could see Miss Lind's dressing room. There's a five dollar gold piece in it for you."

Taking the extend coin the watchman explained, "I can't see any harm in that. Just don't pass the word around. I'll have every man jack in town here bothering me. I won't get my work done and that would mean Miss Lind wouldn't have a clean dressing room. Sure can't have that now can we?"

He let them in, led them through the many ropes and pieces of scenery standing at angles to the stage, then to a small unkempt room with a single gaslight hanging from the wall, nothing like they expected for a famous beauty like Miss Lind.

"You can see I have a little cleaning to do before she gets here," he said wistfully. "Sure hope she ain't too fussy."

"My good man, you can't have a gracious women like Miss Lind use this pig sty for a dressing room. Isn't there any larger, cleaner room in this place?" The words exploded from Harrison's mouth.

"Well, there is one other room, but it's a storage room. Though it's a lot bigger, it's a whole lot dirtier," conceded the caretaker.

"You get another man to help you, get it cleaned up for Miss Lind by the time I get back and you will have earned another five dollar gold piece. I can't have an a gentle lady live in that kind of squalor."

On their way to the museum, the light hearted banter continued until they reached the tall solid stone building that housed some of the most beautiful and strangest art work known to man.

"Wealthy collectors lent much of it to the museum," Harrison told them. "It is the only way we would ever be able to enjoy such great works of art."

They wandered through the great room gazing at the strange, but beautiful paintings and sculptures that graced the vault like room. A lone guard stood near the entrance watching their progress. At the far end of the gallery, a short hallway branched off to the right and at the end of the passage hung a lone painting.

A wraith-like girl gracefully sitting near a pool and behind her, a knight rode toward her. They debated whether he was coming to rescue, love, or slay her. Kate thought the latter was probably true. She had betrayed him and he demanded justice. Lorrie picked the first choice, because everyone needed a knight in armor, and Harrison said he was coming to love her. Couldn't they tell by the girl's expression? He had seen that same look on Sadie's face when she looked at Marcus. They all agreed it was the look of a woman in love.

The mood on the way to the cemetery wasn't as sad as Lorrie expected, thanks to Harrison's light prattle.

He kept a running conversation going with first Kate, then Lorrie, and included James as well. Kate grew quiet as they neared the spot where fresh earth was piled in a slight mound, a make shift cross was pushed into the still wet earth. The name Andrew Johns was barely legible on the raw lumber. Kate stood near the head of the grave, head bowed, lips moving, shoulders trembling, uttering not a word. When she lifted her head, a smile shone on her face. It was as though she had spoken to her Andrew and he had made it right for her

They had one more stop to make before they went back to the saloon.

In the buggy on the way to the opera house, Harrison tried to maintain the same level of lighthearted chatter, but failed miserably.

After several attempts at conversation, he gave up and fell into an uncomfortable silence.

When they got to the opera house, the caretaker was waiting with a proud smile on his face. He ushered them into a room that was not only spotless, but also transformed into a warm, comfortable living area. An emerald green tufted chaise was in one corner. A dressing table had been set up with a beautiful scroll-work mirror hung behind the table, and red velvet fabric was draped dramatically over the wall to hide the scarred wood. Harrison was pleased with what the man had created; a small sanctuary for the famous Miss Jenny Lind, who was so far from home.

It had been an interesting day, but the three of them were tired and a little worried about Sadie. When they reached the saloon, Sadie was waiting, dressed, smiling a welcoming greeting. She and Evan had become better acquainted during the others' absence and were now on a first name basis.

Sadie chatted with her friends about the tour of the town, mentioning that she would like to see the museum before they left. A short time later, pleading a headache she went upstairs to rest.

Kate suggested they take Sadie with them to see Miss Lind, and then they should start thinking about the trip to New York City.

Harrison agreed that while it was all friendly and fun right now, they needed to get there soon to find a house to rent and get settled.

Evan was both sad and relieved to hear these new friends plan their departure. Although he would have liked to get better aquatinted with that Lorrie girl.

They decided to retire early so they would be rested for the next night. Just as they were heading for the stairs, Kate stopped, tapped her forehead and exclaimed loudly, "Harrison what have I been thinking? We can't attend Miss Lind's opening without the proper attire. We need gowns, capes, tiaras and opera glasses."

"You are absolutely right, my love, we can't have you attending a grand affair looking like scullery maids or country bumpkins," teased Harrison.

"James has delivered the gowns you ladies selected and I'm sure that one of those will do just fine," piped in Evan. "Besides, you would be the belle of the ball whatever you wore," he told Lorrie. "Er, all of you ladies would,"

73

he added stuttering and red faced.

Lorrie giggled and hugged herself. Good, he likes me too. I wonder if I should invite him to visit me tonight or wait until tomorrow after the opera. Maybe he will come up on his own. I guess I'll wait and see. It's not like he is a client that I have to succeed in getting him up stairs. This will be for pure pleasure, and I'm ready!

It was decided that even though the gowns were lovely enough, they still needed cloaks and accessories appropriate for the occasion.

Harrison assured Kate, "Don't worry, I will take care of that little chore while you rest up for tomorrow night. I have formal wear all ready for the gala review, but I'm sure no one will be looking at me. I will be escorting three of the most beautiful women in the whole state." Smiling, Harrison with a flourishing bow and a wave of his graceful hand went in search of adornments for the ladies.

Morning came with blazing sunshine, crisp azure blue sky, and a feeling of anticipation. Everyone was in a joyous mood; it signaled a new beginning for the adventurers. Tonight was the Opera and they would spend the whole day making preparations.

Sadie was the first to descend the stairs; everyone stood with mouths agape. She was an angel descending from the gates of heaven.

Next came Lorrie, small, blond, and lovely in her own right.

When Kate came down the stairs the whole saloon full of men stood and bowed to her beauty. Her golden hair was cascading down from a pile of curls topped off with a gold tiara sparkling with diamonds. Her royal blue velvet gown enhanced her china blue eyes and the cold beauty of the diamond necklace she wore contrasted with her warm rosy flesh. The largest pear shaped diamond pointed between her cupped breasts and tempted every man in the room to see what lay further beyond the cold stone.

Harrison walked to the stairs and bowing, offered his arm, "I never tire of seeing the effect you have on men, my sweet."

Kate's smile was reward enough for the compliment that Harrison had voiced. She was a great beauty, that was for sure. Men would be craning their necks throughout the performance.

"I'm glad we have a center balcony seat, so every man in the place can admire you ladies and envy me," he added.

James was on time, parked outside the saloon door waiting for the happy group.

Harrison had chosen well. The cape that Sadie wore over her red velvet

74

gown was a silver, incandescent material with a sprinkle of red stones at the throat.

A gold cape, adorned with gold fur at the collar complimented Lorrie's green velvet gown.

But the star of the group was Kate with a white fur cape over her royal blue gown. She looked like a blue butterfly emerging from a white cloud.

The men in the saloon stood and stared in awe at the three of them. They bowed as the ladies passed them to get to the buggy. When Harrison brought up the rear, the men clapped as he tipped his hat and entered the buggy with a wide smile on his proud face.

James sat on the high bench dressed in his Sunday-go-to-meeting clothes, also wearing a proud smile.

When they arrived at the opera house, the seats on the main floor were filled with finely dressed ladies and gentlemen, most of who were visiting with their neighbors in the seats around them. Some of the other balconies were filled with groups of ladies and gents as well.

Harrison escorted the three ladies to their balcony seats with great pride. After all he was with three of the most beautiful women in the whole house. Most of the men in the audience began raising their heads and staring at the place where the women were seated. Seeing their escorts acting so strangely, the women they had accompanied to the Gala, turned and stared too.

The house lights went down, a golden woman appeared on stage and began to sing in a high sweet voice. She sang one song after another, each more lovely then the first. The evening quickly raced by and before they realized it the adventure was at an end. They left the opera house humming the tunes that Miss Lind had sung so beautifully.

It was an evening they would never forget.

James was waiting for them at the front of the opera house with a smile that lit up his whole face.

"Mr. Harrison, sir, see what Miss Lind gave me." He produced a small lace handkerchief with the initials J.L. embroidered on one corner. He held it to his nose, and exclaimed, "She smells wonderful too!"

"How did you get that from Miss Lind?" Harrison asked. "You didn't make a pest of yourself, did you, son?"

"No, sir, I didn't. She was out at the side of the building during intermission, and I ran and got some water for her. She said she was happy to have a few moments of quiet and would I watch to see that no one disturbed her. I told her I would guard her with my life. She laughed a giggly little laugh and said that wouldn't be necessary. Just make sure she had a few minutes to herself. She tucked this in my shirtfront and went in to finish the show. She said I was the best guard she ever had," he stated proudly.

"I should have known that you would behave yourself. Your mother is raising you right," Harrison told the boy.

James's chest expanded even farther as he watched Harrison's eyes to determine if he were teasing him or if the compliment was real. Satisfied that he had really meant all the things he said, James helped Harrison hand the ladies into the buggy. When all were seated, he jumped up on the bench and began to drive the happy group back to the saloon.

It was late when they reached the saloon, but there were still a few patrons at the bar. The chairs were stacked on top of the empty tables, the spittoons were lined up on the bar ready for clean up, and Evan was pouring the last drink of the evening.

"Did you have a good time?" he asked. "Were there many townsfolk there?"

"It was wonderful," they all piped up in unison.

"It will be the most wonderful night that I will ever remember," Lorrie added. "There were beautiful women, handsome gentlemen, and the songs were wonderful. I feel like humming them over and over."

"Well, tell me about it while I finish the clean up," Evan urged the ladies.

"I guess I will just have to use my imagination to hear the songs," he bemoaned.

"No," chirped Lorrie, "Sadie can sing them just as well as Miss Lind and you won't have to pay the money to hear her."

"Oh, no, Lorrie, I can't sing as well as Miss Jenny Lind, nowhere near as well. I know you are being kind, but there is no comparison between her voice and mine."

Evan coaxed Sadie to sing a couple of songs that they had heard, while he polished the bar, spittoons, and swept the bar room floor.

When he was done, he just stood and listened to the sweet young voice telling the story of unrequited love. Sadie had sung all the songs they had heard at the show earlier. True, her voice was not the trained voice of Miss Lind, but the rendition was just as moving.

Evan took her hand and kissed the upturned palm, and gently closed the fingers around the kiss.

"This is a pass to anything you want or need. Only present it to me or mine and whatever you ask will be given, for I have heard an angel sing tonight."

76

Sadie's face flushed with pleasure while she planted a kiss on Evan's cheek, "My dear friend, you have just given me the greatest treasure on earth. Now I must go to bed, it has been a long day and I'm exhausted."

"Me too," Kate said, "I want to go to bed with the music still ringing in my ears and heart. This evening has been a night of rejuvenation for me. I want to hold on to this warm, contented feeling as long I can."

The tired, but happy group went slowly up the stairs and was soon asleep.

The creaking in the hall awakened Sadie; she lay very still and listened as stealthy footstep crept down the hall. A quiet knock on the door was answered by a murmur from Lorrie. Doors opened and closed softly and then silence.

Sadie smiled. Lorrie has gotten her wish. This is what she wanted to happen and she needs this man to fulfill her needs. She just can't help herself. Sadie rolled over, pictured Marcus in her mind, hugged herself, and went back to sleep with the smile still on her face.

Harrison was the first to rise in the morning; he took care of his toilet in short order and went down stairs for more of Evan's delicious coffee.

"I really must have the secret for this wonderful coffee," he told Evan.

"Come and you can watch me make a fresh pot," Evan told his new friend.

"There is no real secret as I told you. You just add salt and egg shells to the brew, but you can see for yourself. Matter of fact you can make the brew for the ladies." When the great blue porcelain pot was done cooking, they brought it into the bar and put it on top of a small potbellied stove that sat in the far corner of the saloon. The aroma filled the room and wafted up the stairs to the lounging women who were savoring those last few minutes before the day began.

Kate was the next one down, then Sadie and at long last Lorrie, looking slightly rumpled and thoroughly enchanting, floated in.

"What have you been up to that made you so tired out this morning?" Kate teased.

Sadie looked at Lorrie, smiled, but kept silent while the rest kept up the banter until both Lorrie and Evan's faces were crimson. At last when they could no longer stand it, Evan sputtered, "I was fortunate enough to spend an evening with a lovely lady and I'm not ashamed of it. I wish there could be many more nights like that."

Lorrie's face beamed. Sadie could swear Lorrie's eyes were filled with stars when she looked at Evan. Sadie prayed: Dear God, please don't let her fall in love with Evan. I don't want my best friend to be hurt. It's difficult enough for her living with this curse, this driving obsession to bed every man she meets.

Kate saw the look too and decided to move the departure day ahead to tomorrow morning.

"Harrison," she said, "I think we have dallied long enough in this town, bigger and better things are waiting in New York City and we need to get there soon!"

Sadie was more than ready to leave this place that held such torment filled memories.

They spent the day packing, saying goodbye to their new friends, and finally everything was set for the trip.

"When you're covered with this quilt you are covered with the love of your friends," Sadie said as she presented Evan with one of the quilts she had chosen just for him. Evan had tears in the corners of his eyes. They welled up and out, creating trails down his ruddy cheeks. Shaking his head to clear it, he told his newfound friends that he hadn't felt this way with anyone but Andy, until now. He would miss them, but he understood.

Promising to come to New York and pay them a visit, and, looking directly at Lorrie, he said, "That is a promise!"

They all were in a strange mood, excited, but wary of what this move would bring.

James was waiting outside the saloon when Harrison brought the contraption, as they had started to call it (after many bouts with breakdowns and flat tires), to the front door. Harrison loaded the extra baggage on to the already towering pile of belongings; it seemed as though the pyramid of things might topple at any moment. Asking James to fetch a rope he tied a canvas over the mound of clothing that dwarfed the horseless carriage

"Mr. Harrison, if you need help on the way to the big city, I could drive that machine, just give me a chance," James pleaded.

Harrison placed his hand on the lad's shoulder, told him, "I would like nothing better than to have you for a sidekick, but there is no room in the machine for you. Plus your mother and sisters need you. You are the man of the family, and a man doesn't run out on his responsibilities."

James hung his head and murmured, "You're right, sir. They are my kin and I need to see to them. It has been an honor to work for you. I will remember you my whole life."

Harrison shook hands with the young man, who had suddenly grown two feet taller in his eyes. *I would like to have a son like him someday,* he thought as he waved at James on their way out of town and on to a new adventure.

Chapter Seven
New York City

The town was in full fling when they arrived. It was the weekend and the streets were alive with every type of transportation imaginable. Gentleman and ladies were strolling up and down the streets gazing at the storefronts and each other.

The little group in the overburdened Jalopy felt like fools alongside these sophisticated strollers.

Kate urged Harrison to hurry and find a hotel; she didn't like feeling like a country clod.

The first hotel that they came to was full, but the man at the desk told Harrison to go two blocks farther to the south and he would find a clean place to spend the night.

The clerk at the next hotel made arrangements for a place to store the Jalopy, after he had them settled in their rooms. He had a black boy run to the nearest saloon and fetch ice-cold beer for the gentleman, on the house.

Kate looked at Harrison and asked, "Are you very tired, or would you like to wander around the town with me? I suppose things aren't much different here. I can't be seen on the streets alone. I need an escort to walk the damn streets!"

Harrison just chuckled. He had heard this a million times before and he did agree with her, it wasn't fair, but that is the way things were and he really didn't care one way or the other. It just wasn't worth fighting about.

Lorrie and Sadie waved the invitation, pleading exhaustion, but both decided to try the ice-cold ale. Sadie had never tasted ale, so the taste surprised her. She blew it out with a sputter.

"Yuck," she said, "That's awful. Why would anyone drink that yucky stuff?"

Lorrie laughed. "I'll drink that yucky stuff," she said as she reached for

Sadie's glass. She liked the dark bitter German ale because it reminded her of the beer her father used to brew back home. She poured another glass of the strong brew, licking the white froth off the glass and savoring the hops flavor.

A patch of the foam had stuck to her upper lip giving her a comical appearance, and the two glasses of ale were affecting her speech as well.

Sadie watched with amusement as Lorrie giggled at everything they talked about, the trip, the show with Miss Lily and the saloon. Lorrie's face became sad; tears slipped down her cheeks.

"I could have loved that Evan for the rest of my life, you know, but I wonder if I could have stayed true to him."

"Yes, I know, my dear. I think you are the bravest girl in world," Sadie answered.

"And the drunkest!" Lorrie said giggling. "Goodnight."

Sadie went to the bed where Lorrie had been sitting, took the glass from her loose grip, and set it on the nightstand. Picking up Lorrie's legs, she turned them facing the footboard.

"Well, she is still dressed but at least she's in bed," Sadie reasoned. "Now I must get some rest, too. I feel just a little weak from the trip."

Sadie went to her room, changed into a dressing gown and lay on top of the coverlet. Her thoughts drifted back to the farm and the stupid little antic that had set off the series of events that had led to this place. What was his name? I have met so many men over the years. Oh yes, Thomas. He seemed so wonderful then, and now I can't even remember what he looked like.

Would I change anything?

Hell, no! I would never have known that Marcus loved me. We would never have had those wonderful two years together. No! I wouldn't change a thing!"

With the noises from the street in the background and her heart beating with thoughts of Marcus, she was lulled to sleep.

The morning burst into her room on rays of sunlight, accompanied by a street symphony.

What a magical town this is. It's as if the city itself is alive. I can feel the energy in the air. It's saying hurry, come see the day, see what I have for you, there's a party going on and you're going to be left behind.

A sense of urgency came over her; she dressed and went to find the others. She didn't want to miss another minute of the excitement.

When they had all eaten, Harrison went looking for a place to rent, while the ladies went to the dress shops near the hotel. The manager had one of his brothers escort the women around this part of town. They found a small shop that sold curios from other countries. There were dishes from England, clocks from Switzerland, and carved ivory from China. Kate said it reminded her of the carved elephants that Andrew had in his apartment. She said wistfully, "I wish that I had asked for them."

Sadie grinned a delighted smile with the surprise she had for Kate.

"I have them in my suitcase. Evan gave them to me for you when you were gone sightseeing that day before we left. He said he wanted you to have them. Andrew had bought them because they reminded him of you. I was going to surprise you with them when we got settled."

"Oh, my God, I couldn't have had a better gift," said a tearful Kate. "Thank you. Oh thank you for bringing them. They are worth a small fortune according to some of these things that I see here, but they are priceless to me." Kate gently squeezed Sadie's hand and smiled. "Evan turned out to be such a good friend, I'm a lucky woman."

Harrison found them in the small shop searching for treasures. "Ladies, I have found the perfect place. It seems this house was no longer large enough for this newly rich transportation baron and his very young wife, so they built a mansion closer to town. His young wife didn't like being out so far from all the excitement of the city, but it fits our needs to perfection. It is out far enough to be private, yet close enough to be convenient for our clients.

"Kate, you must come and check out the house today. By the way it's called Haven Place. That is a worthy name for this wonderful place. Did I tell you it is completely furnished? There is a balcony that runs around the whole upper story. It's fabulous!"

I've never seen you so excited about a house before. It must be something really special. You have me anxious to see it too!" Kate grabbed Harrison's arm, pulling him toward the door.

"Come along, girls, we can't keep this eager man waiting any longer."

Once again the four acted as one. They were animated and carefree on the way to their new home. Harrison was the first to speak when they rounded the corner of woods and viewed the place they would call home.

"What did I tell you," he said, laughing and proud of his discovery. "Isn't it just about the most perfect place you have ever seen?"

Sadie could not believe her eyes. *They may call it Haven Place*, she thought, *but to me it's "Peaceful Valley," and that will be my secret name for it.*

"When can we see inside?" she asked. "I hope the owner lets us decorate. I would like a lavender room in this house, too. It is such a cheerful color."

Harrison smiled and said, "I was pretty sure you would feel that way, so I put money down to hold it for us," and he proudly produced the key. "We shall look at it right now, and, ladies, I think you will be in for a pleasant surprise."

When he unlocked the door, he bowed low and ushered them into a magnificent hall leading to a great room. Everything was as though the people who had lived there had just gotten up and walked out. There was even a fire in the giant stone fireplace.

They wandered through the rest of the house oohing and aahing; the house was ready to move into right this minute.

Kate exclaimed, "It is wonderful, but it must cost a fortune! We surely can't afford this palace."

"Yes, my dear, we can," Harrison explained. "The old boy was so glad to have it rented and off his mind, so he could get back to his young bride, he practically gave it to me.

"I told him we would check it out and get back to him tomorrow morning early. What do you think, ladies? Is it a deal or should I look further?" he teased. "If you like it you can stay here and get aquatinted with the house and I will bring the rest of our things tomorrow."

"Oh, yes, let's do that. Let's stay here tonight. We can explore the house and maybe find out its secrets," Sadie sang out to Kate as she danced around the room.

"I don't see why we should make the trip back to the hotel when we have such a welcoming home to stay in," Kate agreed.

"Besides we all can use the rest. Harrison, you might as well stay too. Tomorrow you can finish the business of renting the house."

"My dear Kate, I would love to stay, but I have to catch the owner before he leaves on his trip to England on his honeymoon. His ship leaves at noon and I want to find a cook, too. I'll need an early start if I'm to get everything done that needs doing."

"You're right, of course. I was just thinking it could be a little unsettling for three ladies in a strange house. You go ahead," Kate agreed.

"Are you sure you can manage all right until late tomorrow afternoon? I know I can't get back before then?"

"Just go. We will be fine. There are a million things to keep us busy around here, we will be so busy we probably won't even know you're gone,"

Kate teased. "We are three grown women. What can happen that we can't take care of?"

"A lot of things, but we won't go in to that right now," Harrison answered in a serious tone. "I don't even want to think about that. I need all my wits about me when I deal with the owner of this place. I have decided to barter with him and get the house down to a reasonable price, then buy it for us. What do you think about that?"

"Yes," they all shouted. "What a wonderful idea!"

As Harrison left for town, he made them promise to lock all doors and windows, just to be safe and ease his mind.

The women got their heads together and decided which rooms they wanted. Sadie discovered a violet colored room that exactly suited her. Lorrie took the room next to her and said she didn't care what color it was as long as it was clean.

In their wanderings, they found the linen closet. Lo and behold, there were enough sheets, pillowcases, tablecloths, and doilies for the whole house. Their first assumption was correct. The former residents had simply walked out and left everything.

By the time the girls finished putting fresh sheets on the beds and dusting the beautifully hand carved furniture in the rooms, it was after midnight.

Sadie was the first to suggest they search the fruit cellar for something to eat as she felt weak and hungry.

Together they went down into the cold, dank cellar filled with old furniture and trunks that had been discarded by the former tenants. They rummaged around until they found a rotted wooden door that was almost hidden by cobwebs. Behind it was a tunnel leading out into a dark nothingness. The women quickly shut the door and pushed an old piece of furniture in front of it. "We don't want any unexpected visitors, do we?" Kate gasped, out of breath from helping move the extremely heavy commode in front of the door.

Lorrie had found a shelf in the far end of the cellar that contained jars of food sealed with beeswax, crocks of pickles, and dried fruit hanging in mesh bags from the ceiling.

"Come girls," she said, " we have a feast here if everything is well preserved."

They took their treasures up into the kitchen and began opening the containers on the table. The first crock contained sweet pickles; the next one held pickled cucumbers, the next one-held beets that were pickled to perfection. The jars held canned meats, beef in one, rabbit in the second, and partridge in the last.

Kate became the official taster; she had a bit of each and pronounced them delicious.

The women dug in and ate till they thought their stomachs would burst. Sadie pushed back from the table, slid down and back in her chair and showed the others her protruding belly, rubbed it and began to giggle.

"I look like a bloated spider all arms and legs and a huge gut." Kate and Lorrie looked at her for a minute then began to laugh. When the spasms were at last over they felt weak, but tiredly happy.

"I'm ready for bed," Sadie announced. "I will see you people in the morning." She made her way to the stairs and trudged slowly up the spiral staircase to the room she had chosen for her home.

What a pleasant room this is, were the last thoughts Sadie had before she fell into a deep, much needed slumber.

She awoke with a start, hearing people moving around. The sun was shining brightly, birds were singing outside her window, and all seemed right with the world. She hugged herself and thought, how lucky I am: a lovely home, good friends and a job that pays me enough to live comfortably. Gosh, I even have money saved. Sure there are drawbacks to this job, but than I'm sure there are many more advantages to working as I do.

What was that strange sound penetrating her sleep dulled thoughts?

Throwing on a robe, she and made her way down the stairs and into the kitchen where she found to her amazement, a mountain of a woman, so black she shone.

When the woman smiled, the room lit up. She was the source of the low rumble that resounded through the whole house.

"I's be Jessie. I's be the bes' dam cook ina whole dam city of Nu York and who yo' bes?"

Jessie was busily scrubbing pots and pans as she talked, "Yo' would'n believe how nasty dese pots an pans were. They bes lucky they didn' die from the putrids."

"I'm Sadie. I live here. Sorry I'm so late getting up. I will fix myself something to eat, so I won't disturb you."

"Lik hell yo' will," Jessie boomed, "dis here's my kitchen, ain't nobody else cooks in my kitchen, yo' got dat straight? Sit yerself down an have some coffee while I's fix some food fo' yo', yer too skinny anyways. I'll fatten yo' up in no time!"

Sadie hastily sat down and watched this giant of a woman glide around the kitchen as though she was a wisp of a girl. The fear that Sadie first felt when meeting Jessie was soon changed to admiration as she ate the food that Jessie had prepared. There were ham, eggs, toasted homemade bread, home fried potatoes, and a slice of melon with the seeds removed. The coffee was good, but didn't compare with Evan's coffee. Maybe when she knew Jessie better, she might suggest that she try the recipe. For now she had just stopped shaking from her first meeting with the formidable Jessie, and she was in no mood to cross her path again.

Sadie heard a muffled chuckle behind her; turning she saw Kate standing in the doorway watching her eat.

"I see you have met Jessie," she said with amusement.

"She arrived here at the crack of dawn and took over immediately, beginning with the scrubbing of the whole kitchen. The only thing that saved me from a thorough tongue-lashing was the fact that we just took over the house. According to Jessie, the only thing that saved the former dwellers from the creeping crud was luck! She tells me she has never seen such a filthy kitchen, and I for one am not about to argue with her."

Jessie was scrubbing and polishing pots until she could see her reflection in them, humming while she worked. She had heard every word that Kate uttered, but chose to ignore it for the moment, she had more important things to think about than these white women standing around flapping their jawbones.

"When Mr. Harrison asked me to work, he tole me I be my own boss and thet's the way it's gonna be." After announcing that ruling, she burst out in song, loud enough to rattle the dishes on the shelves. That will take care of their tongue wagging for a while. She sang an old spiritual. It was impossible for Kate and Sadie to carry on a conversation in the same room with Jessie's boisterous song, so they went into another room as far from the kitchen as they could, with out leaving the house.

"Isn't she going to be an interesting addition to our household?" Kate said with a chuckle.

"She will be a handful if she doesn't approve of our lifestyle, but I don't think Harrison would hire someone that we couldn't get along with," replied Sadie.

"When I first met her, she scared me so badly I almost wet myself," Sadie giggled.

"Well, think about me," whispered Kate. "I had to answer the door this morning just before daybreak to find her standing on the veranda with a gunny sack on her back. It was so dark out all I could see were two white eyes and a mouth full of teeth smiling at me, and I did wet myself."

"Lorrie met her this morning and liked her on sight. I trust Lorrie's intuition about most people. Lorrie is like a dog I once had. She either likes you or hates you, there is no in between. The only two people I ever saw her hate were Maggie and your friend Robert. She always said he would kill someone, someday, that's why I told you never to let him go too far. That Robert sure was a strange one. He had a bad experience with his mother, and he has been punishing her ever since.

"Whenever he came to the house, he came to punish his mother in the only way he could. The bitch had money and thought that gave her the right to do whatever evil thing she wanted to do. She cheated Robert of his youth, killed his little brother, and then died from an overdose of cocaine when he was fourteen. That embittered old bitch destroyed her whole family and escaped vengeance."

Sadie sat with tears in her eyes, thinking about all the times she had secretly laughed at Robert's bizarre behavior. Now all she could feel is sympathy for the poor man.

"How do you know the story? Kate, did you know the family?"

"Yes, they were a very prominent family in Saginaw, and we were neighbors at the time. The whole town knew she was abusing her children, but no one wanted to do anything because they were wealthy. Robert's father vanished in the middle of the night and was never heard from again. Some folks said she killed him, but that was never proven or even investigated."

"I don't understand how a mother could hurt her own child or any child for that matter. As far as retribution, the good Lord will take care of her."

While they talked, the pleasant sound of Jessie's humming filled the silence of the house and turned it into a home. Both women felt as though Jessie's presence filled the chasm they hadn't realized was there.

A sudden banging on the door startled them out of their pensive mood. Jessie hurled open the great heavy door like it was a piece of parchment on hinges and ushered in two young girls with frightened expressions on their faces.

"Well, git yerselfs in here so's I's kin shut dis door. I's ain got all day ta stan' here. They's some folks got work ta do round here! What the hell do ya want," she asked as she slammed the front door, "and who the hell sent ya?"

. "We were sent by a man named Harrison, he said you needed clean, experienced girls," whispered the tallest girl.

When Kate heard that they were experienced, she thanked Jessie for helping her, and took over the rest of the questioning.

Jessie went back toward the kitchen smiling and crooning a soothing tune; the kind mothers hum while rocking their babies.

Sadie watched as Kate asked them who had hired them, where they had worked before, and how they felt about their former employers?

"I'm Dorothy and this is Phoebe. We worked for a woman called Fancy, and she got the sickness and died. The sheriff nailed the doors and windows closed and run us girls out of town. We worked for Tillie a while back, but she left town with a preacher man; said he was gonna save her soul. Phoebe and me stayed together while we were searching for another house. We met Harrison in town and he sent us out here to see Miss Kate. We are honest, we don't rob our visitors, we keep ourselves clean, and we don't have the sickness. We like our work."

"I'll give you a try after the doctor checks you over just to make sure you're not sick. In the meantime you can stay here, so get your luggage and come back." Kate had been watching them with the eye of an eagle. If they had lied to her, she would have had Jessie throw them out bodily.

They stepped outside the door and reached behind the shrubs that grew alongside the house, pulled out two suitcases, a couple of other parcels, and a basket with a bundle inside. A cry arose from the basket. It sounded like the mewing of a kitten.

Kate was taken aback by the sound. Why would anyone want to bring a kitten on an interview? Peeking beneath the cloth cover, she found to her surprised dismay an infant.

"My God, that's not a kitten, it's a baby! Well, I can't have that. There's no way I can let you stay with that baby. Who's going to care for it?"

"We have tried everywhere and you are our last resort. We can't just leave the baby to die. No one wants the brat of a prostitute. She wouldn't have a chance." Phoebe explained. "At least here she would have Dorothy and me to care for her. That's better then nothing."

"Well, I won't throw you out right now, but if you or the child gives me any trouble, you're out on your ear. Is that understood?" Kate asked.

She turned to Sadie and asked, "What in the hell have I gotten myself into and what in hell does Harrison think he is doing, putting me in a spot like this? Wait until I get my hands on him. He's going to get an earful!"

She turned to the two women saying, "You two better be dammed good at what you do to earn a place in this house for that kid. After all, this is a whorehouse!"

Sadie smiled at the two women, went to the basket and picked up the small bundle that was wrapped so tightly; it was like picking up a giant cocoon. She carefully opened the blanket and discovered the most beautiful child she had ever seen. Phoebe told her that Rachael was her name. Her mother died in childbirth. She was three days old and drinking goat's milk like a little pig.

Sadie's heart melted when she saw the child, and then the child opened her eyes and stared directly into Sadie's soul.

Jessie bounded into the room, took one look at the child Sadie was holding and declared herself "Aunt Jessie" to the little angel.

"We's gotta git a goat, Miss Kate," she thundered. "I ain't got no suckle left in me."

It started slowly, Kate, Sadie and Dorothy made eye contact, and then it began to erupt into full-blown fits of laughter. All three women laughed until they hurt; each would stop for a minute and stifle their giggles, look at each other, and then begin again.

"Can't you just picture this tiny little white creature at your huge black teet," stuttered Sadie. And they were off again laughing and choking; Jessie's laughter was like thunder, shaking the whole house.

"Lookie there now, yo' made me pee my britches" said Jessie, coughing. "I's ain had sech a good laugh in a long time."

This was the scene that greeted Harrison when he walked through the door: Sadie with the baby, the two new girls, Kate and Jessie, the cook, all standing in the front hall surrounded by luggage and laughing like fools.

"What a happy homecoming," declared Harrison. "And where did that child come from?"

"You mean you didn't know about the child when you sent these two? I should have known better than to think you would trick me into accepting a child in the bargain." Kate informed the happy group, "I said you could stay till we see how it works out, and I won't go back on my word, but God help you if it don't work out."

"Ladies," Harrison said, "let us move out of the hall and get ourselves acquainted with each other. There is much to do to get us settled before the rest of the girls come. You two might want to pick your rooms before the others arrive. I would suggest a room at the back of the house, and make sure you're near the back stairway to the kitchen, so you can feed the child in the middle of the night."

The two women exchanged relieved looks and headed for the stairs, the baby forgotten in their haste.

Sadie nuzzled the warm soft neck of the now sleeping child. The baby had that special scent of a newborn that makes mothers want to nurture and protect that child with her life. Sadie felt that primal instinct rise in her. God had sent her a gift to ease the pain of the child He had taken away.

The baby Rachael smiled and the room seemed to glow. Coming down the stairs, Jessie observed that exchange of love between Sadie and the child and she declared "Sadie, you is blessed! Fo' sur' that child is yers. She was sent by God!"

It was decided at that moment that Rachael would be Sadie's responsibility. After all no one dared cross Jessie when she had her mind made up.

Sadie was secretly happy that the baby would be her obligation for a while, she still felt empty inside. She needed this time to mend both body and soul.

Chapter Eight
The Gift

Kate and Harrison went to the room that Kate had chosen for her office, closed the door and in hushed voices exchanged views on what had just happened. They decided to give Sadie a month to get adjusted to the house, the baby, and time for her body to heal.

"It should take about two weeks to get everyone we need to run the business and to gather a clientele. Then we could have Sadie just wander around to help the guests be more comfortable," said Harrison "If that doesn't get the clients interested and vying for her affections, nothing will. In the meantime Lorrie, Dorothy, and Phoebe should be able to handle any early clients that show up.

"By the way, I haggled with the owner of this house so long he became frustrated and sold it to us for a song. Instead of renting, we own it! He wanted to get back to his young bride so bad, he let me bargain down to a ridiculous sum, threw up his hands in frustration, and said, 'All right, all right, it's a bargain.' "

Harrison was grinning ear to ear. "You know, I think this is going to be a very good move for us. The money flows like wine, and they are all looking for ways to spend it. You wouldn't believe how many wealthy men I met just today, and they are hungry for beautiful women to show off at parties and the opera. This town is ready for us!

"We should have no trouble filling the house with clients, as soon as they find out we're here. The others in this business are taking them to the, "outhouse," by stealing from them and watering the whiskey and wine. All we have to do is run the business the same way we always do and they will flock to our door."

The days passed swiftly. Soon the house and grounds were ready for business. Sadie had given Kate, Harrison, and Lorrie each one of her precious quilts, choosing the quilt to match the owner. She gave Lorrie the one that reminded her of a flower garden in spring. Harrison's quilt resembled an English moor, and Kate's quilt was as stately as she, giant columns arranged in symbols of strength, yet glorious to look at. Sadie kept the other quilts tucked away in her room for safekeeping. The quilt she had used in New York, when she was so sick, she kept on her bed as a quiet reminder of a child that God loved enough to take back home with Him. This she had to believe so she could go on.

When she presented the quilts to her friends she told them, "This will make this house our home. We bring a part of our lives to this house that is without memories. I can feel its emptiness. Our love and laughter will fill that void. Even after we are gone from this place, the memories will remain. The house knows we love it and it will love us back."

Lorrie stood with tears in her eyes, so moved was she by Sadie's little speech. She hugged her friend and said, "You are forevermore my sister." Looking at the rest, she shouted, "I love you all, " and dashed up to her room.

Kate and Harrison both thanked Sadie and teased each other about Lorrie's outburst. Kate said, "I know how she feels. This is the closest I've come to having a family."

The men of the town had accepted Haven Place as the best spot to be when ever they needed relaxation or were entertaining clients. Every night was as busy as the weekends used to be back in the old hometown. Money flowed seemingly without end.

The ladies at Haven Place were taken out to grand parties, plays, operas, and even on trips out of the country. Even Lorrie had made two cruises to Europe with one of her favorite clients.

Sadie had refused to go away from Haven Place for even one night; she didn't want to leave Rachael. She had grown used to having the little chubby minx jump into her bed when she woke up in the mornings. That warm, wet, cuddly little person had stolen her heart. She didn't want to miss even one day with her. Rachael's hair had turned darker and curled around her head like a crown. The blue eyes had deepened into a blue green, gem-like color. The child was as even-tempered as she was lovely, and was a joy to be around. Jessie spoiled her every chance she got. She made such a fuss when Rachael was scolded that the household took care never to let her hear them admonish Rachael for anything. Jessie told them all, "Ain' nobody gonna hurt my sweet angel or they gonna deal with me, and thet ain' the bes' thing to do, no. No, sir, thet ain'!"

Sadie was trying to potty train Rachael before her third birthday, but Jessie kept saying, "leave her be, when she ready, she stop, till then let her pee were ever she wan's, I don' min' scrubbing her drawers and her bottom. Mark my word, she most ready."

Sadie had grown used to being treated like a queen by her gentlemen clients and often thought about how badly she had been treated by Robert when she had first started working. He had paid a lot for the privilege of spanking her, but she thanked God that that didn't happen anymore.

"Kate has been looking rather peaked lately. I wonder what's going on with her. She has always been so strong, it scares me to see her this way," Sadie confided to Lorrie.

"Yes, now that you mention it, she does appear to be under the weather lately. I seem to remember when we were in Buffalo, she didn't look too well either, but I chalked it up to hearing the news about Andrew," Lorrie answered. "We better have a talk with Harrison as soon as possible."

They were sitting in the parlor talking over tea, when a rapping on the door interrupted them.

Jessie appeared out of nowhere, as usual, and ushered the caller in, demanding, "Who yo' bes, come here at this time a day, wha' tha hell yo' want?"

Sadie and Lorrie both heard the stuttering voice at the same time, letting out a squeal, they ran to the door to rescue Otto from the clutches of the formidable Jessie.

Otto nearly fainted with relief and laughed heartily, but when he saw Sadie, his face changed abruptly as if he suddenly remembered something. The two women hugged him and coaxed him into the parlor, asking a million questions at once.

"Before you squeeze the vater out of me, show me vhere I can relieve myself."

Laughing Sadie led him to the bathroom, whispering, "She does that to all our friends. Don't let her scare you. She has a heart of gold. We really couldn't manage with out her."

Sadie went back into the parlor to wait with Lorrie; they had three years of gossip to catch up on.

Jessie had brought another cup, saucer, and more scones for the frightened traveler. "Who he bes?" she asked.

Sadie and Lorrie both spurted out, "A friend from home."

"Yo' wan' me ta wake Miss Kate?"

"No, not just yet. She hasn't looked like she has been sleeping very well. We will wake her later, " Sadie responded.

Kate had heard the knocker and wondered who was calling at this early hour, but feeling tired she decided to stay resting. If it were anyone important they would come for her.

Otto made his way back to the doorway of the parlor. Seeing Jessie, he scooted around her and quickly ran and sat next to Sadie.

Jessie's laughter rumbled through the house as she ambled to the kitchen muttering under her breath, "Got thet little piss ant scared an thet's the way I's lik' hit!"

Rachael came bounding in, stopped, looked Otto over, went up to him and hopped up onto his lap, wet bottom and all.

Otto didn't know what to say or do. Again the women came to his rescue.

Taking Rachael by the hand, Sadie led her to Jessie in the kitchen, putting her on a chair she ask the doting Jessie to keep her busy so they could visit with their friend.

Jessie was only too glad to have her little angel to herself.

"Yo' take long as yo' need, little missy and me gonna make meat pies fo' supper. Then we's gonna feed them birds thet been hangin' round all spring. They's got babies by now and they don' have much time ta fatten em up fo' winter. They's God's gift ta us, ta brighten our days and take away bad thoughts."

"You couldn't have a bad thought in your whole body," Sadie replied.

Jessie got a sad, faraway look in her eye. "Don' yo' believe fo' one minute thet I ain' all yo' people think I's is and then some, but I's do hav' thet dark me and I don' ever wan' ta show yo' thet one. She' the devil fo' shor'."

Sadie left the room deep in thought. She believed every word Jessie said, and somehow she knew there was another side to Jessie that was dangerous. She would always keep on the right side of her friend Jessie. Harrison having heard Jessie's voice came in from the garden where he had gone to smoke his cigar and daydream.

Entering the parlor, she felt the tension in the air. They had stopped talking when she came through the door, an uneasy silence hung heavy in the room.

"What is it," Sadie asked "What is going on that I should know?"

Harrison took her hand and Otto patted the seat beside him. She sat down, faced Otto, said," Tell me what is so serious that I have to be prepared to hear it?"

He had terrible news for Sadie. "I haf to deliver hurt to someone I luf.

Vell," stuttered Otto, "I bring you news of your mudder's passing one year ago, dear girl. She didn't suffer. She had a spasm of the heart, fell down und never moved again."

Sadie couldn't believe her ears. Her mind filled with a whirlwind of accusations, her mother dead and she hadn't known that she had been gone for a whole year. Shouldn't she have felt something, known in some way that a part of her was missing? What kind of daughter was she? Why didn't she sense her mother was dead? She tried to think back, where was she and what was she doing at the time of her mother's death. Was there something, some feeling that she had ignored?

"I should have been there," she screamed. "She always worked too hard and I left my chores for her to do, so I could lollygag with Thomas. I will never forgive myself!" She crumpled into a heap against Otto and sobbed. Harrison brought her a glass of brandy. She pushed it away saying, "I feel bad enough already and I don't want to feel worse."

Otto took the glass and pressed it to her lips saying, "Try to take a sip. It vill sooth you und take that cold feeling avay."

Sadie knew her friends were concerned about her, so she took a sip, shuddered as she felt the warmth slide down her throat and spread through her whole body. She took another sip, larger this time and the warmth continued to penetrate her being. She handed Harrison the empty glass and said, "Please." He poured a half glass for her and watched her drink it in one gulp.

A concerned look flashed across his face, but he said nothing.

Kate spoke in a cynical tone saying, "Tell her the rest."

"What else is there to tell?" asked Sadie, "My mother is dead, nothing else is important."

Otto patted her hand and muttered "I vish I didn't haf to tell you this. It breaks my heart."

"What! Just what the hell do you have to tell me?" shouted the distraught Sadie.

Otto stuttered the damaging words out, "Your father married that slut Maggie! She bothered your bruder so much, he left the farm. He vas vorking in town a little bit, but dere isn't much vork dere. He vas tinking of joining the militia when I left."

The color drained from her face, her mouth twitched, and her eyes stared straight ahead. The shocked expression on Sadie's face scared her friends. Slowly the pink inched back into her face. She heaved a wretched sigh, tears began to flood her eyes, and she swallowed that bitter pill. She reached over, picked up the brandy bottle and poured a full glass. She downed it in two swigs, reached for the bottle again and poured another.

Harrison took the bottle away from her and said, "This is no answer. I know, I used it as an excuse for not facing the truth. It doesn't work. The pain is always there when you sober up."

Jessie came into the room saw what was happening, and left again. That amazed the others in the room. There had never been a time, until now, that Jessie didn't have something to say.

Sadie agreed with Harrison and decided she would go to her room, "Just to be alone for a little while." While the others were talking, Sadie slowly wandered toward the stairs. When she knew no one was watching, she quickly grabbed a bottle of brandy and headed for the privacy of her room.

Jessie announced that dinner was ready. The others drifted down to the dining table, sat down, and began to eat. The talk was mostly about the things that had happened in the past week. Nettie, one of the older girls, told the others that her friend had asked her to marry him.

"But I said no because he was too old. Someday I might meet the man of my dreams and I don't want to be married to an old man when and if that happens. Of course I didn't tell him that, he thinks he is the only man who can please me, and I plan on keeping it that way."

"Ladies," Kate said, clapping her hands to get their attention. "Sadie is shattered by her mother's death. We will do everything we can to help her through this crisis. Is that understood?"

Back in her room Sadie was morosely thinking, *he marries a woman who is a slut, but throws his only daughter out for fooling around with the hired man. What kind of justice is that? Damn him! Damn him! God damn him! I could have been there for mother if he hadn't been so pig-headed. Well, they don't have to worry. I won't ever be back to bother them in their little love nest!*

Each time she made a promise to herself, she punctuated it with a drink. She was soon falling into a drunken stupor. She heard knocking on her door but she mumbled, "Go away." They all left her alone.

It was dark when Sadie opened her eyes. Her head hurt, her body ached, and her stomach was growling.

"I feel awful," she whispered. "I better have a little drink to help me shake off this horrible feeling." She felt around in the rumpled bed until she found the empty bottle. "Damn it, I must have spilled it in the bed. I surely couldn't have drunk all of it."

"Well there's plenty more where that came from," she placed her feet on the floor by her bed, stood, and nearly fainted. Hastily sitting down, head reeling, with a sick feeling in her gut, she waited until the agony passed. An intense craving for more brandy pushed her to stand. This time she was steady on her feet. The hunger in her stomach was for food, but the hunger in her brain was for the elixir that promised forgetfulness. The devils brew won. She staggered down to the parlor, found a full bottle of brandy, went back to her room, and started the ritual over again. She cried for what might have been. She raged against her father, cursed the very life of Thomas, and finally fell into unconsciousness. These episodes went on for three days and nights. Everyone tiptoed around the house afraid to wake her and start the cycle over.

The next thing Sadie knew she was in the arms of Jessie and being hauled down the great winding stairs. Jessie had her slung over her shoulder, and Sadie was looking at Jessie's large backside. Opening the door, Jessie sat Sadie on the porch, gave her a push, and said "Yo' kin come bac' in when yo' can behav' yerself. Till then, little missy, yo' arse is outside." She slammed the door and told the others, "I's be answerin' thet door, don' nobody touch hit!" She made her way back to the kitchen and began her ever-present humming.

Sadie couldn't believe what was happening. "Who the hell does that bitch think she is?" she mumbled. "How dare she throw me out of my own home!" Her pathetic ravings landed on the crisp cool breeze.

You're out again, you have no home, you are being punished for the same thing others do. These thoughts ran through her head like a constant drum beat.

The injustice of it was a bitter pill to swallow.

She pounded on the door, begging to be let in and pounded some more, still no answer. Her hands became numb, and her shoulders ached from the constant pounding. After what seemed like days, she crumpled in a heap; her will to fight was gone.

That is what Jessie was waiting for. She hurried from the kitchen, threw open the door and scooped the limp girl up into her arms. She made her way up the stairs to Sadie's room, laid her on the bed, and began to soothe her.

"Honey chil', yo' done got yerself off on the wrong trac', an' the onlyest way to get bac' is ta scare the hellishness out of yo'.

"I's knowd cause I's been there, in thet same place as yo'. It bes a livin' hell! Now, yo' git some rest while I's fix yo' some food and warm milk. Yes, I's said milk, an yo' better drink ever drop!" Jessie picked up the partially empty bottle and headed for the door. "I 's be bac' wit' the bes' damm food yo' ever et."

Sadie lay feeling weak and foolish. "My God, how will I face the others? What will I tell them?" she mumbled as she drifted off into a restless sleep and dreamed of Marcus, her love. In her dream the hunger for his touch swept over her. She felt her fingers running through his dark hair, and tugging on the stray curl that always escaped to lie on his forehead. The dream was so real that she felt the strength of his strong arms holding her close and his lips murmuring words of love. Warmth crept over her; she nestled deep into the rumpled quilt and slept the sleep of the just.

When she awoke, her head ached, her stomach was heaving violently, and she wished she could die! She struggled to get up and make it out to the balcony where she could get rid of this bitter bile that surged up into her throat. She never made it past the edge of the bed. All the bitterness welled up and out.

Although she felt better, she also felt a deep shame, the thought of facing the others made her cringe.

"You got yourself into to this and you have to get yourself out," she told the gaunt faced women in the mirror. "That means facing the rest of the household and apologizing. They are your friends. They'll forgive you. God help me when Jessie sees this mess. I better clean it up now."

"Wha' in hell do yo' think yer doin'?" demanded Jessie as she hurried in with a tray of food, "I don' let no puke stan' ina way of one of my meals. Yo' get yer arse over here and eat these vitals!"

Jessie had entered the room like a whirlwind, "Here is som' of the bes' food yo' ever et and yo' better put it all way. I can' stan' a picky eater, so clean thet plate!" Jessie threw a towel over the mess and told Sadie it could wait till later, when her tummy felt better. Sadie was ravenous; she tore into the food and ate to bursting, an indelicate belch signaling the end of the meal.

Jessie sat watching, occasionally nodding her head in agreement with some unknown presence. Sadie excused herself, and Jessie said, "Better out then in. Same with farts."

She did have to admit to herself that she felt much better. Jessie might be a bossy bitch, but she was right about feeling stronger after eating. I wonder how she knew so much about drinking too much, and what it does to a person?

I'm going to have to ask her about that someday, but not today.

Rachael knocked quietly on her door, asked if she could come in and snuggle. "I miss you when you're sick. I hope you feel better soon."

She motioned the child into her bed. Holding her close, they both drifted off to a place where dreams come true. Too soon Sadie awoke and lay gazing at the small girl beside her. Rachael was so beautiful that Sadie choked with emotion. *I must see to it that she never has to work like this.*

Sadie's eyes were getting heavy, she lay back against the headboard for a minute and woke hours later. The mess was gone, the room smelled fresh and clean, a breeze was gently blowing the curtain, ushering in bird songs. Thank goodness for such good friends. She daydreamed until the child awoke wet and hungry.

Jessie came looking for Rachael. She took her under one arm with her wet bottom sunny side up, and a mass of ringlet's flopping around her face. Rachael was squealing at the top of her lungs. She loved this game they always played; Jessie pretending to be angry with her for wetting her undies. Telling her she was "Gonna hafta wash her own clothes ifin she didn' stop peein' purty soon."

Kate stopped by to see how Sadie was feeling and she told her they were all worried about her and they hated to see the Sadie that she had been the last few days.

"We have all been pretty patient with you, but this behavior can't continue. We love you but we are, after all, running a business here. We can't have drunken women staggering around making a spectacle. From now on you will drink tea when you are working and that is an order."

"Otto is beside himself because he brought you the bad news that set you off. Harrison has taken him to town to take his mind off your little episode. We don't want a repeat of that behavior. Do I make myself clear?"

"Yes," Sadie answered. "I am mortified by my behavior. I will never do that again."

"Good, and I will hold you to that promise," Kate said as she headed for the door. "By the way, the clients know nothing about this and I plan on keeping it that way. Be ready to work tonight. A lot of our clients are asking for you and I wouldn't want to disappoint them again tonight."

A surprised Sadie confided, "I have missed them too. I remember when I used to pretend I was someone else so I could have relations with a man. Now I miss the affection I receive from my clients. I guess my body has grown used to being with a man, now I am eager to share a bed with them.

One at a time of course," she chuckled.

"Damn right we get used to it," Kate grinned and grabbing at her crotch. "We all need a little loving." She sailed out the door and headed toward her room where Harrison was waiting.

Sadie got out of the bed, her hand brushing the spot where Rachael's undies had leaked onto the spread. She touched it gingerly, checked to see if it had seeped through to the sheets. It had, so she busied herself pulling off the damp sheets and piling them by the door. As she did so, she could smell the faint fragrance of the spilled brandy drifting up from the soiled sheets. *Damn,* she thought, *that does smell good. Maybe one little drink would be all right. I don't see what harm one little sip can do. It isn't as though I want to get drunk again. If I can have one little drink maybe it will make my headache go away.* Making her way down to the parlor, she looked around, making sure she was alone, then headed for the brandy. She was reaching for the full bottle when she heard a rustling behind her; she turned and saw Jessie watching her with grief-stricken eyes.

"Baby, yo' ain't agonna get thet bottle if I can hep it. Yo' gonna have ta tak it over my dead body. I know'd what kinda hell yo' goin' through but thet devil's brew won' hep. It jist make hit wors'. Believe me, I knows. Ole Jessie, here wen' through the same thing a few years pas' an' I kilt a man. I hada leave my home, an' the family I lov', all cause I couldn' hol' my liquor. They's some folks like yo' and me thet jist can't drink the devils brew and then stop. We's crave hit like a baby craves the tit. Think we's can't live without hit, but it's the onlyst way we's can live, is without hit."

Harrison came into the room and casually asked what was going on.

"Ain't nothin' we can't take care of," answered Jessie. "We jist chewin' the fat till Kate gits down, thas all." Her tone of voice left no doubt that there would be no answers. Harrison shrugged his shoulders and walked to the fireplace. There on the mantle was a bottle of brandy. He casually picked it up and placed it in the cabinet, locking it. He turned and smiled at the women. "I guess I'm getting old, I forgot to put things away after everyone left last night." He pulled out a cigar from his breast pocket, removed the paper band, and lighting it, sat down to wait for Kate.

The women exchanged glances. Sadie sat down, and Jessie, shaking her head, went toward the kitchen.

Harrison stared at Sadie for a while, then said, "I know what you're going through. I had the same problem for a time. After I learned that alcohol couldn't take away or solve my problems, I never felt the need to drown myself in it again. I am constantly on guard against overdoing it. I allow myself two drinks and that's all. No excuses! Just two. Think about it. You may not want to tempt yourself or you may try the one drink and sip method. One rule I try to follow is never taking a drink when you think you need it badly, which is when you lose control. And for God's sake, don't feel embarrassed by the last few days. Most of us have gone through the same battle and survived. You will, too."

Sadie felt better just hearing those words from her friend. She knew he was right, but she sure would like a drink!

The moment Kate came in she knew that Harrison had talked to the girl. She could always depend on him when the situation was more than she could handle.

"We have decided to add a couple of more girls to our house and we would like you to go with Harrison to help select them. It would mean a few days away, a new place and new people, a chance to get back on your feet. What do you think of that?"

"I would love it, but what about Rachael? Who will care for her?"

"Jessie is chaffing at the bit to be in charge. She will be right in her glory having to care for Rachael, so that isn't a problem."

Jessie, who was just entering the room, heard Kate and burst out, "Dammed right Jessie'll be in her glory, ta be looking after thet little angel. I can' wait ta git my hooks on thet child, she gonna quit pissin' her pants afore the week is out. She final ready!"

Sadie felt as though she was in a dream. Events were moving too fast.

She packed her bags that night. She and Harrison left the next morning for a city called Paterson in New Jersey.

Harrison knew of a woman who had some very lovely young girls, whom she was willing to trade for older, steadier girls. She had put out the word that her clients preferred older, more experienced company.

Sadie asked which girls they would be trading, and did the girls want to be traded?

"Yes, there are two who have asked to be traded. They're getting tired of the fast paced life we live. They want a change of pace, and are ready to live a more sedate existence, maybe even marry, and settle down. It's not unheard of, you know. Dorothy and Nettie have asked me if I would find them a place where they could work and be safe. I told them I would. They are good girls and will be an asset to any house. I will just have to check out the girls and the madam to make sure all is on the up and up. We don't want to take home sick or bad tempered girls. That's not good business. You can interview the girls while I talk to the madam."

"Do you still trust my judgment?" Sadie asked.

"My dear girl, if we didn't, you would not be here."

Somehow this trip was different from the others; she usually looked forward to small trips around the city and countryside. Her heart just wasn't into meeting and being pleasant to total strangers. It must have been the effects of the last week that had dulled her senses. She did make a halfhearted effort to be congenial, but it went nowhere with Harrison. He told her not to worry, just to relax and enjoy the scenery.

Sadie tried but the feeling of doom hung over her.

Chapter Nine
Blood Bath

When the Jalopy pulled up to the house, Sadie felt a shiver of foreboding. She blamed it on the bad week she'd had, mentally shook herself, and got out of the auto with Harrison. The feeling of dread would not leave. She hoped she was wrong, but she'd had these feelings before and they usually meant trouble.

Harrison knocked loudly, waited for a few minutes, and knocked again.

"My God, I've knocked loud enough to wake the dead, surely someone should be up and about by now." They waited a little longer, walked around to the back, and there on the back stoop was the body of a young woman, clothes torn, face slashed, and half scalped. Harrison grabbed Sadie, rushed her to the Jalopy and told her to find the nearest neighbor.

When he was sure Sadie was on her way to find help, he dashed back to the girl. She was sitting up, in a daze, crying softly, for her mama. He took her hand and whispered, "We have to get you out of here."

She looked at him as though she were looking through him, lifted her hand to her face, and began to sob again.

She moaned, "I'm hurt."

"Where are the others? Asked Harrison. "They didn't answer when I called."

"I think the others are dead." The frightened girl continued, "I was asleep when the screams woke me. I didn't know what was happening at first, and then he came into my room and told me I had to pay, too. I ran from him. I still don't know why this happened!"

"Do you know who it was who did this? Was it one of your clients, or a stranger?"

"A client, Robert. He's brutal! He beat Emma till she couldn't walk. Rosy, our madam told him he wasn't welcome here anymore. He threw a holy fit, called us pigs, whores, and sluts. Said we couldn't do that to him, he was tired of being mistreated. He said he could come back any time he wanted too and we couldn't stop him. We didn't believe him. We shoulda listened. Now they're all dead."

"We don't know that yet, but I'm not going in until I get some help. This maniac could still be inside," whispered Harrison.

They heard the sounds of the Jalopy, and a wagon at the front of the house. Voices were shouting to Harrison to call out, if he was still outside the house. Sadie and two men made their way around to where Harrison and the girl were. The men stopped, then moved forward, circling the two people sitting on the porch.

"It's all right, he's my friend," Sadie told them. They came onto the porch, and opened the door to the kitchen.

She had found a farm about a mile down the road, explained the situation, and had pleaded for their help. They lost no time in getting their wagon and following the frantic Sadie back to the house of horror.

The farmer and his son were big of frame and lean as bullwhips. Their occupation had fine-tuned them to all aspects of life and death, but not to the carnage they found when they entered the kitchen.

The floor was splattered with blood. The body of a woman was still sitting on a chair, her head leaning on the table as though she were sleeping, and her throat had been cut from ear to ear. The odor from the dried blood was overpowering.

The farmer's son went white, staggered to the door and vomited on the porch.

He refused to re-enter the kitchen until they had covered the body. The father returned with a blanket, draped it over the body, and called out, "Son, come help me search for more live ones."

Sadie remained silent, shaking inside. Meanwhile her mind was numb from the spectacle that had assailed them. The girl who was so badly wounded had fainted when Sadie pressed her wounds with a scrap of torn petticoat. The white piece of lace on the make shift bandage became pink, then blood red from the slashed face of the unconscious girl.

The men came out of the house and Sadie could tell by the look on their faces that it was bad news. The search was finished and they hadn't found another living soul; the girl on the back porch was the only survivor!

The farmer sat down on the back porch. He slouched down, put his head in his hands, and began to sob. The son joined his father, patting him on his back and trying to sooth the distraught man.

Harrison's red-rimmed eyes, and pinched white face told the whole story. His body was as taunt as a bowstring.

Sadie thought, *if anyone touches him he'll break.*

The farmer finally stopped the racking sobs, struggled to sit erect, the words were torn from his inner being. "We don't even slaughter our farm animals like that. My God what kind of sick beast did this? No one should die like that!"

The young farmer rang the fire bell that would bring the folks from town. The sheriff would need to know right away so he could get some men together for a posse. One person couldn't be expected to go after this maniac alone.

The girl had come out of her swoon and was babbling about Robert and his rage against women. She shook her head in disbelief, and the blood began to spurt out in crimson gushers from her neck.

The sight of the blood exploding from the blood soaked bandage triggered an unknown force in Sadie; she quickly grabbed the girl, pinned her down and demanded someone get flour for the lacerations. The men looked at each other dumbfounded,

"Move, damn you, or she'll die!" she shouted. When Harrison came back with the flour bin, Sadie took a handful and packed the wound till the bleeding stopped. She wrapped the whole, blood sodden mess with the discarded blood saturated bandages.

"There," she said, "I think that will hold her until the doctor gets here."

Sadie wanted to run but she couldn't make her feet obey her mind. *Dear God,* she thought, *did I really hear Harrison say her attacker was named Robert. It couldn't be the Robert I know. He's back in Michigan. It must be someone else named Robert. Please, God, let it be another man with that name.*

The banging of the fire bell rang loud and long. It seemed like a lifetime before the first people from town began to arrive. They approached the people on the porch, ready to ask questions, until they saw the girl's neck. The fear spread through them. They advanced warily, both repelled and fascinated.

Sadie could smell the fear emanating from the newcomers, a rancid odor, very much like the stench of dried blood on the helpless girl.

The townsfolk came in droves, ready to fight that familiar enemy, fire. When they heard the whole story, some retreated in horror, and others became incensed by the savageness.

Sheriff Hopkins asked for men to help him find this rabid killer. A group of men from town gathered around the sheriff while he deputized them. They crowded back into the carts and wagons, and headed for town, looking for a man named Robert, a stranger drenched in blood.

Doc Fredricks had come with the first group and was busy tending to the girl's injuries as best he could. He called for a wagon to carry the wounded girl back to town with him. The young farm lad had not gone with the posse; he had waited to help transport the injured young woman. With Harrison's help they gently carried the girl to the wagon. The young farmer sat close to the girl holding her hand, looking very solemn. Harrison was talking to the farmer when Sadie came unsteadily off the porch, turned her ankle and slipped down the steps.

Throwing herself back down, she began banging the stairs with her fist, and cursing her clumsy self. Frustration, anger and guilt raged in her.

"Why do I have to be so dammed clumsy, don't we have enough problems?"

"Damn it, Sadie! You have to stop taking the weight of the world on your shoulder. You have to stop blaming yourself for every misfortune."

"I know but somehow I do feel to blame. Harrison, could this be the same Robert we know?" Sadie asked thoughtfully, "I truly believe he is capable of this kind of rage. Dear God, why did this have to happen?"

"What makes you so sure it was that Robert anyway, and if it was, you could no more have stopped him than you could push back the sea! Besides, there are lots of men named Robert!"

"I pray you're right," she answered, "but I have this gut feeling it was the man we know. This could have happened to us you know. He was our client for three years, but I swear to God I didn't see this coming. Why didn't I see that Robert was close to breaking? Maybe I could have helped him lose that hateful, cruel nature."

"For God's sake, Sadie, get in the auto and stop thinking that way. It's been years since you've seen him. Surely you don't think he would wait that long to do what he did, if you had hurt him that badly," Harrison told the distraught girl. "We'll wait in town until they catch the person who committed this atrocity. It will give us time to check out some of the other houses in the area. If they don't catch that fellow a lot of ladies will want to leave this town in a hurry."

The hotel clerk, a scruffy, balding little man with a face like a weasel and shifty blue eyes, asked if they wanted separate rooms. They both nodded yes. The man behind the desk raised his eyebrows, leered at them and asked, "Are you sure? It gets mighty crowded in the hallway after midnight, what with folks changing rooms back and forth all night long?"

Harrison had enough distractions for one day. He was in no mood to put up with this slimy fellow's remarks. He grabbed the front of the man's shirt, pulled him up to within an inch of his face, and repeated his request for two rooms.

"Is that understood?" he quietly asked the frightened man. "When I want anything from you I will ask for it. Otherwise keep your foul mouth shut."

"Yes, sir, I understand. Sorry, sir, you won't have any more trouble from me. No, sir, no trouble!"

Under his breath he vowed, "I'll show that pimp and his whore what decent people think of them, waltzing in here like they were as good as other good Christian folks."

The rooms were clean, and just large enough to hold a bed, dresser, and nightstand. The windows looked out on the main street lit with lamps on both sides. There were a few people out walking on the wooden sidewalks, but most of the townsfolk had turned in for the night.

Harrison sat on the bed looking out the window, thinking. *In this small town most folks don't even lock their doors. I bet they will tonight.* He rolled over, stretched out on the bed, and thought about what he had told Sadie about it not being the Robert they knew. He wondered if it had fooled her. He didn't think so, but it had planted some doubt in her mind. Maybe she would be able to sleep a couple of hours, thinking it was a stranger.

Below the desk clerk sat smoking a Cuban Havana, thinking about the woman who had just checked in with the pimp.

Bragging to the skeptical little black shoeshine boy about his imagined conquest, he described elaborate tryst with well-known celebrities and how they always begged him to stay, but he always had to refuse.

"After all, variety is the spice of life lad; ya gotta get all you can get. Now that is some woman upstairs. I could go for some of that! I bet she would be willing to let me play for free, maybe even pay me. I heard that kind of woman wants it all the time and I sure could give it to her. When I finish this cigar I'm gonna take a walk up there and give her a night of pleasure."

The shine boy covered his mouth with his hand so the loudmouth clerk couldn't see his smiling contempt, but his dancing eyes displayed his thoughts. *That the lying old fool was gonna get his ass kicked by a woman.*

Sadie had retired for the night. She lay, remembering the horror of the afternoon. When she closed her eyes she could still see the girl's neck gushing blood. The scene played over and over in her mind. Her mind wandered to her home in Michigan, the farm, her parents, her brother David. I wonder where he is? He must be all grown up by now. She dozed off in a dream like trance.

She faintly heard the door open, footsteps crossing the floor to her bed, a hand reaching out for her. She screamed with all her might.

The figure turned and ran from the room bumping the door. As he ran a mumbled curse escaped his lips.

Sadie recognized the desk clerk's voice.

"Just what I need, a lecherous old fool with lust on his mind," she mumbled.

Harrison was at her door just after the intruder escaped, demanding, "What made you scream. It wasn't Robert was it?"

"My God no! You do believe that it was Robert that did that horrible thing, don't you?"

"Yes, I'm afraid it was. It seems that it was our friend Robert, and he has been here six months searching for someone, but the folks he asked didn't know anyone fitting her description."

"It must be me he was looking for. What did I do to make him hate me? What in god's name did that bitch of a mother do to poor Robert to create such a monster?

Chapter Ten
The Challenge

"I'm going to wait in town a few days to check on the girl and see what will become of her," Harrison decided. He suggested to Sadie that since the girl could no longer work with the clients, she might be able to help out Jessie with the housework and cooking.

Sadie laughed for the first time since they had found the girl and the gruesome scene.

The laughter felt good, she wanted the feeling to last. Unfortunately it didn't, but some of the tension had ebbed away.

"Do you really believe Jessie will let a stranger in her kitchen? She will be lucky if Jessie lets her clean the commodes."

"You don't give Jessie enough credit when it comes to sensing other people's needs. This young woman needs something to make her feel needed. She has gone through the gates of hell and back. If she survives, she will never forget what happened, but she needs to feel safe and protected and Jessie can give her that."

"Thank God we have you with us, Harrison. You know, you're not supposed to care about us, only that we do a good job and satisfy the clients."

"Whoever told you that doesn't know much about running a successful house? We are family. We take care of each other. We need each other," Harrison explained.

"I guess we are responsible in a way for what happened to those women out there. At least I feel that way and if we can give the girl a place to work we will. I know Kate will agree with me," Harrison added.

The next few days were busy, meeting with the sheriff, doctor, and two girls from the town who wanted to travel with them. It kept them from thinking too much about Robert and the shadow he had cast with his violence.

Harrison had sent a message to Kate telling her why they were delayed. She wired back that they had already heard the news. All the newspapers had carried the story, and she hoped that he was bringing the girl, Cathy, back with them. Jessie wanted someone to help with all the work they piled on her. Harrison chuckled all the way back to the hotel, showed the telegram to Sadie and she shared with him the warmth of feeling for their friend Jessie.

Sadie said, "I can see Jessie now, eyes wide, saying, 'Thet por chile gotta come here so's we's can watch over her. Thet Robert ain' gonna git his paws on her agin, I'll break his bac, he comes here.' "

"You do that very well. You should have gone into acting on the stage," Harrison commented. "I could almost see Jessie when you did that."

"Thank you, sir," she said with a low curtsey. It was good to feel a sense of playfulness. They had been too tense these last few days, and maybe the fact that the girl was going to be taken care of gave her a sense of relief. Whatever it was, it prevailed through the next few days.

They had been there a week when Harrison decided to send Sadie and the girls home to New York City. When Harrison put them on the train, he told them, "Give Kate my love and tell her I will bring Cathy home in about a week, or as soon as she can travel."

When they arrived in the train station, Sadie introduced Kitty and Susan to Kate and Otto, who were there to meet them.

They had gotten better aquatinted on the train and Sadie liked both the girls. They were cheerful and looked at their profession as a chance to get ahead in a man's world. They felt no bitterness about being limited in their pursuit of the good life. Sadie felt they would be a welcome addition to their house, and they both behaved like ladies. That had been the deciding factor for Harrison.

Otto took Sadie's hand, kissed it and said, "Ve haf missed you. Ve ver vorried about you. I'm glad you're back vith us."

Sadie put her arms around him and told him they were glad to be back with friends who cared.

"I feel so safe when I'm here with all of you," she said, patting his back.

Kate asked about the girl, Cathy, and how long it would be before she could travel. Did she agree to come and work for Jessie, and did she know what she was getting into?

Sadie had to chuckle as that is exactly what she had thought. When she told Kate her feelings on the matter, Kate raised her eyes heavenward and only sighed.

"Well, let's get going before these two girls are scared off by the talk of Jessie and her temper."

Kitty murmured, "We were happy to get out of that town and have a chance to earn a decent amount of money for our labors."

"Yes," Susan chimed in, "we're just happy to get out of that town of horror. I still get chills when I think about what happened."

Sadie didn't mention that it was she whom Robert was searching for, but she looked at Kate with questions in her eyes. Kate avoided her stare, which told her that Kate knew the whole story.

The quiet group left the train station and headed for home. When they reached Haven Place, the new girls were not only impressed but were awed by its grandeur. They had not worked in such a fine house in Paterson. It was a comfortable place, but it was for farmers, cattlemen, and some coal miners.

Most of the young men had left town to strike it rich in California in 1848, and never returned.

It was a quiet town full of people who were born there and would die there. It was not the sort of place where young woman would find excitement or a husband. New York meant a chance at both.

Jessie met them at the door saying, "Guess which miss smarty-pants ain' pissed her pants since yo' left," holding the proud little girl up for inspection. Rachael was smiling from ear to ear. Her eyes lit up like stars, while a wet stream leaked down her white stockings and into her buckled leather shoes.

"Well, she didn' til now, she's jist het up bout yo' comin' home, thas all," Jessie added.

Sadie didn't care if she were wet or not. She had missed Rachael, pee, and all. She took the child from Jessie and hugged her until she almost peed again. Rachael was struggling to get loose and find the pot that Jessie had said was hers.

"You're like a wiggle worm," Sadie shouted after the disappearing child, "I just wanted a big hug because I missed you so much."

Jessie looked the new girls over and said, "yo'll do. Fin' a room and git cleaned up fo' dinner. Don' ferget ta wash up!"

The two girls went up the stairs and down the hall afraid to open any doors; they stood in the hallway, waiting to be told which rooms to take.

Rachael, who had done her job and returned to Sadie's arms, shook herself loose and ran to them beckoning them to follow her. She up the stairs and to the two rooms at the end of the hall and announced, "This is where you will work."

The people at the bottom of the stairs stood in shocked silence. Where had she picked that up? Had someone told her or was it that obvious? Her announcement had struck fear in Sadie; she never wanted the child to know what they did for a living. She was much too young to know that much. Someone must have let it drop and she had picked it up. It was the only explanation.

"I was planning to send her away to a boarding school when she is old enough to notice what goes on here," she confided to the others. "But she's not ready yet. Well, she isn't, is she?"

The others just stood tongue-tied.

Phoebe had come out of her room when it all started to happen and she piped up, "Her mama was a pretty bright little gal. Smarter than most. Could be she takes after her ma, just way ahead of her time."

"Oh, damn, if it isn't one thing it's another," said Sadie. "I'm so dammed tired of everything happening at once. I need a drink!"

"No, mam, yo' don'. Yo' git up stairs to yo room and res. Yo' bin through a world of trouble and the las' thin' yo' needs is ta make yerself numb. I'll brin' yo' som' tea an toast to hep yo' relax. Now git!"

Otto looked at Kate and shook his head. "Ve have a problem, I tink, I vill be glad ven Harrison is back."

"Me, too," sighed Kate.

The women went back to their old routine, but without the music that Harrison always provided. They were busy every night with most of the newly rich males in the big city. It was exciting to the new girls, for they had never been to plays or the opera and had to borrow gowns to attend.

The gown maker now came to them to do the fitting.

"It certainly has changed since we left Michigan," confided Sadie.

Sadie had not touched alcohol, even though she had craved for it, since she came back from Paterson. She had stuck with her bargain to drink tea instead. "One of these days I will have a drink, but not right now," she promised herself.

Two and a half weeks later, Harrison knocked at the door and ushered in the heavily veiled Cathy. She was shaking from head to toe; her voice was low and raspy when she said hello to Jessie.

Jessie grabbed her, hugged her, and declared, "Yo' is safe now, honey. To git to yo', they's got to go through me! Never did lik' a man thet beats a woman, hates a man thet kills 'em." She hustled Cathy into the back, stopped at a room next to the kitchen and threw open the door. There was the prettiest

111

chamber Cathy had ever seen. The room was painted pale blue with white lace curtains and vases full of flowers everywhere. It smelled like spring, all fresh and clean, ready for Cathy's new start.

The others had followed behind the smiling Jessie, they hadn't known what she had been up to the last few days, and they hadn't dared ask either.

But they were just as excited as she was to have Cathy there with them.

Jessie was justifiably proud of the haven she had created from a storage room. She fluttered around like a butterfly showing Cathy all the tricks she had used to create more space for clothes. Cathy was overwhelmed by the concern shown for her comfort. After giving Jessie a big hug, she suddenly sat down.

"I've never had so many people care before. I don't know how to behave, but I'm glad I'm here." Tears wet the black veil and seeped into the high neck of the dress she was wearing. The others became uncomfortable, wanting to leave and yet not daring to upset Jessie. They knew the girl needed time alone in her new garden-like fortress.

Jessie made it easy when she bellowed, "Yo' others git the hell out and let Cathy res'."

She pushed them into the kitchen, closed the door behind herself, put her forefinger to her lips, "Shush! We needs ta talk when she cain't hear us, thet little girl needs our protection, and we gonna give it ta her."

Harrison said, " I knew I could depend on all of you to accept and protect her."

The weeks flew by, turned into months, and no one had caught Robert. The whole house had pushed the terror that Cathy had gone through to the back of their minds, except Cathy and Sadie.

Otto had invited them all to come to the open house for the hotel he had purchased in the better part of town. He had gone into debt to have it remodeled. It was richly decorated with velvet drapes, gilt adornment, and as plush as a king's palace. Everyone was excited for Otto. He was a good friend and client and they wanted to see him do well. Most of the girls at Kate's place had male friends they had invited to the opening and had gone on ahead.

Cathy and Jessie were sitting in the kitchen with coffee, homemade bread and cheese, recalling what had happened the previous day, when Rachael came romping in, hands full of flowers she had picked from the garden out back.

Both Jessie and Cathy worshiped the ground she trod on. For Cathy it had been an immediate bond. She didn't know why she felt that way, but it took over her life.

"Wha' do my little angel wants," asks Jessie, "are yo' havin' a good time chasing the butterflies?"

"There's a man in the garden, Aunt Jessie. He's all dirty, and he won't talk to me."

"The hell you say," the words spewed out of Jessie's mouth like molten lava. She grabbed a skillet and headed for the back door. She threw the screen door open so hard she tore it off its hinges. It hung at a tilt against the house. Jessie made a trip around the garden, swinging the skillet around her head, like a windmill in a windstorm. She came back to the door, peeked in to make sure Cathy and Rachael were safe, started around the garden again, when to her surprise a man jumped up out of a bed of daisies, ran to the road and disappeared into the woods beyond. Jessie started after him, thought better of it, turned and walked back to the open doorway.

Cathy was holding Rachael and shaking like a leaf in the wind. Her face had lost all color; the scars stood out like roots of a tree that were too near the surface, all nubbed and gnarled. "Oh, God, it was him! I know it was. He wants to finish the job he started."

"Honey, I don believe it twas thet Robert fella cause he wonta runned away lik' thet, but ifn it wer' his fate is rit! Thet basard ain' gonna hurt nobody but hisself if he come bac' round here. Jessie ain't gonna let nothin' happen ta the people she lov '. We's gonna sit right here and finish what we started afore thet man showed up round here. We's don know who hit was but one thin' sur', they is probably a streak of yella down his bac' a mile wide, cause he run from us por, frail, little women." She couldn't contain herself any longer and burst out laughing. "Did yo see how fas' thet jack rabbit run from this little ole black lady?"

She held her stomach and laughed till she cried. Huge tears welled into her eyes, traced paths down her cheeks, and fluttered off her chin from the vibrations of her body.

Cathy still frightened by the man's appearance, reluctantly smiled at the verbal picture Jessie had painted of a jackrabbit with a yellow streak.

Jessie knew that she had to control herself so she wouldn't frighten Rachael, but she did wish they would all come home soon. She too felt much safer with Harrison in the house.

He was the first to arrive home and the two women were waiting for him in the setting room. Cathy was doing needlepoint on a lovely scarf for her hope chest and Jessie was fidgeting with everything that wasn't in the right spot, moving things an inch and then moving them back to there original place, as though her life depended on it. As the frightened women related what happened in the garden, Harrison's mind went back to the horror in Paterson, the sheer terror that had followed Cathy for all these months.

Sadie and her escort were the next to enter, just ahead of the threatening storm. When they heard what the two women told them about the intruder, Sadie's escort decided this was not the best place to be if a maniac was on the loose and left.

The rumble of thunder began in the north sky, lightning soon followed, and large drops began to hit the house, tapping on the windows, adding anxiety to the worried women's awareness. The tap tap of the huge drops sounded like hammer blows to the frightened Cathy.

Jessie grinned at her saying, "Thet tap, tap sounds lik the little people my mama use't ta tell bout. They's only come when it rain, cause if they got dry they 'd dry up and fly way. They always brough' good news, lik' it wern't good news nough that it be rainin'. Course some folks don' ever see the good side of rain. We's lucky the rains come ta nourish the earth and feed the flowrs. The Lord Jesus plan it thet way."

Cathy and Sadie both began to relax and feel the warmth of Jessie's love and humor surround them. They were sure they were safe under her vigilant eye.

Harrison had gone searching the whole house for any sign of entry by some uninvited guest. The search was almost complete when he happened upon a broken window in the very back of the huge house. It had been shattered and the frame meticulously cleaned out so that not a shard of glass remained. Harrison frowned as he remembered how precisely Robert had performed his last deed of terror.

He hurried to the sitting room and finding it empty started toward the stairs where a crashing blow rendered him unconscious. The women sat waiting for Harrison to come back and tell them that all was well. When the wait became unbearable, they moved upstairs to Sadie's room.

Rachael, thumb in mouth, came stumbling into the room rubbing the sleep out of her eyes, her nightdress rumpled and damp, bare feet making scuffing noises on the carpet

A sudden crashing sound filled the whole house. The lights were blown out, the rain came rushing in, soaking the room as well as the people.

Jessie grabbed Rachael, pushed Cathy and Sadie toward the hall, and down the stairs toward the cellar.

"This here is one of those tornadoes I heerd bout," gasped Jessie. "We be safe in the bottom of the house, neath those big timbers. Jist yo' follow me. Move yer arse, girl, the house be fallin' in!"

When they had reached the bottom of the stairs Sadie stumbled over something soft and warm. She felt around the hall table for the glass lamp and the Lucifers that were always kept there, found them, and lit the lamp. When they saw it was Harrison sprawled out on the floor, panic set in. Jessie shoved Rachael into Sadie's waiting arms and grabbing Harrrison hauled the bleeding man down the cellar stairs. The noise of the storm followed them down; crashing and banging like the sky was falling.

Looking around the cellar, and seeing for the first time that the barricade had been removed from the tunnel, Sadie had doubts about their safety in this dark cellar. She could only see into the dark for a few feet, but it looked like someone or something had been there recently. A shiver went up and down her spine. Who had hit Harrison? Could it be the man they saw in the garden? Was he hiding here, and, if so, why?

Jessie could feel eyes watching them. It gave her a creepy feeling, and she felt the hair on the back of her neck rise. *I's gotta git them outta of here.* The thought jumped into her mind and set her in motion.

"Come on honey we's gonna go upstairs where yo gonna be safe from any intruder." They hadn't wanted to leave the warm dark safety of the cellar, but Jessie convinced them that they needed to be where they had weapons handy and knew the layout of the rooms.

She felt better once she reached the kitchen. This was her realm. Here she was in control.

Harrison sat down at the kitchen table, head bleeding, slowly shaking his head, trying to focus his eyes. He had never felt so helpless before in his life. He didn't like leaving his friends vulnerable to whatever or whoever was in this house.

The one lamplight flickered and threatened to go out. The draft from the broken window penetrated the whole house. Rachael was crying softly and shivering uncontrollably. Sadie, seeing her darling Rachael so upset and frightened, felt the anger build in her. How dare somebody enter their home and cause such terror! She stalked out into the foyer and lighting a candle to search the house. Cathy and Jessie called out to her, but she ignored them and continued her search. When she reached the landing on the second floor she spotted muddy footprints leading up the stairs. Heart pounding, hands shaking, she quietly crept up the stairs and put her ear to the solid wooden door of her room. Incredibly, she heard the sobbing of some lost creature wailing for asylum.

Pure terror flashed through her. She knew that if that poor bedeviled creature found her, she would be in mortal danger. Before she could beat a hasty retreat, she heard the sounds of movement on the other side of the door. The turning of the knob set her feet in motion. She darted into the linen closet that separated her room from Lorrie's. The door to the closet was just closing as the door to her room opened and Robert burst forth. The coldly handsome man had disappeared and a raging beast had taken his place. With his face twisted into a maniacal grimace, wild-eyed and filthy, he struck a dreadful fear in the frozen Sadie.

Robert was so bent on destruction he failed to see the movement of the closing door as he beat on his chest and roared an oath of vengeance on all women. He staggered to the stairs, bent on finding someone on which to loose his fury.

Sadie's thoughts flew to the kitchen and the friends who were hiding there. She must divert Robert's attention until Harrison could help her. Where was Harrison?

When Robert reached the bottom step, Sadie eased out of the closet and went to the top of the stairs. Softly calling out his name, she started to descend the staircase leading to the first floor and certain death.

She inched her way down the suddenly too short stairway, never taking her eyes off the cringing Robert. He had jumped as though shot and had huddled into a small knot when she spoke his name.

Sadie could see a sign of recognition light his eyes for a moment then flicker away.

"Please, God," she whispered, "Please, please help us tonight." Slowly she kept inching down the stairs, sweat beaded on her forehead burning her eyes, but she didn't dare blink for fear he would emerge from the trance he seemed to be in.

He jerked up suddenly, taking a deep breath and waving the knife he had pulled from his waistcoat. He lunged toward the frozen Sadie.

She found her voice and let out a blood-curdling scream. Her obvious terror galvanized Harrison, who burst into the hallway on a dead run, arms flailing, eyes darting in every direction. He attacked the crazed Robert with such force that the knife went spinning off into the dark recesses of the room. While Robert was searching for a weapon, Sadie escaped into the kitchen and searched for a weapon with which Harrison could defeat the crazed man. Finding nothing but a broom, she pushed through the door and peered into the dimly lit room. Harrison was there alone! Robert had disappeared. She went back into the hallway and helped Harrison probe the darkest areas with the broom.

"I can't rest until I find that maniac. No one will be safe until he is dead or locked away for good and right now I prefer the former," Harrison said bluntly.

Sadie had to agree with Harrison. She had never known such pure unadulterated hatred was even possible. Having failed to find Robert they headed back to the kitchen to reassure the others that the intruder hadn't murdered them.

The fury of the storm increased until it was impossible even to hear each other when they shouted. It was as though all the wrath of God was all rolled into a giant whirlwind and thrown at Haven House. The house and its occupants shook and trembled. Harrison made them promise to stay together at least until the storm was over.

Propping himself against a wall to keep from falling, he waited for the assault that he expected at any moment.

In the flickering lamplight, the women looked like ghosts from some long forgotten orgy of death, their clothing wet from the rain that had driven through the broken windows and soaked them to the bone, and filthy from the hasty retreat to the cellar. Rachael was hiding her head in Jessie's lap and mewling like a lost kitten. A thunderous crash tore through every timber in the noble old house; it shuddered and became uncannily still. Everyone waited for the next shock but it never came. The storm was over; the silence was almost unbearable. Now they had another disaster to deal with. Robert was still in the house and even more dangerous than the violent weather.

Harrison and Jessie headed the inspection of the house; Sadie, Cathy, and Rachael followed close behind. They couldn't believe the destruction; the front of the house was drenched, rain had poured in from the crushed roof. A giant gnarled limb had crashed into and through the main part of the house and lay in the wet soggy mess that once was the parlor and hall.

While Harrison continued searching for Robert, Jessie got busy making hot coffee and soup to warm the freezing Rachael and Cathy. Jessie noticed Cathy hadn't said a word since they had come up from the cellar; her face was as white as the cotton Jessie used to pick when she was a child. *Thet poor child is going to lose her min if one mor thing happens,* she thought. *We's hasta git her way from here. This ain't the place fo' Rachael either.*

Gotta talk ta Kate bout thet.

When the soup and beverage had warmed them, they carefully made their way through the wet branches to the stairs leading to the bedrooms on the second floor.

As they approached Sadie's room, they swung the door open and saw a man with a branch protruding from his chest. He was as close to death as a man could be and still be able to talk. He smiled a sad little smile and begged, "Sadie, please forgive me."

Jessie knelt on the floor beside him, took his hand and whispered, "God loves ya and fogives ya."

"That's the man in the garden," Rachael piped up.

"I know that man," screamed Cathy. "He's the one who hurt me. That's Robert!" Harrison came running when he heard Cathy's scream and held the terror stricken girl.

Robert died as he lived, violently, but it was not by the hand of man. It was as if Mother Nature stepped in and decreed his life of hell be over.

"Ifen dis was the man hidin' in the garden, then who did the eyes in the cellar belong ta?" Jessie asked, "Firs thins firs, as soon someone gits here ta watch over dese two, I's gonna mak' hit my business ta fin' out. Damn right!"

After what seemed like days, the sounds of axes rang strong and clear as a rescue party worked their way to the house. They were coming through the downed tree limbs, one after the other. First the sheriff, then a whole army of people threaded their way between the limbs and into what was left of the hall.

The sheriff, who was a regular at Haven House, was naturally concerned about the occupants, especially a little charmer named Kitty and said, "Glad you folks are all right. We were worried about you."

"You were right to worry," Sadie exclaimed. "We have a dead man in the room upstairs and his name is Robert. He is the one who murdered all those women over in Paterson a few months ago."

"Who killed him and who do I give the reward to? It's a nice little nest egg, the reward money that is."

"The Lord God done took him home," replied Jessie. "I guess he figer thet por soul suffer nough, even iffen he did kilt them women, the lord fergives' em."

"The Lord may forgive him, but I don't," raged Cathy. "He killed my friends, and he hurt me bad. I will never forgive him till my dying day!"

"We's got mor' important thin's to worry bout sides hatin' a dead man. I got a feelin' they's a live one livin' in the cellar. I cain't prove it, but I felt eyes watchin' when we was hidin' from the storm." This spilled out of Jessie's mouth, words tumbling out over each other, almost like a chant. When she caught her breath, she couldn't believe she'd said that. It had a long time since she felt this kind of fear. *I mus' be gettin' ole*, she mused. *Who the hell do I's thin I's kidding? I's need a drink, no I's don', and yes I's do!* But the argument raged only in her head.

The past came crashing in on Jessie; her thoughts went back to the long ago hell she had left behind. *I's members the las' time I's hada taste. I's kilt a man. My beautiful man, when he bes foolin' round wit som raggidy ass dancer. He made the wrong step when he stepped out on me. Thet dancer don't dance no mo and he bes soakin' up Georgia swamp water. Dam, I's do miss thet man, but he shouldna went messin' roun' with thet bitch. I's don' wanta remember thet turrible night, ever agin.*

Sadie had come into the hall, picked Rachael up and was squeezing her, murmuring, "Thank God, you're safe."

Harrison told the men with the axes to follow him to the cellar, "And be prepared to use them."

They came up after a half-hour of searching; they had found nothing except some soiled clothing and a book of poems.

When they no longer could see to do their work, the men from town left, promising to be back in the morning. After all Mr. Harrison had promised them each a five dollar gold piece for their labors.

Trying to get back some semblance of order for the inhabitants of Haven Place, Kate announced a meeting in the morning.

"There are some serious decisions have to be made and I want everyone's opinion."

Sadie had a sinking feeling in her gut. She knew in the back of her mind that Rachael was one of the problems that needed solving, but she didn't want to face that decision yet.

The storm had cleared the air in more ways than one. The hot smoldering summer night gave way to a clear, cool breeze that reminded Sadie of fall nights on the farm. She felt a vague tug at her heart. Did she really miss that place after all these years? *No*, she thought, *I'm remembering the good times only; there was a lot of hurt back there*. She had trained herself to think of Marcus whenever she felt homesick. She couldn't be with him in body, but she could in spirit. As long as they shared the same earth she would be content to go on. Just knowing he was happy was enough.

After the breakfast hour, the meeting was held in the parlor; Rachael was still sleeping so the house was quiet.

Her mind had wandered back to better times and she had lost the jist of the conversation when she heard Rachael's name and her thoughts flew back to the meeting. "What did you say about Rachael?" she asked. "I was daydreaming, I guess."

Kate answered her with a question; "Do you want Rachael to be raised in this kind of house?"

"No, but she's too small to send to boarding school."

"I've been thinking about buying a little place in the country for when I retire, and I think Cathy and Rachael would be the perfect people to take care of it for me," explained Kate. "I would send them as much as they need to maintain a home, and if you girls want to, you can save for her tuition when she is ready."

"It sounds like the perfect solution to me," Harrison agreed.

"I don't know if I can give her up," cried Sadie, "She has been my life!"

"Yo' hain't the onlyest one gonna miss thet sweet angel," Jessie chided, "but we gotta thin' of what's bes' for her."

"That's right," they all agreed, "we're all gonna miss them both, but they need a chance to live a better life too."

When the meeting was over, they had agreed to start looking for a cottage not too far from New York, where they could visit their friends, Cathy and Rachael, once in a while to make sure all was well.

One of the men from town who had arrived earlier came into the room dragging a young fellow by his collar. The fellow's face was bloody and caked with mud.

"Looky what I found in your cellar," he bragged. "He didn't give me any trouble. He knew what was good for him!"

The captive was thin as a rail and shaking like a leaf. His tattered clothes were rain drenched and filthy. He had tears running down his face, mixed with the rain streaming from his black curly mop of hair. He was the saddest looking individual Kate had ever seen.

Harrison took hold of the intruder's head and tilted it up so he could see the young man's face.

"What are you doing in our cellar?" he questioned. "Don't you know you can be shot for trespassing on your neighbor's property?"

"Yes, sir, I do know that, but I was so hungry and tired that it seemed like a safe place to rest. The only one who came down was the cook and she was always too busy to notice that I was there."

"How'n hell long yo' bes down there?" shouted Jessie, "How come yo' didn' leave fore we's caucht yo'?"

The young man hung his head and answered, "You were too good a cook. I didn't want to leave such good food. I only took a little bit each time so you wouldn't notice."

Jessie burst out laughing. It thundered through the whole house. It was almost as loud as the storm had been.

The tension flowed from the room. The change was visible to everyone. Once Jessie accepted someone, it was a foregone conclusion that he or she was going to be a part of his or her life. Nobody wanted to give her an argument about that or anything else. And so Philip came into their lives.

The men from town cut the tree limbs in smaller pieces and hauled them out. When they had the roof area cleared they began closing the hole that the limb had made. The roof was patched temporarily and the women began cleaning up the rain soaked rugs, sorting the furniture, placing the repairable settees in one area and putting the sofas that the storm had destroyed in another part of the house to be used for fire wood.

Jessie was in her glory with all these people to cook for. She went into the kitchen, humming and still clutching the skillet she had put down in the hall when she heard Harrison coming.

"Jessie, are you sure about this young man? We have really had our fill of strangers lately."

"Y's sir Mr.Harrison, I bes real sure bout thet boy, he gonna bes useful jist yo wait an see."

The days became weeks, then months and still no cottage seemed just right to Kate. She always found something wrong with every place that she was shown.

At last Harrison said, "We are going to look at this cottage in the next town and if it isn't perfect we will fix it so it is, and that's that!" They drove over to a little town called White Plains. The cottage was white washed with flowers on every side of the picket fence, and a vegetable garden in the back yard. An old oak stood guard at the back door, and a rope swing looked lonesomely empty hanging from one low-slung limb. It seemed to beg for a child to give it purpose.

Kate knew this was it. This is where she would like to spend her days and nights when she could no longer work. It seemed like the place had been waiting for her. The old people who had lived there had gone to live with their son and the price was right. She knew in her heart that Cathy and Rachael would love it too.

She had come prepared to find something wrong, but she had to admit it was just what she had wanted. She made arrangements to sign the papers that would make it her own.

When they got back to Haven Place and told Cathy about the cottage, she didn't seem as excited as they thought she would be.

She smiled and said, "That's nice, and maybe we can go to see it sometime."

"Sometime is now," Kate said. "I bought the place and you can go or not, but it's mine. What is going on with you? Are you afraid to live alone out there?"

"Yes, that's it. I'm afraid to be out there alone with only Rachael and me. I think we need a hired man to help and protect us."

"Hum, and do you have anyone in mind?" asked Kate. "Or should Harrison look for someone in town?"

"Oh, no, I have someone who would be interested in the job. He would work for room and board. I know he would!" Cathy stood red faced and eager, "Philip said he would love to be our caretaker. He has become very attached to Rachael and would hate to leave her. I would like you to consider him, too, as we have become great friends these past weeks."

"Yes, I just bet you have," chided Kate. Everyone in the house had noticed the sparks that flew when these two were in the same room.

Harrison told the whole room, "That would solve our whole problem," and with tongue in cheek he added, "I think it will please Cathy and Rachael too. Well then, it is decided they will move to the cottage this week. The house is being cleaned as we speak." Harrison didn't even try to hide his knowing smile.

The next few days flew by in a fury of packing, shopping, hugging, and crying. The whole house would seem empty with these two gone. Everyone had learned to love Cathy almost as much as they loved Rachael, but they also knew that this move was best for all concerned.

Harrison suggested that Sadie should accompany Philip, Cathy, and Rachael to their new home and Kate agreed.

"Good idea, it will give her time to get used to the fact that Rachael is not her responsibility anymore."

As they talked, Harrison became aware of Kate's pallor and lack of enthusiasm. Mentioning that she'd been looking a little peaked lately; he suggested she see a doctor while they were unfettered.

"The best doctors in the world are right here in New York," declared Harrison.

"So, while the folks are moving to White Plains, why not close the house for a week and get some important personal business done? Why we can call it a vacation!" Making light of it, he teased, "Come, old girl. We will run away for a few days and show these gals how to party."

Everyone went along with the suggestion. After all, they had all made quite a bit of money and hadn't had much time to spend it.

Nettie showed the girls her pictures of Paris. "This is where I'm going next year in the spring. I hear it is lovely. I am looking for a dressmaker to fit me for a wardrobe that will be as good as those from a Paris designer. This will give me a chance to visit a few of the shops I've heard about."

Jessie clapped her hands with glee. "I's goin' lookin' fo' a little place ta set up as a restaurant, yo' know, serve the bes' damned food this side a heaven. Then I needs ta find a man ta run it till I's ready ta settle down. Theys got a nigger neighborhood in Nu York City, ain't they?"

A few of the girls were just going to stay home and take it easy, mend a few things, write letters and wander the grounds, now that it was safe again. Robert's body had been taken away by the sheriff and buried in potter's field, but the memory of his deeds would live on in the girls' minds. They had gotten into the habit of going everywhere together. It was a wise decision, but it afforded little privacy.

The moving day came all too soon. They were off in a flurry of suitcases, satchels, more hugs, kisses, and a moaning Jessie, who wailed at the top of her lungs, "wha' I gonna do wit' out my little angel? My heart is gonna break." Her chant followed them for a half mile down the road.

When the doctor had finished his examination of Kate, he took the stethoscope from around his neck, laid it on the desk, hooked one hip on the corner of the desk, cleared his throat, and searched for the right words.

Kate didn't give him that option. She said, "listen, doctor, I know something is wrong, I've known for months, so just tell me what it is and how I can fix it."

"Young lady, I'm afraid there are some things in life that can't be fixed, and you have one of those.

"Your heart is in such a weakened state that just about anything will cause it to stop. Bed rest and no excitement are the orders for the day. Taking my suggestion and treatment, you could live another five years."

"Doctor do you know what I do for a living," asked Kate. "I'm a Madam and I run a whore house. How in the world do you expect me to rest and have no excitement? Excitement is what my business is all about."

"Dear lady, that is your choice. I can only tell you what you should do, not what you have to do. Now I can give you the name of another doctor if you don't trust my diagnosis, but I'm sure he will tell you the same thing." The doctor picked up his note pad, wrote the names of a couple of doctors, handed the paper to Harrison and walked out of the room.

"What am I going to do? I wanted to work a few more years, go get my daughters and live the good life in the country. Now that is out of the question. I've waited so long to see my girls, and now I may never see them."

"You will see them. I'll get them. I'll tell them you're their aunt, and you would like them to visit for a few days. The house will be quiet and you can have a nice visit." Harrison's plan sounded good to Kate, and she felt better already.

Kate rested at the hotel while Harrison made his plans to take the train to Michigan to talk Dorrie into letting the twins come and visit their aunt Kate. When all the arrangements were made, he came back to the hotel to pick Kate up and take her home. She had been sleeping, and to Harrison she looked pale and weak. He felt a pull at his heartstrings. He still loved the woman after all these years. What if they could just quit the business right now, go somewhere new, and start over with the twins? He didn't say these things to Kate, but put them in the back of his mind for later.

On the way back to Haven Place, Kate tried to be cheerful, but failed to fool Harrison. He knew she was trying to pretend that it wasn't as serious as it really was. He had to give her credit; she was a fighter, even when the odds were against her. *Well, of course,* he thought, *that's one of the reasons I love her!*

He played along with her on the ride home, laughing a little too loudly, cheering her on when she said she wanted to learn that new dance that had just come over from Paris. It was the hardest work Harrison had ever done. He was relieved when the house came into sight. At last he could drop this false cheerfulness.

This is not the way to live, he thought, *and I won't do that again. When I come back with the twins, I'll have a talk with Kate. We must be honest with each other. Life is too short to fill it up with make-believe.*

Jessie met them at the door with the news that she had found a storefront in New York City that would be perfect for her restaurant, but she needed a white man to rent it for her.

"Dose damn fools tink I ain't good nough ta rent ta" she ranted. "Theys don' know nothin' bout me, still they say I cain't run a business cause I's black! Wha the hell skin color got to do with cooking? I felt like breaking that liddle piss ant's back, but it won't do no good. Will yo rent it fo' me, Mr. Harrison? I needs to get thins started for the man I hired to run hit fo' me. He ain't much to look at but he can swing a mean skillet, and I's don' wan to lose him. He black too, so we need yo' ta handle the papers and sech."

Harrison patted her shoulder and said, "Sure, Jessie, I'll do that for you, but I can't understand why he won't rent to you, you're a good risk. You have steady employment and we all will be willing to give you references."

"What yo' don' knowed is thet dere is people out there thet don't care how good yo' are. They judge yo' by the color of yer skin. Even yo' folks treat us like we different. Would yo' let a rich black man inta this house? No! Black men can't even diddle whores, but the white women can come down to where we live and diddle our men when theys git a chance. But, thets okay cause most of us don' want ta mix with yo' whiteys either. Yo' is too much a gentleman to hurt my feelin's by treatin' me the way other white folks does, but yo' still think us less then yo'"

Harrison was startled by her accusation but had to admit to himself that most of what she had said was true.

"Dis man, if yo' can call him thet, is ignorant as a box a rocks, but he kin own a piece a land an say no ta me, thet jist wants to git ahead. He tole me thet back home in Georgia I'd be hung fo' askin' ta rent a buildin' fo' business. He say my place was home cookin' fo' white folks." Jessie was shaking so bad Harrison was afraid that she was going to shake herself to pieces.

He put his arms around her, patting her shoulder even harder and crooned, "There, there, there," until she got hold of herself.

Lorrie came in just as this episode was happening. She looked confused. What was Harrison consoling Jessie for?

"Don't tell me something else has happened," she groaned.

Harrison explained what had happened and why Jessie was so upset.

"Oh, is that all?" Lorrie said, " I thought it was something drastic!"

"It bes drastic to me," Jessie exploded. "Yo' don' knows what it feels lik ta be treated like a damn animal all yer life. We good 'nough to suckle yer young, but we's not to be treated like humans!"

"Oh, dear God, I'm sorry, I didn't realize how that sounded. I love you, Jessie. You're part of our family."

"Thets the trouble. Folks don' think. They just use ta treatin us thet way an thet's, thet!"

Harrison with vengeance in his eye told the furious Jessie, "I will take care of that little matter of the rent on my way to the train station. Just tell me where the store front is, and where I can reach this jackass who owns it."

Kate sat without saying a word, which was unusual for her. In better times she would have been outraged that one of her friends was treated so badly. She would have been ready to go to war with that detestable shopkeeper.

"I know you will take care of this, Harrison, and see that you give that fool of a man his come-upence when you deal with him," was all she said.

Harrison saw Kate to her room, made her comfortable, and returned to the parlor. Lorrie, Jessie and Maybelle were in the room talking about the opening of Jessie's new eatery. Jessie was telling them how she was going to decorate it with plants and bright red and white checkered tablecloths with a on every table would be a candle.

"Cause yo knowed how dese lectric lights keeps agoin' out. Cain't depend on em no-how!"

"Will you ladies keep special watch over Kate?" Harrison asked. "She isn't feeling well and I'm worried about her. I'm on my way to Michigan to pick up the twins and bring them to visit their Aunt Kate. I won't be long, so keep an eye on her, but let her rest as much as possible. If I know her, she will need all the rest she can get before the girls get here."

Sadie was happy to see her friends when she returned, but she missed Rachael already. She had taken care of her since she was an infant; it was like losing her own child. She'd nursed her through illness and guided her through the terrible twos, and watched as she became her own person. Now she had to give her up for love, for she did, indeed, love the child.

Sadie had to put her concern for Rachael at the back of her mind when they told her about Kate's malady. She had suspected something was wrong for quite sometime, but didn't want to face the thought of losing her friend.

They all crept around the house like mice trying to be quiet so they wouldn't disturb her. Kate came down for supper, picked at the food on her plate, and declared, "The eagerness and excitement of seeing the girls has stolen my appetite. I wonder if they look like their father. He was a handsome lad. I hope they inherited his dark good looks."

Jessie had made a special dinner for the four of them and topped it off with Kate's favorite dessert, pecan pie. Kate cut a large slice for herself and told Jessie, "I always have an appetite for your pecan pie. It is the best I've ever eaten." She picked at the luscious pie till just a few crumbs were left, patted her tummy, unbuttoned the buttons close to her waist, and groaned with delight. "I'm bloated like a poisoned pup. I've eaten way too much. I believe I'll go up and lie down for a while and let that wonderful pie settle." With that said she made her way to the stairs, slowly pulling her self up each step till she reached the top, turned, smiled a sad little smile, and headed toward her rooms.

Sadie exchanged sympathetic looks with Jessie and Lorrie and silently prayed that Harrison would get back quickly.

Chapter Eleven
A Friend Lost

When Jessie went up to wake Kate several hours later, the whole house heard her wail, "Dearest Jesus, keep her saf' in yor lovin' arms!"

The lament had filtered through every brick and stone in the house called Haven Place, it rang through the gardens, and into the barn at the back of the house. The horses and chickens raised such a clamor that a man going by in a buggy lost control of his team and hung on for dear life, till they ran out of wind.

When he finally did get control, he returned to find out what was happening. He was met with a fierce Jessie, raging at no one in particular, just letting off steam at New York, the fates, and God, in that order.

"Ain't we's got enough trouble without some no-account whitey snoopin' round? Wha the hell do yo' want?"

Sadie came to the poor man's rescue. She explained what had happened and would he please excuse Jessie, as she was mad with grief.

"I understand completely. I, too, have lost friends and know how she feels."

Jessie stared at him, looking him up and down, harrumphed and walked away.

Sadie closed the door in the man's face; her thoughts were on the unexpected death of her friend Kate.

"Oh, dear," she cried, "Harrison, what about Harrison? He's coming with the twins. What are we going to do?"

Lorrie came to the parlor, explaining that Jessie had gone to her room to lie down. She was completely shattered by Kate's demise. Lorrie took charge of Sadie and Maybelle, both of whom were paralyzed by their friend's death, by suggesting that they go to their rooms and rest. It was going to be a long day. Sadie couldn't lie down; her mind was going a mile a minute. She felt lost for the first time in years. What was going to happen now that Kate was gone? She went down to the parlor and looked at the brandy bottle, touched it and ached for just one drink. Her promise to Kate came ringing back into her brain and she walked away from temptation.

Jessie stormed into the parlor shouting, "Food! We's needs ta mak' lots a food, fo' the folks thet's comin' ta pay ther respects ta Miss Kate. Miss Kate was sure loved by these folks. I's hope we's gonna hav' nough room fo' em all."

When she had gotten her menu under way, she set out to do a labor of love, preparing Kate for the showing. She took a basin of fresh water, gathered washcloths, towels, and headed for Kate's room.

Sadie joined her and they undressed their friend, bathed her and redressed her in her finest. Jessie brushed her golden tresses until they shone, braided them into one large braid and wrapped it around her head.

"Dere," she said, "thet the way her hair was the day she say I could sta'. Mr. Harrison hired me, but he said it be her say, if I's stays or no. I's know I's scare the bejesus out of her thet mornin' I's came, it being dark and all, an I don' shows up in the dark thet much, but she jist smil' and say com' on in!"

They laid her out in the parlor in a hand-tooled box that had been delivered by Old Ned. Sadie covered Kate from the waist down with the quilt that she had given her many years ago. Kate had loved it so much and now it became her shroud.

"We all love Kate," Sadie told this woman she had grown to love and trust, "we're going to all need each other just to get through this. What are we going to do about Harrison and the girls?"

"What we gonna ta do is nothin'! When dey git here is time nough ta worry bout thet. Did thet diddle ass thet was here go ta town and tell the authorities thet Miss Kate done pass away?"

"Why do you dislike the man so much? You don't even know him?" Sadie asked.

"Oh, I knowd him alright. I seed his kind afore. They's always round when bad thins happen. They's like vultures circlin' a prey. They's kind at firs', but watch yo' step, they's always ready ta hop in and clean everthin' out, then they's gon'. His kind been round since the beginnin' of time!"

"Jessie, you're just upset about Kate. You're letting it affect your outlook. Besides you didn't even see or talk to him for longer than a minute."

"Honey, thas all the time I's needs ta know the devil when I's meets him, take heed, he not fer us." Jessie gazed at Sadie in such a way that shivers ran up and down her spine.

"Well that's not important right now, we have many things to do before people start arriving to view Kate and say their good-byes." Sadie dashed off to freshen up and change again; she needed to have something to keep her busy so she wouldn't think about the days ahead.

All the girls were down stairs, dressed in their finest, sitting around the parlor waiting for the visitors to arrive. It seemed odd to have Kate lying there so still, looking as though she would rise any minute and begin to circulate through the groups of ladies, telling one to fix her button, another to check the food, and yet another to get more drinks. It was eerie, sitting there waiting. The ladies fidgeted, ironing imaginary wrinkles in their skirts and picking off lint too small to notice.

They waited, and waited. Finally the doorknocker banged. Jessie rushed to the door, flung it wide, and there stood Otto. He was shaking, tears running down his cheeks.

"Is it ttttrue, hhhas she really pppassed avay?" he asked. His stutter had returned with a vengeance. He had loved Kate as much as the rest of them. She had been his dear friend for many years.

They could barely understand him, but they knew he was deeply hurt by the loss of Kate. They surrounded him, hugged, patted and soothed him till he stopped shaking and sat down on one of the settees.

"When are the others coming?" they asked. "You know, the people from town, who invited us to their parties and on trips.

Otto put his head in his hands, sobbing louder, "T-they a-ain't ca-coming. T-they looked at m-me like I vas ca-crazy ven I asked!"

"You must be wrong," Sadie piped up. "They're our friends. They wouldn't do that! I won't believe that. I can't."

Ten o'clock came with still no callers, except Otto. Jessie silently went into the kitchen and began putting the food away. She rattled the pots and pans so loud that they all knew it wasn't safe to go in there. The din ceased and they all waited to see what was coming next.

Sadie felt more comfortable when Jessie was ranting and raving. This silent Jessie was some one she didn't want to have to deal with alone. She would be glad when Harrison did get back, even though he was in for the shock of Kate's death.

It was midnight before they all retired. The offensive way folks were treating the death of Kate had been the gist of their conversation. It was a sickening realization that to the town's folk, they were just highly paid whores, not friends as they were led to believe. Damn them, they will pay for this before I'm through, I can't let them get away with such abusive behavior, and still pretend they are our friends.

The second day passed much as the first. No visitors except Otto.

Sadie, who had retired early, heard pounding and jumped from her bed, grabbed her robe, and headed for the door. Running down the steps, she reached the bottom just as Jessie reached the door. There in the gray light of dawn stood Harrison, hair wet with morning dew, face wet with tears, looking like he'd aged a hundred years.

Jessie grabbed him, pulled him to her ample breast saying, "Por mister Harrison, yo' loved her, too."

Harrison pulled away with a strange look on his face. "Tell me what you're talking about," he demanded.

"Why Miss Kate's passin'. Ain't thet why yo' cryin'?"

A strange look swept over his face, almost joyous, he stood perfectly still, absorbing the tidings. When the full impact of the news hit him, he staggered to a sofa, sat down, placed his head in his hands, his shoulders began to shudder, with what Jessie and Sadie perceived as the ultimate grief.

Sadie sat trying to console him, arms around his shoulders, and crooning, "There, there."

Jessie was the first to recognize the fact that Harrison was not crying, but laughing! She became furious, rage took over, and she grabbed him, jerked him upright, and demanded "wha' the hell is so funny? Has yo' lost yo mind?"

Harrison at once became serious, his frightened eyes searched for Sadie, pleading for understanding. He found none!

Sadie couldn't believe what was happening. Had Harrison gone mad with grief? He could never have fooled them all these years. He cared about Kate. He loved Kate. He's gone mad, that was it!

Harrison pried Jessie's fingers from his coat, sat back down, and began to explain.

"When I first arrived in the small town of Linwood, I asked around for Kate's cousin. The townspeople said they never heard of her or the girls. The local postmaster said the local residents wouldn't answer any questions for strangers anyway.

I next went to the oldest resident's farm and asked if she had ever seen or heard of a women called Dorrie with twin girls about eleven or twelve years old.

The woman looked hard at me for a moment opened the screendoor wider and said, "You best come in and sit a spell while I tell you a story that will tear at your heart." She went to the cupboard, took out two mugs, set them on the table, took the gray granite coffee pot from the back of the stove, shuffled to the table and poured a pungent brew into my coffee mug. She gathered cream and sugar and brought them to the table. She was chewing her lip nervously.

Her hands were shaking, and her eyes were filled with hate. After returning the pot to the stove, she sat down opposite me and began her tale. I will tell you in her own words.

"When I first met that woman, she seemed like the kind of neighbor most folks would like to have. She always doted on the little girls, spoiled them as far as I was concerned. She was here about a year when things began to change. First, we noticed she wasn't keeping the girls clean, and then we noticed they looked skinny. Also some folks said they saw the girls picking berries and they looked like they hadn't eaten in days.

"I went to talk to Dorrie to see if they were having hard times and if I could help. You know how most folks are; they don't want to ask for help, so I figured if I offered, it would be all right.

"When I knocked, a man answered the door asking what the hell I wanted. Well, let me tell you, I sure felt like leaving right then, but the sight of those little girls peeking around the door, all big eyed and hungry looking kept me there. When Miss Dorrie finally came to the door still in her nightclothes looking all frazzled; it didn't take much to figure out what she'd been up to. When I asked her if they were in need of help or if the girls needed to see a doctor, she said she didn't know why I was even asking. The girls were just going through a growing spurt and they would fill out later. Her and her man friend sure didn't look like they had missed a meal," the farm woman said with a sneer.

"What happened to the girls?" I asked.

"Just you let me tell it in my way, so you can live the same horror we went through. Then you will understand why we did what we did," she said with resignation.

"We found out that man (if you can call him that) was forbidding Dorrie to feed the girls anything but gruel. He wanted her to send them away to a workhouse because they got in the way of his hunting and fishing. He wanted Dorrie to travel with him and the girls were dead weight. They picked up and moved to a farm farther out in the woods. By the time we found out where they were, the girls were dead. The doctor said they died of Dysorexy. When we asked what it was, he said it meant reduced appetite. Hell, yes, they had a reduced appetite cause no one gave them food. Two beautiful little girls, about six years old, gone for no reason.

"We were so mad that some of the men got together and tarred and feathered em, and run em out of town. They're lucky we didn't treat them the same way they treated them girls.

"Most folks don't like to remember what they did to those children. We're Christians or we woulda done worse. A few of the white robes wanted to hang em."

"I told the woman that I had come to take the girls to New York City to see their Aunt Kate, who had been sending money all these years to support the girls. Dorrie was still accepting the money even though the girls had been dead for years. The fury rose in my throat, bile filled my mouth, I wanted to kill someone!

"Did you ever hear what had happened to Dorrie and her friend?" I asked the woman.

I picked up the forgotten coffee, now icy cold, drank it, hardly tasting it. My mind was on finding and killing the two people who had taken away Kate's reason for living.

"Yes," she answered. "A traveler passing through town said a couple arrived in Detroit, a few days before he left. They were badly burned. Said they were in a house fire, but the way they behaved, he suspected that they were lying. Didn't take much to figure out who it was. But we ain't heard hide nor hair from or about them since. All I know is they better not come back here even after all these years. Folks don't forget that kind of thing!"

When he finished relating the whole story to Sadie and Jessie, he gave a sigh of relief, and said, "Now you see why I was acting so strangely. All I could think was, I don't have to tell Kate what has happened to her babies. I knew it would kill her. Selfish bastard that I am, I didn't want to be the one to tell her about her cousin's betrayal. I was relieved that she didn't have to know how horribly her little girls had been treated. My God, I'm going to miss that woman. She was my love, my friend and my savior. Thank God she will never know about her girls!" Again he buried his head in his hands, this time he was sobbing.

They didn't try to console him. He needed to get the bitterness out so he could mourn properly.

"Now we's got sumpthin' else important to talk 'bout," announced Jessie. "We hain't had but one mourner to see Miss Kate, an' that was Otto.

Those dandies in town gonna git out here and mourn or else! We's gotta think of a way ta git em to come! Kate gotta have the right send off. Preacher ain't come neither. We's got all thet food. By God somebody gonna eat it!"

Sadie spoke up and said, "Kate wouldn't want them to come if they didn't mean it. She was too damn honest for that."

"Miss Kate hain't here ta run the show. I's gonna see thet she has the bes send off in town. Folks gonna member Miss Kate fo' a lon' time. Now, how we gonna git them out here?"

Lorrie volunteered to deliver invitations to the most prominent households in the city.

"Takes too long," stated Jessie. "We needs ta git their asses movin' today. Miss Kate cain't wait thet long in this kinda weather. Think yo' people, we's a hellva lot smarter then they are, we's can come up with somethin'!"

Violet shyly offered a suggestion: "When I was in New Orleans, they would have wakes where the people wore costumes. They made it a Ball. It was always a popular!"

"Thas it!" declared Jessie. "Them no goods'll fight ta get inside ta a party. We's got plenty of fixens, so if yo' gals'll give me a little help, we be ready in a jiffy."

The doorknocker startled them all. Jessie answered it and the first thing they heard was "Oh, it's yo', what the hell yo' want?" Then they heard, "yo' didn' even know her!" At last they heard, "Well, I guess yo' kin come in. We kin use yo'!"

In walked the stranger that Jessie had taken such a dislike to. He took off his hat, and bowed and said he came to pay his respects to the family.

"Don' give us thet crap, tell us what yo' really wan'," Jessie bellered.

Harrison came forward held out his hand and introduced himself to the stranger, saying, "You're welcome. I'm Harrison and who might you be?"

The stranger shook hands with Harrison, bowed again to the ladies, "Keith is my name. Keith Kendrick at your service."

Sadie was impressed with his manners and suave, debonair way of treating ladies.

Jessie saw the newcomer as a slick, oily, rascal that was up to no good. She vowed to watch that bum at all times, especially since Sadie seemed so interested in him.

They continued discussing the plans for the wake and how they would make the town aware of the costume party to celebrate Kate's departure from this earth.

Keith stepped into the middle of the room and announced that he would spread the news quickly about the costume wake. He guaranteed that everyone who was anyone would be at the house in time for the event.

Jessie eyed him suspiciously, shrugged her shoulders and went to the kitchen, mumbling to herself about jack-asses and fools, and how you had to watch both!

Harrison suddenly looked very tired and weak, saying he needed to have a couple of hours of shuteye or he wouldn't make it either.

While everyone else went off to do his or her assigned duties, Harrison went to Kate's rooms to spend the last few hours alone with the memories of her and the years they had shared. Lying down on the chaise where she would lie and read; he could almost feel the warmth of her body as though this piece of furniture had absorbed the very essence of the woman called Kate. With a sense of belonging, he wriggled deep into the satin chaise and promptly fell into a restful sleep.

The rumble of carriages and wagons woke Harrison. It was late afternoon, and the nap had done him a world of good. He felt rested and ready to go on with this charade. Thank God Kate wasn't here to see it! Well, let the others say good-bye anyway they wanted. He knew in his heart that when he left to go to Michigan, that was really his farewell to a lovely lady.

Sadie was busy greeting guests when Harrison descended the stairs. She had gotten the parlor decorated like a carnival. Streamers were everywhere. The drapes were drawn and the fabric had ribbons looped from window to window. Flowers were on every table and strewn across the aisles between furniture. All that came to his mind was what in the hell am I doing here? Is this the only way we can get Kate a decent send-off? Jesus Christ is this all her life was worth?

The towns' folk casually strode up to where the casket stood on two pillars draped with gold velvet. The inside of the box was covered with white silk and lying in among the flowers that were strewn through out the casket was Kate.

All commented how beautiful she looked, and then hastily made their way to the table where food and drink had been provided. They had taken the time to dress in costume for the occasion, anticipating a fun time and, by heaven, they were going to have it!

Harrison, after much coaxing, sat at the piano and automatically played many of the tunes popular at the time. *What the hell,* he thought, *why not let these idiots have their fun? It can't hurt Kate.*

Every so often Jessie would peek out to watch the revelers, shake her head, and mumble to herself. Sadie had misgivings each time she saw Jessie there. Please, God, don't let her lose her temper. This orgy is bad enough without violence to make it even worse.

The night seemed to go on forever. When the last partygoers had left, the members of the household settled down to remembering the happy times they had shared with Kate. Sadie and Lorrie told the others, suppressing giggles, about how they had moved to New York. How funny the Jalopy had looked all piled high with their goods, how they had met Annie, who had made the beautiful quilts; Millie the widow with small children to raise, and, of course, Evan, the owner of the tavern in Buffalo. They hesitated to talk about Andrew, but it was part of Kate's life, and so they told the others about her love and the twins they had together.

"That reminds me, I must get the ivory elephants. They must be buried with Kate," whispered Sadie. "But we should hide them, or grave robbers will dig her up."

Jessie butted in saying, "Now, wha' in hell is Miss Kate gonna do with dem elephants in her casket? She wouldn' wan' them beautiful things buried way so's no body sees em. I say put em out so's we all kin knowed Miss Kate was here."

Chapter Twelve
The Grave Robber

Dawn came and the weary group moved the coffin onto a wagon, loaded everyone into autos, buckboards and carriages, and made its way to the local cemetery where the coffin was unloaded, and set on two boards that extended across the mouth of the grave. Ropes were placed at each end of the box, the boards were pulled out, and the box was lowered into the yawning hole. The grieving friends each threw a handful of black earth into the gaping maw of mother earth. The dull thud of the dirt striking the casket would be a sound that Sadie would always remember.

Jessie quietly mumbled a few words over the grave, and then said loud enough for everyone to hear, "She's yers now, God. Treat her good. She earned it."

As the mourners began to filter away, Jessie stayed back and stationed herself behind one of the Oak trees that stood guard over the departed souls buried in this consecrated ground.

The gravedigger watched the mourners leave the cemetery. Then he lowered himself into the hole, and using a hammer he tore open the wooden box. He riffled through Kate's clothing, and found nothing of value. Swearing loudly, he began pulling himself up from the hole, only to find himself face to face with Jessie's feet!

He felt his bowels go loose as he tried to pretend he wasn't afraid. Feces ran down his legs and seeped out of his shoes. The stench was a dead give-away. He broke out in a sweat. His eyes looked everywhere but at the mountain of a woman who was about to break his neck! He did the only thing he could think of at the time. He fainted! When he awoke, she was still up there, sitting and waiting. He began to shake. *This is it; I'm about to meet my maker.* He began to cry, begging Jessie to forgive him, promising to never rob a grave again.

She let him go on for some time begging and pleading. When she grew tired of his whining, she grabbed him, pulled him out of the grave and up to her face, so close he could see the pores in her skin. "If I's ever hear of nother grave thets been robbed, I's coming for yor ass and yo' better knows I means it! Now git fore I's changes my mind."

He left the cemetery on a dead run, falling over head stones, stumbling over mounds of earth, eventually reaching the gates to the street. His pace didn't slow till he was out of sight of the black women who had caused him to foul himself. How would he explain that to his cronies? He couldn't admit she caught him robbing graves; they would tar and feather him.

When Jessie came in the parlor, Sadie asked her what had happened to her at the cemetery, had she missed her ride?

"No," replied Jessie. "Jist takin' care of business."

She smiled a secret smile as she remembered what the caretaker had said when she reported the vandalism. He had promised to repair the coffin and see that the grave was properly filled in, and his promise to see that gravedigger's violation would be reported to the sheriff, satisfied Jessie's lust for justice. She knew the men in this town would run him out on a rail when they find out what he had been up to.

Sadie didn't want to go any further. She again felt that warning bell in her brain that told her not to pursue the incident. It was better not to know.

Harrison turned to Sadie, shook her hand, and announced, "You, my girl, are the new madam of this house, and you should decide how things are to be run."

Sadie was in shock. "Why me?" she asked. "What have I done to deserve this business?"

Harrison explained that he and Kate had discussed it many times and she had made the decision to give the business to Sadie because she was caring, honest and the best worker she had ever had. She knew that Sadie would look after the girls and be honest with them.

Will I still bees cooking' fo' yo'?" Asked Jessie. "If no, Mr. Harrison did yo' fin' out bout thet storefront fo' my restaurant?"

"My God, Jessie!" Sadie blurted out. "You can't leave me now. I need you more than ever. Promise me you will stay with me, at least for a while."

The grin on Jessie's face told the whole story. She was there for the long haul.

Keith Kendrick had come back to the house with Sadie and the rest of the mourners and was sitting on the side taking in all the information. His quiet way worried Jessie, but she had decided to hold her tongue and see how far he'd go. She didn't trust him, but Sadie did. *Well, we see who bes right,* she promised herself.

"Yes, my dear Jessie, I have rented the store you chose and it is all arranged for you to get started in the restaurant business whenever you are ready." He then casually announced that he would be taking some time off to make a trip back to Michigan to take care of unfinished business. He wasn't sure how long he would be gone, so he was glad Jessie was staying to help Sadie and the girls.

"I will be leaving in the morning, so I better get some rest in what's left of the day. It's going to be hard going upstairs and not hearing Kate holler good night." Slowly shaking his head, he whispered, "I still can't believe she's gone."

He made his way to the stairs and ascended slowly; his shoulders slumped, head hanging low. Lifting one foot and then another, he dragged himself up the stairs with the carriage of an old man.

They watched him go, agony tearing at his guts. He had known the woman, liked her, loved her, and now she was no more. He was like a rudderless boat on a stormy sea, a helpless casualty to the elements.

Keith walked to Sadie's side, sat down, took her hand, gently stroked it, and in a low voice asked her if she would like him to help out while Harrison was gone. She looked relieved and said, "I hadn't thought about it, but yes, it would be a great help to have a man around in case of trouble."

Jessie was aware of his little play and she watched as Sadie accepted his proposition.

"Oh, hell, we's in fo' it now," she mumbled to Phoebe, "I knowed thet snake in tha grass was gonna try an worm his way in ta Sadie's bed. Well, we's jist gotta watch so's he don cause too much fracas. All my life I's seed these leeches move in an suck the blood outa healthy folks and leave em weak and fragile. Well, he ain't gonna do thet ta Sadie. She' special, we's gotta pertect her agin thet good-for-nothing Keith."

Lorrie, who was sitting near Jessie, not only heard the anger in Jessie's voice but also watched the emotion playing across Jessie's face. She didn't want to be the receiver of that fury, and she sure didn't want to be on the wrong end of that hated. Lorrie tore her eyes away, feeling as though she had invaded a disquieting place.

"It's settled then. While Harrison is away, Keith will be here to help us.

By the way, Keith, do you happen to play the piano?" Sadie asked.

Keith rose, went to the piano, sat down, and played a gay little tune that almost had their feet tapping. When he finished, they clapped their hands. He not only played, but he played very well. *Even better than Harrison,* Sadie thought.

Jessie stood, took a deep breath and said, "Don' know bout yo' folks but I's headed fo' bed. We's got lota work tomorra' to git this place cleaned up, and I's tired!"

When she was safely away, Keith wiped his brow with a handkerchief, breathed a sigh of relief, and stated, "That woman hates my very guts. I can feel it every time she looks at me. What have I done wrong?" he asked with little boy innocence.

Sadie looked at him with the ghost of a smile on her face, and told him that Jessie was always that way with strangers. After he got to know her, he would love her and she him.

"She takes a little while to get acquainted, but once she does, she's a friend for life."

Keith didn't see that happening anytime soon. How did that bitch know that he was here to make a score? He had heard there were some of those niggers in New Orleans who could read your mind. He'd have to watch himself when he was around that woman. Better yet, if I can get rid of her I'd have free reign. I'll have to work on that in a few days. Right now I need to make myself indispensable, starting with that tramp Sadie.

"Jessie's right," Lorrie said between yawns. "I am exhausted, I feel like I've been up for a week! I'll see you folks in a few hours," she tossed over her shoulder as she headed toward the stairs. Then she paused, turned, looked at the others, and through her tears said, "My God, I can't believe she's gone. I'm going to miss her so much." This last was said in nothing more than a whisper, but everyone in the room heard it.

Sadie gave Keith the room that Cathy had once used and made her way to her room. It had always cheered her before, but today it seemed cold and empty.

Her thoughts drifted back to her years with Marcus. I wonder where he is. I hope he is well and happy. She could feel the tears building; the empty feeling in her heart had become so much a part of her she had forgotten why it was there. The emotions raging through her mind exploded into a tremendous spasm of sobs, a torrent of tears and the gut wrenching anguish of loneliness.

"Dear God! Can I still go on without Marcus?" she demanded of herself. She could see him in her mind's eye; the way he tipped his head when he didn't understand, the crooked smile, the sparkle in his eye when he was teasing, the gentle touch of his hands. *Oh, how I miss that man.* After the tears subsided, she felt relieved.

Lorrie was right, a woman needs to let loose and cry once in a while. It does help, but I don't feel like I could lick the world right now, maybe later. One thing it did was bring Marcus closer. She'd buried him so deeply in her heart that she had forgotten what a comfort it was to let her mind wander to the times they had spent together. *I can almost feel his touch, feel his breath on my cheek, the warmth of his love.* At last, near dawn, Sadie had daydreamed herself into a serene state of languor from which she drifted off to sleep.

Keith went to his room, sat on the bed, bent over to remove his shoes, and felt a presence in the room. He jumped up, looked around, but could find no one. Still he felt eyes watching him. *Forget it, that bitch Jessie has me all jumpy.* He finished undressing and climbed into bed. *Too bad we just met. It would be convenient to share a bed with Sadie, or one of the other girls, if she's too busy. I will just have to bide my time till I've worked here a little longer, and then I'll make my move. If my plan works out, I will be running this joint in a month and Mr. Big Shot Harrison will be out on his ear. Keith, my boy you better get yourself some rest, you have a busy day ahead.* He liked that name Keith Kendrick. He was glad he had chosen it. It made him seem like he came from a high-class family. It sure sounded better than John Stump. Keith rolled over and went sound asleep, hunched down in the bed that Cathy used to occupy.

Morning came way too soon for Sadie. She had lain awake most of the night and had fallen asleep just before dawn. She tore herself out of the warm, comfortable bed into the cool morning air. Taking a sponge bath and dressing, she went down to the kitchen for coffee.

In the kitchen Jessie was preparing breakfast for the household. She was humming as usual, but Sadie could tell her heart wasn't in it.

"It shor do seem strange without Miss Kate, don' it, honey?"

"Yes," Sadie answered, " we're going to miss her, but we must get on with our lives."

"I's packing a lunch fo' Harrison to tak with him on his trip ta Michigan. Wonder wat he going there fo'. I's wonder if I's wants to know. Hit ain' none a my business fo' sur'."

"I suspect he is going to find Dorrie, and deal with her for her betrayal of

Kate, but I wouldn't stake my life on it. I just hope nothing happens to Harrison. He is such a dear friend, and we have lost enough when we lost Kate. We need to get back to a normal life here at the house. We must get the word out that we are open for business. I'll put Keith on that as soon as he is up and ready for work."

"Did I hear my name?" asked Keith from the doorway. "Dear Sadie, I'm ready for work as soon as I've had some of that delicious smelling food that Jessie's preparing."

Jessie looked at him with a hard glare, motioned to the table, and slammed a plate in front of him. Next came a cup with a resounding clatter; utensils came last, tossed noisily in front of him. "Now, eat an then git outta my face!"

When she poured the coffee, Keith speculated, if she might end up pouring it in his lap instead of the cup. *Bitch hates me, gotta do something to get her on my side. I can work on that problem on the way to town. Gotta come up with something, that's all there is to it!* When he had eaten, he asked Sadie what plans she had for him, as he liked to stay busy.

She told him the main thing to do was spread the word that Haven Place was open again, then they would worry about the rest of the duties for him.

"While you're in town you might look up another gardener for the grounds. They are starting to look real shabby. The old gardener can't keep up with all the work anymore. He needs help."

"Why don't you let the old gardener go and just hire a new one instead of having two?" Keith asked.

"I can't in good faith do that. Old Ned has been here a long time and he is a good worker and loyal. We need people like that around us. We can't just throw them away when they're no longer useful." She stared hard at Keith, then she smiled and said, " Well, we better get on with the work for the day."

Jessie had overheard the conversation as she stood with her back turned to the two people sitting at the table and snickered to herself. *Sadie is catching on I bet! I's knowd it! I 's promise myself ta keep my tater hole shut. But, it sure gonna be tough. Course, Sadie ain't no fool. She gonna figger him out in time. Jist hope it don tak' too long!*

The girls started filtering in twos and threes. Most had taken the time to dress, but Maybelle, Kitty, and Susan were still in nightclothes and robes. They looked a bit disheveled, but quite lovely. Keith speculated on which one would he conquer first. He would have to watch his step at first with Sadie, but when he tired of her, these girls would provide many hours of enjoyment. He was so busy with his future plans that he forgot to be cautious when he was around Jessie. When he looked up there was Jessie staring at him with a secret smile on her face, but her eyes were hard with black thunderclouds in them. Keith felt a chill run up and down his spine. *I should leave right now*, his panicky mind told him. *There's trouble down the road.* "Hell no," he told himself, "I haven't met a women yet that I can't charm, appeal to, or coerce to do my bidding. I will be all right." He stood and pretended he was finished eating. Damn. He'd liked more food. That bitch sure could cook, but he was getting edgy just being in the same room with her.

"Sadie, my dear, I will head for town and spread the word. Is there anything else to do, other than getting another gardener?"

"You might stop by Jessie's storefront and see if everything is set to start transforming it into a restaurant. I know she's anxious to get started as soon as possible."

Jessie turned from the stove and in a quiet, cold voice stated, "We gonna tek care of tha' business ourselves. We's don need no help from no stranger, no how, and thets thet."

"I'm sorry, Jessie," Sadie apologized, "I thought it would make things easier for you, but if you don't want Keith's help that is your choice. I won't stick my nose in your business again!"

Keith stood by the door thinking, *that is the first wedge in their friendship. A few more and I will have that bitch, Jessie, out.* He retrieved his hat from the hall coat tree, placed it at a jaunty angle, grabbed his coat, placed it over his shoulder, walked out the front door, got into his buggy and headed for town.

The first thing he did was to have posters printed announcing that Haven Place was open again. Then he hired a couple of lads to pick up and post the announcements. Next he went to a tavern on the seamy side of town, where he interviewed a few men for the job as gardener at Haven Place. He had to have the right man, one who would go along with what ever he was told to do by him and him only. The last man seemed to be just what he was looking for: a whiney little man who thought the world owed him a living. The man's name was Asia, and the name reminded Keith of asshole, which he probably was, but that was all right, it would fit right in with his plans. He would be easy to manipulate; all he was looking for was an easy crib. Keith told him to work hard the first month until Sadie was lulled into a sense of acceptance, then Keith didn't give a damn if he did anything or not. Asia greedily drank his ale, while Keith explained the situation at Haven Place. He watched Asia with distaste. The man was a slobbering idiot. He wondered if he was making a mistake in hiring him. He warned the already drunk Asia that there would be no drinking at the house while he is working.

"Sure, sure," Asia muttered, "I can take it or leave it alone. Why just last week I didn't drink for two whole days. Some men can't do that!"

"What the hell have I gotten myself into?" Keith muttered, "but then I didn't expect to find a pure in heart lackey to do my bidding. Gotta just play the cards I'm dealt with just a few Asia's on the bottom," he said, chuckling to himself at the joke he had made.

Asia thinking he was questioning his integrity, stood swaying, holding onto the table, and announced to the whole tavern, "This is my last drink. I will be a teetotaler from now on." He then sat down and finished his tankard of ale.

His cronies in the tavern became boisterous, shouting slurs, telling him he couldn't go dry for one day, much less a lifetime. They were so rowdy that Keith was developing a headache. He paid the owner what he owed him, told Asia to be at Haven Place in the morning sober. He then left.

What a miserable lot that was. How can they let themselves get so low? Well, he would never let himself sink to that level. He had too much pride for that! So, he used a few people to get ahead. That wasn't as bad as those poor creatures. They were no earthly good to anyone. Besides the people he took advantage of knew that was how you get along in this world. After rationalizing his conduct, he felt so much better. He might even reward himself with a trip to a whorehouse, but not Haven Place, not yet anyway. Gotta keep up appearances.

The woman who opened the door looked about thirty-five, unkempt, and slightly drunk. Keith could smell the booze from where he stood on the steps. He told her what he wanted and she offered to be his partner for an hour.

"You ugly old bag of bones, I wouldn't avail myself of your charms for any amount of money. You smell to high heaven. You are revolting!"

Pushing past her, he entered the dilapidated parlor and with distaste he sneered, "Are you the only whore here?"

The hag called out, "Marsha, we got company. Git yerself in here fast!"

A young woman stepped out of the shadows into the glaring light of the parlor; her hair was golden, skin like alabaster, and she had the greenest eyes he had ever seen. He was transfixed for the moment. When she spoke, he knew that this was the woman he wanted. She obviously was a child in a woman's body and that worked real well for Keith. No stupid questioning of his orders, she would do what ever he wanted! Keith decided to play it smart and pretend he was looking for a girl for Haven Place. That way the girl would do her very best, so she could escape from this rat hole. He would pay the price the slut was asking, but he'd make sure he got his moneys worth. After all it might be a while before he got in town again.

When he was satisfied that he had his money's worth and then some, he left the girl sobbing on the bed, went to the lavatory down the hall, freshened up and left.

He hadn't spoken three words after he told her he was searching for girls for the house. Marsha lay beaten and humiliated on the bed. He had made her do things she had never done before, or ever wanted to do again. She had a split lip, her arms were bruised from the force he had used, her whole body ached, and the simple act had become torture for the inexperienced young girl.

"If this is how it is at Haven Place, do I really want to go? I wish I was back home with my mother," she moaned to herself, hugging her wounded arms to her chest. " I hate this work. I wish I were dead!"

The door to her room burst open, and the madam stood weaving drunkenly.

"Well, your highness, did you get what you asked for and where's mine? I need some more to drink. My bottle went empty pretty fast. You sure you ain't been sneaking a few drinks behind my back?" The drunken madam slipped on the rug, hit her head and went unconscious on the floor. She lost control of her bladder; she wet herself, the rug and the floor. She lay there stinking from both booze and urine. The old woman's wrinkled face looked like a wilted jack-a-lantern. Her mouth hung open, and the few black teeth that were left in her mouth finished the disgust that invaded Marsha's soul.

She felt her stomach churn. She stared at the woman on the floor and thought about the previous hours being used by the man called Keith. She knew that she didn't want to end up like this. Stepping over the fallen woman, she went to the lavatory, picked up the straight razor that was kept there for guests and touched the sharp edge. If she did use this to solve her problems, she didn't want to suffer. Yes, it is very sharp. It would only hurt for a minute.

"Now, can I do it?" she asked the empty room. She went back down the hall to her room with the razor in her hand, her thoughts churning.

Who will bury me or will they throw me in a hole and no one will know where I am? Do I care? Will I even know if I'm dead? Will it be important to me any more? No one will look for me any way. Mother doesn't even remember her own name, and she sure won't remember mine.

Marsha lay back on the disheveled bed, staring at the razor glinting in the sunlight coming through the filthy window.

She raised the blade closer to her left wrist, slowly laid the sharp instrument on the white skin and slashed a scarlet ribbon across the alabaster arm.

She marveled at the absence of pain. *Now I can do the other arm. Thank God, it didn't hurt!* The lovely woman-child lay back and waited for release from her agony.

When the police were called the next day, the crone said she had discovered Marsha's body the night before, but she wasn't going anywhere, so it seemed all right to wait till morning to report it.

The news traveled all over town about the prostitute who had taken her own life. Everyone speculated on why. There were as many reasons given, as there were people, but no one asked where she would be buried or if she had family. It was as though another bird had fallen from the sky. It didn't even count. Keith heard the news and thought, *well, there goes one of the people I was going to use. Too bad too, she was lovely to look at, easy to command. She would have given me a lot of enjoyment while I'm here. He just hoped that old bitch hadn't mentioned his visit, which could take some explaining to Sadie. After all, she was still running the place. Later, he wouldn't have to worry about making excuses.*

When they heard the news at Haven Place, Jessie questioned, "I wonder if thet, Keith fella, had anythin' ta do with it. Keith sure hada funny look on his face when one of the girls told em the talk around town. Thet a new client that had used her, then beat her, then used her agin, as though she wer' nothin'. Then threw her aside like a piece of soiled meat."

Jessie knew that Keith was capable of such a deed; the rest would know when they got to know him better, but as for Jessie, she knew him all too well right now! She erupted, "What kinda lowly critter would do thet ta nother human bein'? If'en I ever git my hands on thet kinda critter, he be dead fo' shor'. His ass gonna suck up a lota of ocean. Water don' tell no tales." She sniggered softly, staring directly at Keith.

Sadie wondered if Jessie would ever get over the distrust she had for Keith.

So far he had not done anything to hurt them. She felt Jessie was being unfair to judge him before she really knew him. Everything seemed to be piling up: the killings, the storm, Kate's death most of all, now this with the girl Marsha killing herself.

"What next? I wish Harrison were here. I hope he finishes his business soon," she lamented. Everyone agreed with Sadie on that account, except Keith. He said nothing and just sat with empty eyes, lost in the land where people don't count.

Lorrie brought up the question of what would happen if they got a client like that and what would Keith do to protect them? At first Keith didn't answer. He suddenly felt all eyes on him, waiting for an answer.

"Huh? What did I miss? My mind was wandering, I was thinking of that poor girl and what she went through. I didn't hear what was asked."

"The girls want to know what you will do to keep us safe from that kind of monster?"

"Sadie, you know I will protect you all with my life, even those who hate me!"

"Mister, yo' don knowed what hate be, till yo git me started," Jessie tossed over her shoulder as she left the room muttering, "I's seem to do thet a lot lately, gotta be that slimy Keith gettin' under my skin. He shore's a blown up bag of shet. Where I come from they'd spread thet kinda shet on a rock, cause no good come from hit."

When she got into the kitchen, her mood brightened. This is where she shone. *Can't nobody beat my fried chicken and dumplings,* she thought. *That'll lift our spirits. Thets what we need is good food and less turmoil! I's wonder how Cathy, Rachael, my little angel, and Philip are commin' long with the cottage. What I's wouldn' give ta hav' me a man thet loves me and a whole poke of babies' takin' up space. Hell, jist a man would be okay for a spell, but truth be knowed, I'd druther have a drink. Oh, to feel thet burnin' on my tongue, warm spot in my belly, hell, even in my crotch. Gotta quit thinkin of the drink! It always gits me in trouble, but the yearnin shore stays with yo' longer than a man.*

The delicious smells wafting from the kitchen soon brought the household to the dining room, where Jessie had placed a huge bowl of flowers from the garden.

The room was warm and friendly, filled with the fragrance of flowers and food. When Sadie walked into the room, her mind went back to the first time she ate at Kate's place so many years ago. Her eyes filled with unshed tears and her mind with pleasant memories. She would miss her friend Kate till the day she, herself, died. The dull, bittersweet ache stayed in her heart.

The food was perfect and the conversation was light, full of good-natured laughter. This was going to be the first night open since the wake. The girls were ready to get back to business as usual.

As was quite often true, Otto shared the scrumptious meal with them, teasing the girls about how he had a hard time choosing who would be his partner tonight. Everyone knew Sadie was the only one Otto ever chose. When they teased him back, he blushed and stuttered like a schoolboy, but he enjoyed the banter.

Keith came in as they were finishing their meal and announced, "It's time you ladies got upstairs and got ready for the gentlemen who will be calling. Don't take all day to make yourself presentable either."

Sadie and Jessie just looked at each other as they all sat in shocked silence. Finally Jessie spoke up, "Sadie, yo' wan' me ta throw this jack-ass out on his ear?"

The minute he had spoken he knew he had made a big mistake. He had pushed too soon. When he had the run of the place, this would all change. No more big dinners for the working girls. The help wouldn't eat the same food as the owner, they would eat scraps in kitchen, but for now he would have to go along with the rules Sadie made.

"Sorry, Sadie, I guess I'm a bit anxious about tonight. I didn't mean to sound so rude."

"Sadie, you din' answer me," Jessie demanded, " Yo' wan' I should throw this fool out? I'd love thet job!"

Otto stammered out, "Vote the hell iss going on. Since ven does he gif orders?"

Jessie was half way across the room, when Sadie finally spoke, "Keith, this is a house where everyone is equal. No one gives orders except me, and I try to make them requests. If that doesn't fit your plans, then you should seek employment elsewhere."

"I said I'm sorry. What else do you want me to do?"

"You shouldn't apologize to me. You owe the girls the apology, and you really should try to think of a way to make amends."

"While we're at it, Sadie, did yo' git an eyeful of thet there new gardener, ifen thets what yo' calls him? I don trus' him far as I kin throw him. Keith picked him so thet make me mo distrustful." Jessie didn't want to let him mealy mouth his way out of this mess he got himself into, not if she could help it!

"Now wait a minute, Jessie, I know you don't like me, but don't take it out on that poor fellow. He's down on his luck and needs this job." Keith worked very hard to seem concerned. *Damn it! I've got to do something about that black bitch and soon,* he vowed. *She's going to spoil all my plans if she keeps it up.* "Jessie, I want to do the right thing around here, but I keep making mistakes and you're right there to jump on me for them. Can't you give me a chance?"

"He's right, we do seem to pick at him more than we ever did Harrison. We'll give him some time to get used to the job," Sadie made this statement, much to Jessie's misgivings. "As far as the new gardener, he will be on probation, too."

The girls filed out silently. The fun and good humor was gone and in its place a sense of hostility invaded the house.

Jessie made her way to the parlor to check on the spirits for the night; there on the mantle where the ivory elephants were supposed to be was a cheap set of vases.

"Now, who'n hell would do thet?" she asked herself. Then she started to shake. "Who else, but that no good, slimy creature, Keith!" She barreled into the kitchen looking for him, but he was gone. Next she looked for Sadie. She was nowhere to be found. She went to the parlor again just to make sure her eyes didn't deceive her. No, they were still missing. Jessie went in search of Sadie.

She was mad as hell and somebody was gonna pay for stealing Kate's elephants! She bounded up the stairs, down the hall to Sadie's room, pounded on her door and sang out, "Sadie, som' dirty basard done stol' Kate's elephants. Come quick, we gotta cotch em right now!"

There was no answer from the room beyond the door, only silence. A strange, eerie, feeling stole over Jessie. *There it is agin, somebody jist tramped on my grave.* The thought made her shiver even more. *I's gotta get myself a juju. I's feel some bad times acomin', an' acomin' soon.*

Jessie wasn't the only one who felt something was strange. Lorrie had noticed that some of her things were moved, with nothing missing, just in a different order than she usually kept them. At first she dismissed it as her carelessness, but she became more aware of it each day. She began to put certain things in certain places and later found them moved. She felt uncomfortable with the idea someone was coming into her room when she was not there. And just what were they looking for? *I think I better have a talk with Sadie. This is certain to lead to trouble if it continues.* She too went in search of Sadie.

Lorrie and Jessie met in the hall; both had concerned looks on their faces. Lorrie asked Jessie if she knew where Sadie was.

" No," she answered. "I's lookin' fo' her too. I don' like what's happenin' round here lately. It don' seem right somehow. We's all worried alla time, not lik' afore, then we's happy."

Lorrie agreed with her, "There does seem to be a lot more arguing and quibbling around here lately. I wonder it's because we all miss Kate"

"Well, miss smarty pants, I miss her too, but I's sure's hell knowd she didn' take her elephants off thet mantle!" With that said, she strutted off in a huff.

Keith had come into the hall just as Jessie was leaving and he asked Lorrie what all the fuss was about. Lorrie told him about the statues being missing, her clothes and gee jaws being moved in different places, even her undies were messed up, as though someone were searching for something.

"Well, if they are looking for money, they are out of luck. I put everything in the bank where it is safe."

"You are very wise to put in where it can't be stolen. Do all the girls do the same? I'm only asking because if they don't, I will suggest it to Sadie," Keith said with a smirk.

"Sadie always suggests that the new girls to put their money in an account at the bank, just as Kate did when she was here. We have to protect ourselves any way we can because we deal with a lot of different kinds of men. I don't know if everyone takes her advice, but that is their business, not mine," Lorrie replied."

"Of course, you're right. What they do with their earnings is up to them. You know I have my doubts about Jessie. She has been acting very strange since she started that business about a restaurant. Is she in need of money to get it running? I'm not suggesting she would steal from us. I'm only thinking she might consider it a loan," Keith suggested.

"Keith, I would trust Jessie with my life," Lorrie cried out vehemently. "She would ask if she needed something, just as we would ask her for help if we needed it! We're friends. She sure wouldn't steal from us."

"Well, it was only a thought, but there are some odd things happening around here of late." *All right,* thought Keith, *I've laid the groundwork for suspicion against that black bitch! When they find the statues in her room under the covers where I put them, she will have a hard time explaining how they got there. I just need a few more things to disappear and her ass is gone!*

Lorrie thought about the things Keith had mentioned, then quickly dismissed the idea. She really would trust Jessie with her life. *Besides,* she thought, *we all have known Jessie a hell of a lot longer than we have known Mr. Kieth Kendricks.*

Chapter Thirteen
Viper's Nest

Otto had wandered into the parlor, noticed the statues gone and assumed that Jessie had taken them out to clean them. When Jessie came into the room, he asked about them.

She explained that she hadn't touched them in a week, they had disappeared, and she was, "Damn well gonna fin' em."

"Now don't go off half cocked. It might be dat Sadie took them for safekeeping. Ve must vait till ve talk to Sadie, before ve tink the vorst."

"Well, Otto, ifen she don' hav' em, I's gonna tear this place apar', till I's fin' em!"

They went to Sadie's room, knocked again and still no answer. "Wherein hell could she git hersef off ta?" When they arrived downstairs again, Sadie was waiting in the parlor, pacing back and forth, her hands clasped behind her back.

"I've just been in the cellar. I guess I thought that tunnel had been sealed, after the last storm, but it is still open to anyone that wants to enter. I want it sealed immediately!"

Keith strode in just as Sadie was outlining her plan to close the tunnel, "I will have Asia put up a barricade at the entrance," he said.

"Do you think that someone from outside is coming in to steal? You do know the elephants are missing, don't you?" Lorrie asked.

"No, I didn't know, but someone has been in my rooms and in my things. Whoever it is seems to be looking for something," Sadie answered. "I don't keep anything of value so they're wasting their time, but we do need to find Kate's elephants before Harrison gets back."

"Vell, I tink ve better find out vhy somebody do dis!" Otto face was red with anger.

"The first thing you ought to do is have a search of the house for the elephants, by the way, are they valuable?" Keith asked.

Jessie looked at him with one of her "Evil eye" looks saying, "I's jist bet yo' could tell us rite ta the cent wha' they worth!"

"I don't believe anyone from this house is responsible for taking the statues. They all know how important they were to Kate." Sadie stood, slowly shaking her head in confirmation of her words. "I think someone from outside is snooping through all of our things, and he or she is going to get caught! We are too close knit to suspect one of us."

"Possibly you're right, but we still should search in case the elephants are hidden in the house. Who knows, maybe they haven't had time to get them out yet," Keith insisted.

"All right, let's search the house right now. We'll start with the upper floors and work our way down." Sadie hated to do this, but she knew Keith might be right, and they did have some new girls who hadn't proven themselves yet. Maybe, just maybe, one of them was guilty of stealing the Ivory keepsakes.

Keith was trying so hard to fill Harrison's shoes that Sadie had given him free reign quite often lately. *I wish Harrison were here right now,* she thought. *What would he do? Would he search the girls' rooms or would he ask if anyone knew anything about their disappearance. He always seemed to know the right thing to do.*

She led the small party up the stairs to the third floor, knocked and told the girl answering what they were there for, searching as a group, looking only where it was possible to hide the figures.

Each of the ladies in the rooms was highly indignant that Sadie would suspect them of such a violation of trust. She tried to explain that it was only a way of eliminating them from suspicion. Sadie reassured them that she knew no one in this house would do such a shameful deed.

Lorrie insisted they do her room next, and asked that all the girls join in with the search. When they were done with Lorrie's room, Sadie said, "I'm next," and led them to her room.

Having found nothing in any of the girls' rooms, they turned to Keith and announced, "Your room is next on our list." He bowed and answered, "ladies, be my guest!"

His room was in shambles: clothes everywhere, bed unmade, curtain hanging half out the window, blowing in the wind, shade torn loose at one end, banging on the sill with every breeze, like a rat, tat, tat of a drummer learning his music from the flow.

"Sorry, ladies, I guess I'm not a very good housekeeper. Too busy getting things organized around here to clean this room." Keith's explanation landed on deaf ears, as far as Sadie was concerned. She was reminded of Harrison's room: clean, neat, clothing hung just so, nothing touching. She wished he were back where he belonged!

Sadie spoke to Keith in a whisper, "My God, I thought you had been robbed the way this room looks. I should have known better. Whoever is doing the snooping is a lot neater than this!"

Jessie smiled and said, "My mama always said a cluttered house is a cluttered mind. Nothin' good comes from it."

When they found nothing in Keith's room, he turned in a fury, saying, "Jessie, I don't suppose you would mind if we searched your room now, would you?

"Jist as soon as we's done here,"spat Jessie."I's ain't got nothin to hide. Yo sure can search my place." She led the way to her room and threw open the door. Her sanctuary was as pristine as a nun's, everything in its place, except for two bumps in her bed.

"Well, well, what do we have here?" Keith shouted. "What could be under this mattress that makes it so lumpy? I guess we'll just have to investigate this mystery."

He leered at Jessie, raised the mattress off the springs, and there were the ivory elephants, lying on their sides, gleaming with accusations against the disbelieving Jessie.

Jessie's face took on the shocked look of a deer in flight. "How'd dose tings get dere? I ain't put em dere. Somebody don hid em in my bed!"

Keith smiled a malicious grin and answered her outburst with sarcasm.

"Sure, somebody must have done that. You would never, never steal from your friends would you? But who would do such a thing to you? Why, everybody loves you!"

Lorrie and Sadie both believed Jessie's protest of innocence. They just couldn't guess who else might have done this terrible thing.

Sadie said, "I still think it is somebody from outside the house, but why?"

Jessie felt a sense of guilt, even though she had nothing to do with the theft of the statues. Her mind was racing. *I's jist bets that scum of the earth, Keith, had somethin' ta do wit the whole mess.* Well, she's gonna do some spyin' round herself. *She would prove ta ever man jack thet she ain'no thief.* She stiffened her back, threw out her massive chest and vowed, "I's gonna git to the bottom of dis, or die tryin'."

Otto hadn't said anything through the whole search. He had watched the gathering with a sense of expectancy. The solution lay somewhere in this house and he knew it wasn't Jessie, who had committed the theft of the elephants. She was just too honest and open to steal from anyone. He hadn't liked that fellow Keith since he had met him. He had a sly way about him and Otto felt he was involved in someway. He would bet his life on that.

Sadie told the group of searchers, "Now that we have found the missing articles, let's go on with our business as usual and please watch out for an intruder in our household. We still need to find the culprit!"

They all made their way back to the main hall, then some departed to their rooms to dress, others toward the parlor, gathering in small groups, to discuss the events of the last two hours. Keith pleaded work to discuss with the new gardener and left the house.

Otto took Sadie aside. In a trembling voice he asked, "Do you belief vhat that fellow Keith, iss trying to get you to belief? I don't trust him; it all started after he comes here, before dat ve don't haf any trouble. Jessie still scares the pee outa me, but she's no thief."

"I's heard thet and I's grateful fo yer trust," Jessie said, slapping Otto on the shoulder with her open hand, nearly knocking him off his feet.

"Damn it, voman, you don't know your own strength," he scolded her.

For the next few weeks things went on as usual. The ladies came and went without any more complaints of missing articles or disturbed rooms. The household was almost back to normal, until one eventful Saturday night.

It began as all their Saturdays began, a wholesome dinner, preparing for the evening, and the arrival of the gentlemen. As the evening was getting into full swing, a new man arrived on the scene. To Sadie's experienced eye, he looked young and slightly flustered by the hubbub in the parlor. He was not well dressed, as were the others, and his anxious eyes darted around the room looking for what or whom? Sadie wondered as she introduced herself.

The stranger seemed reluctant to share any information with her at first, but when she told him who she was and that she ran this place, he seemed relieved to talk.

"I'm searching for a girl that I met when I visited a house across town. The house was not as nice as this one, but since it was a prank my friends had played on me, I didn't know the difference. I shared the evening with a slip of a girl named Marsha. She was a sweet, gentle girl, and I couldn't forget her. I hoped to find her and see if she felt the same way. I know I'm being foolish, chasing after a girl I only seen once, but I feel like I've known her forever. I just couldn't let it rest, I have to find her and see if those feelings are still there."

Taking the young man's arm, Sadie led him to the kitchen, sat him at the huge table, and poured him a cup of coffee.

"What made you think she was here?" she asked.

"I went back to the house where I first met her and the woman who answered the door said, "Marsha don't work here anymore. She's moved on to a better place, and then she laughed. Why did she laugh so crazy?"

Sadie sat with tears in her eyes and a lump in her throat. How could she tell this confused young man that the person he had set his heart on was dead? Beaten by a cruel customer, treated badly by her madam, and murdered by her horrible life? *Some days I hate this wretched life I live.*

Never one to put off the inevitable, she began the story just as she had heard it. When she had finished, the man sat with tears streaming down his face, crying for what might have been. He slowly stood, shook Sadie's hand and left by the back door.

" There is a man we will never see again," Sadie predicted.

Keith came into the room as the young man left.

"What was that all about?" he asked. Sadie told him what had happened. While she was telling him, she had a feeling that he had heard it all before. *Was he listening at the door,* she wondered, *and why would he be so interested in the death of a prostitute he didn't know? Or did he?*

She made up her mind right there and then to find out a lot more about this man she'd brought into their midst. Did she invite a viper into the household or a friend? Well, she soon would find out!

He was unimpressed with the story she told him.

"I can't believe a patron would be so interested in one of the whores he had slept with. He had paid for her services, hadn't he? Why would he feel anything else for her?" When he voiced his thoughts to Sadie, she couldn't believe what she was hearing.

"Because we make our living this way, do you think we are less than human? You name any other occupation that would hire unskilled women to work in their business, pay them well, and give them a roof over their heads. In fact, you can't name me one person who would take in one of these girls and help her to survive. I can't expect others to understand, but I certainly would expect understanding and respect from someone who earns his living from the sweat of their brows. I'm afraid I misjudged you. If you can't respond with decency to such a tragic ending as Marsha had, than maybe you're in the wrong business."

Keith realized he had done it again. *Why in hell can't I keep my big mouth shut,* he berated himself. "I'm sorry, I just didn't look at it from your point of view. You know there are a lot of those women who are out to take a man for all they can get. I guess I 've run into too many of them in my day and it has made me bitter." He tried to make Sadie think he repented of his callous feelings. He knelt on one knee, took her hands with his well-manicured ones, and begged her to forgive him for not being considerate and caring enough.

"Please teach me to be the kind of person Harrison is. I have such great respect for him. I will never be the gentleman he is, but I can try."

All the while he was thinking that Harrison was a fool. He had it made: any women he wanted and he was off chasing ghosts. These sluts will get what they deserve when I'm in charge. They get too much for the work they do. After all, they spend most of their time in bed. How hard can that be? He was careful not to let Sadie see his eyes, just in case she was as smart as that black bitch. He chuckled under his breath when he thought about how he had fixed that big black bag of bones, when she was caught with the booty under her mattress.

"I told Asia to keep watch for strangers creeping around the house. He says he's too busy planting and trimming to be a watchman, too. He said the old Ned isn't doing his fair share of work. I told him I would talk to you about it."

"That seems strange. Before Asia came old Ned was doing all the work. True it was taking longer, but he never shirked his duties. Why would he start now?"

Sadie felt as though a weight was bearing down on her shoulders. The last few weeks had seemed like a reprieve, but now the mass of problems was pouring in like a flood. She needed Harrison's common sense solutions. Hell, she needed Harrison here! She could picture him calmly taking over and getting things back to normal.

"Did Asia fix the tunnel under the house?"

"Not yet, but I told him you wanted it done today, or pack up and leave."

"Don't you think you were a little harsh with him? After all, he is new and he does have a lot to catch up on. I really do want it done today. He can leave the garden work till later. Please tell him that." Sadie wandered off in the direction of the stairs and Keith sneaked through the kitchen, down the stairs to the mouth tunnel. There he met with Asia who was hiding in the black void that extended from the mouth of the shaft. When he heard what

Keith told him, he sniggered foolishly, "I hain't never had it so good. Now if only those bitches would give me a good time, I'd never leave."

"You leave those girls alone for now. Maybe later when I run this place you can have one once in a while, if you do what I tell you. Now I want you to make it look like the tunnel is sealed tight, but leave room for a man to get through if need be. Keep it hidden so only you and I know about it. I don't want that snoopy bitch Jessie to find it!"

"You want me to wipe out that big bitch. I can bury her so's they never find her. I got a pal that's a gravedigger. He'll help me get rid of the body. Ole Fred and Asia can hide it in a hole in the ground, dump some dirt on her and bury somebody else on top, jist gotta dig it a little deeper is all."

"Not at this time. Maybe later if my plan doesn't work." Keith liked the idea of having an alternate plan for Jessie's demise.

Jessie stayed in the kitchen most of the time, cooking, baking and cleaning. Her kitchen was always spotless. She prided herself on the fact that you could eat off her floor. It was that clean! She still hummed spirituals, but her heart wasn't in it. The days passed slowly. They were all waiting for Harrison to return.

He sent a wire to Sadie once, saying he was moving on to Chicago to find some people. He would be home as soon as he finished his business. That had been weeks ago and they hadn't heard a word from him since.

September took on a special meaning in Sadie's life, which is when Steven walked into her world. Steven was a tall, handsome German, with curly brown hair, devilish blue eyes, and the gift of gab. He spoke perfect English, even though he had only been in this country for five years.

He had come to the house as a client, seen Sadie, and decided then and there, that she would be his wife. He courted her whenever possible, taking her to plays, parties, dances, and picnics.

Picnics were what she liked best; it gave them a chance to get to know each other better. The utter freedom of a day in the woods appealed to both. When they had known each other for six months, he asked her to marry him.

"Dear sweet Steven, I need more time to make my decision. There is so much to consider. Think about it. This is a totally different life than the one you offer and I'm not sure I'm ready to make that commitment right now." *Please God, send Harrison home to us,* she prayed, *I need him here now more than ever.*

Jessie told her, "Honey picture yerself with Steven when yo' ole and thet will tell ya if ya should bes with him."

Sadie was never able to accomplish that particular feat; her mental picture was blurred when it came to the face of her partner in life. She wondered if that was a bad omen.

"Don yo worry bout it honey, when the right time come yo knows it. Jist let life happen. Frettin' ain't gonna git ya nowhere."

Chapter Fourteen
Retribution

Meanwhile, Harrison was traveling from pillar to post searching for Dorrie and her man. He had almost caught up with them in Indiana. Before that he had just missed them in Cleveland. He had found people who had known them in Detroit when he first set out to find them. Detroit was the only place they had stayed for any length of time. After scouring the city questioning everyone he met, he came to the conclusion that most people didn't want to get involved. They would get this funny look in their eye, shake their heads, and back away. He found out that if he brought the names up casually, he got a better response. Sometimes they even told him where Dorrie lived, but he always seemed to get there too late. One rather scurvy fellow mentioned their planned trip to Chicago.

Chicago was such a large place to find two small people. He was close to the point of giving up when he overheard two men in a booth talking about a couple that sold rum by the case. They made it in vats in their lean-to behind the house. It was not only strong, but it's cheap.

"The old broad, Dorrie by name, makes it, and will barter with you if her old man ain't there. She likes a change of partners every so often, if you know what I mean."

"Ya, I know what you mean, but is it worth it to take the chance of getting shot? She sounds like a frowzy old bag ta me, and I don't want nother dose of crabs, or worse. My old woman will cut me where it hurts, if I give her anything agin."

Harrison didn't know if it was the same Dorrie he was looking for, but there was a chance. He asked the man behind the bar where he could find some cases of rum that didn't cost a fortune.

"I don't know, but the two men over there seem to know where the bootleg rum is made. Just tell them I sent you, and watch your money while you're with them. They don't work for a living, so they have to get their money somewhere."

Harrison sauntered over to the table, leaned down, and whispered; "Do you gentlemen know where I can purchase some inexpensive rum of decent quality? Our friend, the bartender, said you gentlemen just might know of a place."

The two men eyed him suspiciously. The roughest one looked him up and down, deciding Harrison was an easy target. He smiled, showing rotted teeth and swollen gums, and he motioned for Harrison to sit down. The two men worked at being cordial. They offered him a drink of their bottle, asked where he was from, and began to laugh about his visiting the woman Dorrie to buy some of her wares. It was a big joke between the two of them. What they didn't know was the fact that Harrison had heard their conversation and had no intention of buying rum or anything else. His goal was a great deal more complicated. He sat back and let them enjoy their little joke on him. After all, it wasn't these two scoundrels on whom he was seeking revenge. Fate would handle their retribution.

When they had tired of their poking and jabbing each other, when the joke had gotten old, Josh, the first man, stood, grabbed the half empty bottle and told Harrison to come with them. Fredrick, the other vagrant, took Harrison's arm and steered him toward the door.

The bartender pretended not to see them leave. He didn't want anybody asking him questions, if the gent's body turned up in an alley someplace.

They led him through a tangle of streets to a shack on the edge of town.

There they asked for money to buy another bottle. Harrison had seen enough low lives in his travels to know that if they saw any large amount of money, his life would be over. He had planned for just such a predicament. He had a small wad of bills in a pocket of his waistcoat. Harrison apologized for having so little to give them, "But you fellows know how it is when your down on your luck, don't you?"

Harrison could read the disappointment on their faces, but they were used to failure. They had lived with it their whole lives. Josh shrugged his shoulders, put out a grubby hand, took what Harrison offered, and they slithered into the void of their existence.

Harrison approached the shack with a sense of danger, mixed with a feeling of exhilaration. He was glad to see this venture coming to an end. He was tired and he wanted to get home to Haven Place, away from all this filth and poverty. He longed to be with kind, gentle people, share a laugh, a dance, and a song.

He missed the girls at the house, his family of sorts. Well, he would get this mission over with, and if he weren't caught, he would see them in a few days.

The makeshift door flew open before he could knock. A filthy, shaggy haired man stood in the opening, hands on hip, eyes glaring, demanding to know what the hell a dandy like him was doing sneaking around his house, "looking for my old woman, I bet."

"No," Harrison explained, " but I am looking for a woman named Dorrie, who is the cousin of a friend of mine. Her name was Kate."

A shrewd look came into the eye of the man filling the doorway, "What do you want with this woman? Is she in trouble?"

Harrison glanced at the slattern that was lurking in the shadows behind the man; he smiled and answered, "It's her lucky day. When my friend died she left everything she had to her cousin Dorrie and her two children."

The lie came easily to his lips and he mused, *I must tell Kate about this some day. Wait, I can't tell her. She's gone. Dear God, will I ever get over this need to share everything with her? Maybe she already knows.*

Harrison continued, "However there is one stipulation; to get the money and property she must show all the receipts and have the three of them sign a legitimate claim for the estate."

When Harrison saw how Dorrie had ended up in life, his plan to kill her had changed. This way of life would be a better punishment, but he did have to make her life more miserable, thus, the lie about the inheritance.

That should keep her busy the rest of her wretched life, she would have no trouble forging receipts, but scrounging around trying to find twins that would be willing to join her in a plan to steal the money would take her the rest of her greedy life.

He had to chuckle to himself. This is definitely a better retribution then the finality of death.

Dorrie slithered forward and admitted that she was the woman he was looking for. She volunteered the information that the girls were on the other side of town working as maids in a hotel. They would be happy to hear the glad news when they came home.

"You know how hard it is to raise children these days. We had to find them jobs so they could help out." The man was nodding his head and trying to look friendly. She told Harrison how they had struggled to keep a roof over the children's heads. She lied so well, she began to believe it herself. A tear found its way down the mass of wrinkles into the corner of her lip. A sharp tongue flicked out greedily and tasted the foreign nectar, swilled the unfamiliar liquid with delightful surprise.

I deserve that money and I'm going to get it by hook or by crook. Didn't I put up with those brats for six years, even got stuck with this excuse for a man because of them? Well, now it's my turn to live like a queen, like that damn Kate did! Dorrie's rum soaked mind tried to justify her behavior.

Harrison left them thinking about the wealth that would soon be theirs if they could fulfill all the stipulations. Harrison told them he would be in town for two more days; they could get in touch with him at the Ritz. He promptly went back to his hotel, paid the bill and caught the next train for New York. Let them stew in the juice of their own making.

He sure wouldn't want to be around when they finally realized, they didn't know who he was or where he had come from. They had been so busy figuring out how to scam the money they had forgotten to ask.

Harrison knew the pleasing taste of revenge, bittersweet though it may be. He wished he could share it with Kate, but since that was impossible, he would hug it to himself and savor its unfettered intensity.

Damn, I haven't felt this good since I landed in this country. He recalled the anticipation he felt when he first saw this great land to which he had migrated, the hopes and dreams that never seem to die. The intensity that throbs through the whole country, a world alive with the quest to build, expand, and put out tentacles to encompass the wilderness, and create a new world. He needed to be a part of this.

That dream didn't die, but it was pushed into the back of his mind by the necessity to survive. He permitted himself to daydream on the train. Did he really want to return to Haven Place with Kate gone, or was it time to follow his dream? He had saved plenty of money, enough to start a small business, a gift shop, perhaps, or a flower shop. Flowers had really become the rage these past few years.

Meanwhile in New York, Ellis Island opened up in New York Harbor and the town flocked to see this grand building that would become a part of so many millions of people coming to this country to build a new life.

Sadie and Steven felt privileged to be among the throng that went to the Grand Opening of Ellis Island. They saw the first group of immigrants come through from the boat, who were herded into a room away from the crowd, asked to give their names, and wait for further orders. Families huddled together, staring big eyed, and looking half-starved, poorly dressed, yet there was determination in their stance, the way they held their heads. Sadie felt a sense of pride fill her being. She knew if they failed, it wouldn't be from not giving it all they had. These were a proud, dedicated people, the kind a new nation needed to grow. Steven squeezed her hand, almost as though he knew what she was feeling. She found that quite comforting, his knowing what she was feeling was a new sensation, a bonding of souls.

The influx of immigrants spawned a vicious new scam that would panic the gullible, new citizens to be. A man dressed in a uniform would approach the frightened greenhorns as they milled around in the cathedral like building and he asked for their papers. When they had none, the man would tell them they must give him their money and valuables to hold for them until they had their citizenship papers. Most of the newcomers believed what this official looking man told them and would give him their valuables for safekeeping. They learned a bitter lesson when they went in search of the official who so kindly held their goods for them. When questioned about the incident most of the destitute immigrants remembered only the uniform, not the face.

Veteran New Yorkers shook their heads when they heard about the scam, but did nothing about it; their reasoning being, if the newcomers were going to become a part of this town, they better learn right away how to survive in a city made up of people that came from everywhere, some good, some bad, a melting pot of talents and vices and who knows maybe some ambitious cop was working the scam and smart folks didn't cross the coppers.

Harrison was home when they returned to Haven Place. He was waiting in the parlor, brandy glass in hand, sipping slowly, and smiling a strange, satisfying little smile. He seemed somehow at peace with the world. Giving Sadie a bone-crushing hug, he exclaimed "God, it's good to be home! How have things gone while I was away? Did Keith work out well?" Raising one eyebrow and giving Sadie a questioning look he stared directly at Steven.

Sadie introduced Steven to him, told him things were okay, but she was glad he was home. She began by explaining about the elephants being missing, the degrading feeling of being searched, and the uneasiness everyone had felt. She described the finding of the elephants in Jessie's room, the tunnel under the house being opened by someone, and finally about hiring someone to help the gardener to maintain the grounds.

Harrison sat for moment thinking, then with a determined look in his eye he jumped to his feet.

"We will see to this tunnel. Then we will see about this gardener that Keith hired. If he is the rude fellow that I met coming in, he has a lot to explain. I was too tired to take him to task, but I feel much better now that I'm home and with friends. As for Jessie being a thief that is ridiculous. The only way I would believe that is if she told me so herself. Come on, Steven, you can tell me what you think of this country while we check this out."

It seemed to Sadie that Steven and Harrison would become fast friends, at least she hoped so. Two of her favorite people in the whole world becoming friends with each other, that would be perfect.

Sadie felt as though the weight of the world had floated off her shoulders. While she was sitting there enjoying the peace and quiet, a thought occurred to her. *Where was Jessie? She always heard everything that was going on and was in the thick of things. It wasn't like her to miss Harrison's homecoming.*

Lorrie came in asking, "Where is Jessie? Have you seen her? She's not in the kitchen, back yard, or garden. I've searched everywhere."

Sadie felt a chill go down her spine. She hunched her shoulders to fight off the feeling of fright that invaded her mind and heart; her breath came in short pants. *Dear God, nothing must happen to Jessie!* Panic set in, Lorrie could barely talk; when she did say anything it came out in stuttery gibberish between sobs.

"Get hold of yourself," admonished Sadie. "I'm going to need your help, and right now you're too upset to be of any help. First, we must find Harrison and Steven, and then we will search again. Get any of the girls that are here down to the kitchen. We need them and they will want to be in on the search. They love Jessie too."

Lorrie went to get the girls, and Sadie sat with her head bowed, praying to her Lord.

Dear God, let her be safe. I will do what ever you ask me to do, if you keep her safe.

The girls started filtering in one and two at a time, a murmur filled the room and they wanted to know what was going on. Two of the girls had seen Jessie after lunch, but that was the last time anyone had seen her. Sadie told them to pair up and search the whole house. She and Lorrie were going to find Harrison; he would know what they should do next.

May Belle grumbled as she left the room, "This house is turning into a crazy house, always something bad going on. Maybe it's time for me to move on. I don't like this constant turmoil."

Meanwhile Harrison and Steven made their way to the tunnel. There they found Keith and Asia boarding up the tunnel with timbers they had stacked in a corner of the cellar. They seemed pretty engrossed in the job at hand. Both jumped when Harrison spoke.

Keith dropped his hammer, grabbed Harrison's hand and pumped it enthusiastically, "Ole boy, I'm glad your home. We have had some strange things happening around here. Of course, I have held things together. As you can see we are closing the tunnel just to relieve Sadie's mind. I don't think we had an intruder. I think it was someone in the house, but you know how these women are, always thinking they know best."

Steven had the feeling that Keith was talking fast and furious to divert their attention away from the tunnel, so he started to check out the timbers that were nailed in place.

"What are you doing?" Asia asked. "We jist checked to make sure they were solid. You ain't got the right to check my work, you being an outsider and all!"

"You will continue your work, and if I or my friend want to inspect your work, we will do just that. I am no stranger here and what I say goes. We will be back later to check the barricade, and it better be done right!"

He motioned to Steven to follow him, and they left the two men working on closing the tunnel.

As soon as Asia thought they were out of hearing distance he started his tirade. He cursed Harrison, the women, and Steven for thinking they were bettern him.

"Who did they think they were, asking a man to work down here in the pits of hell? Why, it's colder then a well digger's ass down here and they have the nerve to complain about my work." *He was jist as good as any of them, and someday soon he'd show em! Keith too.*

Keith was growing tired of Asia's constant whining. Ignoring the raging fool, he decided right then and there, when the tunnel was nearly sealed, Asia would find his resting-place alongside that bitch Jessie!

Keith looked at the sweaty, smelly Asia with disdain. He wished he didn't have to associate with filth like this. He's making it harder to carry out my plans and I can't allow that.

"Come, my friend, we have to get this job done right for now. Just a slight change in plans, we can always open it later." How he hated being civil to scum like that. Well, not for long!

Harrison and Steven heard the exchange between the two laborers and decided to watch a little longer. Something kept nagging at Harrison. He didn't like the way Keith was behaving. It didn't make sense. Why would

Keith be so patient with the gardener? Were they friends? It seemed unlikely, but something odd was happening. He looked at Steven and shook his head with a questioning look on his face Steven nodded his head. He felt it too.

To the astonishment of the men who were watching when Asia bent to pick up the last board, Keith smashed him in the back of his head with the hammer he was holding. The gardener had a surprised look on his face as he crumpled to the ground. Blood shot everywhere.

Harrison shouted," Stop! What the hell are you doing?"

Keith looked up in shock. It was evident he had thought he was alone. His face took on the cunning look of a cornered fox. He tried to explain his actions. With a futile attempt to cover his involvement, he told them he had discovered Jessie's body in the tunnel.

"I was letting Asia proceed with the work just to see how far he would go. That bastard, Asia, must have done this terrible thing to Jessie. I planned to stop Asia just short of sealing the tunnel forever. In other words, I gave Asia enough rope to hang himself." He knew from the look on the two men's faces, that his lies were not going to get him out of this

Harrison and Steven lost no time tearing off the timbers, pounding the shattered wood to create a safe passage through the barricade.

Jessie lay huddled on the dirt floor, back in a dark corner of the tunnel, eyes closed, head hanging sideways, mouth hunging open, a guttural sound escaping from her throat. Harrison looked for Keith, but he was nowhere to be found.

"That son-of-a-bitch better leave this part of the world if he's hurt Jessie."

They heard a scurrying sound at the mouth of the tunnel. Looking out they saw Sadie and Lorrie staring at the motionless Jessie and clutching each other in fear.

"It's all right," said Harrison. "She is just drugged, not dead, thank God! I've dealt with this type of thing before. All we have to do is get her upstairs, and pour strong coffee into her. She is going to feel like hell for a couple of days, but she'll survive."

Steven was bending over Asia and shaking his head. He looked up and told Harrison, "I don't think he will be bothering anybody ever again."

"Damn good thing because I would have made his life a hell on earth," replied Harrison.

"What about Asia?" asked Sadie. "We can't just leave him here."

"The hell we can't!" answered Harrison. "He can rot in hell for all I care."

The four of them worked on getting Jessie on her feet, which was no small task, and propelled her toward the stairs leading to the kitchen. Pushing and pulling, they worked the great bulk of a woman to the top of the stairway. Lorrie pulled a chair to the opening; they sat her on it and dragged her to the table. Great groves were etched into the wood floor, forever a reminder that even Jessie was vulnerable.

Steven started to make some fresh coffee, but Lorrie said, "no, I want to make Evan's recipe for coffee." She bet it would help Jessie come around, besides she was lonesome for him, and the coffee brought him closer. When the brew was done, a heavenly aroma filled the kitchen. Jessie's nose began to twitch, her eyes opened wide, she stared at her friends surrounding her, shouted, "Who in hell be dirtyin' up my kitchen?"

Harrison burst out laughing from relief and joy.

"Damn it, woman, as much drug as they must have given you, you should have been asleep for a couple of days. I should have known it would take more than those two to beat you! Welcome back, old friend."

Jessie smiled a wide grin, rolled her eyes, and whispered, "I's hongry, and what's thet stuff I's smellin', it smells lik heaven. Thet there sneak Keith tryin' ta git in my good graces, give me a hunk of homemade candy. "Say it were a peace offerin.

Shoulda knowed thet bastard were up ta no good. Thet be my downfall, I's love candy, but not no mo'. I's feelin' kinda tired. Needs a little rest." She leaned her head on her ample arm and began to snore.

They all gave a sigh of relief. They knew how close they had come to losing another friend, and they had lost too much already.

Mugs were handed out to all. They needed the extra boost the mugs afforded them. Save the ladylike cups for guests. Lorrie started to clean the table when they were finished with their coffee.

Harrison said, "Leave it. Jessie will need something to do when she wakes up from this slumber. You know how she likes to scrub pots and pans when she's mad. She's going to have a headache a mile wide, so she will need something quieter to take it out on. We all better stay out of her way for a day or two, but it sure is good to know we have her back safe and sound."

"Harrison, everybody keeps saying rumrunners are using that tunnel, but I want to know why. Why are they smuggling rum? There's no ban or shortage is there?" asked Sadie.

"No, but the mayor and his ilk are demanding a rake-off from each bottle that is sold. If the tavern owners buy it from a rumrunner, they save half of the cost and beat that scurvy bunch out of their booty. That's a dirty lot running city hall. They control the whole state!"

"What are we going to do about Keith? We can't let him get away with this!" Sadie's heart was still pounding, just thinking about the close call Jessie had. *Maybe I ought to start looking for another line of work.*

Harrison went into town and informed the magistrate of the events at Haven Place. He also told him that the body of Asia was still in the tunnel. If they wanted to send someone for it they had better do it quickly because the tunnel was the home of some pretty big rats. When the magistrate asked if he couldn't take care of the burial, Harrison answered with a resounding, "Hell, no, the rats can have him!"

That same day the widow Murphy came in a wagon. She knocked on the door, waited a moment, and knocked again, this time a little harder.

She was dressed all in black, except for a bright red flower pinned to her dress. It gave her an air of rakishness that belied her somber dress. When Jessie answered the door, she jumped back, startled by the woman's small size.

Being four feet tall had never been a problem for Mrs. Murphy. If the truth were told, she used her small stature to her advantage. People just didn't realize that she was very capable of doing whatever she wished. Most people bent over backward to do many of the distasteful jobs she pretended she couldn't handle. It was her private joke on the God that made her so small.

"I'm here to pick up Asia, the gardener, for Christian burial. Not that it would do any good, he was headed straight for hell, but I have to do my Christian duty."

Jessie agreed with the woman as she led her to where Asia was when she had last seen him. As they made their way through the house, the widow Murphy gaped at everything. She had never seen such luxury, never even dreamed it existed.

Jessie chuckled at her obvious incredulity, her furtive touching of everything as she passed. She trailed her rough, work worn fingers along the neck of a vase as they made their way to the kitchen. They went through the kitchen, down the flight of stairs, through the piles of stored furniture, to the tunnel opening and stared at the blood soaked ground where Asia was supposed to be. Jessie was at a loss for words for the first time in her whole life. *Where did thet body git to? Shor couldn' walk off by hit's self.*

They lost no time in getting back up stairs to tell everyone that Asia's body had disappeared!

169

"Thet damn Keith done stole hit," offered Jessie. "Tole ya he was no good!"

"Will it never end? I sure as hell misjudged Keith. Next time I'll listen to you Jessie," Sadie lamented.

"If Keith were smart he would hide the body so the law couldn't do anything to him. No body, no crime. Asia's body is probably floating in the harbor by now," Harrison added.

Weeks went by and still no news of Asia or Keith. Sadie was thankful that things had settled down to business as usual.

Steven stayed with Otto at the hotel, found work as a printer, and was happy to see Sadie whenever she chose.

He had asked her to marry him several times, but she put him off each time saying, "I'm not ready to commit yet, I have responsibilities." Whenever she thought about marrying Steven, Marcus popped into her mind. She tried telling herself that he had made a life of his own and she should too. Steven would be a wonderful husband, but somehow the idea of marriage to him did not sit well. Maybe next year.

Under the competent hands of Mr. George Washington Jones, Jessie's restaurant had grown and become the prime place for the society crowd. Dinner hour was the best time to be seen with or near the wealthy and famous. The dining room was always filled to capacity. Jessie had to hire a man to stand at the door to prevent people from barging in when there was no place to seat them. But Jessie continued to stay and cook for her "Family" at Haven House. That was her home as long as they needed her.

Chapter Fifteen
Greener Pastures

Two years came and went and still no commitment from Sadie. Steven suggested they either marry this year or he was going to start searching for a bride who would be content with one man and a couple of children. His declaration came as no surprise to her. She had known it was coming by his behavior of recent months. She felt a slight twinge when she thought about him with someone else, but her heart knew she would never be content with Steven.

She wished him well, laid her hand on his right cheek, kissed his left cheek, and smelled the fragrance of his soap. It was an aroma that would always remind her of a friend she wished she could have loved.

Christmas came and went without any undue distress. The parties grew more frequent, the business flourished, but Sadie held bitterness in her heart for these callous New Yorkers. She still remembered the insulting way they had treated Kate. She smiled, laughed, and pretended she was interested in their little adventures, but she couldn't forget.

Several months into the New Year, Steven came to visit for the last time. He had met a young lady named Angelina at a recent party and they seemed to get along very well. Her father had seen him here and requested he discontinue his visits if he wanted to court his daughter. Steven knew that it would hurt Sadie to hear it, but the father didn't want a son-in-law of his consorting with prostitutes.

"How do you like that?" he asked Sadie.

"My friend, you need to do what works out for you. I can only wish you well. You have been a good friend and those are hard to find. I hope that this turns out to be the best. You deserve a wonderful life." With tears in her eyes, she left the parlor.

Steven made his way to the kitchen where Jessie and Harrison were talking about the spring ball they were planning for May.

"I've just told Sadie I won't be coming here anymore. I need to get on with my life. As long as I try to hang on to her, I will never be strong enough to break the ties. I love that woman, but clearly she doesn't feel the same way. I could settle for that, but she can't, so I'm going to court a young woman I met a while ago. She's not Sadie, but she is a good woman. She will give me many fine sons. If things go well, I will be taking my bride and moving to Illinois. I plan to start a shoe factory there. I want to thank you for taking me into your house and hearts. You have been good friends, and I will never forget you. Take care of Sadie for me." Steven shook Harrison's hand, gave Jessie a bear hug and head down and with hand raised in final salute, he walked out of their lives.

Jessie was in a pensive mood all the rest of the day. Her mind was in a spin. Why do the ones we love always have to leave? Her mind raced back to her days in Georgia. She had some people back there. Should she go back and let em know she's still liven'. Should she stay 'way, and let um wunder. If she went back, would the law remember her? Could she take the chance? *Hell no, the kin thet wer' lef' would jist as soon thin' she's dead. Sides, I got me a new family, couldn't ask fer better!* Her spirits rose with her decision. "I's gonna mak one hellava dinner fo' thet there shindig," she vowed.

She began to plan for the party of the century. The sounds of joy rang through the whole house.

Everyone was looking askance at each other. What was Jessie so happy about? Did anyone know what was going on? Sadie told them, "We don't need to know, just enjoy the pleasant songs and the feeling of good will. She has really been down hearted, ever since Cathy and Rachael left. She misses that child too much. I wonder if we should plan a visit for her. I'm sure Cathy and Philip would be glad to have her come for a few days. We can't spare her for any longer than that ourselves."

Sadie went into the kitchen, sat at the table, grinned at Jessie and said, "It's good to hear you sing again. We've missed the sound of the humming, too. It always fills the house with warmth and love. You have been so quiet of late, we thought you might be lonesome for Rachael and Cathy. Maybe you would like a few days to visit them. I know we can do with out you that long, but no longer!"

"I's miss my baby, an Cathy, but my place is here. Sides, ifen I sees her now I's just miss her more after. I's better of jist stayin' home and doin' my job. Sides, I's got the place in town to worry me. Mr. George Washington

Jones is doin' good, but I's wants to keep a tight rein on em till I's git to know em better."

That spring came in on a warm gentle breeze filling the house with anticipation for the Mayday party that took place each year. Every waking moment of both Sadie and Jessie's time was filled with plans for the event. This was going to be the biggest party since Mr. Theodore Roosevelt was reelected.

One morning as Sadie sat in the garden reading the invitation list an uneasy feeling come over her. She looked around and seeing no one and she went back to the list. Still she felt as though someone was near, but again she saw nothing moving. The whole garden took on an unnatural quiet. Not one bird sang, not a cricket chirped; even the trees were still. She shivered, pulled her shawl closer around her and headed for the kitchen door. Moving quickly, she pushed the door open just in time to see Keith running to the stairs leading down to the tunnel. His arms were filled with food and blankets; his eyes were wildly searching the room for any diversion. Finding none, he bolted past Sadie to the back door, through it, and disappeared down the path. Sadie was in a stage of shock. She and all the others thought that he had left this part of the country a long time ago. She screamed and ran to tell Harrison what had just happened.

Jessie, Lorrie and Harrison were in the parlor trying out a garland for the upcoming party, stringing it first from the windows, then from the ceiling to the walls in great draping swags. Nothing seemed right, so they were discussing how to make the most of the vines.

They heard the scream and saw the shocked and ashen complexion, and knew something dreadful had happened. The women rushed to her side, begging her to tell them what was wrong. Harrison climbed down from the ladder and went to where Sadie was standing. Looking down at the book she was still clutching, he saw the cover was wet with sweat, and the print of her hand was indelibly outlined on the cover.

"That's it," he exclaimed, "I've had enough of these fellows thinking they can come and go as they please. We're going to get some help from the police or know the reason why."

Harrison made up his mind to leave for town this very day, but before he did, he wanted to check the tunnel. That had to be the way Keith got in. He went to his room, came back with a pistol tucked it into his trouser top, and headed for the basement. The women went with Harrison. Jessie was right behind Harrison, Sadie next and Lorrie in the rear. The candle flame wavered in the drafty cellar. When they came to the tunnel, the boards were pried away and the earth was packed hard from activity. Jessie couldn't believe what she was seeing.

"I's down here ever day I's sur' would've seed somethin'," she declared.

"Well, I can't leave with this all open. It's too dangerous," Harrison told the women.

"Jist yo' gwon ta town, I's gonna set here wit' thet there pistol of yern and don' nobody wanta com' through thet there hole. I's haint scared of thet snake ina grass." Jessie had the look of an avenging angel. Harrison knew they would be all right till he got back. He handed her the pistol, brought a chair that had been wedged into a corner and asked if she knew how to shoot the pistol.

"Shor do, kin shoot the whiskers offa flea. First husband showed me how."

"Why, Jessie, I didn't know you were ever married," teased Harrison.

"They's lots yo' don' know bout ole Jessie. Some yo' don' wanta know," she teased back. It was said in a friendly tone, but it held a warning ring.

They all knew enough to drop the subject; besides, they had more important things to worry about. Jessie's business was her own.

Harrison left for town. Sadie, Lorrie and Jessie held the fort at the tunnel entrance.

"I don't think Keith would be stupid enough to come back, do you?" Sadie ask.

"I's shor do! He stupid nough ta do anythin'. His kind thin' the world owe him what he want. He gonna grab hit, if he want hit! I's jist hope he come while I's here. Never did trust thet snake. Lik' to make shor' he won' bother us agin!"

"If we lived closer to town, we could have one of those telephones, then when something happens, we could call the police," Lorrie offered.

"I could never leave Haven Place," exclaimed Sadie. "This is my home!"

"You're going to have to leave someday. You can't stay in this business forever." Lorrie stared hard at the tunnel, avoiding Sadie's eyes. She wanted to say more, but Sadie's attitude told her to wait for a more opportune time. She didn't want to hurt her friend, but she had been thinking of leaving the house and traveling to Buffalo to visit Evan, find a nice boarding house to run and settle down. She didn't need to work at the house anymore, she had enough saved to last her a very long time, if she had an added income. She could tell people she was a widow that would take care of the gossip.

After what seemed like a lifetime, Harrison and ten policemen arrived.

They spread out all through the house, tunnel, and gardens. They searched the house from top to bottom; the garden was scoured as well. The tunnel was lit with candles every few feet. They found a cot, some blankets, a box of food wrapped with a tarp to keep the rats away.

"From the evidence, it seems this man has been using this as his home base. He probably doesn't stay here all the time, but he sure makes it homey when he is here," the officer in charge intoned in an Irish brogue, which Sadie found charming.

She asked if they were planning on looking for Keith until they found him. She explained she hoped they would find him soon; he could be a very real threat to both her and her girls. She wanted that information, but she also wanted to hear his voice again.

"Madam," he said with a smile and a bow, "we plan to stay on this until we catch him, or my name isn't John O'Shonessy."

His smile lit Sadie's world. She drank in his features, basked in his eyes, felt her soul blend into his essence. *My God,* she reflected, *you're behaving like a simpering child. Get hold of yourself. He wouldn't be interested in a prostitute. They're plenty of young ladies in town who would kill for his attentions.*

Harrison noticed the attraction Sadie displayed for the young officer. *Well, why not,* he thought, *she deserves some love in her life, and she has been too long without some real affection. I'll sound out this young fellow; see where he stands with our profession. I hope he can put aside any prejudice he may have against her.*

Lorrie also noticed the way Sadie was behaving. *Yes,* she thought, *she has finally found someone she could care about. She hoped it would work out for both their sakes.*

Taking Sadie's arm, John guided her up the stairs and into the parlor. There he sat on a settee, patted the seat next to him. She was more than happy to comply. He began to question her about Keith. Was he any one special to her, did she have any reservations about how he would be captured? He may have to issue a dead or alive proclamation. Did that upset her?

Sadie found the questions a little unusual, but she didn't care. All she wanted to hear was that musical, lilting voice speaking to her. She could listen to him forever.

When he finished questioning her, he took her hand, squeezed it gently, led her to the door, held her hand silently for a moment, opened the door, slowly released the grip, stepped out on the verandah and the world darkened for Sadie.

Several days passed and still no word from John O'Shonessy. Sadie was fidgety, high strung, and irritable. She jumped at the slightest noise and became angry when questioned about her nervousness.

Jessie had enough of this foolishness. She cornered Sadie in the hall, "Damit, girl yo' is makin' us miserable with yo' persnickety ways, what yo' needs is ta git thet fellow in bed, then tha jitters go way. I's had thet same ailment oncet, all thet save me, is a roll in the hay. Hitched up with him, too, fo' a little while. Sho was good in the hay! Gotta git hit outa yo' head, an thets the bes' way."

Lorrie came down the hall and heard most of the conversation, she nodded her head in agreement and she teased, "Sadie's in love!" She grabbed her friend, hugged her, and told her to go to town to find out if he is married because she just might have met her mate.

"I's has ta go long with Lorrie, yo' is hooked!" Jessie chimed in.

"I can't do that. It would look as though I were chasing him. I would feel so foolish if he were just being friendly."

"Well, yo' is chasin' him, honey. Thets part of tha game, he may not know thet, but hit's a game as ole as life."

"I suppose I could visit town to find out if there is any progress in the search for Keith. After all, it is important to all of us."

Jessie looked at Lorrie, grinned and said, "Sho, sho, you needs ta find out fo' all us." She made her way to the kitchen chuckling, body shaking from repressed hilarity.

"That woman knows me too well, damn her helpful soul!" exclaimed a smiling Sadie. She suddenly made up her mind she would make that trip today and get it out of her craw. *I have been a bitch around here long enough. Besides; it would be a pleasant change to make love with a young, handsome man.*

When she got to her room to prepare herself for town, she scanned the closet full of gowns. Nothing suited her. She wanted to look especially young and fresh for this man.

"I've lost my mind," she mused.

Maybelle, hearing about the plan, knocked on Sadie's door, pushed it open, and stuck a gown in through the crack of the door.

"I've never worn this new gown because it never quite seemed like me. It's too girlish for my wide shoulders and big breasts. If it fits you, it would be perfect. With all its sprigs of flowers and the white cotton background, it looks so virginal. Not like we aren't in a way," she teased.

Sadie grabbed it saying, "That's exactly what I had in mind. I will make it fit." Maybelle helped Sadie get dressed for the big adventure. When they were finished, she looked like any other young lady in town, sweet and pure. She yearned to be the young lady in the mirror but knew it was impossible, still, at that moment she hungered for the love and respect of a husband and family.

Her delight changed to melancholy. She stared into the mirror one more time, grabbed her shawl and ran to the stairs as though the devil himself was pursuing her. The old gardener met her as she came out the door, his hat in hand.

He declared, "Don't we look lovely this spring morn. Don't know when I've seen a prettier day or lady either. We need a lot more of both."

"Thank you. I really needed to hear that. I'm on my way to town to check on the news about Keith."

"Oh, that one! Good riddance to him. Never did like him or that fella he hired. Both were jack snipes if you asked me!"

Sadie found her spirits lifted by the friendly old man and his obvious admiration. Her footsteps tapped down the steps to the stone walkway. There the automobile was waiting like a chariot to sweep the goddess to her Mount Olympus.

She was so glad she had learned to operate the automobile so many years ago. It gave her a sense of freedom. She drove with abandon, her hat barely staying in place in the warm breeze that filtered into the machine. The faster she drove, the lighter her thoughts became and she was almost giddy from the thrill of the ride and the anticipation of seeing John. When she neared town, she slowed down so her hair would not be in disarray from the wind, and tucked in the few stray strands. It was important to Sadie that she look her best. She had always been very particular about her hair, attire, and everything around her, but now she was demanding perfection of herself. When she pulled up in front of the great stone building with its wide stone steps, she felt overwhelmed with doubt.

Did I make a mistake coming here, she asked herself. *Am I being foolish to chase after this man? There are plenty of men out there who would be happy if I just smiled at them. Am I being disloyal to Marcus?* She'd loved him so long. She felt a pang of regret when she thought of the time they spent together. *No, it's not over. He will always have a special place in my heart. Fate meant for us to be one, but not in this lifetime, maybe in the next.* As her mind was spinning with the problems of the heart, her face wore the absorbed look of a woman coming to a decision.

She did not see John come out of the building and walk over to where she was standing, lean over and whisper in her ear, "I thought you would never come. It has been too many days since I last saw your beautiful face. I have been in pure hell waiting to see if you felt the same things that I felt stirring in my heart. Am I being too foreword. Have I overstepped my bounds?"

"Oh!" with a muffled cry, she turned and found herself being drawn into John's wonder filled eyes. "Are we taking chances or is this the real thing?" John asked in a lilting voice. "I can't believe this is happening to me, us, oh, you know what I mean!"

"Yes, John, I'm afraid I do, but there are many things that could stand in our way. Let's just take it slowly, see if there is anything to be concerned about. It may only be an attraction that will go away in time." She knew when she said it that her heart had already made room for him. She was already picturing in her mind how their children would look. Same dancing eyes, as John, her hair, she hoped, and his marvelous smile.

Her reason finally restored, she asked John about Keith.

"Have they found him yet?" The girls as well as she were nervous all the time thinking he will find a way back into the house. Even Harrison seemed troubled by the thought that he may come back and harm someone.

Asking her to walk with him, John took her arm and led her to a sidewalk cafe near the station. After he had seated her and found a waiter, he ordered two lemonades and brought them to the table. When he sat down, Sadie felt a rush of love engulf her very being. She wanted this to last forever.

They agreed to take their time, see each other often and wait and see what evolved. They sipped their drinks, lost in each other. Passersby's smiled with knowing looks at the two oblivious people.

Days went by and grew into weeks, then matured into months and still Sadie and John found new and exciting charms to enthrall each other. When they had known each other a year, John asked Sadie to marry him. One thing he demanded, she must leave the house. He wanted to support his wife and he didn't want her in that business anymore.

"It wouldn't look right to the children," he teased. While he said it in a teasing manner, the hard look in his eyes told Sadie that he meant it with all his heart. She began to make plans with Harrison to leave the house and the life of a prostitute.

Lorrie had warned her that this was coming someday; she just didn't think it would be so soon. Lorrie was the ideal one to pass the business on to; she would be in business a long time. Her sex drive wouldn't permit her to retire. As Lorrie had told Sadie many years ago, she loved men, all men. Sadie knew she was a natural to take over the house.

Lorrie was not only excited, but also grateful for the gift. She begged Harrison to stay and help her run the business and he agreed.

New York definitely knew how to usher in the New Year. There were parties and many new faces. Taverns were filled with rejoicing clientele, stores, and cafes were teeming with people. Shoeshine boys with their wooden boxes, containing metal cans of polish, shine rags, and sheepskin brushes, were raking in more money than they had ever earned before. News Boys were hustling papers on every corner and New York was an exciting place to live.

This is the world that Sadie and John were leaving. She was eager, yet a little wary of this new life. Hers had been so opposite. Could she adjust to the humdrum world of a housewife and mother?

They were to be married in the Court Street Church by the Reverend David Alan Schmidt. That is really strange. That is the same name as my brother, but David isn't a cripple, like John said the Reverend is. Oh, well, there must be a lot of people out there with the same name. Besides, my brother isn't old enough to be a reverend. She put it out of her mind.

The wedding day came. She was waiting in the back of the church, when to her surprise, in walked her brother David. Limping up to her, he touched her shoulder with a mangled hand, and in a soft voice said, "Hello, Sadie, I knew it had to be you as soon as I saw that gracious walk. You always did carry yourself like a queen."

Sadie nearly fainted. She had never thought about David as a grown man even though Otto had told her that David was grown and had joined the militia. To her, he was the little boy at the kitchen table. She threw her arms around him, hugged him, kissed his cheek, and patted him on the back as if to sooth his injuries.

"I am so fortunate, not only do I have a member of my family at my wedding, my brother is performing the rite. I have so many questions to ask you. How did you get here, when did you become a minister, what is new in your life? Wife maybe. Children? Tell me everything!"

"Slow down, sister dear, there's plenty of time for questions later. Let's get the ceremony over first, and then we can swap the stories of our life.

"Your groom is waiting, woman. Let's get this poor man out of his misery and into bondage before he changes his mind."

The music started. Sadie slowly walked down the aisle toward the man who would become her whole world. She wore the same white dress with the sprigs of spring flowers that she had worn that first day she went to meet John on the station house steps. She shone with the radiance that only love can fuel. The friends in the church pews were awed by the brilliance.

When David said the words, "You may kiss the bride," the whole church resounded with the cheers. They pushed foreword, engulfed the happy couple and swept them into the street with their eagerness to be the first to congratulate them. David stood at the entrance to the church, smiled and waved, motioned that he would wait for the reunion, turned and entered his place of sanctuary.

The celebration at the house was the greatest party that they had ever had. Jessie kept the food in good supply and the wine, ale, and Irish whiskey were in abundance. John became a little drunk with the excitement and more drunk with the whiskey. He apologized to everyone, over and over for his bad behavior. Sadie felt a twinge of apprehension, but put it aside for the moment. She would have many times in the future to take it out and examine it again.

The night was a complete success for Jessie. Her food was in high demand, and the guests were, for the most part, on their best behavior. The only fly in the ointment was John's obvious over indulgence in the devil's own brew.

"I's knowd dey wer' som' folks could do thet, git drunk and still not hav' a problem wit' the stuff, but he shor will bear watchin'." *She wouldn' want her friend Sadie ta hav' ta deal wit' thet crap,* she speculated.

The newlyweds settled in a flat not far from the station. Those were the happiest months of Sadie's life; they were hoping to start a family right away, as neither was interested in the party circuit.

David was their first caller. He brought with him a sweet-faced young woman and a boy of five. He introduced them as his wife and son. Sadie was delighted to see her little brother, happily married with a son to carry on the line. Sarah was a gentle, giving woman, perfect for the wife of a reverend.

The boy was shy at first, but soon was making friends with the rough looking cat Sadie had rescued. It had one ear half torn off, was bald in patches all over it's body and it worshipped Sadie. It followed her around as though afraid to be out of her protection. She had saved it from a gang of toughs that were torturing it in an alley. They had run off when they saw her coming with parasol swinging

David laughed when he heard the story.

"I remember those looks you used to get when you were upset. If I saw you coming at me with a weapon I'd be running too."

Sarah smiled at Sadie and added, "Don't you believe that. David is the bravest person I know, even when he was severely wounded, he helped Steven and me to survive. My husband left us in Spanish territory during the war to chase a dream of gold. We had no one. We were starving. David saw what dire straights we were in and took over the chores and defended us against marauders. When news came that my husband was killed over a hand of cards, David asked me to marry him. I said, yes, yes, yes, for I had grown to love him and his gentle ways." She looked at David with stars in her eyes and at that moment this plain woman became beautiful.

When a year had come and gone with still no sign of child, John asked Sadie if she were doing something to prevent it. Sadie's look should have been enough to tell him that she was just as disappointed as he. Pressing the matter, he told her he had heard that the sluts that worked in those houses had ways to keep from getting that way. She better not be doing that because he wanted sons to carry on his name.

Sadie straightened her shoulders and threw back her head. Going to him she kissed him with such abandon that he was left without any doubts. He kissed her mouth, held her tight. Scooping her up, he carried her to the bedroom, saying, "This night will be our son's beginning. I can feel it in my bones."

The few parties they did attend were not very comfortable for Sadie. Most of the time the other women huddled in groups, gossiping about friends, neighbors, any one that wasn't there to defend themselves. Sadie had the feeling she was quite often the subject of their conversation.

Whenever she joined the group, there was an uneasy silence. She knew it wasn't going to be easy, but these women were downright rude in many ways. John told her that she had to try and understand these women. They never had much in the way of clothes, grand parties, or knew famous people, and so they were a bit resentful of her and her advantages.

What John didn't know is that they often called her slut, bitch, and trollop, just loud enough for her to hear, but then pretended that they had said something else. She began to find reasons not to go to the parties by telling John she had a headache, or cramps, anything to stay away from those vicious females.

John began coming home later and later, often drunk and wanting to make love. Sadie hated to see him that way. He was abusive when he drank. The next morning he would be contrite and would fall all over himself to make amends.

"I would never put up with this behavior when I was at Haven Place. Sometimes I wish I were back there. Jessie, I love John, but he is changing into someone I don't know. Maybe I was too much in love to notice his behavior. You of all people know I must help him fight this drinking habit. I know he does it because of me, but he can beat it with my help. I must be more patient with him, if only I were with child that would solve everything."

Shaking her head Jessie advised Sadie to hold off having a baby.

"Honey, havin a chile don' fix anything it only mak it worser to git away."

Violent heaving, nausea, and terrible headaches ushered in that following month. John was beside himself with pride. He had been right, that was the night his son was conceived. He walked around with his chest stuck out, a goofy smile on his face and the drinking stopped. *Thank God*, thought Sadie, *I don't think I could be in the same room with the smell of alcohol.*

The next six months were just as exhausting as the first three. She spent much of her time lying on the bed with cold cloths for the severe pain behind her eyes. John did not welcome most of the people from Haven Place, but Jessie did come often bringing food to tempt her appetite. Sadie had only Harrison, Jessie, and Lorrie from the house, and her brother David and Sarah to care for her wellbeing.

She would be glad when this child was born; maybe she would feel like a human being, instead of a lump of pain.

John tried to be patient with her, but he liked his meals on time, the flat in ship shape order, and his breakfast on the table when he was dressed. Sadie wished she had a girl to help while she was incapacitated. She offered to pay the girl herself but John said, "No, you will live on my salary and there is no extra money for a hired girl. We will never use the money you earned being a trollop."

He made me sound so dirty when he called me that. Why did he ever marry me?

His attitude continued to change. At first Sadie thought she was just oversensitive, but David noticed it too. He asked Sadie if John had anything on his mind that was making him so irritable. She could only answer, "it must be the baby coming that is bothering him. I don't know of anything else."

In the later part of her ninth month, John began coming home smelling of liquor. He slept late, rushed off to work, late there, too. He started badgering

Sadie about who the baby's father was. One particular night he drunkenly told her what the fellows at the station were saying. They were ragging on him all the time. Telling him he wasn't man enough to make a baby. The more he thought about it the more sense it made. She must have been seeing other men when he was working cause she didn't get with child till he complained about it and began working late.

Sadie couldn't believe her ears. What is he talking about. When he wasn't working he was at the tavern with these same wonderful friends that are taunting him. Her heart was breaking. Not too long ago he was declaring his undying love and now he was acting as though he hated her.

Jessie came in one day when John was ranting and raving. She stood in silent amazement, fists doubled, her face like a thundercloud.

"John, why yo' marry Sadie, don' yo' know thet she never have another man, but yo' since she marry yo'. She give her heart ta yo' an' yo' tear it ta pieces. Dammit, man, stay way from the liquor an' yo' kin see straight."

She turned and left the flat, her mind in a whirl. "Thet man gonna make her lose thet chile, him an' his drunken' ways."

"I's knowed if I's stayed, hit be lot harder fo' Sadie, but I's shor hated ta leave." she said aloud to no one in particular, receiving stares from people passing her on the street. She slowly made her way back to the restaurant, where George Washington Jones was waiting to have her taste his newest concoction. It was a broth with shrimp, barley, and tomatoes combined. He had been working on it all morning, adding a pinch of this, a pinch of that, till it reached the flavor he was searching for. At last he discovered the precise tang, heady, but savory, a perfect appetizer for the luncheon crowd. He was so busy with his new brew, he didn't notice Jessie sitting at one of the tables crying. She had her head bowed, elbow on the table, leaning on her right hand; her whole demeanor a picture of despair. She began to murmur, low at first, than a little louder, finally shouting, "Dearest Jesus, hain't she had nough sorrow? She need some solace in her life. Ifen yo' give her thet, I'll do what ever yo' wan'ts me ta. I's yo' servant, precious Savior."

Some of the less sophisticated dinner crowd stared in wide-eyed curiosity. Seeing it was just a sad old black woman, they turned back to what they were doing previously, occasionally glancing over to see if the woman was doing anything more interesting than crying and praying.

Mr. George Washington Jones continued his work with one eye on his boss. He knew the woman was hurting, but he also knew that if she wanted to talk about it no one on God's green earth could stop her. She needed time to come to peace with her problem. She fought a personal battle with grief every time she came back from visiting Sadie.

Chapter Sixteen
A Miracle

Sadie was alone when she went into labor. She had gotten up that morning feeling wonderful, full of ambition, and cleaned the flat from top to bottom. She was just finishing the dusting when the first wave of pain hit. It nearly floored her. The piercing, stabbing agony felt as though she were being torn apart. It came in nauseating waves of pure torture. She dropped to the floor, writhing in the most excruciating torment that childbirth could bring. She felt a bursting sensation below, water gushed on her nice clean floor. *I don't give a damn. Right now all I want is to get to the bed before the baby comes. Dear God, I wish someone would come to help me.* She pulled herself across the wet floor between convulsions and onto the bed. When the next pain ceased, she lay panting from the exertion. When the next wave hit, she knew it was the one. The exquisite agony was almost too much to bear. The next thing she knew, she was holding her red and glistening child. She must cut the cord, but how? She was too weak to go to the kitchen. With trembling hands she pulled the cord to her mouth, and bit through the rubbery texture. She felt fluid gush into her mouth. *Spiting it on the floor,* she thought, *there goes more mess of my nice clean floor.*

Oh, to hell with the floor, I've got one more thing to do. With shaking hands, she tied the cord, tucked the little new life in her exhausted arms and promptly fell asleep.

She awakened with the baby snuffling deep into her breast. It was the most beautiful child in the world. A sense of wonderment stole over her. This little human being came out of her. This wonderful little person was the results of their love. Wait till John sees what we have created. Her heart was full.

John came in the flat, found the mess on the floor and in a drunken rage he cursed the day he ever met such a pig as Sadie. When he stumbled into the

185

bedroom he stopped. Weaving drunkenly, he stared at the woman and child lying in the bed, threw his cap on the floor, and shouted, "My son is here! That calls for a drink!"

Sadie watched in disgust. Here was a miracle and all he could think of was another drink. She felt sick at the thought of having to share this gift with such a man.

In a low voice, full of distaste, she told him the child was not a boy, but a wonderful little girl with his eyes. He was too drunk to notice her tone of voice, but the thought of a girl was too much for his sodden mind to accept.

"I knew that thing wasn't mine. All the men at the station told me you would sleep with anyone. You're nothing but a whore!" With that he slammed out of the flat.

Sadie lay in shocked silence. *Did he think he was marrying a virgin? My god, why didn't I see this coming? Who am I kidding? I did see it coming. I just didn't want to admit it. Well, that's all changed. You will never have to go through this, little girl. I think I will call you Katherine and I vow you will never know pain and disappointment as long as I have anything to do with it. Your life will be as perfect as I can make it.*

Sadie drifted back to sleep holding the child in her arms. She awakened with a soft nuzzling sensation at her breast, felt the vigorous searching of a hungry mouth, the satisfying clasp of child to nipple and the ferocious foraging for the nectar of life. Her whole body took on a new meaning. She felt the exquisite pleasure flood her whole being. This is what I was born for. She held the suckling child closer to her breast.

When Katherine finished her meal, she urinated, had a bowel movement, snuggled closer to the source of her comfort, and drifted off to sleep. Sadie stayed perfectly still for as long as she could until the smell of feces pierced her sense of well being. She hated to disturb the child, but she could no longer stand the stench. She struggled out of bed, taking care not to wake Katherine, made her way into the kitchen, found the basin John used to soak his tired feet, filled it with water and returned to the sleeping baby.

Katherine was wide-awake, staring at her new surroundings. Her eyes found Sadie and their eyes locked, something passed between them, a gift that only God can explain. Sadie felt complete peace settle into her soul. Nothing could ever hurt her again as long as she had Katherine. Thinking that Katherine seemed like such a large name for such a small being, she decided to call her Katy until she grows into the name Katherine. She began the routine of cleaning up. It was such a pleasure to smell the sweet, fresh odor of baby again. Her mind went back to the time, many years a go when Rachael was a babe. It brought back bittersweet memories of Marcus and Sadie's lost child. For a moment she felt sadness invade her spirit. Shrugging it off, she told herself, "This is the moment I must treasure, hold it close, clutch it to my heart, let it enfold my being, this is what women were created for." The beauty of the moment astonished her.

"Sadie, you're becoming profound in your old age," she told the girl inside. Her ministrations finished, she bundled the watchful infant in a soft blanket she had made, sat in the rocker by the window, and sang softly to the now sleeping child. She sat for hours, rocking and humming. The child didn't need soothing, but the mother did.

When John came in at last, they were both sleeping in the rocker. He felt deep shame penetrate his soul. How could he be such a bastard to this woman he loved? The child was as beautiful as her mother; he should get down on his knees and beg their forgiveness. He went into the kitchen to find some food. He hadn't eaten all day. He spied the brandy bottle. One little sip to ease the agitation, then he would eat. His next thought was, just one more to help me decide what to say to that wonderful woman, who is my wife.

He sat at the table drinking until the bottle was empty. His mind told him that she thought she was too good for him. Well, he'd show her who was too good for who; he'd throw that bitch and her brat out of his flat. After all, he paid for it and she didn't give a red cent to help! His head drooped; he slid sideways in the chair, slid off onto the floor and lay in a drunken stupor until Sadie found him the next morning. He remorsefully promised he would never do that again. He hurriedly put on his uniform and left the flat quickly, late for work again. "Well," he reasoned, "as long as he was already late, he could stop at the tavern on the way. There he could get a pick-me-up, just one," he vowed, "to start the day."

When he finally arrived at the station, the captain told him to, "Go home, sober up, and don't come back till you do! I've put up with your malarkey long enough. You get yourself straightened out or get a new job!"

John's head was in a whirl. *How can I support a wife and child without a job? I'm scared. I have to think. Some of my cronies should be at the tavern. Maybe they can tell me what I should do.* He made his way back to his refuge of choice. There in the dim lit tavern, his thoughts became as dark as the dreary retreat. He had a shot of whiskey, then told the man behind the bar to leave the bottle. He tossed down the first drink, picked up the bottle and found a table in the corner, where he could nurse his fragile ego. A hag that had been standing at the end of the bar staggered over to his table.

"For a sip of that magic potion, I will read your fortune," she told him. "I have the gift. I can see into the future."

"Well, if you can see the future, then you know you ain't getting any of my hooch, so get the hell outa here."

She wandered off muttering to herself about cops thinking they are too good for other folks. She stopped suddenly, turned around, and with wide eyes and a frantic look on her face, she screamed, "I see you dead, bleeding in an alley, your throat slashed." She staggered out of the tavern, giggling crazily.

"Saints alive," John shouted, "Am I always going to be bothered by crazy women? First that bitch I'm married to, then this harpy predicting doom and gloom. God save a good Irish boy from the likes of those two vipers. Sadie probably sent her to scare me." His muddled mind made it the truth. " Those kinds all know each other," he mumbled. "Well, it won't work. I'm not afraid of gypsies and their predictions. The hell with everybody! That calls for a drink," he proudly told himself. "I wonder if the bartender will trust me for one."

Harrison heard the news about John's drunken binge from Otto.

"I vould haf gone to help her, but John had changed so much, I vas afraid it might cause Sadie more trouble." Harrison hurried to Sadie's flat, taking Lorrie and Maybelle along for moral support.

What they found there astounded all of them. Sadie had always been a beautiful woman, now she glowed with an inner radiance and they could sense the peace in her soul. They begged her to come home with them back to Haven Place. She was tempted, but she sadly told them no, she must try to make this marriage work for all their sakes.

"John has a problem and as his wife it becomes my problem too. Remember I went through it, and with the help of my friends, I overcame it. John can too.

After much talk and persuading, they gave up and went back to the house. Sadie waited for John to come home to her and Katy. A week passed and no word came from John. Otto sneaked in every so often, bringing food and news of John's escapades. He had picked up with a tart called Dolly. She was supporting his habit by selling herself to every man the ships brought in to port.

David came as soon as he heard he was an uncle. His smile told her how proud he was of her beautiful little girl.

"We must set a date to baptize her; after all, she is a gift of God."

The next few weeks flew by. Sadie was in her glory taking care of Katy. She doted on every burp, grunt and smile the tiny bundle made.

"If only John were here to see his daughter grow each day. He's missing so much." Before she knew it, Katy was three months old and a happy contented baby struggling to lift herself, to see what this new world was all about. Sadie set aside a playtime just before putting her down for the night. This is what they were doing when John came staggering in.

He took one look at them on the floor playing on a quilt and he sneered, "That's where you and your brat belong, at my feet." He shouted as he stumbled to the kitchen, opened the icebox and grabbed some food, shouting for Sadie to heat it up. "I'm hungry!"

Katy began to cry. She was not used to the loud noises her father was making.

Sadie went to the kitchen, got the fire started, and prepared to heat the food in a skillet when John grabbed her, shouting, "You dirty bitch, why did I ever marry you in the first place? I must have been crazy to think you could be faithful. Pack your rags and get out. Take that bawling brat with you, it ain't mine anyway." John pushed her into the bedroom and slammed the door. Sadie was frantic over John's callus disregard for both her and the child. Her anger overwhelmed her. While taking his clothes from the clothes press with the intention of requesting him to leave, a wild thought struck her. Her anger turned to cold calculating rage as she looked at the two carefully pressed uniforms. Taking the scissors from her mending basket, she laid the trousers on bed where she carefully cut one leg off of each of the garments. Lifting them by the waist she carefully laid them on hangers with only the uncut leg showing. A sense of elation enveloped her. That will serve that lying, drunken bastard right.

Hurriedly she stuffed a few things into an empty laundry bag that hung on the doorknob and went quickly to the frightened, sobbing child, wrapped her in the quilt and made her way to the door. Looking back at the man she had once loved, she felt only pity. John read the disgust in her eyes. With a snarl, he reeled across the floor toward the door, hitting walls, as he staggered to reach her before the door closed. Sadie ran down to the street, still clutching her precious bundles and huddled in a doorway hoping he wouldn't follow. When she felt it was safe, she left the doorway and walked toward Otto's hotel. With Otto, she knew, she and Katy would be safe and welcome.

"Dear God, after so many years, here I am walking away from my home again, carrying my life in two small bundles."

As she walked, she thought of all the things that had happened in her life, both good and bad. She had to admit that most of the things that happened had happened for the best. Losing Kate was one of the bad things; the death of a friend is always harder on the people who are left behind. They are left with just memories of that person, but thank God there are memories! Sadie made up her mind then and there that Katy would get to know Kate, just as well as she had. Sadie would tell her little stories of the real Kate, not the hardhearted Kate that she pretended to be. The child had snuggled her head close to her mother's breast and had finally calmed down.

As Sadie walked, she talked to herself and Katy.

"This will never happen again, to either of us, I swear to God. I won't let it happen again." She repeated it over and over again in a singsong vow.

When she finally reached the hotel, it was close to midnight. The bar was still open; a few men were leaning on it, smoking cigars and finishing what they were drinking. Otto was behind the bar wiping glasses. When he saw Sadie and the bundles she carried he threw the towel over his right shoulder and dashed to them as fast as his stout body would permit. He gently took the sleeping child and holding her pressed against his shoulder, led Sadie to the lounge, sat her on a sofa, and asked, "vot the hell are you doink out at thiss hour? Don't you know that bad tings can happen to a voman and child on the streets?"

"Otto, it was safer on the street than it was in the flat with John in one of his drunken rages. We are leaving him for good!"

Otto couldn't believe that John would treat Sadie and the child so badly. Shaking his head in sympathy he cursed the ground John walked on. Taking them to the front desk he had the clerk assign her a suite. He personally led them to the rooms that would become their home for as long as they needed it.

When Sadie told Lorrie about her willful revenge against John on last day at the apartment, Lorrie burst out giggling.

"I can't believe our sweet, even tempered little Sadie did that, cut off his pant legs." She shook her head in delighted admiration. "Your lucky he didn't find them before you left, he would have raised holy heil."

"I know, I can't believe I really did it. I had to get us out of there as quickly as possible. God only knows what he would have done if he had found them. I'm not proud of myself for what I did, but I was so furious with him I had to do something, and it did make me feel better at the time!"

On Katy's first birthday, Sadie went to the courthouse to arrange a bill of divorcement against John O'Shonessy. When she finished signing all the papers, she paid the fee the clerk named and walked out feeling free.

Going back a few weeks later to get the legal documents, she was told that she was still married to John. He had refused to sign. He wanted her and the child back. John claimed she had abandoned him, but he was willing to give her another chance. The clerk looked down his nose at Sadie and told her, "You're a lucky woman. Most men wouldn't forgive their wife leaving them for any amount of time, much less a year. You go home to your loving husband, be a good wife, and thank God he is so forgiving."

The fury built in Sadie's mind. *Damn him*, she thought, *why would he want me back there? He doesn't care about Katy or me. He just wants to torture us some more. Well, he's not going to get the chance. I'll see him in hell first!*

She went to the hotel, told Otto what the clerk had said, went up to her rooms and packed. She would not stay in this town another day. Thank God she had enough money in the bank to go anywhere she chose. She asked Otto if he minded watching Katy a little while longer, she wanted to go to the bank and withdraw her money.

The clerk behind the grill at the bank asked to see her passbook took one look and said, "That account has been closed for some time. Your husband and his sister came in and withdrew all of it about four months ago. I remembered him from the time you brought him in to put his name on the account. He was so upset to have to use your money to help his sister with her operations. By the way, is she well now?"

Sadie felt the room move. It began to revolve and she slid to the floor in a faint. When she awoke the clerk was kneeling over her, concern written all over her face.

"Are you alright? Was I mistaken? Was it you who was ill? Let me call your husband. He is such a caring man."

She felt the bitterness rise in her throat, almost choking her.

"Yes, isn't he?" she said with disdain. "A real loving husband and father!" She sat up, straightened her clothing, took the hand the man offered, rose from the floor, made her way out of the bank amid protests from the clerk who was muttering to himself, "Such a well mannered, charming husband, and she takes him for granted. Some folks don't know when they have it good!"

Back at the hotel, Otto couldn't believe what she was saying. He offered to go talk to John and see if he would return the money. She knew it would be futile for him to even try, but he insisted, so she finally said, "Yes, okay, go, but don't say I didn't warn you!"

Otto found him in his favorite tavern, sleeping at a table, smelling of booze and unwashed body.

Looking at the sleeping man, Otto wondered how a man could slip so low in such a short time. It was as if he was never the man they knew in the beginning.

Otto gently shook the sleeping man, but nothing happened. He shook him again, a little harder. This time John woke up, peered at the man standing over him and with a roar, lunged at the trembling man. His fist found Otto's chin, knocking him over a table, and smashing a chair, he took the leg and swung it at Otto's head, screaming, "I'll kill you, you German bastard. You stole my wife away!"

"I come to tell you dat she needs her money dat you stole from her. I didn't stole your vife. You threw her avay, und the child, too."

"She'll never get that money. I plan to spend it all, if she don't come back. You can keep the kid; it's probably yours anyway. Now git the hell out of here before I kill you."

As Otto struggled to stand, a woman came to his side took his arm, helped him up, brushed him off, and motioned toward the door. Her eyes held understanding and compassion for his dilemma.

John shouted at the woman, "Dolly, you bitch, get the hell away from that kraut. He stole Sadie from me and now he wants you. Get away from him. I'll kill that bastard!"

Otto lost no time getting out of the tavern. Leaning against the brick building, he used his handkerchief to stop the blood that flowed from his split lip. *Damn, I must haf bit my lip,* he thought. As he stood there, a shadow moved closer, blending in with the dark street. He felt a presence near him, turned just in time to see a pipe, in upraised hands, swinging toward him. He ran away as fast as his short, fat legs would carry him. When he got to his hotel, he felt a sense of relief. Those people who lived in that part of town, were dangerous; they had no respect for anyone.

Sadie was upset when she saw Otto's swollen lip and bruised ego. She knew how he felt about her. She never felt so low in her life. Her husband was swearing to kill her friend, wanting her back to torture her and her savings gone. She was in tears.

Jessie heard the news from one of the men who visited Haven Place, and she made the trip into town that very same day. She rolled into town like a black thundercloud, didn't nobody want to get in her way. Sadie had to smile in spite of her troubles. Here was Jessie, her shining black knight, ready to go to war for her. John would stand a better chance of surviving if Jessie were a man. Women are always more vicious when riled.

"Honey, don' yo' worries bout that John, he gonna give back yo' money ifen he wants to draw nother breath, I's gonna see ta thet." Jessie stomped out of the room, left the hotel and was gone for two days. When she came back, she told Sadie, "Yo' troubles are over. I's goin' back home to git ta work, those gals must be starvin' by now."

That afternoon a knock came at the door. Katy ran to open it; a man in uniform was standing in the hall, hat in hand.

Sadie walked into the room, stopped in the doorway, reached out for the archway wall, put her hand to her throat, and ask in a low voice, "Did you want to see me, sir?"

"Mam, I have terrible news. Maybe the child should leave the room."

"Yes, yes, I will be right back." Taking Katy's hand she led her from the room. She was back in a moment. With a trembling voice she said, "Please, tell me what you have to say, no beating around the bush, right straight out!"

"Well mam, as you wish. Your husband was found in an alley with his throat slashed; he's dead. A woman named Dolly identified him. You can come and see if it's him, but I wouldn't if I were you. The owner of the tavern said it was John O'Shonessy and said he's been hanging around there for a long time. Oh, he knew him alright!"

"Did you catch the person who did it?"

"No mam, and probably never will. That happens a lot down there, they kill each other for a drink, and I say let'em. Good riddance to bad rubbish! Sorry, mam, that's how I feel."

"What you don't understand, sir, is that he was a good man with a bad habit. He couldn't help himself; he was addicted to alcohol. When I married him, he was a kind, gentle, man. When I left him, the alcohol had turned him into a monster.

" I prefer to remember the man I married, thank you, and, no, I will not come down and view the body of that man. I will take your word for his death."

When the officer left the hotel room, Sadie let herself relax. The feelings of grief began to seep into her mind and heart. Tears were building behind closed lids; they filled her eyes, pushed out, slid down her cheeks, but there was no sobbing, only deep regret for what might have been.

Katy came running into the room, curls bouncing, eyes smiling, and feet pitter-pattering across the tile floor. She picked Katy up and squeezed her till she squealed with delight. *This is who I must concern myself with, not that stranger in the morgue.* Putting the child down for her nap, Sadie asked Otto to keep an eye on the sleeping child. Sadie went to the flat where she and John had lived. There she found Dolly, packing and crying.

Dolly seemed to shrink before Sadie's eyes. She started to say something, then stopped and looked at Sadie a long moment, handed her a valise, and scurried out the door.

Sadie held the bag for a long time. She suspected what was in it and wanted to savor the feeling. She opened the valise. Deep inside the small black bag was a bankbook with her savings. It was the account with both John and Sadie's names.

"Thank God and thank you, John. I knew you weren't all bad," she murmured. She dug through the cedar chest, and finding her precious quilts, she murmured silent thanks to an already generous God. Aloud she promised herself to send someone for her quilts. I can't lose them now; we have been through too much together.

The stray cat that Sadie had saved came bouncing in, mewing and rubbing itself against her legs in greeting. It's mangy fur smelled of fish, but Sadie didn't care. It was welcome back into her life. She picked up the scruffy animal, tucked it under her arm and squeezed it gently. She went to the door of the flat, turned, and took a final look at the place that had held for her, both happiness and pain. The tears started to build. *No,* she thought, *no time for such foolishness.*

Her next move was to place her money in the hotel safe. She told Otto she wasn't sure about banks anymore. She had thought her money was safe in the bank the first time and found out differently.

"Sadie, be fair, if you didn't put John's name on de account, he vouldn't be able to touch it. Can't blame the banks for dat."

"You're right, my friend, I'm just looking for someone to blame." She sat with Katy on her lap, the ratty looking cat at her feet, a picture of contentment.

Otto's heart was filled with contentment and joy; he had the most important person and her child in his world. What more could he ask for? They both were welcome to stay forever. *Got, I lufe that voman, I vish I could be the kind of man that she could lufe!* Otto let his mind drift. *If I vas tall und handsome, then she could maybe be my vife. I vould gladly die for that vomen.*

Enough vith the daydreams, just being her friend vill haf to do! If I can just keep her here at the hotel, I can see her everyday, und that vill be enough.

The years were slipping away. That thought kept popping up in Sadie's mind. She began to have feelings of haste, as if there was never enough time. She rushed around doing nothing, and was exhausted from the pace. She sensed that something was going to happen, but she didn't know what. It gave her an uneasy sense of impending doom. Or maybe I'm hungry for the home and life I once knew. She talked with David about her feelings of discontent. He didn't think it was a yearning for the farm, but there was only one way to find out. Go there! Katy was four years old, certainly old enough to leave for a little while. She could leave her with Jessie and Harrison and not have a single worry.

"Your absolutely right, David, I will make that trip. Maybe that is exactly what I need to get the old Sadie back." She began to prepare for the train ride back to Michigan. So much to do and so little time kept running through her brain. She didn't want to delay the trip another moment. Lorrie teasingly suggested she take only her very best frocks.

"You never knew who you would meet along the way."

Katy was delighted to be going to stay with Aunt Lorrie, Aunt Jessie and Uncle Harrison again. There she was the center of attention; the whole household was always at her beck and call. The garden surrounding the house was the perfect place to play in complete freedom, not like at the hotel where she could only play in the small courtyard behind the building. Sadie and Uncle Otto were forever saying, "Katy stay in the back away from the buggies and automobiles." Here she could run and frolic at will, no autos and buggies came near the spacious gardens.

Chapter Seventeen
Valley of Emptiness

Now that she had decided to make the trip, she was looking forward to visiting old friends and familiar places with great anticipation.

She wondered if she should stop to see Phoebe, her childhood friend. Now that they were both older, maybe now she would understand that what had happened to Sadie could have happened to anyone. Phoebe must know by now that Sadie wasn't bad, just daring and foolish. As the time got closer, she became more agitated. She knew that she was making herself sick, but she couldn't stop thinking about what might happen.

Jessie told her, "Yo's a dam fool to put yerself through thet agin, but go if yo' gotta, git it outta yo' craw, maybe then yo' git on with life here were yo' belongs. Yo' kin leave thet child with Jessie. I's care fo' her like my own."

"It is so beautiful here and she does love to play in the gardens just as Rachael did." Sadie still felt a pull at her heartstrings every time she thought about that first child she had cared for. Maybe on her way home she would stop and visit Rachael, Philip, and Cathy.

Harrison had given them the cottage after Kate died. When Philip had called last month, using Mr. Bell's gadget called the telephone, he said they had decided to marry.

"We had a quiet ceremony in the church, just the minister, his wife and sister for witnesses. We are making friends in town. I'm becoming involved in town politics. The wounds on Cathy's face and neck have healed until there is just a trace, but the scars in her heart are still as raw as the day they were slashed there. I had hoped that my playing an active roll in government would enable her to meet all kinds of people and realize that everybody has a cross to bear, some just heavier than others. She needs to get the hate out of her heart or it will destroy her.

"She is so gentle and loving to me and Rachael," he explained, "but she holds everyone else away with her coldness. She needs to see old friends. We would be glad to have you all visit. Rachael is growing like a bad weed and doing well in school. She still talks about all of you. Sometimes she even cries for the old times."

The trip back to Michigan was uneventful, except for four slightly inebriated young men hoping to find work as ship builders. They had gotten on the train in Detroit, heading farther north for the Saginaw Valley. They were young Frenchmen from Windsor, full of anticipation, rowdy, but friendly and most people just turned their heads, smiled, and shrugged their shoulders, as though saying, "Boys will be boys!"

One gentleman was extremely upset over their behavior; he called the conductor, complained loudly and sat with his back to the jovial band. His cigar was making Sadie ill from the stench of bad tobacco and the more upset he got the more he puffed on the stinking thing. She didn't usually mind a good cigar smell, but the man's stogie smelled like burning oily rags. Sadie was afraid that the man's behavior was going to cause more trouble than the four young men's conduct.

Sadie moved to the dining car, sat at a window far to the back of the compartment. Her mind was lost in memories. She did not see the bad-tempered man enter, look around, and head in her direction. When he slammed himself down in a seat facing her, she jumped, startled out of her reveries.

"Sir," she said, "I did not invite you to join me. Please leave."

"Fine. Now a slut insults me. What must a gentleman do to get some respect around here?" the man shouted loudly.

Quietly, Sadie said, "Behave like a gentleman." She stood and made her way out of the dining car, through the passenger cars to the open platform at the end of the train; there she stayed until they reached the next station.

The closer she got to her hometown, the tenser she became. What would she find here, would they even remember her? Why in the hell did she even come back? Her mind was swirling with questions that could only be answered by being there.

When the train pulled into Bay City, she was shocked at the change in the town. There were many new stores, hotels, taverns, and people everywhere. She searched until she found a livery stable where she hired a man to drive her the rest of the way home to her father's farm. The trip was a lot shorter than she had remembered. Of course she had been walking, toting all her belongings in grain sacks the last time she had passed this way. The memory made her a little bitter, until she thought about what she would have missed if it hadn't happened.

When they rounded the turn to her father's house, she saw a tumbled down shack that had once been a neat, clean farmhouse. The yard was littered with garbage, broken down machinery, and a few scraggly chickens. The barn that once held so many good memories had settled down like a tired camel with its hump still in the air, its roof had slid sideways to provide an overhang, under which a lonely cow had taken refuge. Sadie couldn't believe this was the same house she had so often pictured in her dreams. The house seemed to have shrunk as did that wonderful old barn that had held so many good memories. She remembered the rope that hung from the hay loft that they used for a swing, playing hide and seek in the barn, the smell of new mown hay. Bile surged into the back of her throat. This was a mistake. She should leave right now.

A bent old man came out of the house shading his eyes. He peered out of the shadows to see who was coming. The door flew open again. The hag who emerged didn't wait on the porch. She came running out to meet Sadie saying, "I knew you would come back to flaunt yourself. You always did think you were bettern everybody else! Well, you ain't no bettern me, cause I'm your mama now. How'd you like that?"

Her father just stood there, a foolish smile on his face, his eyes begging for forgiveness.

Sadie walked over to the old man, gently touched his cheek, turned and walked back to the man who drove her there, saying, "Wrong place, sorry!"

On the way back to town, Sadie felt an inner peace settle through her whole being. That's the end of that old life, no more tears for what might have been.

She couldn't believe how much the town had grown; it had become a thriving city. Shipbuilders were in high demand and the trains were inching into small towns, bringing in people and industry; maybe Michigan would be a welcome change for her and Katy. Not here though, some other city. This town held too many bad memories.

She checked into the Astor House and told the clerk she was just looking up old friends and would only be here for a couple of days. She retired early, wanting to get a fresh start as she felt a great sense of anticipation for the events that she hoped would take place, meeting with Phoebe again after all these years. Did Phoebe still feel the same? Maybe, just maybe, she might hear something about Marcus. *It could prove to be an interesting day*, she told herself as she drifted off to sleep.

The noise from the street tore her out of a deep sleep. It sounded almost as if she was back in New York with its hustle and bustle. Peeking out of the window, she saw huge wagons hauling wood slabs. "For Sale," the sign said for cooking and heating. The sounds are the same, but the purpose different. *I keep forgetting I'm in the back woods,* she mused. She went to the basin to freshen herself for the day. When she had bathed and dressed, she went down to the dining room for breakfast. She had a leisurely meal, watching people come and go, seeing no one she knew. *What did I expect, I've been gone eight, no, nine, oh, my God, I've been gone almost fifteen years! I can't believe it. Where did the time go? Why didn't I realize it?* Now she remembered her mother saying, *"Time slips quickly away. I never remember getting old. One day I looked in the mirror and I was an old woman."*

Sadie took out her makeup bag, sneaked a quick peek in the mirror, and saw her mother looking back. She rose up quickly, shaking like a leaf in the wind and went to her room where she packed her bag, paid her bill and headed for the train station.

While waiting for the next train, a woman entered the station with three children tagging along behind her. The woman told them to sit while she purchased their tickets. She glanced at Sadie, started for the ticket master, looked back again, a puzzled look on her face, shook her head, and proceeded to buy the tickets.

Sadie recognized Phoebe right away; her red hair and receding chin were a dead giveaway. When she came back to where the children were sitting, she looked again, walked over and said to Sadie, "You look very familiar. Do I know you?"

Sadie smiled and answered, "No, I'm afraid you don't."

The woman went back to her seat, busied herself with wiping noses, straightening clothing and nagging the children to sit up straight.

"Well, so much for hashing over old memories with best friends," she said softly. Her voice carried to the woman, who paused, glanced again, recognition flashing in her eyes. Her face turned crimson, she ducked her head and nervously patted imaginary wrinkles from her skirt.

The train for Detroit came first. Sadie climbed aboard with the help of the porter, turned around once she was aboard and raised her hand in a farewell gesture to Bay City.

When they finally reached Detroit the stationmaster told her the train for New York would be late. It had hit a cow and was derailed. It would be a day or two till they got it back on track. Although Sadie was anxious to get back to her daughter, Katy, she decided to see some of the sights while she was here. Detroit too had grown since she had passed through many years ago. There were hotels, restaurants, opera houses, and even a few bawdyhouses, too.

"How the world is changing," she murmured.

She wandered into a restaurant near the station and sat at a table waiting for someone to come and take her order. The proprietor came over, asked where her escort was and would she feel more comfortable waiting in the back?

Sadie was about to tell him what she thought, when a young man walked up saying, "Sorry I'm late, my dear. I was held up longer than I planned."

She looked at him, debated whether she should accept his help or continue her response to the owner. She decided to let it go and see what happened.

He sat down, ordered two lemonades and introduced himself as John Davis, a local banker. He just happened to have the day free; would she consider seeing the town with him?

Just what I need is another John in my life. No thanks, she thought as she introduced herself as Mrs. John O'Shonessy. He simply smiled, said, "I won't tell if you don't!"

Sadie stared at him, picked up her bag, made ready to get up and leave when John touched her arm, "Sorry, I just had to find out if you were willing to stray off the beaten path. Please forgive me, I promise to behave myself from now on."

He is handsome and does seem like a gentleman, now that I have put him in his place. He really does sound remorseful, Sadie thought, *and I do have free time on my hands. Face the facts old girl you no longer know anyone in this town, and why not give him a chance to show you around?* They spent most of the day together. He was charming, thoughtful, and considerate of her every wish. Later in the afternoon they went back to the train station to check on the progress of the train to New York. Tomorrow, they told her. She would need to find a room for the night. She and John went to the nearest hotel, booked a room for her, had dinner in their dining room, shook hands, said their good nights and parted company for the evening.

The next morning he was waiting for her when she came down for breakfast.

"Good morning, my dear. Did you sleep well? I, on the other hand, didn't sleep a wink. Every time I closed my eyes, you were there, smiling, looking beautiful. How can a man rest when he has such beauty with him through the night?"

Sadie was flattered but apprehensive. The last time she listened to that kind of talk, she had married John O'Shonassy, which had proven to be a big mistake. The only good that came from that union was Katy! Was it time to lay her cards on the table and tell him what she used to do for a living? No, she decided, she didn't know him well enough, and she would never see him again after today, so leave well enough alone.

Again, they spent the day together, sightseeing, and eating at small tables on the wooden sidewalks, taking advantage of the warm spring breezes. John explained that many of the shop owners were from other countries and brought many of their customs with them. It made the town more interesting and colorful to him. What did she think?

Sadie agreed with him. She told him New York was the same, a hodgepodge of people, strange and delightful.

The wonderful day was coming to an end when John took her hand and apologized for misrepresenting himself. He was just a teller in the bank; not the owner as he had led her to believe, but he did have higher aspirations.

"I have had experience in running a newspaper and hope to own one of my own very soon."

"I forgive you and I'm sure your little lie has done no harm. Sadie added, "We have had a lovely time and I will remember the day and not the lie."

She checked the train station again and found out the train was in and waiting for passengers. The train would leave within the hour. She and John rushed back to the hotel, packed her bag, paid the bill and got to the station just in time to board the train. Sadie looked out the window and waved with a feeling of regret. It would have been nice to spend more time with him, but why dream useless dreams? Besides, she had little Katy to worry about, not some man she had met in a restaurant. The trip was much longer than she remembered. She knew why, she was leaving with regret, and that made the world move in slow motion. She changed her mind about visiting Philip and Cathy, she couldn't wait to get home to Katy. She needed to be near her daughter more than anything else right now.

All her friends welcomed her home; everyone was talking at once, asking questions, commenting on how well she looked,

Noticing her high color, Jessie stated, "Honey yo looks like a woman in luv'!"

Sadie felt the blush warm her face.

She stuttered out, "Well, I did meet a charming man, but it meant nothing."

She avoided any more questions, and headed for her room with Jessie right behind her.

Jessie, hands on hips, stared at Sadie with a glint in her laughing eyes. "Now little missy, yo tell Jessie all bout it, an don leave out anythin'."

"Yes, my nosey friend. We did spend time together and I enjoyed his company very much. I think I could love John Davis, but I'm afraid to take the chance. I never told him what I used to do for a living. That could change him completely. He might end up hating me, too. That thought alone scares the hell out of me. This could turn out just as badly as last time," admitted Sadie.

Jessie poo, pooed the excuses Sadie gave. " Yer Katy needs a pa, yo' cain't go without a man furever. Take a chance. Hit's natural ta bees scairt, but life goes on."

She stayed the night at Haven Place and headed for Otto's hotel the next morning. Katy chattering all the way, full of stories about Haven Place gardens, the dark place in the cellar, where the ghost hides, the tunnel that goes down to the water. Sadie had been daydreaming, nodding her head every so often, throwing in a few uh, huhs, once in a while, until what Katy was saying filtered into her mind.

"What! Did you say the tunnel is open so you could go through to the water?" she shrieked, not really believing what she was hearing. She tried to stay calm, but her hands were shaking, sweat stood out like raindrops on her forehead, a cold chill ran up and down her spine. All she could think about was Keith was still out there somewhere, lying in wait. She couldn't get to the hotel fast enough; she would go to the police station as soon as she made arrangements for someone to watch Katy. She had to find out about Keith! God, please let him be caught. That man was dangerous to everyone.

The driver took her to the hotel, helped her and Katy out of the dray, handed out the bags to a lad who was shining shoes in front of the hotel, tipped his cap and drove away. Otto and a young man from the desk came dashing out, grabbed her bags and hurried Sadie and the child into the lobby. The dining rcom was full, but Otto pushed the crowd aside to escort Sadie and Katy to a reserved table. When he had them settled, he told them, "Ve haf missed you so much, ve haf a special lunch prepared for you. Sit und enjoy."

Sadie wanted to rush to the police station, but she didn't want to hurt Otto's feelings, and she was hungry, so why not wait till Katy was taking her nap? That decided, she dug into the delicious meal they had prepared. *Dear*

God, she thought, *I still eat like a thrasher. I'm a pig when it comes to good food.* She watched her daughter with delight. Katy looked more like her father every day. She had his same charming smile, dancing eyes, and a sweet manner. She felt pride swell in her breast and she took a deep breath to keep from crying out with joy.

The meal finally ended with praise for the cook, the waiter, and their host.

Sadie took Katy upstairs to their rooms lying down, while she was waiting for the girl who would be staying with Katy; they both fell fast asleep. Waking up to the sound of pounding, she stumbled to the door to find Otto hanging on to the wall, clothes torn, blood on the front of his suit, eyes glazed, searching for the sight of Sadie. She was the last person Otto ever saw. He died there on the floor with Sadie's arms wrapped around him, a confused look on his face.

Sadie didn't have to go to the police station they came to her. The police found the cash register open; the money was missing, and a few bottles of liquor were also gone. They searched the hotel from the cellar to the attic and found nothing. They questioned everyone who had been in the hotel at the time Otto was stabbed. No one saw anything.

She couldn't believe it; almost everyone she loved was dead. She would have to keep a better eye on Katy; she couldn't go on if anything happened to her child.

Harrison and Jessie heard the news and came immediately, bustling around like mother hens, protecting their chicks. Jessie took complete charge of Sadie and Katy, packing their clothes and moving them out to Haven Place. Harrison stayed in town taking care of Otto's business and settling the will with the lawyer.

The next few days were a blur for Sadie. She remembered eating, sleeping, but she couldn't tell you how or when. Jessie kept Katy busy every minute. She helping to make cookies, peel the vegetables, snap peas, and wash pots as big as she was. Jessie had tied one of her aprons on Katy. It went around her little body three times, folded at the waist, and it still reached the ground. Jessie had to pinch herself to keep from bursting out laughing. She was in her glory with Katy in her charge.

Sadie was lying on the bed thinking about all the things that had happened to her and her friends over the years when a stray thought came sliding in. The tunnel, what was it about the tunnel?

"Oh, my, God, now I remember. The tunnel is where Katy said the ghost lives!" She jumped up, raced down to the kitchen, grabbed Jessie, shook her, screaming, "When did you check the tunnel last?"

Jessie almost went white. She shook her head, "Not fo' while, don' hav' no need, it blocked off las' time I's look." Looking at Katy, she saw fear in the child's eyes and went for her pistol.

Harrison walked in just as the women were going to the cellar; he took out his pistol, led the way into the tall, dank cellar with huge beams holding up the ceiling. The floor was earth, packed down from many years of use. There were pieces of broken furniture strewn everywhere. The last time they were down there, it had been stacked in an orderly manner, now it looked like a giant hand had picked up the cellar and turned it upside down. The kerosene lamps that Harrison had ordered placed along the walls helped to brighten the darkness somewhat, but it still gave them an eerie feeling as though there were unseen eyes on them all the way to the tunnel. There they found it wide open and obviously being used. The women wanted to leave right away, but Harrison said, "We must block this off at least temporarily, then we will call the police. This may tie in with Otto's murder."

Jessie nodded her head in agreement. "I's betcha thet Keith scum don kilt old Otto. They hain't cotched em yet, has they?"

"No, they haven't and I'm at the point where nothing would surprise me. This has been a really strange past few years. I'm thinking of finding us another place to live."

"Harrison, you can't blame the house for what has happened to us. I love this house, I wish I could live here forever," Sadie said with tears in her eyes.

They hurriedly stacked broken furniture in front of the tunnel entrance. It wasn't completely blocked, but a person would have to climb over some very unsteady pieces of furniture to enter the cellar. Retreating toward the stairs, Harrison motioned for the women to go ahead of him. When they reached the kitchen Harrison slammed the door leading to the cellar, and put a chair under the knob.

"Now we wont have uninvited guest." With that he went to the wall where the telephone hung, cranked it up, and ask the operator for the police station. The call made, he sat down to think over all that had happened. The only thing he could think of was the fact that some scoundrels were smuggling rum in from Canada. Could this be the place they were using? If so, they were a real rough bunch of rowdies, who would just as soon kill you as look at you.

Jessie was thinking along those same lines.

She told Harrison, "I's don care what yo-all think, thet snake Keith is up to no good, I's knows it! Till he dead, I's don trust nothin bout him, he know bout thet tunnel, right from the git go."

When the police finally did arrive, they searched the tunnel again and found evidence that someone had been there, but couldn't find a thing to support the idea that it was rumrunners or Keith for that matter. The officer told Harrison he might be farther ahead to post a guard at the entrance of the tunnel, and maybe one at the exit.

"We can't spare men for that job. We're still looking for that Keith fellow, but his name isn't Keith at all, it's John Stump. He's a criminal from Ohio. He got out of the state before they hung him. They are still looking for him. That's why changed his name. Killed a fella in Cleveland awhile back. Cut his throat in an alley."

Sadie looked at Harrison, then at Jessie, who quickly lowered her eyes.

Could it be true? But why kill John? He didn't even know him or did he? Sadie's mind was racing, trying to find a reason why Keith would kill John and in such a horrible way. When she spoke her thoughts out loud, Harrison explained, "Those people don't need a reason to kill. If John was standing in his way, it was reason enough. Maybe John flashed money in the tavern, who knows?"

The young officer nodded his head in agreement, "But, I will say one thing, that female John was living with might know something or may even have seen the killer. She must have packed up and left town in a hurry, ain't nobody seen hide ner hair of her since the killing. One thing good about it, one less slut walking the streets of New York."

The silence was deafening, when he realized what he said and to whom, his face flushed a crimson color. He stuttered, "Oh, I don't mean you ladies. I mean the tramps that walk the streets and give us diseases. That kind we can live without." The more he tried to explain, the worse he made it. Finally he said, "Oh, you know what I mean!"

"Yes, I'm afraid we do," replied Sadie.

Jessie grabbed the coffee mug she had just filled with hot coffee, slopped most of it in the officer's lap and said, "I's so sorry thet mus' bees hot, let me cool it wit' water."

"No, no, that's okay, I gotta get back to town, lots of work to do." His mind searched for a reasonable excuse for his hasty exit. "Those meat packers are giving us a hard time; they don't want to let us inspect their work place. Been a lot of sickness from meat lately." He put on his cap, brushed the front of his trousers, and quickly made his way to the front hall. Looking around disoriented, he searched for the door to the outside. His eyes landed on Maybelle in a flimsy negligee, coming down the stairs and blushing he bolted for the door jamming his fist into his wet trousers in an effort to hide his embarrassing erection. He could hear peals of laughter following him down the path to his motorcar. *Why in hell can't he keep his pecker from doing that every time he saw a beautiful woman? What was wrong with him? Was he a pervert or something? Well, one thing for sure, they can solve their own problems. He wasn't getting involved. That Keith, John, or whatever the hell his name is was a dangerous man and he didn't want any part of him.* His thoughts kept him busy all the way back to town, first with the search, then that nigger throwing hot coffee on his pecker, then the way it stood at attention for that whore. *Damn, he would like some of that slut's ass!*

Maybelle was still giggling when she came into the kitchen. She saw the grave look on everyone's faces and asked, "What's going on? What happened?"

Harrison told her about the ghost Katy said she saw in the cellar, the tunnel being opened, and the signs of people being in there. Katy piped up with a description of the ghost.

"He's a raggy old man, with a big scar on his head. He talks out loud. Says they's owes him shelter, cause they's the ones thet kilt him."

" My God, could it be Asia? We never did find his body," asked Sadie. And all the time we thought it was Keith, err, John Stump. But why wouldn't he find another place to hide. Is he planning something?"

"Probably crazy from the hit on the head. He didn't have many brains to start with, and they were soaked in booze." Harrison looked relieved when the talk got around to Asia and the ghost. His mind made up; he went into town to hire a couple of guards for the tunnel. Two guards came back with Harrison; big, burly black men who worked on the docks.

They were happy-go-lucky young men and ready for anything that came their way. When Jessie met them, she gave them her stern, no monkey business look that put them in their place with her. "I's de boss of yo' an' thet is thet. Yo' cross me an' yo' fin' out what hell bes lik'."

Thoroughly cowed, they stood near the door to the cellar, bobbing their heads up and down, like two corks in the sea. When she had them completely intimidated, she asked, "Yo' et yet? Yo' gonna needs yo' strength to fight thet haunt thets don there."

They looked at each other, shrugged, and answered, "We's sure nough hongry. We's ain't et since yesterday noon. Didn' nobody says nothin' 'bout no haunts."

Jessie laughed. "Thets what I's calls em. He suppose ta be dead, jist too ornery to lay down." The relief was evident on both the men's faces. They were young and strong, but also leery of anything that was of the other world. They had seen many strange things happen when folks messed with juju.

Jessie fed them a meal fit for a king. They couldn't believe that all that food was for them. When they could eat no more, one of the men began wrapping up bread and hiding it in his shirt. Jessie saw him squirreling food away and smiled. She remembered those days. *Let em fill they's guts,* she thought. *They's gonna bees busy watchin' thet hole ina groun'.*

The men worked one on watch every eight hours, the other resting. Harrison spelled them every couple of days. They were getting bored with the job, but not the food. Jessie took a lunch to them on watch, always careful to sing a little something while coming down, so they wouldn't shoot her by mistake. One afternoon on the third day of the watch, she was bringing pie and coffee to the man named Seth, when she heard scuffling in the tunnel. She dropped the food and ran to the entrance, where she saw Seth and Asia wrestling. It looked funny to Jessie, almost as if they were dancing. Seth towering over Asia and reaching down half his height trying to keep the wiry little man from slipping away. When the man saw Jessie he suddenly stopped his useless fighting and whined to her about not getting paid for his work in the tunnel.

"What yo' talkin' bout?" she asked, "what kin' work yo' doin' in the tunnel, an' fo' who?"

"Why for Keith, of course. By the way, why did Mr. Harrison hit me with the hammer? Keith told me all about it. Said he didn't know why either!"

"What yo' do fo' Keith in thet tunnel, so's I's know what to pay yo'."

Asia smiled showing a mouth full of rotted teeth, "Sure, pretend you don't know he's bringing rum in to town from over the water. Those Canucks sure do make good drinkin' liquor. Keith told me Mr. Harrison supposed to pay me, not him. All I get from him is some food and all I can drink. Course that's a goodly amount, heh, heh, heh."

Seth was holding Asia as far away as he could, by the man's bony arm, but he still could smell the unbathed man, the stench was filling the tunnel. Seth's stomach began to undulate, his throat filled with bile. He handed Jessie his gun, pointing at the man he had thrown on the ground, and ran to another part of the tunnel. Jessie could hear Seth vomiting. She couldn't blame him for being upset. The odor was offensive. Asia was in no mood to run. He had an audience and the chance of getting paid, so he was content to stay and see what happened. Besides, if no one remembered the fallen pie, he would get that later.

When the sounds of retching finally stopped, Seth returned, grabbed the crazed gardener, pulled him up the stairs to the kitchen, out the door to the backyard, and waited for Harrison to come and deal with the man who was causing so much trouble.

Harrison walked into the back yard, thumbs hooked in his vest pockets, and his eyes burning a hole into the frail man's conscience.

"Why would you do all these things to the very people that hired you, gave you a place to stay, and welcomed you into our home. Have you no loyalty?"

"Oh, I'm loyal all right to the man that hired me. He told me you tried to kill me, and he saved my life!" The old man peered up at Harrison through rheumy, bloodshot eyes.

"You fool! Your friend Keith is the one who hit you. He was trying to kill you and you don't have sense enough to realize it," Harrison said with distain.

"Mr. Harrison, git that smelly jackass outta here, take him ta town and ta the station house, I can't stan' ta have im here no mo. I's had all of thet smell I's kin take." Jessie shook her head in disgust.

Seth and Harrison escorted Asia to the motorcar, put him in and made the trip to town with all the windows wide open. When they got to the station, they got everyone's attention. The odor filled the post. People who had been in the station carrying on business, left quickly as his stench filled room.

"I know how to solve this problem," said the captain. He called the fire department, took the reeking man outside to the alley, and washed him down with the fire hose. When he could no longer stand, they picked up the drenched man and placed him in a cell. "He won't appreciate the bath we gave him, but we do, and he sure as hell smells better.

"We can ask him questions till we're blue in the face, but if he ain't smart in the head, it won't do no good. We're going to keep an eye on that tunnel from the water's edge, and see if we can't catch ourselves some rumrunners. They must get a healthy price for that swill to bring it in all the way from Canada.

"I wonder if this is tied in with the murder of Otto," Harrison questioned. "If it is, I hope you catch who ever did it and hang him from a tree! That bastard killed a kind, gentle man!"

"Oh, we'll catch em all right. It just might take a while. We're still working on John O'Shonessy's murder. You don't kill one of our own and get away with it."

Chapter Eighteen
Second Chance

When Harrison returned to Haven Place he found a visitor, a man whom Sadie had met in Detroit while waiting for her train.

"How do you do Sir, my name is John Davis," he said as he shook hands with Harrison. "I hope I'm not intruding. I'm in town for a couple of days and thought maybe Sadie could show me around."

Harrison answered him, "I have no say over Sadie. She is free to entertain anyone she wishes. Have you asked her if she wanted to show you our city?"

"No, but I will right now. Sadie, would you be good enough to show me the sights of New York? I have a few days to spend here, and I can think of no one I'd rather spend them with."

Sadie agreed to show him the town, but first she had to find out what the police had to say about Asia, Keith and the now dreaded tunnel.

Katy came in while Harrison was telling Sadie what the captain had told him. She ran over to her mother, pulled herself up on Sadie's lap and began playing with the lapel watch pinned to her dress. It was a small, delicate timepiece with diamonds marking the hours, twelve, three, six and nine.

The child loved the way the rays of light flashed when she turned it to the light.

John watched Sadie and the child while he listened to the report Harrison gave to the woman who had captured his heart. *This woman was created to be a mother,* he thought. *See how gentle she is with the child. This is the kind of wife I want.*

Jessie wandered into the parlor, spotted the guest, looked quickly at Sadie and gave a smile that lit the whole room.

"Why yo' don' tell Jessie we's got company. I's jist baked a cake thet gonna melt in yo' mouth," she said, heading for the kitchen. In what seemed like seconds, she was back with a tray on which sat a pineapple upside-down

210

cake, a coffee urn, cups, saucers, cream, sugar, and a silver cake server. How Jessie could move so fast when she wanted to still amazed everyone who knew her. She cut a huge piece for the guest, a smaller piece for Katy, and began to pour coffee for all while humming in a low voice, was a welcome sound for Sadie. It meant she approved of John, at least for now.

Jessie was right. The cake was delicious. It did melt in their mouths, and they sat and talked comfortably. Jessie busied herself cleaning up the clutter left from the repast and Katy asked if she could help her carry some of the dishes.

"Sho, honey, yo can carry thet pile a forks." Taking the heavy tray loaded with left over cake, coffee urn, and silverware, Jessie headed toward the kitchen.

John was telling them about the trip from Detroit to New York, how the train had to stop every so often for broken rails and cattle on the tracks.

"Someday we won't have that problem. Folks are starting to fence in their livestock, it is already causing range wars in the west."

Sadie was fascinated. John seemed so abreast of the world around him. He had impressed her with his knowledge of the history of Detroit when they first met, but she thought he was just showing off for her. Now it seemed he knew a lot about other areas of the country as well. The longer she knew him, the better she liked him. True, he wasn't the handsomest man around, but he seemed to look better to Sadie each time she saw him. His smile was his best feature; it made you want to smile too. She was lost in contemplation.

Harrison broke into her reverie repeating the question he had asked before, "Would you be willing to do that?"

"I'm sorry, I was deep in thought. What did I miss?" she asked.

"John asked if we were willing to become a partners in a hometown newspaper in Detroit. I said I thought it was too risky a venture to sink money into. There is too much competition in the news business already and being a newcomer makes it twice as risky."

From the kitchen came screams, the clattering of silverware, and the explosive sound of breaking dishes. John, racing toward the source of the noise arrived first. Jessie was kneeling over the limp body of Keith, her huge knee was on his throat, and her hands pinning his arms to the floor. Sadie ran to Katy, scooped her up into her arms, squeezing her till she struggled to get free.

Seth came up from the cellar carrying a case of rum, set it on the table, motioned Jessie off the man, grabbed Keith off the floor, hauled him to the motor car and tied him to the front fender. He came in dry washing his hands, saying, "That takes care of the haunt in the cellar." He grinned at Jessie; his eyes were alight with admiration. She chuckled with delight. "We's gonna hav' our self's a party. We's gonna celebrate."

Harrison and John drove the captured man to the station. The officer grinned. "See, I told you all you needed was a couple of guards and you would catch him. Now we gotta give him a trial before we hang 'em."

He walked away thinking, *the man is caught and with no harm to me. I like this job better and better each day. Now if I can only figure out a way to cash in on the rewards, if there is one or some of that big bribe money that is floating around this town.*

"There goes a man that will either become a big man in this town or will get hung. I think I would prefer the latter!" said Harrison. John was thinking along similar lines.

On the way back to Haven Place, John asked a million questions about Sadie. Harrison told him only what he felt was common knowledge, informing John that he must ask Sadie himself for any other information.

John answered, "I don't care about her past; I was no saint myself, and I am definitely interested in making her my wife. "

Harrison was silent the rest of the way home, his mind going back to the first time he saw Sadie when she was but a child. She had come a long way in this world, in spite of being on her own so early in life. She had matured as a woman as well as a human being. He was proud to call her friend. If this was her chance to get out of this kind of life, he was pleased for her. What he hadn't told her yet was that Otto had left the hotel, money and all his other goods to her and Katy. With what she had saved over the years, unless something catastrophic happened, they need never worry again. He decided to wait to see what she decided before he told her the news. John seemed like a stout fellow, but you just couldn't tell anymore. Of course Jessie's instant acceptance was a pretty good sign. She was usually right.

Back at the house, there was such a feeling of relief for everyone that the house became a beehive of activity. Jessie filled it with songs of praise while she cooked, baked, and found jobs for Seth and Samuel. She had them helping in the gardens and gathering flowers for the many vases scattered though out. She liked having the boys around and treated them as though they were the sons she never had.

The party was the talk of the town. Everyone who was anyone came, some just came to find out what Haven Place looked like inside. Many of the wives stared; gathered in a cluster, put their heads together and compared notes. Most of the husbands sat and pretended it was new to them too. The working girls of the house all had orders to recognize no one, just smile and nod their heads at everyone. That way no one would know for sure if a person was a client or not.

The next morning at breakfast, John asked Sadie to go for a ride with him.

Katy hearing his invitation, asked, " May I go to too?"

"Why not?" he said. "I'll need you around for help when I ask your mother an important question."

Sadie was shaking while she made herself ready for the ride. *What shall I say? He must know what my life has been; still he wants to spend the rest of his life with me. What shall I do?* Her mind was whirling by the time they left for the ride. When they had driven for a short while with out speaking, John glanced at Sadie, winked at her and smiled. She suddenly knew what she was going to say when he asked her to be his wife.

The doubt was gone; her heart was filled with delight and a feeling of contentment. She took a deep breath, turned to the back seat and smiled at Katy. The child put her hand out to John, touching his neck, and giggling planted a big, wet kiss on the same spot. John broke out in an upsurge of laughter. Katy crawled over the seat, slid in between John and Sadie and she snuggled closer. It was settled then and there. They were a family! When they reached their destination, John hauled out a picnic basket, blanket, grape juice and a bottle of wine. Katy and Sadie were surprised and delighted. This was going to be a lovely day after all.

The wedding plans kept Haven Place in an uproar for days. John said he couldn't see why they would have to wait; they had their family started already. Sadie felt the same need for haste. She had let too many years fly by. Both she and Katy needed some stability in their lives. Jessie filled the house with flowers and song.

Sadie couldn't believe that Otto left everything to her and Katy. The tears came quickly, followed by fond memories of the wonderfully, funny, charming, loyal friend who would never be forgotten. Sadie knew in her heart that she loved Otto in a special way, and his memory would be with her until the day she died.

John gently teased her, saying, "I was jealous of Otto because I knew you loved him so dearly, and I can't fault you. He was a great gentleman!" Sadie knew right then that she was marrying not only a lover, but also an understanding friend. Her heart was so full it felt as though it might burst. It was with a sweet, pleasant ache as she remembered Otto, Kate and, yes, John O'Shonssey, too, who, after all, was Katy's father. John had been a good man with a hurtful, destructive problem.

The day of the wedding was as beautiful as it gets in New York. The sun shone brightly, with clear skies and warm breezes; it was as if God was smiling down on this union. Jessie made sure everything was perfect. When she checked everything twice, then once again, she went to the kitchen, sat down, took off her shoes, wriggled her toes, gave a big sigh, and bowed her head in prayer for Sadie, John, and Katy.

When she finished her meditations, she poured herself a mug of coffee and let her thoughts run rampant. She remembered the day she met her man. *There never was a real weddin' fo' us. Jumpin' the broomstick counted back then.* She chuckled, *we's jist got down to tha nitty gritty rite from the start. "Thet man shor could giv' a woman a lotta lovin'. Too bad he got ta passin' it round. Thet was wha' set me ta frettin', hell, I's coulda come up wit' somthin' ta take care of his wants, but no, he hadda mak' me the fool an' run round. Thet was tha las' straw. Shor could go fer a drink rite now. No I's don wan thet kinda trouble agin, better stick ta coffee, it don' mak me crazy. Shor do wish thet man was here rite now, I could shor use som' of thet lovin'."*

The wedding couple, plus one happy little girl, left for a trip to San Francisco. The year was 1906 and a time of upheaval. The nation was having growing pains and people were just beginning to realize that they had a choice in selecting jobs, housing, and mates.

The trip was long and arduous, but as John explained, "Well worth the discomfort," because he was seriously thinking of relocating to some part of California, such a beautiful state, with perfect weather to boot!

When they reached their destination, both Sadie and Katy agreed with John, it was gorgeous scenery and wonderfully pleasant weather. They couldn't get over the fact that it was warm all the time. Huge flowers grew wild and it never seemed to rain during the day. "Just perfect" became everyday words in their conversation. John spent his mornings exploring the town while Sadie and Katy spent most of their time at the seashore. They had been at the water's edge a couple of hours, Sadie reading and Katy playing in the shallow water near a huge rock, when Katy felt something odd, "Mommy, why is the sky moving?" she asked.

"Why, honey, I don't know what you mean, I don't see anything unusual." Then she too felt the earth move slightly. She grabbed Katy's hand, left everything where it fell, and ran toward the hotel.

The hotel manager was waiting for the guests to begin filtering into the lounge, assuring them that it was just a slight tremor and would be over soon.

"We have these little vibrations every so often. They stop in a short while. In the meantime I suggest you enjoy lunch in the dining room."

"Oh God, I wish John were here." It seemed suddenly to have grown too quiet. Even the birds had stopped singing. Jessie had once told her, "The critters know when something bad is going to happen." She felt the need to hold Katy close, so she picked her up and put her right arm beneath her bottom to support the weight of the growing child, who wrapped her arms around her mother's neck, hanging on for dear life.

John came in just as the earth began to move again. This time it went on for a few seconds, which seemed like a lifetime to Sadie. She ran to John, carrying Katy clutched to her breast.

"Oh, John, thank God you're here. I was so afraid you were going to be hurt. We were out by the shore when it started. We just got inside a few minutes ago. This fool wants us to eat lunch as though nothing has happened."

"From what the people I talked to say, this does happen quite often. They have gotten used to it and go on as though it is another shift in the wind. I must admit it did agitate me for a moment, but I guess every place must have its bad point, and this seems to be it. If we decide to live here we will have to accept it like the others do."

"Please, John, even though it is beautiful, I don't think I could live here and feel safe ever again." Katy was hanging on to Sadie's neck, her face white, and frozen in fear.

"Please, Daddy, take us home, I'm scared," she whispered, "Mommy, I wet my pants!"

Sadie squeezed her even more, "That's all right, I almost did, too. Don't you worry, we will get you changed and we are going to leave this place, aren't we, John?"

John stared long and hard at his wife and child, and his smile told them the answer. They went to their rooms, packed and headed back to New York.

"Darling," said Sadie, "the weather is wonderful here in California, I love being near the ocean. The flowers are wonderful and I love the fresh fruit at our beck and call, but I really love the changing seasons. New York is exciting, but I really do miss my home state. Please, Darling, consider Michigan, it, too, is a beautiful place to live and it's home. It is a state that is growing in transit and industry and would be a great place to make a new start."

They discussed the many aspects of living in New York, versus Michigan; John agreed they should move to a place that would offer the most opportunities for new business. It was settled. They would go back to New York, sell the hotel, close out their bank accounts and start their new lives in Michigan. The trip home took on a holiday atmosphere. They sang songs to occupy their time, Katy's favorite being "A Bird in A Gilded Cage." Her voice was strong and sweet. She had Sadie's gift for singing. John sang off-key, but his rhythm was good and he put his whole heart into the words. Every time he glanced at his two girls, his heart filled to the bursting point; thank God he had braved that sick feeling in his gut when Sadie almost walked away from him. If he hadn't begged her to stay and see the town with him, he hated to think of what his life would be without them.

On the third night of their travel, they reached the place where they would spend the night. As John checked in, the clerk asked if they had heard the news that California had split apart from an earthquake; part had washed into the ocean. Thousands were killed, and many, many more were hurt. As the clerk talked he became more agitated, forgetting that Katy was standing there with eyes wide, mouth open, panting like a wild thing caught in a trap.

Sadie started to tremble. "Thank you, Lord," she whispered softly. She caught sight of Katy's face; pure terror was reflected there. Sadie bundled her off to the elevator that would take them to their rooms. John stayed and listened to the rest of news.

The next morning John got up early, dressed, and went out for the newspaper. The newsboys in the neighborhood all had extra editions telling everything about the earthquake that had struck San Francisco in the early morning hours. It had completely devastated Knob Hill. One home survived the quake, that of James C. Flood, who made his money in silver mines. The telegraph reports indicated that 250,000 people were homeless and the death count was in the thousands. The city was still burning, and people banded together to fight the fires that would destroy even more lives and property.

John read of the disaster, thankful for their escape from the horrendous disaster, yet also with a feeling of guilt.

A vague feeling of responsibility crowded into his conscience, was this another obstacle he was supposed to overcome? It seemed to him that he was always avoiding the real tough adventures in life. He yearned for the chance to "Slay the dragon." When he talked to Sadie about his feelings, she told him that right now she and Katy needed him more than a lot of strangers, but if he felt that strongly about it, he was free to return to San Francisco. She came as close to pouting as she ever had. She was slightly ashamed of herself, but if it worked, all well and good.

When they got back to New York City all their friends welcomed them. They had been missed greatly and they were told by Jessie, "tha sun dint shine so bright when yo was gone." After the welcome home party, Sadie told Lorrie, Jessie, and Harrison about their decision to relocate.

"Where?" Harrison asked,

"We have decided on Detroit."

Harrison was thoughtfully reassuring, saying many an industrious enterprise began in a small town. The next week they took the train for Michigan. For John it was coming home.

Their next few years were idyllic, except for the fact that Sadie had not become pregnant. John hoped for a son and Sadie wanted to grant him his wish. Katy dearly wished for a little brother or sister, and nearly drove them crazy with questions about how babies get here. Sadie wanted to explain some of it to the child, but John said it wasn't the thing to do yet.

"You explain that to the daughter on her wedding night." The usually compliant John was unyielding about this.

John's many friends in and around Detroit kept their lives busy with church picnics and parties. Their summers were spent in a cottage in Northern Michigan near a small body of water, called Little Sand Lake. Many of their friends had cottages there as well. These were the happy days for Sadie, the relaxed way of life, all the children swimming, learning to row, playing hide and seek, chasing butterflies in the surrounding woods.

John told Sadie he was considering buying a weekly newspaper in a small town called Bay City, "Honey isn't that where you were born? It seems that a runaway horse had trampled the owner. He is forced to sell the business and return to Pennsylvania where he has children to care for him."

John didn't notice the apprehension that flashed across Sadie's face as she nodded yes to his question.

When he finally got back to the subject, they were in the final negotiations. She was hurt of course, but held her tongue. *Dear God, back to Bay City! Would anyone remember?*

She loved and respected John, and knew any decision he made would be for their best interest, but she did wish he would talk to her about decisions that affected their future. He announced the purchase that night at dinner, telling Sadie they would also have a place to live, behind the newspaper. The house wasn't much, but it would serve the purpose until the paper made enough profit to build what they needed.

Her friends all sympathized with her. Moving to the backwoods was the death knell to society. She put on a brave face and told them, "I will start a group of ladies' meetings, and we will do just fine!" In her heart she knew she was going to be lonely so far from her friends in New York and Detroit. There were no happy memories left of that place, and she had planned never to return, ever again! The only good memories left to her was Marcus. Folks said he had gotten filthy rich on land speculations; he spent most of his time in Washington, hobnobbing with the big wigs. The R.R. had bought the right-of-way from him when it first came into the area, which had gotten him started buying and selling land for profit. She still felt the same when she heard his name, but he had his life and she had John and Katy to fill her lonely hours.

John went ahead to get things ready for the move. Sadie and Katy were to follow in a week. They visited as many of the sites as they could before they left. They had dinner with friends and went to the library Mr. Andrew Carnegie financed for the city. It was a fabulous stone building, looking like a huge castle, which made Katy's imagination run rampant. She began making up stories of knights and ladies, jousts and missions of adventure. Sadie was both pleased and a little apprehensive; she didn't want her child living in a fantasy world. Life was too hard for dreamers. People seemed to crush their spirit, label them strange in most cases. She would do anything to protect her child from the unsympathetic world.

The day to move came all too quickly for Sadie. Her heart just wasn't in it. She kept her thoughts to herself, but it was uppermost in her mind.

Her stomach was even affected by the tension over this move. She felt like she had eaten something bad and it lay like a stone in the pit of her gut. She wanted to cry all the time and the feeling of dread hung over her like a mourning veil, darkening even the brightest day ever so slightly. When she saw the house where they were to live, the feeling grew even more oppressive. John commented on her lack luster attitude.

"Sadie, I know it isn't what you are used to, but it will only be for a little while. I know this paper is needed. We will be able to move to a better neighborhood soon."

When she called Harrison and Jessie to tell them about her new home, they in turn had news, saying, "Lorrie is marrying Evan and moving to Buffalo.

Remember Evan, the one she took a shine to?" Sadie not only remembered, but was pleased and happy as well. Her friend Lorrie deserved a good life, too. She only hoped that Lorrie would be content with just one man in her life, and now she had another friend to talk to when she got lonely or things got too much for her to handle.

Katy was delighted with the new house. It was right in the center of town. There was something going on at all hours. The fishermen, lumberjacks, and voyagers were a lusty bunch, drinking, singing, and fighting, all of which soon became her nightly show. She spent many a night at the window when she was supposed to be sleeping. One voyager had a parrot that swore all the time. Katy had never heard such foul language before. It was her delightful secret, which she hugged tightly to herself. She could hear this forbidden talk without being scolded by her parents. She loved the waterfront, the wooden ramps where they unloaded the goods, mysterious shapes bound in canvas, old torn sails rolled into logs that were piled in a stand at the end of the pier. What Katy loved most were the strangely dressed people who came to trade goods for food grown by farmers in the rich, fertile valley.

Huge logs were floated in the river to mills that lined the shore, there to be cut into boards, then sold to shipbuilders, barrel makers, and homebuilders. The lumber barons used much of the lumber to build great castle-like homes as a tribute to their industrial prudence.

Sadie tried her best to keep Katy away from the waterfront, fearing some harm would befall her.

John on the other hand felt the exposure was good for the child. She needed to learn how other folks lived. Sadie agreed with him, but her protective instinct said otherwise. She had gotten over the stomach problems, but now her back ached all the time, which she attributed to doing all her own housework. One morning in their fourth month of living behind the newspaper shop, Sadie tapped on the dividing door, poked her head into the office where John sat working on an article, whispered, "Guess who's going to be a father," pulled her head back out and closed the door. It took him three seconds to register and shout, "Whoopee, by God, I'm going to have a son!" He came bursting into the sitting room, knelt by Sadie's chair and said, "Thank you, my wonderful wife, I couldn't be happier."

Sadie patted his slightly thinning hair, "Please be just as happy if it is another girl. I know I will be because it will be a symbol of our love."

Sadie knew in her heart that something was different with this pregnancy. Her stomach was always on the verge of vomiting, her feet and ankles swelled almost double and she dreaded the intimacy that John seemed to crave even more now that he was going to be a father.

She dragged herself through the endless days and sleepless nights praying that her baby would be healthy and strong.

Katy helped her mother as much as she could and took this time to learn what she could about cooking and preserving the food from the small garden behind the house.

"You know, Katy, I hated working in my mother's garden on the farm, but I love watching the plants grow and produce fruit from my own garden. It makes the yard look nice and the flowers do brighten the parlor."

"Mama we are the only ones in town with flowers around our house, the neighbor kids say that's cause we're rich."

"We're not rich, but we do like nice things, if that makes us rich, then so be it."

Chapter Nineteen
Double the Joy

The time went slowly for Sadie in her last few uncomfortable months. She had gained more weight for this child than she had for Katy, and dreaded the ordeal of birth, but kept silent. When her time came to deliver, John went to get a woman known for her success in delivering babies. Her brag was, "Never lost a mother, child or father,"

Flora Smith was her name; her husband ran a tavern in West Bay City called the Frog Town Inn by the local inhabitants. It was the favorite watering hole of the Frenchmen who had settled in this area. It was also well known for brawls, shootings, and killings.

Flora was a big woman with large breasts, huge buttocks and an ample waist. She resembled the stevedores who loaded and unloaded cargo from the ships. It was rumored that she acted as bouncer when her husband was too drunk to handle the job.

Sadie took one look at Flora and nearly fainted. All she could see was the top half of the midwife, but that was enough. Then the hard pains began; and Sadie forgot everything except the job at hand. Her stomach was throbbing. She had an excruciating headache, and her back felt as though it would break in two. She feared the touch of this giant of a woman. She would rather deliver the child herself. At least she wouldn't have to suffer the rough treatment this tavern woman would inflict on her.

Flora came to her bedside with a damp rag soaked in alcohol, laid it on her forehead, gently raising Sadie's knees to an upright position and spreading them to make room for her hands and arms. When the pain subsided, she told Sadie to take a deep breath, hold it for a second, and then start panting like a dog when the next pain came. Sadie thought the woman was crazy. Pant like a dog? What was this? Oh, hell, she would try anything to keep Flora from giving more orders. The next pain came in waves, almost taking her breath away. She tried what the crazy woman said. It didn't take away the pain, but it made it tolerable. Maybe the woman did know what she was talking about. She was gentle so far. The pain increased to a crescendo of violent convulsion. Flora was there in the space between Sadie's legs, talking in a low soothing voice, "There, there, you're doing fine. That's it, pant, keep it up, good girl, just a little more, push! Push! That's it! We got him! A boy, and what a boy, looks like a three month old. Biggest baby I ever delivered."

John was waiting outside the door until he heard the word "Boy." Wild horses couldn't have held him back! He burst into the room and took the bundle wrapped in the blanket that Sadie had dug out of the cedar chest. It had been Katy's when she was born and it was one of Sadie's favorites. The colors had stayed bright over the years. Washing and airing had made it as fresh and pliable as when she had first made it.

John held his son close to his chest vowing, "You will have all the love and affection your family can give you. You will grow up strong and fair, you will be a son that we can be proud of. Now you must meet your big sister." After gazing at Sadie for a few moments with tender, worshipping looks, he left the room and the women to the chore of cleaning both mother and bed in that order. The after birth wasn't coming; it needed to be forced from Sadie by pressure on the stomach. Flora slowly began to press on the still rounded Sadie. Suddenly she turned and gave the exhausted mother a look of concern, "Sadie, you are not done yet, there's another child in there, wanting to come out. It's weak, but it's there. Do you want me to help you, or can you force the baby out by yourself?"

"I'm so tired, I don't know if I have the strength, maybe you should help. What will happen to the baby if you help? Will it be all right?"

"I'm not sure of the outcome of this child, but I do know, I will do all I can to have it born into this world with a fighting chance. After all, my reputation is in jeopardy!" The two silent women went back to the work of delivering a small, red-faced stranger into a world full of joys, mysteries, and eternal conflicts.

When the second child finally emerged from his dark safe, haven, into the cold, white world of life, he came kicking, screaming, full of protests.

"If this child survives he is going to be a handful," Flora mused.

John came back into the room, still holding the first child, a look of amazement on his face. Katy was with him, hanging onto the corner of the blanket, her eyes wide with wonder. "Another son! How wonderful, so much more than I expected." John knelt by the bed, placed the bundle by Sadie's right arm, took the wrapped, second son, held him as though weighing him, and asked Flora if he were too small to live.

Flora answered, "That's God's will, I have nothing to do with if he lives or dies."

John took the small baby to Katy, placed him in her arms for a moment and saw the look of wonder on her face. He drank in the pure pleasure, he saw there. Gently taking the bundle from Katy, he placed the nuzzling little creature on the left side of the bed next to his mother and grinned from ear to ear. His face alight with pride, he announced, "We are a complete family. The Lord has been good to us."

The boys grew strong and healthy. Jonathan and James were inseparable, and Katy worshipped them both. Jonathan was the natural leader. He was the older, larger, and more reckless, which caused Sadie great concern. James, the follower, was the cautious one, always hesitant to take a chance, but he followed his brother's lead, sometimes to his regret. Sadie often mused about how wrong the midwife was. Jonathan was the handful and James was her dependable one.

As John had promised when they wed, she made her weekly call to Harrison, Jessie and Lorrie, to let them know how everything was going: the latest news from the Michigan woods as they teasingly called 'her stories of the town.' One morning she called Lorrie and Evan to chat, and Evan told her Lorrie wasn't feeling well.

"Sadie, Lorrie has been working too hard keeping house and helping out in the tavern. Both Lorrie and little Sadie," Sadie's namesake, "need a vacation." The child was now six years old and needed other children to play with. She had friends at school but she needed the freedom that the country provided. Both Sadie and John insisted they come for the summer. Sadie and the children would spend the summer at Little Sand Lake, Lorrie and little Sadie could join them. It was the best time they all could ever remember. The children, ran around with very little on, were always barefoot. They had meals whenever they were hungry and bedtime was when it got too dark to see each other. Too soon the day came when they all had to leave. Everyone cried, kissed and hugged, and promised to do it again next summer. The years went by. Each spring they talked about spending another summer together, but something always came up to prevent it. Maybe next year, they would promise each other.

One morning in April, after a long hard winter, the boys, bored with the games that kept them in the small house and under their mother's watchful eye decided to go outdoors to watch the men harvest ice from the river. Dressing warmly with coats, boots, and gloves, mufflers and hats that Sadie had knitted for them, red for Jonathan, green for James. They promised that they would stay out of harm's way and ran pushing and shoving each other to the river.

The men who harvested the chunks of ice for the businesses and households of the area, waved a greeting to the boys, shouting, "Stay off the ice, it be mushy!"

The boys shouted back, "We will," and ran farther down the shore. Once away from adults, Jonathan started to make small dashes onto the ice, farther each time until he was about fifteen feet from shore.

"This ice is perfectly safe," he announced in a superior voice, sure of himself as only a boy of ten can be. "I want to visit the Indians that pitched their camp on that strip of land near the crossing. We can cut across the river to West Bay City on the ice. It will save us time. Come on, don't be such a sissy. No one will know. We can be there and back in no time!"

James was hesitant. He had a bad feeling about this ice. He kept hearing cracking sounds, but it was a wonderfully warm day to be outside after such a hard winter. Maybe it was his imagination.

He was always such a scardy-cat, not brave like Jonathan. I wish I had been born first, and then maybe I would be the brave one. He stepped out on the pock marked ice. The regular cuttings had weakened the layers, and the current beneath had further undermined the solid looking sheet of ice. It was no place for two young boys to be on this spring day. They inched out slowly at first, and then becoming more confident, began playing tag, chasing and punching each other, forgetting fear. They did not hear the ominous steady cracking, signaling the break away of the chunk they were on, which was floating toward the mouth of the river. When they finally looked around and realized the danger, the ice floe was shrinking to raft size, and men were running along the shore, shouting at the boys to stay on the ice until someone could row out to them. A canoe was hauled to the edge of the river, on sturdy shoulders, and hastily put into the water. Two men with oars jumped into the birch bark rescue skiff and began paddling toward the two fear frozen lads on the small floating chunk of frozen water. People hearing the shouting had gathered at the shoreline to watch and pray for the safe rescue of the two foolhardy young boys.

Katy had been wandering around the docks when the shouting began and ran to the place on shore where everyone had gathered. Seeing her brothers on the ice floe, she began to pray, shaking, not from cold, but from fear. She begged the Lord to save her siblings from certain death in the river. In her mind she promised everything she could think of, if only He would save her brothers.

John, having heard the commotion, came to see if he could get a story for the newspaper. When he saw his sons were the reason for all the turmoil, he lost all interest in a story. All he could think of was the rescue of his flesh and blood from the shrinking stand of ice, which was now just large enough to hold the boys as they stood together, arms, wrapped around each other. When the canoe reached the sobbing ten-year-olds, there was a cheer from shore that filled the spring day with explosive gladness. Once they reached shore, John rushed to the canoe, grabbed the boys, and hugged them till they squealed from discomfort, and then whacked them both on the seat of their britches.

"Thank God, you're safe! If you ever do anything like that again, you will live to regret it. Now let's go home. Come Katy, right now we need to be together as a family."

Sadie knew something was wrong when she opened the door. John's face was a mixture of fear and anger, with another look that she didn't recognize. She had never seen John so upset before and it scared her. She mentally counted heads. Everyone was here, safe, so what could it be? John explained what had happened, how close to death the boys had come, and then announced that he was going to find a larger house with some land for the boys to explore, plant a garden, a place where they could run and play without risking death!

Katy was a little disappointed, but Papa was right. Those brothers of hers needed more room to run and some work to keep them busy, so they didn't go out of their way to find trouble. *I guess I must be growing up,* she thought, *last year I would have screamed, and put up a fuss, because we had to move. This house is way too small for a girl going on fifteen and two younger brothers. I need my privacy, too.*

Sadie opened her arms and encircled her family.

"Thanks be to God you're all safe. I would like to do something to show my appreciation to those men who rescued our children."

"My God, Sadie, in my haste to get these rascals home, I forgot to thank them! I will do that right now, if I can find them. Not only thank them, but also invite them to dinner! My love, prepare a feast they will never forget!" John dashed out the door, hat in hand, running toward the docks.

Sadie started the meal preparations with Katy helping pare the vegetables that came from the fruit cellar; she brought up winter apples for pies and apple cobbler. Katy had learned how to cook, clean, and keep house from her mother. Sadie told Katy she had learned the art of putting up preserves from her mother, an excellent cook, wife, and mother. Katy suspected that she praised her grandmother because she was no longer living. Nobody could be that perfect. Mother had a way of remembering people the way she would like them to be, instead of seeing them for what they really were. *Maybe that's where I got my imagination,* she thought. *If so, I'm glad because it takes me away from these dull surroundings.*

The only interesting place in this whole town is the docks. There I can pretend I'm leaving on one of the boats that come up-river. Going to exciting places, meeting new people, maybe even meeting the man of my dreams. *There I go, daydreaming again,* she scolded herself, and got back to the business of helping mother. *I do wonder why mother left home if it was so wonderful there.*

Her mother's voice interrupted her fanciful thoughts.

"Hurry, Katy, set the table. Your father is coming with two young men in tow and they look hungry. I'll see to the boys while you finish with the table arrangement. Don't forget to put the napkins on. We must keep up our manners. We can't have our guests thinking we're uncivilized."

Chapter Twenty
A Bitter Lesson

Sadie had noticed that Katy was already watching the young men that came into town. When she had mentioned it to John a few times, he pooh-poohed the idea.

"She just turned fifteen. She has plenty of time later to think about men. She's too young!"

"Katy doesn't seem to be unhappy, but she does spend a lot of time writing in her diary. It's as though she escapes in her writing. She doesn't seem to need the friendship of the other girls. I wonder if she's lonely. What do you think, John?"

"I don't really know that much about young girls. That's the woman's job. I do think you're looking for trouble where there is none." These thoughts all whirled around in Sadie's mind while she called the boys; told them to wash up for dinner, hurried back just in time to take the biscuits out of the oven. Katy had put wildflowers on the table, folded the napkins just so, and placed the silver in the right order. *She sets a nice table,* Sadie mused. *All her training didn't go to waste.*

John had taken the two men into his office to give the women time to finish the niceties of the meal and to offer them a drink of brandy to "whet the appetite."

Jared, the younger of the two men, heartily accepted the glass of brandy. Christian, the other of the rescuers, refused, saying, "I prefer not to dull my brain with alcohol."

"As you wish," answered John, pouring himself a small amount and tossing it down his throat to keep from spitting out, "What a pompous prig!" His thoughts jumped to the reason they were here and quickly swallowed his temporary anger.

"Thank God, you two came along when you did," he told them. "We will be eternally grateful."

"It was God's will," intoned Christian. "If it weren't for Him, we wouldn't even be in this part of the country. He has sent us to save these heathens from hell and damnation." His face took on a look of recrimination, even though no one had attacked him.

I am going to find it difficult to be courteous to this Bible thumper, John told himself. *I just hope the meal doesn't drag on all night. The other fellow seems like a good egg. Wonder how he got stuck with this, "Holier than thou," Christian, although, the name fit.*

"Katy, go tell the men the food is ready and be sure and call your foolish brothers."

Jared's face took on a look of pleasant surprise when he saw Katy; he had visions of this being a long, boring evening. Now he wasn't so anxious for the dinner to start.

Sadie had called Harrison and Jessie much earlier, telling them about the near death incident with the boys. They were very upset and called back while she was serving the dessert. John took the call and explained that they had the young rescuers here at this moment, having dinner as a partial thank you for their heroic venture. Both Harrison and Jessie wished to thank the men in person. John gave the telephone first to Jared and he responded, "Jared Meyer at your service, ma'am. You're very welcome sir and ma'am." He then handed it to Christian, who listened, and said, "It was God's will, sir. As for you, madam, I do not congregate with niggers. They are the offspring of the devil."

John was shocked, too surprised to move, but Katy and Sadie both jumped up, clutched their fists against their breast and left the room.

When John regained his composure he announced, in a quiet voice, "Gentleman, this evening has come to an end. Thank you again for being there when my children were in such dire straights. We will never be able to repay you, but this evening is over. Goodnight and goodbye." He promptly left the room leaving the two men standing there looking at the two boys they had saved.

Jonathan spoke first, "What's a nigger?"

Christian answered, "People as black as the devil's heart. They are the spawn of the devil!"

Jared spoke up. "You're wrong, Christian. They are black skinned, but they are a good, religious people, just the same as you and me."

Christian's face became beet red. He stammered, sputtered, almost suffered from apoplexy.

"You dare to compare those savages to me, how dare you, sir! They are the devil's creation and were sent here to vex us." When he realized he was getting nowhere, he grabbed his hat from the peg, and jamming it on his head, he dashed out the door.

Jared hung back hoping he might see Katy once more and maybe even have time to apologize for Christian's behavior. The boys badgered him with more questions all the way to the door.

"Will you be coming back again? Are you staying in town? How long are you going to be here? Will you take us out in your canoe?"

Jared was flustered by the boys' onslaught. All he could think of was to leave before he made a fool of himself.

"Yes, yes, if it is all right with your father. From what I saw, he probably thinks you have had enough of the river to last quite a while!"

When he was outside the house, he wiped his brow, straightened his shoulders, took a deep breath, and whistled his way to the boarding house where he and Christian were staying. His thoughts were churning.

I guess I will have to make some decisions pretty soon about my friend Christian, who is becoming insufferable. The more he studies the Bible, the stranger he gets. I have heard it does that to some men, they believe just the words, not the meanings behind them. If God wanted us to hate black people he would show us that. Besides we don't know what color God was or if He were any color at all.

Mrs. Brown was waiting with his satchel in her hand, when he reached the boarding house.

"Young fella, yer friend says he won't share a room with a nigger lover. Yer gonna hafta find another place."

"It's so late, don't you have a place where I can spend the night? I'll find a room tomorrow."

"All my rooms are filled. My old man don't want no nigger lovers in his house!"

"Have you ever seen a black person, Mrs. Brown?"

"Cain't say as I have, but that there parson, Mr. Christian, says they're evil works of the devil and he should know!"

"Yes, he should know, but, what he should know is better than to think that the color of his skin makes a man good or evil. I'm sure you have heard of some really bad men and they were as white as you or I."

"Don't make a difference, you gotta leave now, or my old man will toss you out, bag and baggage, when he gets home from the tavern."

Jared picked up his satchel, and made his way to the docks where he found an old sail fluttering in the wind. He wrapped himself in it, found a coil of rope, which made a perfect cradle. The sail was an unexpected luxury. It kept him warm and cozy and protected him from the cool, damp fog that drifted in from the river. He was soon fast asleep where he danced, picnicked with, and held a lovely girl who resembled that charming young woman named Katy.

When he awoke, the first thing he saw was Katy's face looking down at him questioningly. He thought he was still dreaming. Shaking his head to clear the cobwebs from his brain, he smiled and asked if she would like to dance again.

"Sir," she said, "we have never danced, so how could we dance again?"

"I'm sorry, " he stuttered, face burning with embarrassment. "I thought I was still dreaming, I, I, oh, my gosh, I mean, oh, well, the more I say the worse it gets. I give up!"

Katy giggled at his obvious discomfort. Her eyes had a twinkle that Jared could swear came from the stars he had seen last night, while he lay waiting for sleep. His heart felt strange, happy, yet sad, full, and yet empty. What was happening to him? He had never felt this way before.

All he knew was he never wanted this laughing, sparkling beauty in front of him ever to be out of his sight.

"Why are you sleeping on the docks? Don't you know it's dangerous at night?" Katy asked the still foggy brained Jarod.

"I had to sleep somewhere. It seems Christian no longer craves my company. We see things so differently. He believes his way is the only way. I believe there are many ways to love our God, and we must respect all of his creations.

"I know he is a very unhappy man, his bitterness is contagious, so it is just as well that we part ways. I have come to help him build a church. But I suppose he won't want my help now, so there is nothing holding me here. Unless I can find work, I will have to move on." The local mill was Jared's very first try at being hired and he started work that very same day.

Katy began to find reasons to visit the lumber mill where Jared had found employment. She often packed a lunch and saying she was going on a picnic, and went to share her lunch with her new friend.

He had proven to be a conscientious worker. The mill owner, J.C. Bartock, soon began to depend on Jared and his dedication to the safety of his crew.

Mr. Bartock always had great difficulty finding replacements when a man was hurt on the job. Jared's safety measures had cut down on the work-related injuries. As he praised Jared's hard work and loyalty one Monday morning, he added, "Now if they would only stay out of the gin mills, maybe production would increase."

Jared's courtship began soon after he had found suitable lodging, and had been employed for three months. He began having Sunday dinner with the Davis family after attending church and that ritual soon became an accepted part of the family weekend. The Widow St. James had graciously allowed the traveling preacher to hold prayer meetings and church services in her large unused barn. The bugs and spiders that visited the attendance did little to ensure the tranquility of the service. One Sunday afternoon as John and Jared were discussing the building of a church building Jared stated, "I'm not a preacher, but I am a believer, and I believe He will show us the way to build a church of our own."

Katy couldn't get over this young man's sincere, dedicated feelings about his beliefs.

Her family was religious too, but there was always that little feeling of embarrassment when they discussed religion or worshiping God. She had seen nothing of this when Jared talked about his beliefs. His words came so easily, without even the slightest hesitation, almost as if he were a preacher.

Sadie had seen the relaxed way he discussed everything with John and hoped Katy was looking at the young man as a potential suitor. After all, there wasn't much to choose from in this small town and he did seem like a good catch.

When she talked to Lorrie one Saturday afternoon as usual, she told her what had happened with Jessie and the preacher. Lorrie said some things the operator shouldn't hear, which made Sadie giggle, then burst out laughing. When she finally caught her breath, she said, "It seems like old times back in New York. Lord, I miss that place every once in a while. Don't misunderstand, I'm happy here with John and the children. It's just that we were so young and foolhardy; we didn't realize what a carefree life we had. I wouldn't have missed it for the world! We had some wonderful times, made a lot of lasting friendships along the way, but I wouldn't want my daughter to live that life."

Lorrie had to agree with her; not everyone could survive in that kind of lifestyle. The parties and the glamour were one thing, but the degradation and the scorn were another. They were lucky. They had lived the life and gotten away before it gobbled them up and spit them out.

Lorrie confided that her Evan was by far the best lover she had ever met and that was the only thing that kept her from straying.

Sadie told Lorrie about her hopes for Katy's future with Jared, and the plans to help build a church so they could invite the preacher to come and live in this town of loggers, miners and farmers. "It's exciting to be in on the growth of a new city."

Katy heard her mother tell Lorrie about her hopes for her future, but didn't let on that she was already involved with Jared. She only smiled a secret little smile, but the twinkle in her eye gave her away.

The building that would house the church was erected in a week by the able bodied men of the town. The younger men did the whitewashing of the building when it was finished. But the design of the building and intricate carving of the pulpit was done by an older skilled carpenter named Henry Oaks Russell; newly arrived from Canada. Russell was a large, burly Irishman, who had learned his trades from his father and grandfather. His temper was explosive, but his workmanship was exquisite.

Christian had found solace and quarters with the Browns and lived off the handouts of a small group of people who were as gullible as the host family. He had made an effort to be appointed preacher of the new church, but saner heads prevailed. Word was sent out that the town was searching for a permanent preacher.

The preacher who rode the circuit heard the news and rode in on a Saturday late in the afternoon. After he had checked out the church, he declared it wonderful and just what he was searching for. He announced his intention to make this his home if that was acceptable to the city fathers.

Bitter because of his rejection by the town fathers, Christian decided to lie low and see what the future would bring. He tried placing hate articles in the newspaper but they too, were rejected. To his utter chagrin a Negro blacksmith moved into the house across the street from the local hardware store.

At first the townsfolk crossed the street when they went passed the house. But they soon learned that the man and his family were an asset to the town. The two small children who played in the yard were always clean and polite. The wife always had a clean wash on the line, and that was what the woman folk of the town went by.

Oh, sure they had heard what that Christian fellow said, but what did he know about women's work and the day to day living in a small town? Feeling brave and adventurous, several of the women got together and made a welcome call on the family, mainly to see if what that Christian fellow had said was true.

"The woman was spotless," said Mrs. Bartock. "I didn't see any strange idols on her mantle place either. That preacher fellow is teched in the head."

The other brave souls that had accompanied her nodded their heads in agreement. The matter was settled as far as they were concerned. "Live and let live," was their motto.

Chapter Twenty-One
Impending Doom

Sadie was usually happy when she finished talking with her friends from the old days, but today she felt depressed. A lost, sinking feeling settled in her very being. She went about her daily duties the same as any other day but her heart wasn't in it. She felt as though some terrible thing was stalking her, waiting to jump out and destroy her peaceful, well-adjusted world.

Meanwhile, Christian had completely enraged the Brown household against Jared; they didn't want that betrayer of the white man to stay in their town. He told the small collection of hangers on, "The new Preacher was handpicked by the devil. He must be to declare that God created all men equal. Why, everyone knew that the black man was a savage."

Mr. Brown, in a drunken stupor, nodded his head, agreeing with every word Christian said, even though he had never seen a black, red or even yellow man until now. The only men who counted on this green earth were the white men. The fiery young man hypnotized Mrs. Brown. He seemed to fill a vacuum in her life. He was son she never had, and now was thankful that she never bore the bitter fruit from this marriage. She sat mesmerized while Christian raved on and on about the sins of the father being placed on the sons, that Jared was the fruit of a bad seed, and he would come to a no good end. When he finished his maniacal tirade, he slammed off to bed. That was one of his tricks to keep his audience spellbound, make a memorable entrance and exit, and always leave them wanting more. His plan to discredit Jared was beginning to take shape. He couldn't have that fool stay in town. Jared really believed all those lies about all God's children being the same. Well, he'd show him where the bear shit in the buckwheat!

Mr. Brown sat at the kitchen table sucking on his lip, thinking over what the preacher said about Jared, that betrayer of the white man. How could he go against his own? Why, every man in town should know what a crime that young fool had done. He hurried off to the tavern to let them all in on the news. Wait till all the red-blooded men in town heard about that traitor Jared. The faster he walked the more he thought of the things that he could have done to undermine the good white folks of this town. By the time he got to the tavern he had a mental list of the outrages Jared had performed against the town folk. It didn't matter that they were untrue; it just mattered that he would have done 'em if he could. When he rushed into the tavern, the cronies hanging out there teased him about having his tail on fire. Mr. Brown started to tell his pals about the abuses that the white man suffered at the hands of that nigger loving Jared. They looked at each other, then they began to laugh.

"What's a nigger? Who cared anyway? We ain't never seed one. Don't care if I ever do. Ain't one here so why should we worry?" One fellow chimed in; "I seed one down Georgia way. They ain't nothin to be scairt of. Poor scared black folks that's all!"

Mr. Brown was furious with his friends for laughing at him, taking up for the black devils, those spawns of Satan.

"There's one livin right here in this town. I saw him the other morning, working on his anvil, nothing on but a pair of trousers. Our wives are going by seeing that black son-of-a-buck near ta naked, and we cain't do a thing about it. I say that ain't right, they shouldn't be allowed to congregate with white folks at all!" He was so angry, he left his drink and went home to the house and wife that he drank to escape. When he walked into the house, his wife started ragging on him about the evils of drink. That was too much for poor Mr. Brown. He lost all control over his violent temper. He grabbed the Mrs. by her hair, threw her at the wall, grabbed a handful of her dress at the throat, and slammed her head against the wall until it gave way. Another hole was added to the once smooth papered wall that now held pictures of strangers to cover holes made by frequent beatings. When his arms became too tired to lift them for one more slap, or punch, he dropped her on the floor, went to the shed for his jug of hooch and headed for bed. That way he didn't have far to go when he got too tired.

Mrs. Brown picked herself up from the bloody floor, leaned against the wall, tipping pictures left and right.

"What the hell do I care?" she muttered through broken teeth and lips. "I don't know those people anyway. Why in hell did I marry that old man in the first place? I should have stayed an old maid. Might just as well be. He don't give me any diddling anyway. I sure would like some from that preacher man. A course he's too holy for that kind of fooling around. Well, better get to bed. Sure hope I feel better in the morning." She shuffled off to the bed she shared with the stranger she called husband.

Christian, hearing the noise of the beating, believed a good husband should beat his wife once a week to keep her in line. His sharp ears also heard her muttering to herself about the lack of physical contact from her husband, and he, being always on the lookout for another way to bind his followers to him, filed that scrap of information away for future use. *A man would have to be desperate to stick it in her, but I have been in some pretty dire straits at times,* he reminded himself. *I'll keep her in mind.*

Sadie couldn't shake this feeling of doom hanging over her every thought. "Dear Lord," she prayed, "Please keep my children safe from harm." Uppermost in her mind was the close call the boys had on the river. Her heart jumped into her throat every time she thought of the danger the river offered.

John came home early one afternoon saying he had a surprise for her. Oh God, now what? Please not another move to some God-forsaken hole in the world? John just smiled, held her coat for her, bundled her into the automobile, slammed the door, and ran around to the driver's side. Settling in, leaning over, he planted a kiss on her cheek and said, "Mrs. Davis, prepare to view your new home. It is a secret I've kept for much too long. I hope you will love it as much as you did Haven Place."

John drove out of town, heading north to the river, over the bridge through a patch of woods. Just the other side of the many trees sat a wonderful dream-like home, all brick and stucco. A garden stretched out around the house like a giant moat protecting a palace. Sadie couldn't believe her eyes. It was a dream come true. A house large enough to raise a family and still have overnight guests. She threw her arms around his waist and hugged him with such enthusiasm that he groaned at a twinge that struck his side. Hiding his discomfort, he grinned with pleasure.

John escorted her into the foyer with a wave of his arm. The house was everything Sadie had ever hoped for: a great room for entertaining and family reunions, a large kitchen with all the latest in fixtures, even inside bathrooms, what a wonderful surprise!

Sadie talked all the way home about the house, the drapes, curtains, and decorations. The first thing that they would move into the house was her very last quilt. She had saved it for a special time and this was it. She was so busy furnishing the home in her mind, she didn't notice John's face turn red, then white from pain. He tried not to spoil the surprise he had worked so hard on, but he had no choice. He grabbed her hand, put it on the steering wheel and fainted. She stared at him for a second, realized what was happening, put her foot over his and pressed the brake. Jumping out she ran around to the driver's side and tried to waken the unconscious John. He wasn't moving. She frantically looked around for help. Seeing Christian walking down the wooden sidewalk near the newspaper office, she shouted for him to come and help. He looked at her, saw the situation was drastic, smiled, tipped his hat and sauntered away toward the docks, leaving Sadie in shock at his behavior.

But she didn't have time to worry about him right now; she needed someone to help her get John into the house. The boys, who were in the back of the house, heard their mother shouting and came running to see what all the excitement was about. They grabbed their father's arms and Sadie held his legs. Struggling with his weight, they inched their way into the house. They got as far as the sofa in the small living room and put him down. Jonathan ran for Doctor Ruggles. Sadie placed cold cloths on John's burning brow while James loosened his waistcoat and vest. The doctor came bursting in after what seemed like a lifetime, pushing everyone out except Sadie. He began to examine the still unconscious John.

Sadie couldn't control the tears that slid from her tightly squeezed lids, "God, please take care of John. Please don't take him away from his family that loves and needs him." All the while she prayed she knew that this was the dread that had hung over her these last few weeks. We are going to be alone again. This thought crept into her mind and heart and it took up permanent residence.

The doctor, a thin man with a beard that he stroked when he was deep in thought, held out his hand to Sadie, took her elbow, steered her into the kitchen, sat her at the table and gave her the news.

"It's his appendix, I'm afraid. He is in a coma now. I've never performed this operation, but I have seen it done. I sure don't have any other choice, I've gotta operate or he's gonna die. He might die anyway, but at least he will stand a chance. It is up to you, Mrs. Davis."

"Please do what ever you have to do to save my husband, Doctor." Even as she said the words, she knew what the outcome would be, but she had to hold some hope or she couldn't bear to stay in that room and this is where she had to be!

They heard a strangling noise from the unconscious man running into the room Sadie saw green bile erupting from the semi-conscious John's mouth.

Screaming, she ran to John, propped him up so he could spew out the infection and not strangle on the noxious liquid bursting from him. Sadie cried out, "Do whatever you have to do and hurry."

The boys were in the back yard, peeking in the window, trying to see what was happening to their father. The door suddenly banged open, and in marched Christian waving a Bible, chanting, "I'm here to give him absolution and save his soul."

At that moment in came Katy, Jared and Flora Smith, the mid-wife. Jared had summoned her when he heard what was happening at the Davis house. Jared took Christian's arm and tried to steer him out of the room. He resisted, so Jared twisted his arm behind his back and walked him, protesting loudly, from the room. He went out the door shouting, "You are condemning that sinner to Hell's portals." He continued his tirade all the way to Mrs. Brown's rooming house.

Katy and Flora were helping the doctor prepare for the surgery that must follow. Sadie went into the backyard, knelt down and began to pray and was soon joined by the twins. All stayed in that position until the surgery was over.

Doctor Ruggles finally came out wiping his blood stained hands on his apron. He was shaking his head in defeat. "I've failed to get it in time, the poison is all through him. It's only a matter of time now."

Katy rushed to her mother's side, throwing her arms around her, sobbed as though her heart would break. Sadie let her daughter's pain take precedence over her own deep grief. The children must come first had always been her creed. Putting aside her anguish, she gathered her children to her breast and soothed them as only a mother can.

The doctor went into the kitchen looking in all the cupboards until he found a bottle of brandy; poured a stiff drink, tipped it into his open mouth, swished it around, then swallowed. He looked at the bloody table that had become the makeshift operating table, poured another and quickly tossed that one down his parched throat.

He had done everything that he was supposed to do, but it was too late to save John. *Why does it always have to be the good ones who die? There is a goodly few that needs dying just to make the world a better place. Take that Bible thumper that came in here to save John's soul. I would like to get him on the receiving end of my scalpel; I would save his soul for him. Damn, that is good brandy. Better have one more before I leave.* His mind raced with reasons why, excuses, and regrets over his personal failure to save every patient he tended. The bottle helped him to forget for a little while.

John never regained consciousness. He lay for two days burning up with fever, moaning, filling the household with an intense awareness of their own vulnerability.

Sadie sat with him, touching his fevered brow with her cool hands, wiping the sweat away from his eyes, brushing his thinning hair back away from his face. *Funny,* she thought, *I never noticed how thin his hair was getting. I only saw his dear sweet face, always so handsome to me. Dear God, please make a special place in your house for this good man. He has always been the best he could possibly be. It was as if God heard her. John stopped moaning, a slow smile drifted across his calm face, and he was at peace.* Sadie's eyes filled with tears. She bent her head, and murmured, "Thank you."

Jared became the mainstay for the family, running errands, making arrangements for the paper to be printed, and seeing to the church service. Sadie wanted to handle all the viewing arrangements. She handled the chore of bathing, shaving, and dressing her beloved John. She needed to be close to him for the last time. When she had finished her labor of love, she bent and kissed his mouth, whispered against his cheek, "I will see you again someday, wait for me."

When she retired that night the bed seemed large and empty. She twisted and turned, trying to find a comfortable spot to help her sleep. Her mind was full of the vast business arrangements to be done; the tremendous responsibilities that raising three children alone can bring. She didn't wish John back, he had suffered too much for that, but she did wish they had talked more about what she should do in case of just this circumstance. While she lay pondering her next move, she felt a weight gently press against her shoulder, snuggle tighter against her whole body, yet there was no one in the bed with her. Her hand reached out behind her, patted the warm spot that had been John's favorite part of the bed, as close as he could get to her. She felt a sense of relief sweep over her, she could sleep now, John was there to guide her, she need never be afraid again. Sadie drifted off to a restful land where the sun was shining, the flowers were the brightest of colors and misery was unheard of.

After the funeral, Katy and Jared came to Sadie and announced their plan to marry in a month.

"You're just a child," she pleaded. But even as the words came out she knew that she was wrong. Katy was a young woman and a capable one at that. She hugged them, gave them her blessing, and started making plans for

239

the wedding.

"No, mother," said Katy, " we are not going to have a big wedding. I am with child. We want to go away and have the ceremony. It will be less embarrassing. We really do love each other and that's all that counts. We would go right away, but we want to respect the month of mourning. Father was very important to us both."

Jared took Sadie's hand begging her forgiveness.

"Katy's right. We do love each other and I promise I will be the best husband and father that I can possibly be."

"That's all anyone can hope for. I know you love each other, but it is going to be so hard to have you leave. I had planned on having you around for a couple more years. Your father and I believe in long engagements."

Katy looked at her in astonishment, "Mother, I can't believe you said that. You and father knew each other for such a short time. Were you so unhappy?"

Sadie's face flushed a bright pink; she had forgotten Katy was old enough to remember how she and John had met, when they had wed and where she had worked. To Sadie that was another lifetime, almost a dream or a story she had read.

"You're right again, Katy. Your father and I didn't know each other very long, but when you love as we did, it seems as though you knew them forever."

The month flew by for Sadie and Katy; the wedding day came and went quietly, a simple ceremony in Saginaw with Sadie and Flora Smith as witnesses. A small celebration was held at the house and Katy became Mrs. Jared Meijer. The boys teased the newlyweds about Katy not even knowing how to cook, but Jared just smiled and winked at Katy.

The new home that John had been so proud of held no great warmth for Sadie or the boys. They discussed it at length, decided it should be sold and the money used to pay the bills. Any money left over was to be put in the bank for an education for the boys.

Jonathan declared, "I want no part of any la-de-da college. I am going to be a lumberjack. Now there's the life. Work in the fresh air, get free room and board, paid a big wad of cash once a month. That's the only life for a red blooded man."

James shyly said, "I thought we we're too poor to even think about college. Dad was always saying we don't have money for this or that. I guess we're not poor at all. I think I would like to be an engineer someday. You know, build great impressive buildings."

"That's it," teased Jonathan, "I will cut the lumber and you use it to build temples to the sky."

To Sadie's surprise the house sold quickly. After the bills were paid there would be two thousand dollars left.

Sadie decided, "I will put this in the bank next time I get I a spare moment," even though she still held a distrust for banks.

Days flew by and the blistering hot summer had burnt its way into fall, leaves were beginning to fade and vees of gray geese split the sky with their signaling honks of exodus.

Sadie awoke this morning with a feeling of great urgency. *What is it? Have I forgotten something? I wish this feeling would go away. I'm frightened, and I don't know why. Just lonely and missing Katy, I expect. She seems so happy with her Jared, she has the look of a woman in love, and the radiance of a soon to be mother, that's probably what it is.* She looked at the newspaper lying on the table. It didn't give her any clue as to why she should be upset. It had a story about a young man drowning in the river, but she didn't know the family. It brought back memories of the near death experiences the boys had a while back. *I'll say a prayer for that poor mother. She has no one to turn to, and the boy had no father.*

The local newspaper had printed, "Bastard son of Sarah Jane Wolf" in the obituary. *Dear God, there has to be a better way of writing an account of a young man's life. Thank God her children never had to suffer that humiliation! Was there something special about the date? The man who had taken over the paper for her had changed the whole format and she had a hard time locating the date. Thursday, Oct. 24th, 1929 that was nothing special, I just wish this eerie feeling would go away.* She finished getting breakfast for the boys, called them again, and sat drinking her coffee and contemplating the future.

Jared and Katy came beating on the door, shouting something about the bank being closed, and the whole town ready to lynch the banker. Sadie couldn't believe what they were telling her, her heart began to pound, her breath came in short gasps, "O my God, I was going to put money in the bank today, but I didn't feel like getting dressed for town, something made me wait. What about the money we had in the bank? Will we be able to get that out?"

"No, that is what the townsfolk are so upset about. The bank is closed, and the sheriff and a couple of his deputies are guarding the door with guns drawn. The banker is inside, but he won't give us our money."

241

Sadie slowly sat down, put her head in her hands and took a deep breath.

"I have saved that money for years, I even had Otto's money in that bank. Your father wouldn't use it. It was supposed to be for our old age. Dear God, am I being punished for hoarding it? "

Sadie felt a warm gushing wave dampen her underclothes. She excused herself, went to her room and removed her bloodstained undergarments and tucked them into a basin sitting on the dresser. She bathed herself, put on a pad made of old torn up sheets, wiping away the tears, she reentered the kitchen, and resumed the conversation. They must never know she had lost the child that she and John had prayed for.

Sadie asked if there was a chance that they would be able to collect some of the money they had saved for so many years. She just couldn't believe that all that money was gone, just like that, gone.

"I feel like I'm being punished for having such a good life, such a good family, and having been so lucky till now. I feel as though my world is slowly falling apart."

"Mother, the whole town, no, the whole country is in the same situation as we are. Are they being punished, too? It is time to think of what we are going to do next, not blame ourselves."

"Katy is right," Jared said reassuringly. "We have to decide on a plan to survive for the next few days. I'm sure by then the government will have this all straightened out." Jared's confidence would soon be tested as the days turned into weeks, weeks into months, months into years.

The two thousand dollars plus the household money became the income for the whole family. Jared and Katy moved back home with Sadie and the boys. Sadie silently worried that the money she had was dwindling away with no hope of more to come. Jared cut wood to heat the house and did whatever odd jobs he could line up. Katy took in wash for the single men of the town. The boys scrounged around for any job they could find. James helped Mr. Carter at the local store delivering groceries, stocking shelves, and sweeping the wooden floor till it shone. Jonathan, being a big lad for his age, found work at the tavern. He stacked the kegs into the back room, tended bar, swept the floor, cleaned the brass spittoons, and doubled as bouncer when a patron got out of hand.

Sadie wished there was something she could do to help with the income, but they all assured her she was doing an important job making good meals and maintaining the house and garden.

One cold morning in December she received a telephone call. It was from a lawyer in New York. She was barely awake when she answered, but was soon wide-awake. The attorney told her she was the heir to the estate of Jessie Jonas. For a moment it didn't register, she had never known Jessie's last name, didn't need to, she just knew she loved her like a second mother. When she was done talking to the lawyer, she placed the earpiece in its cradle and sat down in a daze. She had promised to come to New York for the reading of the will. He had assured her she wouldn't be wasting her last few dollars foolishly.

The telephone was their only luxury. The bill was long past due and the company was dunning them all the time, but Sadie somehow kept stalling them until she could scrape together a dollar to pay on the bill. Thank God, the company hadn't taken it out yet. When she woke the others, they couldn't believe their stroke of good luck. They were excited about her trip to New York and couldn't understand her lack of joy until she reminded them her good friend Jessie had died. She hadn't even known Jessie was ill. She had lost a very old and dear friend and she could never be replaced with money. How like dear, sweet Jessie, not to let anyone know she was sick, to suffer alone, yet give the gift of her everlasting love. Sadie could almost hear her low, soothing chant to the God that she had made an important part of her life. The hymns she sang and hummed had become such a part of Sadie's life, that when she left Haven Place, the world was strangely quiet and empty. It took her a while to realize it was Jessie she missed most. She savored the emotion and closeness she felt at that moment. Jessie had saved her life once before. And now it looked as though she were reaching beyond the grave to save her and her family again. Oh, how I miss that woman! Why do we have to lose friends before we realize how important those friends are to our world, she pondered? I wish I could reach out and hug her right this minute!

Chapter Twenty-Two
New Life

On the morning of her trip to New York, she cautioned the family not to expect too much. She didn't see how Jessie could have saved a huge amount in a city that only tolerated blacks. The trip was going to be difficult for Sadie. She always expected to find all of her friends' there waiting. This time one would be missing, an empty chair at the table in the Haven House kitchen. Good heavens, she'd done it again, forgotten that the old house was empty, closed for so many years. Deserted by the last madam. The lump in her chest grew larger. It had started when the lawyer had called and each memory added to its density. At times Sadie found it difficult to breathe and the tears came too easily.

As she prepared for the journey she glanced into the mirror in the hall, saw for the first time an older woman, not the Sadie she was, but the Sadie she had become. The shock was great. Is this the person everyone sees? She almost cancelled her trip.

Sadie hadn't packed much for the trip, one change of clothes, so she was able to carry the satchel to the train station. No one could see her off. They all had jobs. Work was sparse and they must grab whatever was available.

When the train pulled into the station, the conductor swung off, picked up her bag, and led her to the train. She sat facing the bright red engine, her whole body taut with anticipation. She soon began to relax to the hum of the mighty machine pulling them along the tracks like a toy on an invisible string. Her head began to droop, her eyelids were getting heavy, and the steady hum lulled her into a state of half sleep. She was there in the train, but not there, somewhere in between. A space in time where she was young, beautiful and running free, running to a misty place where he waited for her. The place she did not know, but she knew she had to get there. She ran faster, her feet were flying, but the faster she ran, the farther away the mist drifted.

She cried out, "Stop, I can't run any faster," and she awoke with a start. Her face flushed. *Fool, you were only dreaming,* she told herself. *You are getting old!* The elderly man in the seat across the aisle smiled, nodded his head and went back to reading his newspaper.

The long tedious pilgrimage gave Sadie time to think of all the wonderful people who had come into her life and had shared a part of themselves. How lucky she was to have known them, and how hard it was to say goodbye to the ones who had gone on ahead. The parade of the dead started in Sadie's mind. *First there was Kate, then John O'Shonessy, her first husband, then Robert, or was it Robert first then John? She didn't remember. Oh well, it dosen't matter anymore, they were just as gone. Mama passing and the news that father and Maggie had frozen to death one winter caused some unhappy memories for Sadie, but that was in the past and better left there. David, Sarah and Steven had come to take care of the farm until it could be sold. They said it hadn't been cleaned in years. Poor Mama, she had kept it spotless. Then there was poor Otto. She wished she could have loved him as he so richly deserved. He would have climbed to the moon if she had asked him. And now, her poor John. Had it really been four years that he had been gone? It seemed like yesterday.*

I can still feel his arms around me when I go to sleep. It is so comforting to have his spirit there with me. Oh, I know I'm being foolish, his spirit went on a long time ago, but I can pretend he is still here with me. God, old girl, you are getting daffy in the head, talking to yourself, and even answering. Funny, but I've never given a thought to Jessie passing.

I thought she would go on forever. I wonder if Lorrie and Evan will be there. Cathy and Philip should be there too. I wonder if they will bring Rachael. I have missed that child so much. One of the hardest things I ever had to do was give up that child to Cathy and Philip. I know it was for the best in the long run, but it did hurt. Thank God I have Katy and the boys. I don't think I could go on if it weren't for them.

She wrinkled her brow, thought back to the good times at Haven Place. *I will go there to see the old place again. How did I get so morbid all of a sudden? I can't let life get me down. I'm going back to New York, my second home. How can I be sad?* The excitement began to build; she could feel the joy of life filling the empty spaces that had taken over her existence the last couple of years.

She dozed off again, dreamed of a sunlit meadow where the blossoms grew in great splashes of color, the trees gave refreshing shade, and the grass was the greenest she had ever seen. She wanted to tarry there forever. She woke with a start, someone was touching her hand, shaking it as though to introduce themselves, she jerked her hand away, let out a startled scream and half rising, pushed the gentleman away. When she was fully awake she peered at the shaking, red-faced man, and recognized him as one of her first clients when she worked at Kate's House in Lower Saginaw. She couldn't believe her eyes. This trembling, old man was in his seventies. Where was the handsome young man she knew? She patted his hand, apologized for her behavior, told him she had just come out of a dream and didn't recognize him. Time had not been good to him.

Then she remembered the woman who looked back at her from the mirror. I'm an old woman right along with him. *I will be glad when we get to New York,* she brooded. *If there is enough money, I'm going to get a new hairdo and some new clothes. I wonder if the others have changed as much as I have.*

The old man sat with her the rest of the way to New York City. The gossip was a good way to stay awake, but much of it she already knew. What? What was that he said about Marcus? Just hearing his name caused her to tremble. She asked him to repeat what he just said. He told her that the scandal was all over town Marcus had gotten a divorce from his wife of twenty years and moved to New York City and didn't she used to know him years ago?

Sadie's hands were shaking, her mind in a whirl. Was there a chance they finally could be together? The rest of the miles were a blur for Sadie. The thought of being held close again, in his strong, gentle arms sent a thrill through her whole body Would Marcus remember her and the love they shared? I must be a wreck. She hadn't worried how she looked until now, but suddenly she felt like a frowzy old woman. She touched her hair, straightened her dress as well as she could. Tears filled her eyes as she turned and stared out the window.

The scenery flying by the window became a stage for her fantasies. She saw herself and Marcus meeting, looking deeply into each other's eyes, remembering the cascade of emotions they had shared, touching, making love, and falling into that all consuming love, all over again. When she turned her head away from the window and came back to the present, she felt drained but content; she would see her Marcus again, soon.

At long last, the conductor announced, "Ten minutes to New York City." With shaking hands she took her bag from the rack, set it next to her seat waiting for the last few jerks of the train to subside, so she could step off and into whatever adventure that fate had in store.

She stared around in amazement. The city had grown skyscrapers, which dotted the skyline, and there were people everywhere. She hired a taxicab to take her to the attorney's office. Mr. St James office was in the Flat Iron Building.

He had said, "Just tell any cabbie that, and he will bring you right to me."

He was right. The building was shaped like a flat iron and matched the property it was built upon. What a clever way to make your building a showpiece, she marveled.

The excitement she always felt when she was in New York came rushing back. She felt young and ready for whatever fate had to dish out, now that she knew Marcus was here too. *First things first,* she thought. *See the lawyer, get that settled, arrange to move her family here, if she could afford it, and then worry about the future. Sadie was always a mother first, wife second, her own person last.*

Mr. St. James was a large man with a protruding stomach, small eyes almost hidden by bushy brows, and a beard streaked with red and gray that looked like it contained tobacco juice. He made little sucking sounds around the cud of tobacco that he shifted from one side of his mouth to the other as he talked.

Sadie hadn't eaten since breakfast and her stomach began to churn as he explained Jessie's will. He spat toward a bronze spittoon as he talked, shooting rivers of brown fluid in the direction of the container, missing much of the time, as the rug on the floor testified.

Sadie, pleading a severe headache, dashed out of the office, barely making it to the crowded sidewalk and around a corner where she lost all control in a wooden box that had been left in the alley way. She made her way to a hotel where Mr. St James had booked a room for her. It was lovely; it reminded her of Haven Place. She lay down on the huge bed pulled the coverlet over her shoulders and drifted off to sleep. The ringing of the telephone awakened her. It was the desk clerk, someone had telephoned for her and would she like to take the call?

"Yes," she answered, "but I don't know who it could be, everyone I know is in Michigan. Hello," she whispered. "Who is this calling?"

"That's for me to know and you to find out," the caller teased. The moment Sadie heard the voice she knew it was Lorrie, and then another voice chimed in, "And who is this, miss smarty pants?"

"Cathy!" Sadie screamed, "Where are you and how soon can you get here?"

"We're downstairs in the lobby. We wanted to surprise you, we'll be right up!"

Sadie scurried around trying to freshen up before her friends got up to her room. She looked in the mirror and saw the stranger who resembled her. No time to worry about that right now. Later she would have to sort this out, but right now she just wanted to be with friends who loved her. When she opened the door there stood a group of people who looked strangely familiar, but she just couldn't place them. *Another one of Lorrie's tricks,* she thought. *No, wait, that is Lorrie. She, too, has changed. Evan looks the same, just a little wider and grayer. Is that Cathy? She has grown lovely in her passing years, the scars had all but faded, and she shines with an inner glow. I wonder what the secret is. Who is that astonishingly beautiful girl with them, and why is she here? This was supposed to be a meeting among old friends.*

Moments passed, but the group knew what she was experiencing, for they had gone through the same question and answer game when they met in St James' office. Philip broke the silence with a hug and presented their daughter Rachael to an astonished Sadie. The great, wide eyes and jet-black hair should have told her that this was Rachael. She is gorgeous, not the pretty little girl Sadie remembered. She had forgotten that other lives go on at the same time her life was unreeling like the film on those new picture shows.

Exchanging hugs all around, they coaxed Sadie to have dinner with them. She told them about her meeting with Mr. St. James and the result of his use of the spittoon while he talked to her.

"I know. Isn't he awful? I wonder how Aunt Jessie ever picked him to be her lawyer," said Rachael. "If I remember correctly, she didn't hold with booze or chewing tobacco."

"You're right, Rachael, do you think we dare ask him to go with us when we go to dinner? Sadie questioned. "And just where are we going to eat, I don't have a great deal of money and I don't think we can wash dishes or sing for our supper."

Lorrie settled the question of dinner when she announced, "Sadie's buying dinner for us at her eatery downtown."

"What are you talking about? I don't own a restaurant. I barely had enough money to come to New York, much less buy a restaurant in this town!"

"Whoa, girl, Jessie owned one of the finest eateries in this town and now it is yours. St. James told us yesterday. The bulk of her estate went to you, her special child. We meet tomorrow to find out what she left us, but whatever it turns out to be will be undeserved. Having her for a friend was enough."

Sadie quickly readied herself for the excursion to Jessie's Place. The building was the same one Harrison had helped her rent many years ago and now occupied the whole block. The restaurant covered the main floor; the upper rooms were offices and apartments. Jessie had long ago decided to buy the building, so a landlord could never rule her life again.

When they entered the door music began to play, a saxophone greeted her with a rendition of "Ain't She Sweet." The crowd stood and cheered. Harrison, looking older but just as handsome, stepped forward and taking her arm, led her to a table near the dance floor, where Seth and Samuel played in the band.

"When did you have the time to plan all this," Sadie asked.

Don't forget most of us still live here. It was no hardship to get together and make plans for a surprise party for you, my dear," replied Harrison

They had it all planned! How long has it been since she'd seen some of these people? She had completely forgotten the two boys, Seth and Samuel, but evidently Jessie hadn't. What a remarkable woman she was.

The evening was a fantastic blur of friends and acquaintances, most she remembered, a few she didn't but the others did, so they were made to feel welcome as well. Sadie felt a vague feeling of guilt come over her. Here she was dining in a fabulous restaurant and her family at home barely had enough to eat. Tomorrow she must send them some money to tide them over till she got back. But did she really want to go back to Michigan? Better she should bring her family here where she could run the business, and live in one of the apartments in the building. It would solve all their problems. Coming to that decision she let herself relax, drink some wine, and feel the warmth fill her whole body. She wondered why she hadn't enjoyed this pleasant surge of well being more often. She didn't have to crawl into a bottle like she had seen some people do; she would only have a drink once in a while to cheer her up. *Sure,* she thought, I *had a problem when I was younger, but now I know what too much can do. I've learned my lesson.*

When the food came she was too excited to eat, but sipped at her second glass of wine. Her head began to whirl, the people in the room began to change shape, her head refused to stay up, and she went face first into a plate of fried chicken and dumplings. Her friends pulled her head out of the food, cleaned her face and hair, and carried her to her room.

When she awoke the next morning, her head hurt, her stomach was growling and she couldn't remember coming to her room, undressing or getting into bed. She had felt this way twice before and both times it was from strong drink. Never again! She hurried and dressed for the meeting with Mr. St. James. The clock was just striking one when she entered his office. The others were there, waiting for her to arrive so he could read the will. It was pretty much as her friends had told her except for a codicil, stating she must change the name of the restaurant from "Aunt Jessie's" to something more fitting, "Cuz I's don' owns it no mo."

Sadie broke down and cried, great, agonizing cries tore from her.

"If I had only known that she was ill, I would have come to her. Why didn't you let me know when I talked to you? Is that where you were when you took that vacation so abruptly, here with Jessie?"

Lorrie nodded her head. "That's when you were having your last miscarriage, John had just died and you didn't need any more heartache at that time. Besides, Jessie didn't want you to know. She said if you knew, you would hurt yourself coming here to be with her and she wouldn't hurt you for the world. We all took turns visiting with her till the end. It took her three years to lose that battle. She fought right up to the end."

Harrison pulled up a chair next to Sadie, put his arm around her shoulder and squeezed her gently, "One thing that worried Jessie was your obvious danger of being poisoned by the grape. She informed me she had that same problem and I should warn you that she had to fight it to her dying day."

"What happened last night? Did I make a fool of myself, and how did I get to my room?" She didn't want to know, but she had to ask. She had already made up her mind that the warm feeling wine gave her did not compensate for the humiliation she felt the next day. Jessie had saved her from this evil once and now she was coming back from the grave to do it again.

"Your friends know how hard Jessie's death has hit you, plus you hadn't eaten much in the last two days, so the wine hit you especially hard." Harrison's words of excuse made her all the more embarrassed. She stood up as tall as she could, looked each one of her friends straight in the eye, and swore her life long abstinence from any kind of alcohol.

"Jessie was right. For me it's the devil's brew and I won't let it destroy my life.

Mr. St. James spoke to the group in his office for the first time since they had arrived. "That is how I met Jessie. She picked me out of the gutter, cleaned me up, and gave me a place to stay. Her only rule was no alcohol.

She kicked me in the seat of the pants, told me to get out there and pass the bar exam, and stop feeling sorry for myself. I fell off the wagon once and believe me she did everything except kick me out on the street. She said that came next! I loved and respected that woman even when she gave me hell for being such a slob with my tobacco. She said I was worse than a rutting pig with that dam cud in my mouth. She knew I chewed when I wanted a drink so damn bad I ached, but she gave me hell anyway." He chuckled just thinking of Jessie raising Cain.

"I would have married her if she had been white and would have me. She was some woman! A rutting pig, indeed!" he blustered.

Lorrie and Sadie burst out in laughter. "That is exactly what we were thinking when we saw you chewing that cud," stuttered Sadie. She was laughing so hard she could barely talk.

"Well, ladies, you can't change me. It has been tried by the best and she failed. The only time I ever did see that women fail at anything she set her mind to."

Rachael smiled at him and said, "If Aunt Jessie could put up with it, then I can, too."

It was decided they would all go out and celebrate Sadie's good fortune, although they warned Francis (for that was his given name) St. James, he could not take his chew with him to the party. He chuckled at their concerns; he was in too good a mood to be upset by their request. He hadn't felt this good in years. Damn, it was great to be in the company of friends. He hadn't realized how much he missed that sense of belonging.

When Sadie had called Katy and Jared to tell them the news, she had gotten a long silence at the other end, then happy congratulations from her daughter.

"What's going on? Aren't you happy we won't have to worry about a place to live, food for our table, an education for the boys?"

"Yes, Mama, we are, but Jarod and I have talked about our future. We've decided it is right here in Michigan, not in New York."

"Then I will give you the newspaper, that fool running it hasn't payed rent for a year and that's long enough. That way Jared will have employment and you will have a roof over your head. I do wish you would be closer when the new baby is born, but I can come there when it is almost time. Of course, that won't stop me from worrying."

"Mama, The boys are old enough to ride the train by themselves, and will jump at the chance to have an adventure on their own."

"Oh, I know. It's just that I would feel less apprehensive if you and Jared were coming, too. While I'm on the telephone, do you need anything else?"

"No, Mother, Jared wants to make it on his own as much as possible. I know he will pay you back someday for the gift of the newspaper."

"Katy, he never has to pay me back. All he has to do is be a good husband and father. You know I love him like a son."

Jonathan and James boarded the train for New York the very next day. They could hardly contain themselves during the trip. The times were getting better, and more people were beginning to travel. Young men and women were going away to school. Young women were just beginning to fight for their independence in the academic world. They now had hope for a better life in the future. The desire to become doctors, lawyers, and judges was no longer just a dream.

The brothers watched wide-eyed and opened mouth at the antics of their fellow travelers. The young students, away from home for the first time, were in a playful mood and no one was exempt from their horseplay. They began by singing rowdy tunes just to see the ladies blush. When they became bored with that ploy, they arm wrestled in the dining coach, the winner ordering sarsaparilla for the ladies brave enough to watch

One young lady, with the most beautiful eyes he had ever seen, watched Jonathon instead of the two boys who were struggling to overcome the other with brute strength, and putting on quite a show for the crowd. When their eyes met, Jonathan felt as though he had been hit with a bale of hay, no damage done, just numb from shock. What was it about this girl that made him feel as if he had always known her? He had been searching for her his whole life. He wasn't comfortable with this situation; he was used to being in charge of what happened in his life. He was the leader who made things happen, not the other way around.

James watched his brother, thinking to himself, *what is going on between these two that can happen with out knowing, touching, or even smiling at each other?* Whatever it was it scared him. *I hope it never happens to me. Jonathan was brave enough to handle it. I would fall all over myself if a girl stared at me like that. I will say one thing: it's the first time he has been silent in years. It just isn't natural. Oh, well, it will be over when we get to New York.*

James felt himself getting sleepy. His head nodded several times, the rhythmic pulse of the rails lulled him to that place between sleep and wakefulness. His head grew too heavy to hold erect. He felt it slip sideways, gave up the fight, and slipped into a deep dream filled slumber. When he awakened, Jonathan was sitting with the girl with the beautiful emerald colored eyes. Her jet-black hair was piled high on her head, her suit was the same shade of violet as her eyes, and she wore a small pin on her lapel. It was shaped like a heart, she opened it and showed Jonathan what was inside, and he laughed, took her hand, and shook it vigorously.

Waving his hand, motioning for James to join them, he introduced the young lady, "This young lady is Aunt Lorrie and Uncle Evan's daughter Sadie. Remember, they spent one summer with us at the cottage. Can you believe this; we knew each other since we were children. Small world, isn't it? Sadie, show James the picture in your locket. You won't believe this. It's like we're all family!" The picture was of Sadie and John taken on their wedding day. It had been sent to Sadie on her fifth birthday and was a treasure to the wearer.

The girl grinned. "I wish I were as beautiful as my namesake, your mother. Her name is perfect for her. I prefer everyone call me Sid. I'd feel more comfortable with it. Then I won't feel like a turkey with a swan's name."

The brothers fell all over each other trying to convince her that she was more beautiful than their mother. After all, their Sadie was just mother to them. They began to see mother through the eyes of the girl. Mother had been a beauty in her day, but she had changed from a beautiful girl to a lovely, mature, graceful woman whom they loved and respected. They couldn't imagine men being head over heels in love with Mother. After all she was old, and old people didn't really think about those things, or did they?

When the train arrived at the station in Buffalo, Sid was torn between wanting to stay with these newly found old friends and seeing her parents. Visiting her grandparents had been wonderful, but she had gotten lonesome after the first two weeks. The next two weeks had dragged into a month and Sid was ready to start walking home by the time the ticket finally came. She was a little hurt by her father's attitude when she spoke to him on the Saturday night before she had left. He had seemed so distant as though he really didn't want her to come home at all. Well, she would show him. First, she would find out what was happening to make them change so much, then she would make arrangements to go somewhere else to live if they didn't want her there. She was putting on a good front for the brothers, but her heart was breaking.

As the newfound friends waved their good-byes, the fates were conjuring up a delightful twist for the girl with the violet eyes. Her father met her at the station, looking suddenly very old and drawn. Her heart gave a lurch when she saw him.

"Papa, what has happened, why are you looking so tired? Is something wrong with Mama? I have been so worried about you both, why didn't you let me come home to help?" Evan just smiled a tired smile and answered, " You will know very soon what has been happening since you were gone. It will be a pleasant surprise, I hope."

The first sound she heard when she entered the house was the muffled cry of a baby. She gave Evan a questioning glance and rushed into the parlor. There on the chaise lay her mother with a tiny bundle tucked into her arm. The bundle began to squirm like a cotton caterpillar edging toward the engorged breast that was filled with the elixir of life.

Sid couldn't believe her eyes. When did this happen, and why didn't she know her mother was having a child? Why did they keep it a secret from her? She turned on her father, angry beyond words, "How dare you make me miss this important part of our lives!" With that outburst hanging in the deathly still room, she ran to the stairs. Taking two at a time she ascended to her room and flung herself on the bed, floating in a sea of self-pity and wailing as if her heart were breaking.

In the room below the worried parents tried to console each other. They each knew Sid had been deeply hurt by their secret, but they also felt they did the right thing in keeping the news from her until the live, healthy baby was on the scene. When the doctor told them they may never see this child alive, they made their decision to keep it from their "little Sadie," or Sid as she preferred to be called. She had wanted a brother or sister for so long and now there was a chance the child would be born dead.

"The irony of it, my dear, is she's almost old enough to have her own child."

When Evan said that to his beloved Lorrie, both were shocked. He repeated slowly, "She is almost old enough to have her own child. My God, Lorrie, what have we done? No wonder she's angry. She is a young woman now, and we excluded her from something she should have shared with us. Can we ever forgive ourselves? More important, can Sid forgive us for our foolishness in thinking we were saving her from heart break?"

"I don't know, Evan, but I do know we need her to forgive us and get on with living our lives as a family. We have wasted enough time these last few months hiding and pretending nothing was wrong. Now we must explain to her all the things the doctor said could happen, the chance that Michael would never be a normal child, might need care for the rest of his life. This is too important to keep secret from Sid. I hope she doesn't hate us." The pressure in her breast filled Lorrie with contentment. They could weather any storm as long as they were a close-knit family. Their love for each other would help them over the pitfalls of life.

Evan went to Sid's room, knocked gently on the door, waited a few minutes, then opened it a crack. Sid had cried herself to sleep, her right hand was over her head, as if to ward off a blow. Evan felt his stomach flip, a sense of depression swept over him, so much tension these last few months. He wondered if they had done the right thing, trying to have another child so late in life. Had they brought all this on themselves? He let Sadie sleep and went down to Lorrie, took the sleeping child, sat in the rocker near the fireplace, tucked Michael into his left arm, all the while slowly rocking and humming a lullaby he had learned from Jessie.

Lorrie lay watching her husband and child, thinking, *I'm the luckiest woman in the world. With this wonderful family we can survive whatever the world throws at us. Sid, damn, I wish she would let us call her Sadie. Oh, well, Sid is too sensible to let this stand in the way for very long. She will forgive us when we explain everything.*

When Sid first awakened, she couldn't understand why she had slept in her clothes and then she remembered what had happened. It didn't seem so bad in the morning light. They must have had a really good reason to keep this from her, and she was going down right now to find out what that reason was! She washed her face, tidied her hair, noticed the dark shadows beneath her puffy eyes, shrugged her shoulders and stuck out her tongue at the girl in the mirror, feeling suddenly warm and happy to be home.

Jonathan couldn't wait to see his mother and tell her whom they had met on the train. James shyly kept his thoughts to himself. He thought, *Sid was the most beautiful girl in the whole world, but, of course, she hardly even noticed him, her attention was hogged by that show off brother of his. Oh, well, Jonathan was always the center of attention when they met someone new.* "I will always be standing in his shadow, second in birth, second in life, but I'll be damned if I'll be second with Sid. She is too real to be bamboozled by him.

Sadie watched her boys while they were relating the adventure on the train; she saw the quiet determination in James's eye and the set of his chin. She had seen that same look in her own eyes when she thought of Marcus. *Dearest Marcus, how long has it been since I've seen you, and yet you're still here in my heart, and mind? I still feel you holding me; the taste of your lips will never leave me. I still catch a whiff of the bay rum you used after shaving. I seem to know when your thoughts are with me. When things are settled, I must find out what has happened to you and if you're happy. Maybe, just maybe, there is still a chance for us.*

James saw his mother leave, going to that hidden world she sometimes escaped to when things were moving too fast. True, she was here in the room listening, or at least she seemed to be, but James knew she had that secret place in her mind that she didn't share with anyone. He first noticed it when he was still a child; she had a way of retreating. She seemed to be withdrawing from the room and people who were there. Her eyes were seeing other places and times. How he wished he could share that place with her. He had mentioned it to Jonathan once, but he was sorry he had. Jonathan thought he was getting loony like that kid down the street in Bay City who talked to his invisible dog.

Chapter Twenty-Three
The Meeting

Sadie came back to the conversation just as Jonathan said, "and the girl was Sadie, I mean Sid. That's what she likes to be called now. You know, Aunt Lorrie and Uncle Evan's daughter!"

"How wonderful that you should meet that way. Did you remember each other at first?"

"No, Mother, but as soon as we began talking, I just felt so at home with her, it seemed as if I knew her all my life and I did!" He jumped up, danced around the table, shouting "I'm gonna get that girl and make her mine!"

Oh, my God, thought Sadie. *Lorrie and Evan have enough to worry about without Jonathan busting into the picture, wanting to court their young daughter. Besides, these children are too young to be thinking about that sort of thing right now.* She glanced in James's direction and saw the knowing look. *He knows*, she told herself. *He is so observant; some day I will share my secret with him.*

He would understand. He is caring and considerate, not like his wild, brash, insensitive brother. They are both good boys, but the midwife had the wrong son in mind when she predicted that James would be my problem child.

That was a moment James would come to cherish, the momentary sharing between his mother and himself. In that instant he knew his mother was in tune with him in a way that she and Jonathan could never be. Warmth engulfed him, bathing him in acceptance. For the first time in his life he felt like the superior brother. He knew he would never look at Jonathan again without feeling pity.

Jonathan was still talking, parading around the room, so tied up in his own dreams and adventures that he never noticed the gradual change in his once shy brother. James was standing taller, shoulders thrown back, ready to meet whatever fate had in store for him.

Sadie just smiled. She had seen her son James grow before her very eyes. It was a welcome sadness that wretched her gut in a gentle way. The sadness that she felt when Katy married was not her first experience with the loss of a child, but it was more meaningful because it was her first birth child. The loss of Rachael to Philip and Cathy was nothing compared to the emptiness she felt when Katy and Jared decided to stay in Michigan. It was as if an important piece of her flesh was being torn from her body, an extension of her love was being ripped away, never to be a part of her person again. She mentally shook herself, brought her attention back to her older son who was still strutting around the room like a peacock; unaware of how childish he looked in his mother's eyes.

Sadie slowly explained to her sons the circumstances of Sid's homecoming and the painful secret Lorrie and Evan had kept from Sid to protect her. When she had finished her report of the events, James came to his mother, placed his hand on her shoulder, and squeezed it gently.

"Growing up isn't always as wonderfully or exciting as we like to think. I wish we could be there for all of them. Is the baby well? Is there anything we can do?"

"What fun," exclaimed Jonathan. "Can we travel to Buffalo to see them? That would give me a chance to see Sid again."

"For God's sake, Jonathan, think of someone else for a change. This isn't the time to intrude on other people's lives," Sadie said disdainfully. "They are going to need time together. They don't need the three of us barging in on them!"

"We could stay at a hotel," Jonathan said sullenly. "We wouldn't be in their way. We can afford that now, can't we?"

"Well, we are not going yet and that's that!" Casting a disgusted look at her elder son, Sadie left the room.

"What's her problem?" asked Jonathan. "We wouldn't be in the way, maybe we could help. I'm getting tired of Mother always telling us what to do. She doesn't know everything. She don't know about young love or she don't remember what it is like to be young and full of passion." The angry young man stalked out of the room and headed for the street, bound to find out about this New World called New York City. He made his way to the subway entrance and descended to the platform. Strolling the length of the station, he decided he liked this mode of transportation the best. Besides, he was sure Mother would not buy him an automobile; she would say he was too young. *Dammit, when would he be old enough to do the fun things?* As he strode the walkway, thinking of a girl with violet eyes, he caught a flurry of movement out on the platform ahead.

Two cocky young toughs were accosting a young girl accompanied by an elderly woman; they were frightened, cowering against the marble walls, their packages strewn on the floor around them. The attackers were tearing into the packages, holding up underthings and making obscene remarks to the terrified women. The enraged Jonathan let out a howl that echoed through the tunnels that made up the station. He charged the offenders like a wild bull, head down, and shoulders hunched, looking very much like a wild animal. The two ragged villains dropped their spoils and ran toward the opposite entrance, looking back with naked fear in their eyes.

Jonathan braked at the point where the women were shakily trying to pick up their belongings and hastily shoving them into torn boxes. Both embarrassed and distressed, they thanked their brave rescuer, stumbling over the words while trying to hide the undergarments from his sight. He started to help them pick up their clothing, but was not permitted to touch the delicate wisps of lace and satin. The girl took his arm, led him a few steps away from the place where the older woman was gathering up the intimate things. The old woman continued retrieving the wispy garments and deposited them in a canvas bag she carried over her arm.

When the whole incident was over, the girl told him that she and her Nanny had gone shopping without permission, so her father must never hear of this.

"I must admit, I am responsible for this whole mess. Nanny didn't want to go, but I made her. I told her I would go alone if she didn't go with me. I was being a spoiled, childish little fool. I have learned my lesson. From now on I will listen to Papa."

Jonathan understood exactly how the repentant girl felt, but he was thankful that he was on the spot when she needed him. He had to admit to himself, she wasn't as lovely as Sid was, but there was something about her that made him feel all queasy inside. *What was that all about,* he asked himself. *Was he as fickle as the young girls he flirted with back home? No, it had to be the excitement of the chase, just a reaction, nothing more.* The women were standing waiting for him to escort them from the station, clutching their bundles looking a little worse for the fracas they had been through.

A thoroughly confident Jonathan took the girl's arm, then dropped it, tipped his hat and introduced himself, first to nanny, and then to the girl, saying, "I'm Jonathan Davis. We just moved here from Michigan. You must meet my family. My mother will love you."

A delighted giggle escaped the girl's lips. She extended her hand, took his, and announced, "I'm Josie Vandermeer. My father, nanny, and I live together. We must figure out a way to introduce you to my father without telling him how we met. Nanny will go along with anything I say.

"I would just tell him the truth, if I were you. Sure, you're in trouble at first, but what happens when he finds out you lied to him? Then he will really be angry. It is always better to face the music and get it over with. All he can do is scold you." *Am I really giving this advice to a total stranger?* Jonathan asked himself. *I sound like a namby pamby little mama's boy. Oh, hell, if she wants to lie to her father it's up to her. Why should I give advice? I've done enough stretching the truth myself from time to time.*

Nanny stepped up and stated, "I vill tell your fader vhere we vere and vot happened, so you should do the same, ya?"

"Oh, all right, I will tell him, but I really don't want to."

The trio made their way to the street above, turned right walked toward the trolley car stop, sat on the bench and waited for the next car that would take them to meet Josie's father and the punishment she would receive.

Meanwhile Sadie walked the floor trying to keep calm, and picture where her eldest son could be, her imagination running wild. He was in an accident, he was mugged and lying in an alley someplace bleeding to death. *Dear God, don't let that be so,* she prayed as she remembered many years ago the way John O'Shonessy died. She seemed to spend a lot of time remembering how her friends had died. So much violence. She shook away the thoughts of death, but a sense of foreboding lingered in the back of her mind. She jumped when she heard the door burst open. An exuberant Jonathan grabbed her up, whirled her around in a wild dance of joyous frenzy. She fought to keep the fury from her voice.

"Where in hell have you been? I've been half-crazy wondering what had happened to you! I could just beat you within an inch of your life for making me worry so!"

Shock filled his face. "Mother, I never heard you use foul language before. You must really be upset with me. I didn't think you would worry about me. You know I can take care of myself. As matter of fact, I saved a young girl and her nanny from being manhandled by two toughs in the subway station today. Oh, yes, and I also met her father, Mr. Vandermeer, quite a gentleman. I must admit he wasn't too happy to meet me until Josie, by the way that's the girl's name, explained how she met me. He was very grateful that I was there to save his daughter and her nanny. We are all invited to dinner next Wednesday, if it is convenient for you."

"You will be lucky if you are able to walk after I strap you for all the worry you caused me," she sputtered. "I know I'm not making much sense, but you have to remember I was worried sick. A young man in a strange town, out on his own, without a inkling as to what can happen in a big city."

"I'm sorry, Mother, I didn't think. I won't do that again. I will let you know where I am or call from now on. I promise, swear to God," he said crossing his heart.

James walked into the room as his brother was swearing his promise. He looked askance at his mother and she returned his puzzled look with the sweetest smile and said, "I think your brother has grown up a little!"

Jonathan called and confirmed the dinner invitation, then went to his room to dream about the lovely Josie.

The night of the dinner came all too soon for Sadie; she was not in the mood to meet someone who thought her son was a hero. She still hadn't reconciled herself to the fact that her family had grown up and no longer needed her. When they entered the Vandermeer apartment she was impressed with the quiet elegance. Mr. Vandermeer's friendly greeting helped them get over the awkward introductions.

He was rather straitlaced, in her opinion, but she was courteous to him. *The evening had gone rather well,* she thought as she was preparing herself some cocoa before she went to bed. She needed something to calm her down after the wild ride home. When they left the dinner party, Jonathan asked if he could drive home to the hotel. Sadie absentmindedly said yes. Much to her dismay he drove like he lived: fast and furiously attacking each street as though it was a racetrack. James reminded him he was driving way too fast with their mother in the auto. Slowing down, he apologized to Sadie and James saying, "I'm sorry, I guess I still haven't grown up all the way. I love driving fast. I guess I'll have to learn to fly, so there won't be anyone in my way."

Sadie had taken over the ownership of the restaurant, feeling right at home in her dealings with the patrons. One of her first obligations was to change the name of the business. After much soul searching she decided on a name she had heard in connection with Mr. Roosevelt, and his campaign to get people back to work and out of the bread lines. She called it "The New Deal." The name fit her business perfectly. She had a sign maker start on it immediately.

"The New Deal" became the place to go for everyone who was someone, or wanted to be seen. Through the front door walked most of the prominent people in New York, but at the back door, the hungry, wretched and poor found a meal and a few coins to tide them over. The important people were willing to pay the inflated prices just to be seen in the company of Sadie and her friends. That made it possible for Sadie to help a few families survive the devastating years of the Depression.

"Katy and Jared had called this morning. I'm grandmother to a healthy seven-pound girl named Bethany Ann. Jared told me she is beautiful just like her mother and me."

Chuckling, Sadie told James and Jonathon, "I'm happy that he loves our Katy so much that he sees her beauty, but I fear he is full of blarney when it comes to the truth about his mother-in-law." A surge of love for the child she hadn't seen coursed through Sadie, but she also experienced a strange feeling of jealousy toward Katy. She knew she was being silly, but she remembered the warmth that entered her mind and soul when she became a mother, and she knew she would never experience it again, but Katy would.

She suddenly felt old and tired. She sat in the rocker and thought about the path that had brought her here to this place in her life. She got up and searched through the cedar chest for her one last quilt. It was one she was saving for a special time in her life.

Well, she thought, *it couldn't get more special than being a grandmother for the first time.* "Should I send it to Katy for the child or should I keep it till I see her? No, I'll keep it for her until I'm ready to let go of it. There's no rush, and she has plenty of time to wait for it." She folded it the long way and put it at the foot of her bed. She went back to the rocker and slowly moved the chair closer to the window. Tears were running down her cheeks. She was happy and sad. Happy for the gift of a granddaughter and sad for her youth that she had lost along the way.

Sid called once in a while, wanting to talk to Jonathan, but he usually was out when she called, and she ended up talking to James most of the time. James had decided on a career in law instead of architecture and spent most of his nights studying. He would tell her how school was going; he was in his third year of law school, looking forward to getting out into the "real world" as he called it. Sid began looking forward to their talks and was glad when she missed catching Jonathan at home. Soon James began to call her, always finding an excuse for calling. One night, after he had given a very poor excuse for calling, she whispered, "But I love talking to you and hope you will continue to call."

He hung up the earpiece after a half-hour of conversation, did a little jig and hugged his mother. "She wants me to call her every week, can you believe that?"

"Yes, son, I can believe that. Lorrie and Evan didn't raise a fool. That girl knows a good man when she sees one. By the way how are they doing with little Michael?"

"He is learning more and more every day. He will never be a doctor or lawyer, but he will be able to earn a living. He is a gentle, happy little boy whom everybody loves."

Jonathan was busy getting himself elected to every office that came his way; he was becoming quite an influence in the Democratic Party. His charming ways and gift of gab took him to many influential meetings and house parties. He managed to convince Josie to attend with him, even though she was bored and felt out of place at these events. Her schooling finished, she was working in her father's clothing store. She had excellent taste in colors and style, but her father made her apprentice under his long time buyer, George. George was a loud, effeminate bully, but he had made a fair amount of currency for Mr. Vandermeer, so, as her father said, "You don't change horses in mid-stream, especially when he makes you money."

Josie always hated those darn parties, all those stinky men and their stinky cigars, those old codgers were always trying to look down the front of her dress. Well, she made sure they didn't see anything they weren't supposed to. Some of the women at the parties bent just a little to let them peer into those forbidden places, but not her. If they want to see that, they should be at home with their wives! Besides, she belonged to Jonathan; he was the only one who could see the mysteries she possessed. She just hoped father wouldn't find out. He would kill them both.

Sometimes she wished mother were here. She missed her terribly. Jonathan's mother was good to her and seemed to like her, but there was nothing like you own mother. Father never said why she left, but Josie heard the cook and Nanny talking when they thought they were alone. Was it too hard for her to live with father and his rules? Why didn't she take me with her? Didn't she love me? When Josie got in a pensive mood not much could get her out of it; Jonathan called it her whiney mood and refused to discuss it.

Sadie often wondered what happened to change Josie; she had liked the girl when she first met her, but she had changed into a whiney, clinging female that seemed to need Jonathan's constant attention. *She'll be all right,* Sadie told herself, *she's just in love and doesn't know it. When that son of mine wakes ups and realizes that she loves him, all will work out.*

Chapter Twenty-Four
Fate Steps In

Sadie had been working all morning getting ready for the busy night ahead at the restaurant when in walked Marcus. On his arm was a lovely young woman, dressed in the latest fashion. Her hair was golden blonde, her eyes were aquamarine blue and she smiled up at him as if he were the only man on earth.

Sadie's heart leaped in her breast. Would he recognize her? Dear God, she must look a fright. Maybe God will be merciful and he won't recognize me. She ducked her head a little, yet wanted to savor the sight of him after so many years. The hunger for his touch raged in her veins, an overwhelming feeling of lust swept through her whole being. She went weak with desire.

Marcus glanced her way, stared hard at the woman behind the counter, looked again, and burst out laughing.

Sadie wanted to shrink up and blow away. She knew she had changed, but not so much that it was laughable. Had she turned that unattractive?

He ran to the counter, came round the end, grabbed the shaking Sadie, pulled her to his open arms and enfolded her to his chest. He was both laughing and crying now, his tears and hers mingling on the wet surface of each other's lips.

The blonde girl stood back watching with a smile on her face. Her eyes watched his every move, enjoying the scene to which she was privy. At last the two lovers tore themselves apart, still touching hands, afraid to lose each other for even a moment.

Marcus motioned the girl to come to the counter. When she got close enough, Sadie could see the resemblance in her face.

"Sadie, I would like you to meet my eldest daughter Stephanie. Her brother and sister live with their mother, but Stephanie lives here in New York with me.

"Do you know how long I've searched for you? When I finally found you in Michigan, you were happily married and had a family. There was no way I could intrude on your life at that time. I recently heard you are a widow, are you still alone?

Heart pounding, Sadie enthusiastically nodded yes.

Marcus's liquid brown eyes reflected his undying love for a joyful Sadie.

"When can we meet? How long have you worked here? So many questions I want answered, but, thank God, I found you!"

Stephanie reached out and took Sadie's hand, squeezed it gently, and smiled at her father.

"You're right, Father, she is as lovely as you said, but we must let her get back to work." With a low laugh she teased her exultant Father, "come Papa, we don't want to cause her trouble or God forbid, make her lose her job. Maybe we can meet her for a quiet dinner later."

It was Sadie's turn to express amusement as she told them that she was the employer and they could have dinner right now. She was buying!

The meal was a combination of wonderful food and marvelous company; Sadie couldn't remember when she was so happy. Stephanie was a delight. She not only knew about her father's love for Sadie, but she was in favor of it. For so many unhappy years she had watched her father long for the love of his life.

Sadie had this sense of unreality, a vague unrest that hounded her whenever she felt that life was starting to turn out the way it should. *Oh, dear God*, she thought, *not now. Please let us spend the rest of our lives loving each other. Our being together won't hurt anyone. We deserve a little of the contentment that others share.*

All too soon the meal ended and they walked out into the brisk night air. Marcus hailed a cabbie, tucked Stephanie into the seat, instructed the driver where to take her and turned to Sadie.

"We, my girl, are going to spend the rest of the night getting reacquainted." Hand in hand they began to walk toward Central Park exchanging reminiscences of the good times and the bad times in their separate lives; sometimes laughing, sometimes murmuring sympathetic regret. When they came to the fountain in the park, they stood staring at the water dancing out of the angel on top. She seemed to be reaching out her hand in blessing, her face shining down on the lovers with compassion for the years lost, extending the fragile cord that still bound them for the rest of their lives.

The streets were teeming with people from all walks of life: the well dressed businessman and his companion, the dock workers up town to see the "Swells" on their night out, the ragged urchin selling flowers, and shoeshine boys with their boxes slung over their shoulders or tucked beneath their bottoms while they polished the gents' shoes. Sadie was really seeing all this for the first time. It was as if she hadn't really lived until now and had only gone through the motions. Her heart was full, almost to bursting. Please let it last, she prayed. At the height of five foot eight inches, Sadie was usually face to face with most men. She secretly delighted in the fact that she had to look up to see Marcus' wonderfully crooked smile. She wanted to reach out and brush the crisp curly lock of hair from his forehead. His once dark hair was now streaked with silver, which only made him more attractive to Sadie.

Marcus found a small café just off the beaten path. They took a table in the dim corner, where he ordered coffee and they sat consuming each other with their eyes. After the coffee had been served, Marcus broke the silence. Taking her hand he touched the white area where her wedding ring used to be. Rubbing it gently, he said, "I know I shouldn't be jealous of a dead man, but I am. He had you for so many years and I could only stay away and yearn for what he had. Our lives have taken so many twists and turns, but now we are back together to stay forever. I hope you feel that way, too."

"Yes, my darling, I do, but I don't regret those years with John. I loved him, too, in a different way, but love just the same. We had our children to keep us united. I wouldn't trade them for anything. You must meet my children. You will love them as I do. Katy, my oldest is married and has a little girl; my twin boys are getting on with their lives, too. I was beginning to feel life passing me by. They no longer need me," she said wistfully.

"Well, I do," Marcus, whispered quietly. "I need you for the rest of my life." They left the café, slowly walking toward Sadie's apartment.

The doorman held the door. As they moved through the opening toward the elevator, he heard Marcus say, "The beginning of a love that has no end."

David called the next morning. He and Sarah would be in the city for a couple of days and he wondered if they could stay with Sadie. She wanted to tell her brother about Marcus, but she decided to wait until she could tell him face to face. She didn't know how he would take it, but he would just have to understand. She needed Marcus to complete her existence. She wanted David and Sarah to meet Marcus. After all, David was so young when he had last seen his cousin Marcus. Would he remember him? Would he hate him for loving her? Well, time would tell. Just have to wait and see.

Why can't life ever be easy? Kate had not crossed her mind in many years, but now she seemed as if she were right here in this room, cautioning her against being too happy, too giving.

Marcus left before the sun rose, "To protect your name," he said. Sadie laughed at the very thought. She reminded him where they had loved so many years ago. Placing her hands on Marcus's slightly wrinkled cheeks, gazing into his warm brown eyes, she spoke softly, as though to a child. "True, I have been a respected wife and mother all these years, but that young, daring, wisp of a girl is still inside, peeping out of these tired old eyes and she still adores you, my love."

Sadie wondered what her brother David's reaction would be to her and Marcus' love, and plans to marry. Sadie invited him and James to have lunch with her at, "The New Deal."

No time like the present to find out, she thought as she blurted out, "David, Marcus and I have been seeing each other and would like to continue, but I also would like your blessing on the relationship. I value your opinion and hope you will see this as our only chance for real love."

"My dear sister, I not only give my blessing, but I would like to perform the nuptials when the time is right. Sarah will be ecstatic when she hears the news; she has been hoping that you two would get together. He made quite an impression on my Sarah. She has talked about nothing else since meeting him last night."

"I wouldn't have anyone else marry us, but we would like to wait a little while. We need to get reacquainted and I have a business to run. I can't just throw everything aside and elope like a young girl, much as I would like to."

"James, Marcus has asked me to spend a few weeks with him in Boston, while he is on business there and I'm thinking of going. Do you think you could look in on the restaurant while I'm away?"

"Of course, Mother, I would be glad to. You need some time away to rest, relax, and explore your feelings."

David earnestly exclaimed, "Yes, big sister, the time away together will do you both a world of good!"

The next morning, Sadie went to Jonathon's office to inform and discuss her plans for the trip with Marcus. When she broached the subject of her trip, Jonathon exploded with a tornado of abuse.

"Mother, you can't be serious! Going away with a man you're not married to just before the election is unforgivable. What will it do to my voting public's impression of me? My voters will think I'm not of high moral character when they find out my mother is running off with a divorced man and behaving like a common whore."

Sadie couldn't believe her ears. This is the same lad that just a few years ago had broken every rule and flaunted his misdeeds in the face of authority, and now he was judging her. She turned on her heel and marched out of his office, determined to make that trip come hell or high water.

Sadie and Marcus, giggling like giddy newly weds, left the next day on the first train to Boston.

Sadie didn't tell Marcus about her discussion with Jonathon, but somehow he knew. He was especially gentle with her and proudly introduced her to everyone they came in contact with as, "My future wife."

During the day they visited art museums, attended plays, and were entertained by business partners as though they were royalty. A couple of days were spent window-shopping for furniture. Their nights were spent sharing the love they had for each other.

"The nights are never long enough," Sadie complained to Marcus.

"I know, my darling, but I love waking up and finding you lying next to me, I hope that pleasure never has to end. Do you know that you smile that crooked little smile I love so much even when you're sleeping?"

"Have you been lying here watching me sleep? I do believe you are smitten," she teased.

"Guilty as charged," Marcus teased back. "Darling, please call home and ask James if he would mind watching out for things one more week. If we can extend the trip for an extra seven days, I will be content until the wedding day."

As usual James was more then happy to comply with their wishes.

"It's a shame your boys aren't more alike when it comes to giving," Marcus whispered as he stroked her cheek, "One gives and the other takes."

"I know, my sweet, but I love them equally, and one of these days Jonathon will grow up and realize he isn't the center of the universe. Hope springs eternal in a mother."

Being held and loved by Marcus was to Sadie the most complete time in her life. She, too, hated the thought of going back to reality, but they must. These three weeks had been heaven to the lovers, but the real world was waiting.

Two weeks had gone by and Jonathon still hadn't called his mother, even though he was well aware they were back from their trip to Boston. Sadie was hurt by his callous behavior and stated her unhappiness over the situation to Marcus as they were having dinner.

"Give him time," consoled Marcus, "you know he likes to shoot his mouth off with out thinking. He will come around in time. Meanwhile you have all the rest of the family with you, and they understand our feelings for each other. We should set the day for our marriage. Maybe that will sooth the savage beast."

After escorting Sadie up to her flat above the restaurant, Marcus made his way back to his apartment across town. Stephanie greeted her father with a hug, kiss and a question, "Daddy when Are you two going to tie the knot? I see how happy you are when you're with Sadie, and how lonely you are without her and I have to wonder why you're waiting "

"Whoa, little miss nosey posy. Yes we are as you young ones say, going to tie the knot, but not for a while. Sadie hasn't set the date yet. I would have the nuptials tomorrow if it was up to me, but it isn't. Meanwhile, I'm going to keep busy working while I'm waiting for her answer. It will make the time pass faster. God, I miss that woman already and we have only been apart for two hours. Soon we will be together for the rest of our lives. In the mean time there is an oilrig in Texas that needs my attention. I'm headed out there day after tomorrow and I hope I have her answer before I get back. We are having one last night together before I leave, so don't expect me home tonight."

Sadie had spent the day at "The New Deal," chatting with diners, greeting newcomers to the now famous eatery, and looking forward to her evening with Marcus. When they were together the world stood still.

Looking up from the newspaper she was reading, Sadie watched as Marcus approached the booth where she was sitting. The sight of his slim hips and broad shoulders sent a shiver of anticipation through her. His smile warmed her heart; she had never known such a feeling of belonging body and soul. She didn't think it was possible, until now, to give your complete self to another human being.

Their dinner over, the lovers went out to the street and Marcus hailed a cab to take them to their "Home away from home" as Marcus called it.

"Darling, anywhere you are is home to me," Sadie had answered. It was the most glorious night they had ever spent together and both hated to see it end. They lay in each other's arms and talked until dawn. When Marcus finally pulled away saying, "My darling, we will have the rest of our days together when I get back from this trip. All we need now is for you to set the date."

Sadie watched unashamedly, while he bathed and dressed, all the while sending loving looks her way. Planting a kiss on the tearful Sadie's lips, he tipped his hat, grinned and walked out the door, leaving Sadie lying on the disheveled bed yearning for his safe return.

With the closing of the door, a dreadful sense of doom invaded her whole mind and body. She wanted to run after him, call him back to the safety of her arms, hold him against her bare breast, never letting anything separate them again. *Foolish woman,* she berated herself. *Why must you always look for trouble? Because it always finds me,* her heart answered.

Jonathan checked his calendar; he was busy in the weeks before the election. Dinner parties filled his whole calendar for the month of October and the first week in November. He was still undecided about his treatment of his Mother. Should he call her or just let things work themselves out. After much thought and consultations with his political cronies he decided Mother's money and influence could be an asset to his campaign.

Calling her, he ignored his own rude behavior and told her.

"I was planning a short trip to see Sid in Buffalo, but my busy schedule won't permit it. Maybe I'll be able to see her after the election. She's been behaving rather strangely when I do call. It's as though I'm talking with a stranger. True, we are not betrothed yet, but I get the feeling she's drifting away. Josie fills the gap for the time being, whenever I need an attractive woman to impress the others, but she isn't smart enough to marry. I have high aspirations and I need a clever woman by my side." Confident that he had mended the rift in his relationship, he bade her goodbye. Pushing back his chair, he sat fiddling with his watch chain and staring around at the posters in his office. All were pictures of him looking down, smiling, and looking prosperous. That was the message he had hoped to convey to the little people, when he ordered the largest posters he could get. Finishing his paperwork for the day, he shoved it into a leather briefcase, gathered his overcoat and homburg from the coat rack just inside the hall door, jammed the hat on his head and made his way to the street.

Walking in the brisk cool air gave him a sense of confidence; he was pleased with the world he was creating for himself. As he passed the couples strolling on the crowded street, he tipped his hat and smiled. You could never be sure who was out walking on the avenue. He couldn't take a chance on slighting someone of importance; after all, he was running for a very important office. Mayor of New York City was nothing to sneeze at. With Sid at his side, who knew maybe Governor next? He was so busy planning for the future; he forgot to be aware of the present, until it was too late. He had wandered into a section of town that was known for its rapes, fights, and killings. They came at him with wooden clubs swinging first one then the other. He felt the club connect with his head. There was no pain, only the sensation of falling into a world of black.

A passerby found Jonathan and thought the man huddled in a bloody ball was dead. He debated walking on by, letting some other poor bastard find him. He walked a few steps away, turned back and saw the corpse blink. *Oh, hell,* he thought. *I better get a cop to check this out as long as he don't try to lay it on me.*

Sadie was getting ready for a long day at the New Deal where there was a knock at the door. A young man in uniform stood in the hall, hat in hand, and a humble look on his face.

"Sorry I am to have ta bring this bad news to ya, ma'am, but a battered up body was discovered in an alley off Broadway. I'm led to believe it belongs to your son Jonathan. He was beaten, robbed and left for dead sometime last night. If he lives, it will be a miracle. He's in Sisters of Mercy Hospital downtown. Now, ma'am, please don't faint!"

"Don't be a fool, I don't have time for such foolishness. I must get to get my son; leave the fainting for some other day. She bolted out the door leaving the young cop standing with his mouth open and a look of admiration in his eyes.

Sadie called James as soon as she finished talking to the doctor; her heart was filled with fear for her poor, wounded Jonathan. The doctor had explained that with a head trauma such as this, one never knew what the end result would be. He could be fine or he might never remember even his own name. Some victims stayed a child for the rest of their lives.

"We just never know until they recover consciousness."

James assured her they all would do whatever was needed to help Jonathan back to health. She sat in the hall waiting for the nurses to finish getting him cleaned up and comfortable. The wounds were too serious to worry about cleanliness when he was first brought in, but now it took precedent over visitors. When they were done with the bath and medications, one of the women in the gray nurses uniform waved Sadie into the room.

Her heart leaped in her breast. Her boy looked like an old, beaten rug that had been thrown away in an alley. She cursed the men who did this to her boy. May God strike them dead! Tears traced wet patterns down her cheeks. Her trembling hands took his broad hand into hers. He squeezed her index finger and tried to smile. She began to sob, the effort to contain herself was causing her whole body to convulse, and she couldn't swallow the mountain that was lodged in her throat.

"Oh, God," she prayed, "Don't let me fall apart now when he needs me so much." He moved his hand, took hers, touched his feverish, swollen lips, tried to wink, and dozed off to sleep.

It was mid-day when she left the bedside. Going into the hall she saw Marcus sitting on a bench, head tipped back, staring at the cold white ceiling. His hat sat on the bench beside him crushed, as though he had wrung water out of it. *Why in the world am I thinking about his hat at a time like this she asked herself? What is the matter with me? My boy is lying in there close to death and I'm fretting about a dammed hat!*

Marcus jumped to his feet, dashed to her side, taking her in his arms he guided her to the bench and sat next to her, saying nothing. Just his being there was enough. Sadie knew this man would be there when she needed him most, but her son had to come first. After many tears had been shed, Marcus explained, "I came as soon as I heard, I was in the depot and read the newspaper's account of his attack. I caught the next train back. I knew you would need me now, more than ever.

"Yes, darling, I do need you, but my son needs me more. I can't turn my back on him now. There is so much I have to think about, to sort out in my mind. Oh, dear God, it seems we are always being torn apart by fate. Maybe we are not supposed to be together." The anguish in her voice was so tangible, it could have been sliced into layers.

"Nonsense! We were destined for each other. I know how you feel my sweet, but now is not the time. Jonathan should be your only priority. I can wait. After all, we have waited all these years, what are a few more months?"

"I can always depend on you to do the right thing. That is one of the many reasons I love you, dear heart."

Marcus went back to Texas the next day, leaving Sadie in the competent hands of James and Sid. "Call me if you get time, my dear, and take good care of yourself too, after all, you are my one and only love."

Sadie's days were spent between the hospital and the restaurant. She heard from Marcus every week. He called often, but he stayed in the background. The sound of his voice always made her feel important and loved. This is what she would have to settle for, until her boy was well and she was free to share her life with Marcus. Every night after she said her prayers, she had her talk with God, telling him of her hopes and dreams. When she finished on this night she chuckled.

"Yes, Father, I know I'm telling you how to do your job. Forgive me. You know what is best for me. Let Thy will be done, Amen."

When Marcus returned from his trip, he and Sadie spent the night together, but Sadie explained to Marcus that this would be their last night together until Jonathon was well. She must devote all her time to making sure he was able to care for himself, before she could seek a life for herself.

Katy had called that morning, just to check on her brother's progress, as she did every weekend. She had wanted to come when she had first heard about Jonathan's incident with the muggers, but having a brood of four now kept both her and Jared not only tied down, but very busy just keeping up with them. She giggled when she told her mother about Christian and Mrs. Brown.

"You won't believe what happened. Well, Mr. Brown spent his evening at the Frog Town Inn as usual, drank until he ran out of money and friends to buy for him, left his cronies hanging on the bar at the tavern and wandered out into the dark night. The next morning a fisherman found him floating in the Saginaw River. It looked as though he fell and struck his head, got up dazed, made a wrong turn and fell off the dock into the freezing water. Mrs. Brown carried on like she really cared. She mourned for about as long as it took to bury him, and then she offered that hypocrite Christian free room and board if he helped out around the house. So far all the townsfolk can see is that he surely is helping Mrs. Brown with her problems. She even smiles now and then. He talks as though he owns the boarding house and Mrs. Brown, too. We can't wait to see what happens next. You know how it is in a small town; everybody knows everybody else's business. After all, what else is there to talk about? Oh, and I must tell you about this, it gave the whole town a much needed laugh.

"Mrs.DuFrain, you remember Mrs.DuFrain, the one with nine children and no husband, she takes in laundry for a living. Well, a peddler from the Jewel Tea Co was harassing her. He had talked her into buying linens for her household. He told her he understood she didn't have the money and he would fix it with the company to only collect ten cents a month until they were paid for. The first month he came and told her that he had to have a dollar for that first month. The company wanted to see if her credit was good. She paid even though she had to take it out of her food allowance. The next month he came and demanded two dollars, just to prove she was a good risk. She told him she couldn't do that and he began coming every week, asking for money. Well, you know they don't have inside facilities; they still use a pot for the nighttime visits, and with a large family it fills up pretty fast.

This fateful morning her sister Nora was visiting from Linwood. The two women were upstairs making beds and cleaning the washbasins when she heard a pounding on the door. She looked out and there was the Jewel Tea man standing on the stoop below, hat in hand waiting for her to open the door. 'Oh, my God, what am I going to do?' she asked her sister.'

"'I'll show you what we are going to do,' Nora answered. 'You open the window quietly, and I will take care of Mr. Jewel Tea!' She lifted the full pot to the windowsill, slid it forward until it was directly over the man, tilted it until the liquid inside reached the very edge, then she dumped the whole pot over. It rained urine and feces all over the salesman, covering him head to foot with the night deposits of the entire DuFrain family. The two women hung out the window, watching the sopping, furious man rushing down the road, cursing and swearing. They were laughing so hard, they almost fell out the window. They couldn't wait to tell everyone in town why the drummer was in such a hurry to leave town. Mama, I can picture it and every time I do, I have to giggle." Katy was giggling so much she could barely tell her mother that, "the last time the man was seen he was running out of town, tearing off clothing and screaming something about this town being nothing but a shit hole anyway."

Sadie had been depressed when she answered the phone, but talking with Katy always cheered her up. Katy was such a good wife and mother, but she was also a wonderful daughter and friend.

Jonathan was doing better than the doctor expected. He would always have a limp, but his mind was sound. That was the important thing to Sadie.

The police officer in charge of the investigation said he didn't have any suspects for the brutal beating, but he did suspect it was political in nature. Jonathan was becoming too powerful in the Democratic Party. The officer had information from an anonymous source that Jonathan's stand on immigration and prohibition pitted him against some very dangerous people.

Sadie knew it would do no good to plead with him to stay out of the political ring. She just hoped they were done trying to convince him to change sides. The stone building felt damp and cold as she left the police station for what she prayed was the last time.

She wanted to call Marcus every night to tell him of the day's events, but forced herself to wait for his call. He was called on Friday to make sure she was well and to see if she needed anything. He was always prompt with his calls. He prided himself on being dependable. This particular Friday when he did call, he explained to Sadie that he must go out of town for a few days, a business trip. It shouldn't keep him away any more than a week. He would call every night if she wanted him to, but he wanted to be sure it was all right with her.

She answered his question with a question, "Do you still want to marry me, when you get back?"

"My God, yes!" he answered, "I've waited so long for this day."

"Then save everything you want to tell me until you get back. In the meantime, I will be shopping for a dress that is appropriate for a mature bride."

Sadie moved Jonathan from the hospital into her apartment when he was feeling better. He teased her about having a beau, fixing her hair differently, and wearing the latest glad rags. Sadie loved the comaradie that Jonathon was displaying. *Maybe the knock on the head did him some good,* she mused. The telephone ringing broke their teasing contest and Sadie ran to answer it. Standing in the kitchen leaning on the door jam, she watched her damaged son lying on his bed drifting off to sleep.

She whispered, "Guess what Bethany, it seems Jonathan has accepted the fact that Marcus and I will be wed. Thanks be to God. Why, just this morning he wanted to know when I was going to learn the Black Bottom and the Lindy Hop. I told him that just goes to shows how much he knew, I already know how to dance those particular dances. I'm hoping to teach them to Marcus and for once Jonathon didn't sneer. Come to think of it, I don't know if Marcus can even dance. Well, I'll take care of that little matter as soon as he gets back."

While they were having their evening tea a knock came at the door. Sadie opened it a crack and was promptly pushed back. Josie's father bulldozed his way into the room, stomped over to the table, grabbed Jonathan by the front of his shirt and pulled him up to meet his angry blood red face.

"What the hell have you done to my innocent daughter? Sir, you have dishonored my name. Our family doctor tells me that her stomachaches are perfectly natural when she's three months with child. My sweet daughter tells me you are the father. Well, Mr. Big Shot, you will marry my daughter this Saturday. I have the preacher ready and Josie is past ready! Now! Any arguments?"

Jonathon changed color, and stammered, "No, sir, I am ready to do the right thing. The child is mine and I am sorry I dishonored your good name."

Sadie stood with her mouth open, eyes wide, staring from one to the other. *My God,* she thought. *Jonathan doesn't even love her and now he is forced to marry her. It was a foolish thing to do but now he will have to pay for the rest of his life.* Her heart sank while she made Mr. Vandermeer comfortable, served him coffee, offered him scones, fruit, anything to keep her mind and hands busy. When the man left, Jonathan held his head and wailed, "How am I going to tell Sid? You know we are seeing each other, don't you?"

"I don't know how you figure you're seeing each other when you haven't even been here for her calls in six months. You never call back; you take Josie to every party and outing, in fact, everywhere you go. I think Sid will be relieved to have it settled. She is a strong young lady and won't fall apart when she hears the news."

Sadie didn't mention the fact that James and Sid had already formed a close relationship. If it became any more than friendship, which Sadie hoped, then they must decide for themselves when they wanted the world to know.

The week flew by and Saturday came in with a fury. Huge drops of rain pelted the wedding party; everyone was soaked from the sudden spring storm.

God's crying! The depressed mother of the groom thought. She did have to admit to herself the undeniable fact that Josie made a beautiful bride. She had worn white in spite of her father's threats and radiated that special aura that makes some pregnant women glow. Josie's eyes followed her new husband everywhere, worship shining on her face.

Rushing from the church to the New Deal, where the party sat at long tables eating, drinking and pretending that this was a marriage made in heaven.

Sadie longed for Marcus. The hasty wedding plans and prior commitments didn't allow time for Marcus to return in time for the event. Sadie needed his calm, strong, common sense attitude to help her through this ordeal.

James had invited Sid to be his guest at the wedding; Jonathon did a double take when he saw them together. With wrinkled brow, Jonathon came over to their table, "Brother, I see you have brought the most beautiful woman in the world to our wedding. Please make sure she has a good time." Curling his lip into a sneer he added, "Now I must get back to my lovely bride."

James reached for Sid's hand and squeezed it gently, saying, "Everything will be all right."

Katy and Jared had gotten on the train almost as soon as they heard the news. A neighbor offered to watch the children while they were away. It would be a welcome vacation from the rowdy brood. Their home was a noisy house, full of happy children, theirs and the neighbors! The ladies of the church always commented on how the children of the town seemed to gravitate to the smallest house in town. Sometimes it seemed as though the house was leaking children from every door and window. Katy just laughed at the mental picture the ladies drew.

She was perfectly happy to have the children underfoot. It meant she knew where her children were and that was important to both her and Jared.

"After all, there are bad people out there, and you can't take a chance with such precious, little people," she would reply to their pointed remarks. She knew they thought her house could use a better cleaning. It always seemed to be dusty when they came to tea, but Katy wanted to be known as the best cookie maker, not the best housekeeper. *Let them put that in their pipe and smoke it! She rewarded herself with a cookie and smiled a secret smile. Wait until I tell Mama that another child is on the way. She's going to raise holy hell, but Jared and I are happy and that's all that counts.* She brought the tray into the dining area where her mother, Jared, Jonathan, and Josie sat making plans for the honeymoon. The dinner had gone very well, the guests ate, toasted the bride and groom a little too often and Jonathan, who had kept up with every toast, had become quite drunk, singing and laughing too loudly at everything that was said.

Sadie's heart felt heavy. She knew he resented the marriage and was trying to put on a brave face. He tried to stay awake while they poured cup after cup of coffee to help him keep his eyes open. Josie couldn't drink the coffee, but the cookies sounded good to her. Jonathon groaned when he heard the grandfather clock strike the hour, midnight, and he realized he was going home with the wrong woman.

James had invited Sid to a walk in Central Park after the wedding supper. They strolled around the fountain watching other couples holding hands, touching cheeks, and showing signs of more intimate knowledge of each other. Sid stood it as long as she could; she doubled up her fist, shook it in James' face, demanding, "And just when are you going to tell me you love me? I know you do, but you're so damned afraid of hurting your brother. You sure don't mind hurting me, so to hell with you!" As that torrent of words spewed out of her, she seemed to shrivel into a shadow of herself, then sat on the nearest park bench and sobbed as though her heart would break.

The shocked James stood as though frozen; his face slowly began to melt into a look of utter disbelief.

"Me? You love me? My prayers have been answered! I have loved you since we first met on the train. No, I think I loved you when we were children, but I didn't realize it."

Sid looked up through her tears and whispered, "Will you stop all that talking and kiss me!" Grabbing the now smiling girl, James wrapped her in his arms, pressed his lips against hers, and the world stood still. Without a word they started walking again, this time arm in arm as though they were melded together. Sid broke the silence, "Darling, when will we tell the others?"

"As soon as we get home. That will give them a lot of time to get used to our engagement." Nodding his head vigorously, "We are, you know. Engaged I mean. I'm a hell of a lawyer! I can't even talk straight when I'm around you. You make me all tongue-tied, and I'm loving every minute."

When they entered Sadie's apartment, she knew something had changed in a subtle way. An aura seemed to flow from the happy couple, engulfing the whole room with its gentle warmth.

Josie sat eating her cookies and rubbing her barely noticeable little potbelly. She stared at the couple for a second and in a teasing voice said, "I know what is making James and Sid look so happy. Sid's expecting, too. Am I right?"

"No, dammit! You're not right! Sid's not that kind of girl," Jonathan's face turned scarlet, his hands began to shake. He stood up, knocking the table over, shook his fist at his brother and limped from the room.

Sadie started after him, rage etched on her face, but James gently took her arm.

"No, Mother, this is between Jonathan and me. It's always been there. If it weren't Sid, it would be something else. Now is the time to bring it all out, get it settled."

"You're right, of course, but a mother always thinks she needs to solve her children's problems. I don't think that feeling ever goes away. I'm so sorry this had to happen to you, Sid. I hope you will forgive us."

Josie sat with tears streaming down her face, hands clenched, mouth working, but nothing was coming out. James went to her, touched her shoulder saying, "My brother didn't mean what he said. He has been through a lot this last year, and had too much to drink tonight. It will be better in the morning."

"That bastard meant every word he said. Sometimes he even called me Sid when we were making love. Now I know where I stand. I sure didn't get this way alone, so what does that make him? I'll make him pay for that remark, you can be sure!" She stood up lifted her gown, and looked at the filthy coffee soaked hem.

"Looks just like the bride, soiled beyond repair."

When Marcus called Saturday morning, the operator asked for Sadie.

She had spent the early part of the morning cleaning the coffee and food out of the Persian rug, which had been under the table the night before and was depressed over the whole situation. She needed to hear his voice.

"Darling," he explained, "I've run into a problem here and need to spend a few more days. The well we were drilling came up dry. The oil is there, but we need to go a lot deeper and to do that we have to order more equipment. I promise to be home in a couple of days. You sound different. What has happened?"

"I'll tell you all about it when you get home. Take care." She was tempted to beg him to come home now, this very minute. That old feeling of doom came over her. She pushed it away. She was just being a foolish bride to be.

Sadie had a sudden urge to see Haven Place, see if it was still there and just as wonderful as she remembered.

Everyone was still asleep when she slipped out of the house, drove back over the years to a place where she had always felt safe and loved.

From a distance the house looked the same. As she drew closer she saw the rickety porch, as close to falling down as it could be and still stand. The garden had gone to weeds, the roof needed repair, the paint hung in strips from the windowsills, and the glass windowpanes were broken. Curtains, torn and filthy, were blowing in the wind that tore at the very heart of the house. She felt betrayed. The house had gotten old just as she had. It had no one to care for it, so it had lost its special gift of elegance.

Is that what happens to humans, too? Do they just shrivel up and wait for death? My God, I'm getting morbid. After all, it's only an old abandoned house, but it still holds many wonderful memories for me.

When she arrived back at her apartment the air was filled with tension. Josie sat eating the eggs, toast, and fried potatoes that Sid had prepared for her. Jonathan sat sipping coffee, head bowed in abject misery.

After hanging up her cape, Sadie walked quietly into the room and selected a slice of the homemade bread that had been toasted to golden perfection. She glanced at Sid and nodded her head. Sid smiled her recognition of the soundless Thank You and brought out a carafe of freshly squeezed orange juice, poured a small glass and raised it to her lips in a toast to the newlyweds. James walked in just as they emptied their glasses and asked, "What's the occasion? I thought we did all that last night."

"Reinforcement, my dear brother, just reinforcement," murmured the relieved Jonathan.

He and Josie had come to an agreement in the confines of their room. He swore he meant no harm to her or her good name.

She blamed herself for letting him lead her astray.

"After all, it is the woman's place to say no." They agreed that from now on they would treat each other with the greatest respect. To Josie, the whole mess was over. He would never treat her so shabbily again.

"Mother, I called here early this morning and there was no answer. I heard all the clicks of the party line waiting for you to pick up, but you must have gone out before I called. Is Marcus back in town?"

"No, I just felt the need to visit a place that I knew many years ago in a different time and place. I was very happy there. I don't know why it came to mind, but I couldn't resist the urge to see it again. Now, I'm sorry I did. It is so run down and sad, like a beautiful flower that has withered and died. I wish I had kept it alive and lovely, in my memory."

Chapter Twenty-Five
Empty Arms

The telephone interrupted them. Sid jumped up saying, "That's probably Mom and Dad. They said they would call to see how I am." She grabbed the earpiece, put it to her ear and stood in shocked silence, disbelief registering on her face. James rushed to her side, took the earpiece from her delicate hand, placed it to his head, listened and slowly shaking his head, he told the person on the other end, "Come to the apartment now. Did you want me to send someone or can you make it alright?"

"What is going on?" demanded the pacing Sadie. With dread in her heart she waited for James to answer.

"Mother, please sit down. Sid, will you get Mom some water or better yet some brandy?" He took his mother's hand. Gently rubbing it, and told her, "We have some bad news about Marcus. He was hurt while working on the oil rig they were putting up."

Sadie pushed the brandy away and stood facing the window, staring out into the void that suddenly became her life. She asked, "What about Marcus, is he all right? Is he alive? Maybe it's a mistake. Oh, God, please let it be a mistake."

"Mother, please sit down and be calm. There was a terrible accident and Marcus was killed. I have some terrible news. That was Stephanie on the telephone; there has been a terrible accident and Marcus was killed. The job foreman called Stephanie and told her that Marcus fell from the rigging, hitting the engine below. He died instantly. Thank God, he didn't suffer. Poor Stephanie was alone when they gave her the news and I told her to come and be with us. She needs us right now."

Hands shaking, Sadie took the brandy bottle, poured herself a drink, tossed it down, poured another and started to lift it to her mouth. Then she remembered Harrison's warning, "When you want it most is when you must say no." *Good old Harrison,* she thought, *still saving me after all these years.* She slowly set the half filled glass down and wiped her lips with her handkerchief.

The family clustered around Sadie, comforting her in every way they could with the exception of Josie; she sat still eating as though nothing had happened. She was shoveling the food in as though she hadn't eaten in a week.

Jonathan looked at her with disgust.

"Please don't let us disturb you," he said with a sneer.

"There's nothing I can do to help her," she whined. "Besides, I'm hungry. This baby is making a pig out of me."

"You're so right!" he said, shaking his head sadly.

She began to howl, not just cry, but bellow at the top of her lungs. "You don't love me, if you did, you wouldn't talk to me this way. I hate you! I wish I were dead!"

"Get her out of here before I do something I'll be sorry for," James was shaking his fist at his brother, his eyes displaying his fury.

Jonathan grabbed his hat and his wife and jerked her out the room.

"We are going home to my place, no damned honeymoon for us!" He limped into the hall with Josie trailing behind, sobbing like a penitent child.

James went back to his mother's side, took her into his arms, cradling her like a small child. He would become her rock in the days to come.

Sadie let the comfort of his arms soothe her as she remembered the man whom she had loved forever. Marcus had been her first love, now he was her last love, and that thought brought the tears gushing again. He was her whole world. As long as Marcus was in this world she could go on. Now she wasn't sure she wanted to.

The numbness seemed to penetrate her whole being. She knew how Josie felt; she too wished she were dead. That thought seeped into her mind, took root and began to grow. Stephanie walked into the room, took one look at Sadie, and rushed to her side.

"Sadie, why did it have to happen to Daddy just when he finally found happiness?"

"Oh God, I wish I knew. My dear child, I know how you feel. My heart is broken, too," she sobbed. "But we need to be strong right now. We can help each other survive this horrible time in our lives. I feel like giving up, but we can't. Marcus was a fighter and we must be too. Your mother will need your support when she hears about it."

"No, she already knows and all she said was, 'That's too bad, he was too young to die.' I think she's still bitter about the divorce. She's never remarried and she has grown more miserable every day. I wished to God that she had found someone else, it would have made Papa's life a little easier." Choking back the tears, she circled Sadie and James in an open arm hug. Mustering a sad little smile, she whispered, "I feel as though I'm home at last, Papa was right, you do emanate love."

Three people joined in grief, bonded in love and became forever part of each other. Their days and nights were filled with both laughter and tears. Stephanie regaled them with stories of Marcus and his exploits in the oil fields, and some of the strange people who were his friends, like One Ear Johnny, a weird little man who claimed he could divine oil with a willow switch and sniffing in the air. Stephanie stood, and assumed the stance of a man with a cigar in his hand. With a hat jammed on her curls, she posed in the doorway, and said, "Yes, ladies and gents, I lost me ear in a bar room brawl. When the other fellow couldn't whip me arse, he bit off me ear to show his friends he gave as much as he got." The three of them laughed till they cried. When they had recovered enough, she told them of the odd little woman who tended the dry goods store in a small town in Wisconsin. When she walked by you, she reached out and slapped your cheek. Some said she lost her husband to another woman and she was forever punishing any woman crossed her path.

Sadie remembered the many stories that Marcus told her, both sad and happy and they decided to write a book in his memory. As they waited for Marcus' body to arrive in New York, they brought together all the people who knew him and listened to stories of his remarkable life. Even Stephanie wasn't aware of the impact her father had on the lives of others. There were loans made that never were expected to be repaid, jobs given that were created just so a friend could work and keep his pride, there were nights when he sat with a friend to keep away the bad dreams and temptations from his door. One woman came because she wanted to thank his family for the care he had given her and her son after a horse trampled his leg. She told them she was a widow with an eight-year-old son, she took in laundry and her son helped out by delivering the baskets of clothes when they were ironed.

"One morning," she continued, "on his way to a client's house to deliver their clothes, a horse became frightened by an automobile backfire. Kicking and screaming as only a wild animal can do, it knocked over the wagon that my child was pulling, thrashing and leaping wildly as its hooves came down repeatedly on my unlucky boy. His foot and leg were mangled. Skin shredded from bone, the boy lay in an unconscious heap in the street. People gathered around but no one moved to aid my son. That is until Marcus came upon the scene. Folks said he ordered a cabby to help him get my son into an automobile that was near by, straightened the wagon and paid a newsboy to bring it home and tell me that he and my son would be at the hospital.

Thank God for that man's prompt action, today my son can walk; he only has a few scars from the accident. Doc said Marcus got him to the hospital just in time. He even paid the hospital bill and for the two surgeries my son needed to help him walk. God bless that man!"

Sadie knew that the next few days were going to be hell with the strain of the funeral. She hated the fact that Marcus had to be frozen to preserve him for transport; every time it crossed her mind the chills would start.

James watched her closely to make sure she was well enough to get through this ordeal. He knew she was more deeply affected by this death than she showed. He would have to take special care to ensure her safety from herself, she just didn't seem to care very much about anything except that the funeral would be perfect. "A tribute to a great man," she said.

Jonathan and Josie came to the funeral, sat in the back and left as soon as the prayers were over. The rest of the mourners followed the horse drawn hearse to the cemetery, and watched as they lowered the beautifully carved box into the open grave. The many friends walked to the gaping hole, took a handful of freshly dug earth, and sprinkled it into the final resting-place of Sadie's destiny. When the last of the long line of mourners had passed, she knelt beside the grave, bowed her head, praying silently.

James and Sid came; taking her gently by the arms, they drew her away from the chasm that held her bound to it. She didn't want to leave her love so cold and alone, she needed to be there with him, holding him, warming him, making sure he would never be alone again. *Oh, God*, she thought, *please let me join him soon.*

The days dragged slowly for Sadie, she spent most of her time sleeping; there wasn't any reason to get up, get dressed, and face people. Her life had ended with Marcus' death.

On the eighth day after the funeral as Sadie lay on the settee, mind somewhere between sleep and wakefulness, she heard humming, low at first, then louder, until it became a roar. She sat up and shook her head as though to shake the noise away. Then she heard a voice say, "Wha' yo' think yo' doin', layin' on yo' arse like dis, git offen yo' arse an' do som' livin', time nough for dyin' when it yo' time!"

She looked all around the room. No one was there, the dishes were rattling in the kitchen, the typewriter in the den was clacking away at a steady beat, the hall clock struck five times, all seemed normal, but where did Jessie's voice come from? Did I dream it? No, I was awake, at least I think I was. She made her way to the den where James sat working on the final drafts for the book they had written about the life of Marcus.

"Did you hear any humming a few minutes ago?" she asked James.

"No, I didn't, was I supposed to?" he asked with a puzzled look on his face. "I guess I wouldn't hear much with the noise from this machine. Is there something wrong? Are you all right?"

"I'm all right, I must have been dreaming. I could swear I heard Jessie's voice giving me holy hell for giving up after Marcus's death. But I could hear her so clearly!" Still shaking her head she went into the kitchen where Sid was preparing dinner. *That girl is like a daughter to me,* she thought, *with any kind of luck she will be one day soon.* "Did you hear any humming a few minutes ago," she asked again, "and then a voice talking?"

"No, but I was using the egg beater for the cake I'm making. I'm sorry if I disturbed you. I tried to be quiet, but I must have made more noise than I intended."

"Did I dream or imagine it? I swear to God that I heard Jessie giving me what for, for still mourning my wonderful Marcus. If she were here right now I'd give her a big hug and a piece of my mind."

Sid tried to hide the smile that flitted across her face, "I don't know what you heard, real or imagined, but if it got you out of that lost mood you were in then I say hallelujah! We need you to make the family complete. Without your experience and friendly smile to run the restaurant, business has fallen off. Besides, you're too young to curl up and die. Now that you're out of your funk, I can go home to Buffalo. I've been here too long already."

James came to the doorway just as she announced her decision to leave New York City and go home to Buffalo, where her parents probably needed her help. He stared wide-eyed at her for a moment, then went to her, took her hand, knelt on one knee, and asked her to be his wife.

She watched her son and as he waited for Sid's answer, Sadie knew what it would be before the girl answered. Her very being was filled with the beauty of the scene before her. The phrase "He replenishes my soul," sang in her heart and she knew then that she would never be far from Marcus, for he lived in her heart and her mind. Every time she saw young lovers she would remember Marcus and as long as she lived, he would too. *Oh, God, it hurts so much to remember.*

The wedding took place in a small church in Buffalo, near the falls; the hotel where they were staying was crowded with guests from both sides of the family, all but Lorrie's family; they had never forgiven her for her past profession. Evan's parents, brothers and their wives more than made up for the lack of Lorrie's folks. Evan had sent for his brothers the first year after he and Lorrie had wed. They were delighted and came as quickly as they could book passage. After settling in, they had joined the police department, found wives, married and each were raising a brood of youngsters. In the first year of working in their adopted country they had gotten together and pooled their savings to bring their parents over to this wonderful young land. After all, the grandchildren needed grandparents to spoil them.

Jonathan and Josie sent their regrets, Josie was having difficulties with her pregnancy and Jonathan didn't want to leave her home alone.

Sadie was glad to hear Jonathan was concerned with Josie's distress, she hadn't been too sure about that marriage, but it seemed to be going smoothly, so far. *I must remember to put them in my prayers tonight,* she thought.

Sid asked Rachael if she would be her maid of honor, and she said yes if Gilbert, her intended, could stand with her. James and Rachael both were delighted. They had gone on outings and to theatre with the engaged couple and found them very compatible. James especially liked Gilbert's position on preserving the wilderness for future generations, and found him knowledgeable and a good conversationalist.

Rachael had met him at a seminar for the preservation the forests and rivers. Gilbert had taken one look at Rachael from across the room, forgotten his speech completely, stumbled through a few words at the podium, apologized to the next speaker and dashed to the place where she was standing. With trembling hands and stuttering voice he introduced himself to Rachael and the lady friend she was with. They pretended to ignore him, until Rachael could no longer bear seeing how miserable he was. She smiled at him, told him their names and asked him if he would like to take tea with them. Gilbert was in seventh heaven just being near the girl of his dreams. They had been seeing each other for six months when he asked for her hand in marriage. Philip was a little hesitant about giving his permission, but he saw how much in love they were and he had taken an instant liking to the fellow. Rachael and Gilbert would make a handsome addition to the wedding party.

Sid was a beautiful bride, and of course the groom was as handsome as he could be. Standing so proudly, their faces reflecting the love they felt for each other.

Sadie had worn her favorite color dress, a simple lavender gown with white rosebuds sewn here and there on the skirt.

The wedding dinner was in the hotel dining room. The food was delicious and everyone came away well fed and content with the several toasts to the newlyweds. Folks said it was a perfect wedding.

The next morning Sadie caught the train for New York City; she wanted to be home where she felt at peace. She loved the many friends that she had, but she enjoyed her solitude even more these days. Katy begged her mother to come and spend a few weeks with them, but Sadie declined, "No, I really want some quiet time to think and sort out my life. I think I've earned it."

The book was finished. Many people said they had captured the man and his deeds in the writing of his story. Sadie cried as she read it, tears that washed away all the bitterness she felt about once again being separated from the love of her life. She firmly believed that they were lovers in a past life and would someday be together in another life. That was the only thing that kept her from going mad.

Haven House crept in and out of her mind through the next few weeks. It was as though it were calling to her, "Remember me, remember me, I was your haven in time of need, come home." She began to plan for the future; she would sell "The New Deal."

It was worth a great deal of money now that the Depression was nearly over. If I keep the rest of the property, I can use that rent money to live on for the rest of my life and the money from the sale of the restaurant will restore Haven House, only this time it will be called "Peaceful Valley," my secret name for that marvelous old house.

When she told the others about her plan, they thought she had gone mad, but James figured that would not only keep her busy, but alive a lot longer. As he explained it to the rest of the family, "Mom has earned every cent of that money and if she wants to spend it on an old house, it's hers to spend!"

The restaurant sold faster than anyone thought. Sadie wasn't quite ready to make the move to the old house yet. She needed to locate the final owner of the house, line up repairmen, find a cook, and a gardener. With so much to do, her world came alive with joyous anticipation.

At last her lawyer called to let her know that the house was hers. The last owner had not paid his taxes for many years and the house had reverted to the city. He had gotten it for next to nothing as it was in such disrepair. He questioned her again about her decision to purchase such a run down place when there were perfectly maintained houses for sale for just a few thousand dollars more. Sadie's answer to him was, "Money won't replace the wonderful memories, nor the feeling of contentment I get when I think of that grand old place." She began packing the very day the call came. She dragged out trunks that she had collected over the years. She sorted clothes she had squirreled away, throwing out most of the items she had packed away for later use.

"Now why did I save that, I must have known it would be out of style when I finally dug it out. Look at this, a blue dress, why in heavens name did I keep this?" Then the memories came flooding back.

"Why, I remember this dress. I wore it on the day Marcus first came to Kate's house, no wonder I saved it, and here is the first flower he gave me. I don't remember pressing it into this Bible. Look at the size of that waist, dear God. I would never fit into that today." Slowly, the tension of the past few months drained from her body. She leaned against the bedpost, shaking like a leaf, slid onto the dress-laden bed, sobbed and beat the pillow, letting out all the rage, disappointments and loneliness she had buried within her for so many years. At long last she was free, free to build a new life for herself.

Her step had a bounce when she walked away from that room filled with the pain and misery of lost love. The only things she took from the now discarded items were the cape she had worn to see Miss Jenny Lind, the opera glasses, and the last quilt, the one that kept her warm the night she lost her first child, Marcus' child. These are the only memories I want to salvage from that other life, my children, and grandchildren are enough for me now.

With James helping interview the cooks and gardeners, she soon was ready to move to Haven House. The repairmen had started to work immediately; the roof and two of the upstairs bedrooms were finished.

The old house was coming alive under the capable hands of the carpenters and the talented directions of Sid. Sadie was so impressed with Sid's decorating talents, she encouraged her to seek employment as a decorator. James didn't like the idea, but said if that were what she wanted, he wouldn't stand in Sid's way. They came out on weekends to help her get settled in and for James to reassure himself that his mother would be safe in this isolated setting.

The cook they finally settled on was a far cry from her old friend Jessie, but she did make delicious meals, kept the kitchen clean and loved to gossip about the neighbors. She never repeated anything bad about them, only the funny things that happened. She took delight in a good old-fashioned joke as she called it.

Sadie was always a little surprised to see Goldie in the kitchen. She still could picture Jessie humming and scrubbing the pans.

"God, I miss that woman," she often told herself, "If she were only here now."

Goldie was the complete opposite of Jessie. Where Jessie was a huge black woman with dark hair streaked with gray, Goldie was fair skinned with red hair and small in stature. *I wonder if I did that on purpose, Sadie speculated. No, it just turned out that way. Don't go looking for things that aren't there. Jessie would give me hell for that; I can hear her say, 'Don't go stirren' up thins better lef' alon'.'* "Oh God, I wish she were here! It seems whenever I think of Jessie, I come away safe and happy, she said to the empty room. I've been doing this a lot lately, talking to myself, a sure sign of old age," she chuckled to no one in particular.

It took a year, but the house was finally finished, the gardens were in full bloom and the summer was one of those rare times when the temperature was always mild with a light breeze blowing in from the ocean. It was the perfect time for a house warming party.

James and Sid helped with the guest list and the decorations.

Jonathan said he and Josie were too busy to help, but they would have time for the party. His campaign to run for mayor of the city was in full gear. Now with a wife and child, the party considered him a perfect candidate and with his standing as a good family man, he was pretty much a shoe in.

Sadie just shook her head when she heard this. She kept silent, but James knew she was hurt by his brother's selfishness.

He wished there were something he could do to change him, but he was afraid it was too late. He too kept silent.

The week before the party the weather was mild, a gentle breeze drifted through the gardens, spreading the perfume of a thousand roses throughout the open windows, enhancing the aroma of many other flowers placed strategically throughout the lower part of the house. It reminded Sadie of a night many years ago, the night of her marriage to her second husband, John Davis. That had been a good marriage; we should have grown old together. Marcus was the dream one always chases and never catches. He was the elusive perfect lover. If we had lived together, the picture of perfection would have become etched with the scars of truth. Now the memory of him can remain unsullied in my mind and heart forever.

Harrison arrived a day early for the party, knowing full well he would be more than welcome to stay at the house. Sadie gave him his old room, newly remodeled, but decorated the same as it had been in years gone by. Tears came to his eyes when he saw the room that held so many memories, both good and bad.

Sadie looked at her old friend, seeing him as he was so many years ago. *I guess I'm looking through the eyes of love because he hasn't changed that much. Dear friends never change when we see them with our hearts. Harrison should be in his seventies,* mused Sadie, *and yet he looks much younger. Sad, that he never married, but he never seemed to get over Kate's death. I must ask him to stay for a while now that he has retired. James tells me he did very well in his import business. I'm glad he succeeded in something important in his life. I really should ask him about his trip back to England. He did mention it when he called, but he didn't seem too happy about it. Well, here I stand daydreaming again and my guests are fending for themselves.* She took a loving look around her wonderful house, felt the comfort it offered, and descended to join her guest.

Lorrie, Evan, and Michael arrived the morning of the party and insisted on helping with the last minute touchups on the decorations. Michael, being a sweet mannered man-child was excited to be allowed to string the lights around the patio roof and the rose garden fence. The pride showing on his face was worth all the concern Sadie felt at giving him that project.

The housewarming party was a huge success; the only one missing was Mr. Vandermeer, who had declined the invitation saying he was too ill to attend. Peaceful Valley came alive with warmth and the sounds of laughter.

Sadie's children stayed after the party broke up; taking rooms that could have told a far different story forty years ago. The house still held the welcome feeling for Sadie, but it was obvious Lorrie, Harrison, and she were the only ones who felt that way. As Harrison had said, "You have to have a history with a house to sense its ambiance, and we three are the only ones here who have that."

The morning after the party came in on a spring shower, it rained softly and the trees stretched their branches skyward to catch the precious nectar, the liquid of life.

Sadie woke very early, went to her window, threw open the drapes, and said "God, it's good to be alive. I haven't felt this way in a long time."

Goldie had made an enormous breakfast, scrambled eggs, slices of ham, and bacon, toast, fruit of every kind and Evan's coffee. Even after all these years, and all the modern inventions, coffee makers indeed, Evan's recipe was the best!

The children came down as she was having her second cup of coffee.

"Wonderful party, Mother," praised James. "Everything went perfectly."

"Yes, it did, didn't it? But I always feel as if I forgot someone or something. I guess it's just old age. We mothers must have something to fret over."

Jonathan came down after his mother and was standing in the door way listening.

"Mother, you don't have a thing to worry about. We both are set as far as life goes. I know what I'm going to do from here on out. Once I get elected mayor, it's only a matter of time until I go for governor and then who knows. All we have to do is sit back and take it easy. So, you see we have it made!"

"Oh, Jonathan, I wish life were that simple," was all that Sadie could say. *I could say a lot more on that subject,* she thought, *but he would never believe it anyway. He's one of those hardheaded people who only learn by experience. He has to fall down before he will believe it could happen.*

"Well, my life is that simple. I have it all laid out in my mind. Josie is going to make a handsome first lady someday."

After a hearty lunch, they all decided they had eaten too much. A good game of Croquet would help them work off that stuffed feeling. While getting the little metal hoops pushed into the ground, Sadie suddenly felt a chill race through her whole body. She stood up clasping her chest, her eyes racing around counting heads. They're all here so why do I feel this dreadful sense of loss? Harrison, where is Harrison? Dear God, please let him be all right.

"Mother, what is it, are you all right?" James and Sid were at her side in an instant, took her arm, and led her to one of the many stone benches that dotted the gardens. Sid poured ice water on her handkerchief and was patting Sadie's brow.

"James, will you please go check on Harrison. I can't seem to get it out of my head that something is dreadfully wrong and he's the only one missing."

James was back in a few moments with the welcome news that Harrison was regaling Goldie with some of his adventures.

"They seemed quite intrigued with each other, if I do say so myself"

"Thank You, God, thank you. I was so afraid I had lost another friend. There aren't many of us left anymore. I'm glad he is having a good time on his visit.

"James, I really don't feel like playing right now. I think I will lie down for a while. That gave me quite a start, I need time to recoup my mood"

"Are you sure you're feeling well? We can't have you getting sick on us. We need you around to keep us on a straight course."

"No, son. I'm fine. Just a little shaken. I will be fine after I gather my wits about me. Maybe a nap will help."

"Yes, Mother you go have a nice nap, but we won't be here when you wake up. Me and Josie have to get back to town. I start on the campaign trail tomorrow and I need to get some rest, and Josie has to get back to the child. She's been away too long already."

"Don't worry about me, Jonathan, just go and do what you have to do to make your lives complete. It is what makes you the person you are."

"We will be back after the election and we then can have a victory party." He laughed as he headed to the motorcar, which would carry him and Josie back to the city.

Sadie felt that sense of loss again. Don't be an old fool, she berated herself. You, my girl, are definitely getting dotty in your old age! Find something else to think about or you will be a wet blanket on the rest of the family.

Jonathan's day started early that Monday; his campaign manager had arranged the many stops he would make on the train tour. He kissed Josie and the child goodbye and began his campaign for the Mayor of New York City.

His first day on the campaign trail proved much harder than he expected. There were hired ruffians all along the way, shouting slurs and stirring up the crowds. His second day was even worse; it was frightening to see the crowds that came rushing at him when he offered to shake hands with his constituents. On the third day he decided to carry a pistol with him, just in case. The morning went as he expected. The hecklers were there in full force and the people who wanted to hear him were driven away by fear. He had decided to try moving on to another area when a shot rang out. He felt the sting of the bullet. *Strange,* he thought. *It doesn't hurt. It was the last thing he ever felt.*

Sadie heard the news on the radio. She stopped in her tracks clutched her hands to her breast and fainted.

Harrison was with her when she heard the announcement. He went quickly to where she had fallen. He sat beside her on the floor and tried to soothe the unconscious Sadie.

Goldie came running into the sitting room with ashen face making her red hair look even redder. She rushed to Harrison's side asking, "What happened, what can I do?"

"Not a thing. We can't do a damn thing to help her," Harrison sobbed.

"All we can do is be here for her."

When Sadie came back to consciousness, she pleaded with Harrison, "Please tell me it isn't true! Dear God, please tell me it was a mistake."

"Sadie, I wish I could. I would give anything if I could make it all right."

"Harrison, we have to find out if Josie knows. That poor child will go out of her mind with grief and Sadie's in no condition to call."

"You're right, Goldie. I'll call her father's house and see if she has heard the news yet. She is staying with him while Jonathan was on the road, isn't she?"

Harrison finally reached Mr. Vandermeer. "Yes," he said, "She found out about an hour ago and has not stopped screaming. I have sent for the doctor, but he hasn't arrived. I think she is going mad. We don't know what to do with her. The child is just sitting there watching her mother. She hasn't made a sound."

"Let us know what is going on as soon as you know. Sadie's in pretty bad shape too."

"I will keep in touch. Thank you so much for calling."

"The poor fellow is in shock too; he just thanked me for calling."

Sadie lay as if in a trance, her mind continually going back to the day when the boys were born. She remembered the pain, but it wasn't half as bad as the pain she was feeling now. *Dear God, I know you have a plan for us, but how can the death of my son fit into your plan? Is that punishment for the life I have lived, or is this retribution you seek? If I could only take those years back, I would. Father, show me how to go on with this guilt on my soul.*

The rap on the door was soft but insistent. Finally Sadie whispered, "Come in"

Harrison appeared in the half open doorway, "I need to talk to you young lady." Making his way to the bedside he began to give Sadie the much-needed therapy she would understand.

"Knowing you like I do, I'm sure you have found some way to take the blame for this. In the first place, you did not shoot your son. Some crazy son-of-a-bitch did that for God knows what reason, and in the second place you have been a decent human being all your life. You accepted what life threw at you and did your very best. No one could ask for more. If Kate and Jessie were here, they would agree with me"

"I know you are trying to make me feel better but I don't think I will ever get over this. It's so unnatural. The children are supposed to outlive the parents. This is a grief too hard to bear. It should have been me," she lamented. With this said she began to sob, her body was wracked with great convulsive sobs of agony. She sobbed herself to sleep.

Harrison tiptoed out of her room and down the stairs to the others below. James was the first to ask, "How is she taking it? I worry about her now more than ever."

"She is a strong woman; she will survive, believe me. This is the hardest thing she has ever had to accept, but she will come out of it even stronger."

Sid sat quietly watching the two men as her mind planned strategies to make Sadie's agony bearable. She hurt for her mother-in-law with a pain as deep as any mother could. No one knew that she and James were going to become parents, and now was not the time to announce the news. She would tell James tonight and let him decide when to tell his mother.

Goldie kept staring at Sid. When she caught the girl's eye, she winked. *What was that all about,* Sid wondered. *Has she guessed my secret? She couldn't possibly know that I'm with child. James doesn't even know yet.*

"My God, Harrison, whatever possessed that fool to kill my brother? I know these are violent times but murder never solved anything! I have such a rage in me that if that fool was here right now I'd want to kill him! I don't savor that emotion. It makes me feel less than human."

"I know, son, I feel the same way, but you can't lower yourself to their level. We must remain rational even in times like these."

James sat at the table with his head in his hands, his shoulders shaking, but not a sound was heard. Sid wanted to go to him and take him in her arms till the pain was gone but she knew he must get the bitterness out before he could begin to mend. Why can't men just give in and weep freely? Why must they give in to convention? Damn it, whoever said that men shouldn't cry, should be hung!

"Has anyone heard from Mr. Vandermeer," asked Goldie, hoping to ease the tensions in the room, "I wonder how things are going at their place."

"I talked to him this morning,"answered Harrison, "both he and the doctor have decided it would be best if Josie were placed in a sanatorium until she came come to terms with Jonathan's death. That poor woman has completely gone over the edge with this and who can blame her. I only hope for the child's sake she comes out of it soon."

The morning of the funeral started out with a cold rain, which soon turned into a full-fledged storm. The wind ripped at the umbrella of the people in line out side the church waiting to pay their respects to a notable politician and friend to labor. Others came to see the great laid low as people have done since the beginning of time.

One of the men in line began to tell his wife about the gossip that was circulating how Jonathan's stand on immigration for the Jews is what got him killed or at least that was the theory the police were going on. It was said one of the men in the crowd on that fatal day had identified the shooter as a Nazi hothead who had been recruiting around the docks for the last year. Another of the dockhands reported to police the existence of a Bund forming here in the city. The police stated that they have been watching it and its members for some time but found no cause to do more. Gossip ran rampant through the waiting mourners; it helped to keep their minds off the drenching rain.

The church was silent except for a cough or two, a clearing of throats once in a while and a strangled sob from the line of mourners filing by the casket. It seemed to echo through the hushed church.

Sadie stood very stiff and still, taking each hand that was offered, showing a sad little smile and nodding her head. She didn't hear a word they said but she nodded anyway. When she could no longer stand she made her way with James's help to the nearest pew and sat down. The line continued to file past the bier and then to where Sadie sat waiting to acknowledge them.

Sadie could tell the difference between the mourners. Even in her state of shock she held a sense of resentment toward those who came to gape at the important people who were honoring her son. She also knew that they were waiting like vultures for one of the family to cause a scene or behave badly. *Damn them,* she thought. *We are made of sterner stuff than that; we'll show them.* She kept her head held high when she left the church with James at her side.

He felt her tighten her shoulders, stand a little taller and he unconsciously joined her in the demonstration of pride.

Sadie's brother David and his wife Sarah and child were at the funeral, but had to leave right after the closing of the grave. David had accepted an offer to go to Africa as a missionary and their boat was leaving that same day. When they put their belongings aboard, the Captain told him that the sailing time could not be changed, be there or he would sail without them.

Sadie wished them well on their endeavor, but she didn't realize what she was saying or how far they were going away from the family. She was still in a fog of disbelief.

Josie was not at the funeral. She had never stopped screaming. Her voice was gone, but her face was frozen in a grimace of the primal scream.

The days dragged exceedingly slowly for Sadie. James and Sid had to get back to their home and work and the house was quiet as a tomb for Harrison and Sadie.

Goldie did her best to cheer them, but to no avail. *Hell,* she thought, *I'm no singer but if it will make this house sound lived in I'll sing to high heaven!*

The winter dragged by for Sadie, but when James called and announced the news that Sid was pregnant she now had something to look forward to.

In the spring, the gardener tried to interest Sadie in some special roses he was cultivating and splicing, but she couldn't seem to concentrate on what he was telling her. All she could think of was the many times she had chastised Jonathan for his foolhardy adventures. She wished in her heart that she could remember herself praising him more. *Regrets always seem to follow the loss of someone we love,* she reflected.

James couldn't wait to call and tell his mother the wonderful news. He was father to a little girl and her name was April. Sadie felt a stirring in her numbed brain and heart, *a child, new life, Thank You, God! She had always heard that God sends a new soul to replace the one He had chosen to call home with Him. Maybe this child will help me to survive the loss of my adventuresome son, Jonathan. Lord, please keep this child safe. I don't think I can survive the loss of another loved one. April,* she mused *born in the month of April and she will be a harbinger of spring and new life. How appropriate.*

Chapter Twenty-Six
Breath of Life

On the morning of the third week after the funeral, Mr. Vandermeer called Sadie and asked if they could meet for dinner that evening.

"Yes," she answered, "but I really don't feel like having dinner in town. Could you please come to Peaceful Valley and have dinner with Harrison and me?"

"Yes, I will do that and thank you for seeing me so soon after your great loss."

She hung up the telephone and pondered what he could want now. He had always been a private man even with his daughter. Why would he be coming to see her? Well, no sense in worrying about it right now. I will find out soon enough. I'd better let Goldie know we are having a guest for dinner.

Goldie was ecstatic; she was more than ready to cook for a guest and she needed to keep busy. The way these two picked at their food, they really don't need a cook. Beside, she would like to fatten up that Harrison; he could use another ten pounds on that tall frame.

When Mr. Vandermeer arrived, Goldie took his coat and hat, hung them in the closet and showed him to the den where Sadie and Harrison were waiting.

Harrison was leaning against the fireplace mantle, wineglass in hand looking very old and tired.

Sadie sat in a chair close to the burning logs, her hair shining with the reflections of the bright flame. She too looked old and tired, worn from the battle of life.

After accepting some wine, Mr. Vandeermeer got right to the reason for his visit.

"The doctor has told me it may take years before Josie will be well enough to care for the child and Josie's nanny is too old to care for such a small girl.

298

I was hoping you would consent to take the child and raise her here away from the city."

The shock on Sadie's face told the whole story; she had completely forgotten the child in her own selfish grief.

"Of course we will. She's welcome here as long as she needs us." The words burst forth from her mouth in a torrent of excitement.

Suddenly the room took on an aura of new life. *This is what we need,* Sadie thought, *the presence of youth to help us mend our broken hearts.*

All through the dinner they discussed moving the child to Peaceful Valley as quickly as possible. The three of them felt a sense of accomplishment. Goldie had heard the news as she served the meal and was delighted.

"Thanks be to God," she exclaimed, "a little one is just what we need to brighten our days."

Sadie agreed with her; it always brought her a sense of rejuvenation when she had a child to care for. She remembered the day so many years ago when she first saw Rachael, and the satisfaction she felt when that child became her responsibility. She felt the coldness begin to thaw at the idea of another child in the house and a grandchild at that.

Harrison fell in love with the very idea of being uncle to this little ball of energy.

From the moment Emily was carried in, the household became hers. She dominated their very existence.

Sadie knew she shouldn't get too attached to Emily, but she couldn't help herself. No one had called the little girl anything except "the child" till now. "Well, we'll change that," she promised the baby sleeping in her lap.

"The world is changing all around us, but the process of life goes on," Sadie commented to Harrison one afternoon while working in the den. "We have been through so many changes over the years and still we go on. A lot of our friends are gone and here we are raising Emily. Can you believe that?"

"I didn't know if you wanted me to stay and help you with our girl," whispered Harrison. "I'm so attached to her it would be difficult to leave, but I will if you want me to."

"Oh my God, no, Harrison, please don't even think of leaving me with this little handful to raise by myself."

It was settled. Harrison became a permanent part of the household.

Goldie was in seventh heaven, the family was growing larger instead of smaller, and she wouldn't have to leave and find another place to work. Besides she felt like family here. Her days became a round of cooking, baking and fixing special foods for Emily. Since she had gotten over the sleepless nights of teething, she was like a bottomless pit. They couldn't fill her up.

The first step she took was a major event in the household and telephone calls went out to everyone in the family.

The years seemed to melt away with the busy schedule of Peaceful Valley.

When Emily turned seven, Sadie hired a tutor for her, a plain little woman named Jane who spoke French and German fluently. She taught her student reading, and writing in English, French and German. She worshiped the ground Emily walked on. Jane became an important part of Emily's young life. The years flew by on the laughter of the delightful Emily.

One evening as they sat reading and discussing the news, Sadie stopped rocking and laid the paper down on the floor by her chair. Turning to face Harrison she announced, "I have been thinking of deeding this place over to a charity for the placement of homeless young women. How does that sound to you? You know John always said he wanted to do something for the lord. Well, maybe this is it. We could do it in his name."

"Are you sure you want to give this lovely old home to a bunch of girls that come from nowhere," asked Harrison?

"Old friend, don't you remember where you found me. I was homeless. Without any means of support and you took me under your wing and helped me to survive. Now you look down your nose at girls in similar situations. You fussy old poop, I suppose you're going to tell me you knew I was going to survive all along," she teased.

"Well, I know you're not going to believe me, but I swear to God you were something special. Everyone who ever came in contact felt the same way. Sadie, you know I would go along with whatever you suggest because you always have worried about the downtrodden. Besides, James is the one you should be talking to, James and Katy both."

"I'm planning a surprise trip back to Michigan for Emily's fourteenth birthday next week and I will talk to Katy while we are out there visiting. I know James will agree.

"I need to get my affairs straightened out for the future of the family. James is doing very well and doesn't need my help. Emily only needs me for day-to-day support, she will inherit all the Vandermeer money and I've made a sizable bequest to Goldie for her years of service to our family. I really don't know what we would have done without her all these years. She is like one of the family to me. Remember when she even tried to sing when I was so withdrawn after the funeral? She couldn't carry a tune, but she didn't care. I thanked God when she stopped though, I didn't want to ask her to stop and hurt her feelings, but I was thankful when she did." Harrison had to chuckle at the memory. He had wanted to ask Goldie to please stop, too, but hadn't had the heart.

The day that Emily turned fourteen, Sadie told her about the surprise trip. She and her grandmother were going to visit her cousins in Michigan. They would be gone a month; Harrison was not feeling up to the trip, so he would wait for them at home.

Emily was excited about the trip. She confided in her cousin and best friend April that she wanted to see her other cousins again, especially her favorite cousin, Seth. They had often come here to visit, but now she could see where they lived.

Seth said lakes almost surround the state where he lives. Bethany Ann is the oldest and Emily thought she was the prettiest and smartest girl in the whole world and adored the ground she walked on. She had a whole lot of cousins, but she liked Seth the best. He seemed to know her every thought and mood. He was her constant companion when his family visited New York.

She was anxious to see her cousins again, but she was going to miss Uncle Harrison, the only Papa she ever knew. Miss Jane was going on vacation for that month leaving Goldie and Harrison to take care of the house.

The morning of their trip came none too soon for Emily. She hugged Harrison as though she would never let go. Tears welled in his eyes when he thought about that long month ahead, without his adopted family.

Emily talked all the way to Michigan, while Sadie stared through the train window, her mind wandering back to the trip to New York so many years ago. She remembered with apprehension the changes and the attitudes they would encounter in that strange place. Her mind dredged up memories, both good and bad, which had molded her life. *Some made me stronger,* she admitted to herself, *but they also tore away a piece of my heart.* A sad little smile crossed her face when she thought about the first trip back to her home state. God, she had expected so much and was sorely disappointed when it didn't work out. *What a foolish young girl I was,* she mused. *I thought the world was centered on what I wanted. That surely was a big mistake!*

When they reached the train depot in Detroit, a cascade of memories washed over Sadie. John, my dear John, he loved this town so much; he wouldn't recognize it today, it has grown into a metropolis. *Now where did I pick up that word,* she asked herself?

The ride to Bay City was in one of the new fleet of Balcer buses, designed for comfort during the long trip. They even had headrests so you could sleep if you cared to. The driver was a pleasant young man with a warm smile, and a cheery voice that announced the sites as they passed them. After they left the city the drone of the motor was the only sound they heard.

Sadie wished the young fellow would keep on talking; it kept her mind occupied with thoughts other than the painful old memories.

Katy and Jared were waiting at the bus terminal; the other children were at home with Bethany, she was their eldest, no longer a child, but her parents refused to see her any other way.

Jared had long ago sold the newspaper and gone into the salt mine business, did well and sold that enterprise and bought a coal mine. That was the business that allowed him to live well and support their ten children.

Katy was very active in the Ladies Benevolence Society, a club for the prominent ladies in town to show their goodness and mercy for the less fortunate.

"Mother, why didn't you fly home for this vacation? You can certainly afford it and it would have saved you and Emily a long tedious trip."

"My dear, I know I can afford to fly, but I'm just not comfortable with the thought of being so high in the sky. You young people are in too much of a hurry these days anyway."

"May we fly home, Grandma?" asked Emily. "Please, please, please?"

"We'll see," answered Sadie, " but in the meantime, let's just enjoy our visit."

The days flew by in a flurry of parties, picnics and lazy days spent at the beach in Linwood. Jared had built a lovely bungalow on the water in Linwood and it was the ideal setting for getting reacquainted with Michigan.

Emily fell in love with the woods and streams of the northern part of the state. She and Seth spent hours fishing and wading in the Au Sable River.

"She is so much like her father." Sadie told Katy, "Sometimes it breaks my heart."

"Jared and I noticed it, too, but that's a good thing, Mom, because every once in a while I forget what he looked like. She looks enough like him to remind me."

"Well, I can see his every feature. Every funny look, the lock of hair that always stuck up no matter how often he wet it down, even the crooked tooth he showed when he smiled." After a moment she murmured, "Mothers are like that. You are, too. You are a good mother. I hope you never have to go through the hell of losing a child. It's against all the laws of nature."

Jared went with Sadie to help her get the tickets for the trip back to New York and home. Emily had won; they were flying home on the following Saturday.

The last few days were bittersweet for Emily and Seth. They spent much of their time wandering hand in hand through the woods surrounding the Meijer House.

Sadie watched with some concern, remembering how she felt at that age. She knew that love can start in the very young, as it had done for her. She never remembered a time she didn't love Marcus. Even now she could feel his presence with her. Some loves can transcend the ages. She firmly believed that. *Dear God, if Emily is destined to have such a love, please let it be a love she will not regret.*

Katy came up behind her mother at the window. Looking out she saw the two young people hand in hand, strolling toward the house. She squeezed her mother's hand saying, "I know, I worry too."

Sadie and Emily boarded the plane in Detroit, both silent, both thinking of time spent with loved ones. In what seemed like moments to Sadie and they were at the airport in New York. Harrison was waiting in the depot, wearing a silly, playful grin. He teased Emily, winked at Sadie, and she wondered what he was up to now.

At the house they found out! Goldie was a bit shy about telling Sadie, but her glowing face told the whole story.

She and Harrison had opened their hearts to each other, went to the Justice of the Peace, and became husband and wife. Harrison was ecstatic; his face didn't seem wide enough for the grin he was wearing.

Emily ran to them and wrapped her arms around them in a bear hug and giggling, wished them a long and happy life.

Sadie sat in shock. It never occurred to her that Harrison would ever marry. She pulled her thoughts together and wished them both well. Goldie noticed her reserved attitude, but held her tongue.

When they had settled down from all the excitement of the homecoming and announcement, Sadie apologized for not being as excited as they were but it had come as such a shock.

"Harrison has always been single and I guess I thought he would continue that way, but I am very happy for you both."

"We will have to consider finding another cook. We can't have your wife working here as a domestic," Sadie added

"The hell you say," piped up Goldie. "I know what this family likes and how to fix it. No stranger is going to take my place. The only change that needs to take place is moving my things to Harrison's rooms. Right, Honey?"

"My Dear, what ever you say," Honey said, with a foolish grin.

Sadie was happy for her friends; each day seemed better for both of them. Their happiness lit up every room they entered.

One morning, while having tea on the balcony with Goldie, she broached the subject of the age difference, and slyly asked Goldie how old she was.

Goldie smiled and answered, "I know what you're getting at Sadie, Harrison is much older than I, but I've gone over all that in my mind. I'm ready to face the world without him, if need be. In the meantime, we're together. Harrison tells me he has never been happier. If I can give him that, I'll take my chances on the rest. Nobody knows how long he or she has on this earth. If we can grab a little happiness without hurting anyone, that's what we are going to do."

"You're right, of course, I have only to look at him to see he is happy and content. I'm glad that I was here to see that. He has had so many disappointments in his life. It is a blessing to see him finally win a little tranquility

Life in Pleasant Valley was just that, pleasant and fulfilling. The days were filled with the gardens, piano recitals, and visits from friends and family. Picnics and short jaunts around the ever-growing city of New York were the many fairs in the summer and skiing and bobsledding in winter.

Sadie had gone into town to see her attorney about the final codicil of her will. She wanted to make sure everything was set for the house to be used as a home for homeless girls, once she was gone. She planned on the rents from the building she still owned to maintain the house and grounds. She had planned everything down to the last tee so why was she feeling so apprehensive today? She racked her brain trying to think of anything she could have forgotten. I hate it when I get these feelings; nothing good ever comes from them. I hope I'm wrong but so far they always precede a bad event. I guess I'll just have to wait and see what it is. I'm getting too old for this.

The morning of Emily's fifteenth birthday the doorbell rang and rang again insistently.

Goldie hurried from the kitchen wiping her hands on a towel that was tucked in the belt at her waist.

"Just a minute, for Pete's sake, I'm coming, I'm coming." She opened the door and there stood a young woman, wild eyed and fidgeting with the buttons on her coat. She pushed past the outraged Goldie and headed for the stairs.

"Now just a darn minute, who are you and what do you want here?"

"I'm here to get my daughter, I know she's here. I've watched this house for two days and I saw that bitch Sadie coming and going. I want Emily now!"

Harrison hearing the shouting came in from the garden, where he had been smoking a cigar, stopped in his tracks, took a second look, then greeted Josie.

Taking her arm, he led her struggling against his firm grip, into the drawing room, sat her in a large winged chair, and poured her a brandy.

She slapped the glass out of his hand and it shattered into a million pieces against the fireplace. He stood still for a moment, then spun on his heel and headed for the kitchen to get a broom to clean up the mess.

Goldie braced herself to prevent the woman from going up to Emily's room. The child had been in her bed for a couple of days with a cold and didn't need this wild woman bursting in on her. When Harrison came back into the room, he introduced Goldie to Josie as an after thought.

"Oh, I know who she is, I remember her very well. I also remember how bad mannered she was and still is!" Goldie shot out in Josie's direction.

Josie's face flamed with embarrassment, but her manner became more hostile. She hunched forward in the chair as if ready to make a dash for the stairs guarded by Goldie.

Walking in, Sadie took one look at her daughter-in-law and went to her. Taking Josie in her arms she tried to soothe the distraught woman. She hugged the frail young woman, telling her how glad she was to have her back home.

"We must go up and see Emily. She has been fighting a bad cold, but I'm sure she will be delighted to see you."

Josie pulled away from the surprised Sadie and shouted, "You have stolen my baby, she is mine and you can't have her. You just wait until Jonathon gets home and finds out what you're up to."

Sadie and Harrison both tried to talk to the irate woman but to no avail.

Josie began to cry, moan and then the screaming started.

It almost shattered everyone's eardrums.

"Oh God, Harrison, she still is not well. I wonder why she has been released."

The doorbell rang again and it was Mr. Vandermeer and two young men in white uniforms, they tipped their hats and waited for Mr. Vandermeer to tell them what to do.

"I'm so sorry, Sadie, but Josie was released from the sanitarium last week and I was hoping to catch her before she found her way here. I would have told you, but I didn't want you to worry. These men will take her back to the hospital and we don't even have to tell Emily she was here."

"No, Grandfather, you can't do that." Emily, having heard the shouting, came down unnoticed and was standing just inside the door. "I already know who she is and why she's here. Hello, Mother, I'm sorry to see you're not feeling well, but I know you will be better soon."

"You're not my child," the woman screamed. "My baby is somewhere here in this house and I'm going to find her! You can't keep my baby from me any longer. She's mine. Do you understand me? She's mine! Mine! Mine!"

The two men looked to Mr. Vandermeer for direction; he nodded his head toward the door. They held the struggling woman and forcibly dragged her to the waiting ambulance. She fought like a wild woman, but they finally got her into the back and strapped her down so she couldn't hurt herself or them.

Sadie went to her granddaughter and held her. She knew the feeling of rejection, Emily must be feeling and she wanted to protect her from any more hurt.

Miss Jane walked in, took one look at her charge and hustled her back to bed. Her face was filled with rage at the suffering that her little Emily had gone through. Why couldn't that bitch have stayed away from this house? Why did she have to come and upset everyone? Miss Jane's mind was filled with unanswerable questions.

Mr. Vandermeer couldn't apologize enough; he kept blaming himself for everything.

Sadie asked, "When did she get released? Did the doctors think she was well? What happened?"

He explained the puzzle as well as he could, but some of the pieces were missing.

"Josie's mother, Adie, had returned from Europe a month ago and claimed she wanted to reunite with her family. She had spent all her settlement from the separation on high living and willing young men. Now that she was no longer the belle of the ball she wanted to return to her child and me. She didn't have time for us when Josie was small or when she first fell ill, but now she wants to intrude herself back into our lives. Adie slyly talked the doctors into releasing Josie to her. She said she was taking Josie to Europe with her. Adie must have figured that's the only way I would let her back into my house. It seems that Josie had other plans and here we are."

306

"God, what a mess," exclaimed Harrison.

"What are we going to tell Emily?" asked Mr. Vandermeer.

"That's easy. We tell her the truth, just not all of it. There is no earthly reason why she has to know the sordid side of her grandmother's life," replied Sadie. "We all have things in our lives that are better left buried."

"You're right," agreed Emily's grandfather. "You know, it seems like a thousand years ago that I loved that woman. Adie was sweet and kind and oh, so beautiful, but she changed as soon as we got back from our honeymoon in Europe. We spent a month in Paris and she fell in love with the country and the people. She never was the same after we came home. I guess she loved Paris more than Josie and me."

Harrison watched this lonely, abandoned old man and silently thanked God for Goldie.

Goldie went to Harrison, sat on the arm of his chair, and reached for his hand in recognition of his thoughts.

Sadie felt a twinge of jealousy when she saw the melding of spirit between these two lovers. Marcus and I had that, and I'm glad Harrison and Goldie can share that gift.

"You know, Mr. Vandermeer, Josie's mother reminds me of a cat I once had. I picked it up in an alley, fed it and gave it my love. When it was well, it would follow me around like a dog, but when the call of nature came, the cat left. It couldn't help itself. It had to follow the call. Some people are like that; they love us but that siren call is too strong in them. They must answer that call even if it hurts them."

"Thank you, Sadie, that is the first time I have ever heard it put like that. I know Adie loved us at one time, but I thought she had stopped caring when she left us. Now I know she must have heard that siren call and couldn't resist. You have lifted a weight from my heart. Thank you, thank you!"

Emily took the news of her mother's relapse much better than anyone expected.

Miss Jane watched over her every move, ready to step in at the first sign of distress. She need not have worried about the resilient young lady; Emily was growing more lovely and self-confident every day. She excelled in both French and German and was a willing student. The whole household was very proud of their little girl.

As the months went tumbling by, one after another, the whole incident was forgotten until the news of Josie's suicide by hanging was blasted across the front page of the New York Times one Saturday morning. The private hospital had tried to keep the story from reaching the press, but failed to realize that one of the attendants was married to a reporter on the newspaper.

Emily had just celebrated her seventeenth birthday and was planning a trip back to Michigan to visit her Aunt Katy when she read the news. The story included the death of her father, the breakdown of her mother and an estimate of her grandfather's wealth and her grandmother's vast holdings.

Sadie felt that the paper had abused her privilege of privacy and caused irreparable harm. Emily was now a sitting duck for anyone who wanted to kidnap her or even worse, marry her for her money.

Katy was furious when she read it and immediately phoned both the owner and the editor to vent her anger about their highhanded manner.

Sadie didn't say anything to anyone; she just bought the paper and fired the editor and the reporter.

Emily left for Michigan on the next available flight. Her heart was singing. She was about to see Seth again.

"It has been three years, I wonder if he has changed much," she mused. "The last time we were together we made a lot of silly promises to each other. I wonder if Seth remembers. Probably not, we were so young."

Seth met her at the airport and gently took her in his arms. Cradling her head on his shoulder, he kissed her cheek.

Emily could feel his heart wildly beating, matching her own thump, thump, thump. *Dear God, he hasn't forgotten, we still care for each other. What will happen now?*

Out of the crowd stepped a lovely young woman with friendly gray eyes and bright red hair, her hand held out in a gesture of welcome. With questioning eyes, Emily took the extended hand and searched the depth of the soft gray eyes and found an answer she didn't want to see. Seth placed his arm around the woman's shoulder, and squeezing gently, he introduced his wife Linda to Emily.

She managed to acknowledge her cousin's wife and not faint dead away. She didn't want to admit that she was broken hearted. She had foolishly dreamed of coming here, being greeted with open arms and rushed to the altar. It was going to be a long two weeks for the devastated Emily.

Katy knew the moment she saw the girl that the pain of rejection and loneliness heavy on her shoulders. If only she could have spared the child she would have, but she also knew that the only way Emily would accept it was to be here and see Seth and Linda together. She had talked to Sadie about it and they had decided the only way for Emily to be given a chance to get over her love for Seth was to see him as someone else's husband. After all, first cousins aren't supposed to marry.

Emily came home a different person. The joy no longer radiated from her face and her smile came slowly now. She didn't sing when she worked in the garden and she spent too much time alone in her room.

As the weeks went by she began to change back into the happy smiling girl that they all knew and loved, but there was a small part that remained reserved, she was growing up. Emily was becoming a woman.

On her eighteenth birthday, she decided to go to a university to study to be a doctor. When she told Uncle Harrison he was delighted and very supportive.

Sadie and Goldie were happy she had found something important to occupy her time and hoped that she would meet a handsome young doctor, who would sweep her off her feet.

While they helped her with her shopping and packing, they teased her about the fun and parties that she would be going to and the people she would meet.

"Why, I bet you won't be there a week before you will meet some one exciting," predicted Goldie.

"Don't be ridiculous, I'm going to school to study, not chase boys," retorted Emily.

Harrison was looking drawn and frail these last couple of months, but his mind was as clear as ever. He teased Emily about studying too much, playing too little and about the young men who began showing up at their doorstep.

Chapter Twenty-Seven
Home At Last

One spring day, in the early morning hours, Harrison went home. His spirit had left him while Goldie was holding his body in a loving embrace. He had wakened with a twinge in his chest and tried to lie quietly so as not to disturb her, but she was always sensitive to his every movement.

To Harrison it felt like a kink he had once had in his back, but this time it was in the front beneath his rib cage. He slowly shifted around to relieve pressure, but it stayed where it was and grew stronger.

Goldie was lying still, hoping against hope that it was not what she thought it was.

Maybe if I lie still he will go back to sleep and the discomfort will be gone when he wakes up, she reasoned.

When the pressure turned into pain Harrison could no longer ignore the ripping, tearing spasms that tore through his frail body. He moaned in agony. Goldie turned and took him in her arms, patted him and crooned to him as though he were a child.

He looked into her eyes and said, "You know this is goodbye, don't you? You have made me very happy, but it's time to go home. I love you, my little wife." He closed his eyes, no longer in pain. Goldie lay there for some time with the still warm body of Harrison until her arms could no longer support the limp frame of the kindest man she had ever known.

She slowly got up from her side of the bed, rearranged the blankets around the peaceful looking Harrison and made her way to the bathroom. Sitting on the side of the tub, she let the tears come. When she was nearly drained of grief she went down to prepare the morning meal.

When Sadie came down, Emily and Goldie were sitting on the terrace eating breakfast and watching white clouds scuttling across an azure blue sky.

310

The day was like any other to Sadie, except Harrison must have overslept because he wasn't here to join the conversation. That wasn't like Harrison. He loves the mornings, he must really be tired.

"Isn't Harrison feeling well?" asked Sadie. "Maybe I should send for the doctor."

"That won't be necessary, dear. Harrison passed on this morning," Goldie said quietly. "He knew and was ready to go." Tears spilled down both cheeks and fell on her pink dress leaving a blood-like stain.

Sadie stared at the stain, for a second, watched it grow, her mind repeating, *he's gone.* Harrison is gone. That can't be. He has always been there for me and now he is gone! Sadie rushed to her old friend's side and taking her into her arms she let Goldie release all the pent-up emotions that she had tried to bury out of concern for Emily and Sadie.

Emily sat wide-eyed and waiting. She had never really known anyone, except Mama, who had died and she hadn't really known her. She was at a loss as to what to do. Then the realization set in; she would never see Uncle Harrison again, never again have him tease her, teach her tunes on the piano and join her in those crazy little songs when they were walking. The tears began to fall.

Goldie stood in Sadie's comforting arms and waited for her tears to subside before she began to speak.

"We all loved Harrison, but we have to let go. His spirit was old and in need of rest. Now he's with the Lord. You know Harrison as well as I, and you know as long as we need him he will be here. We must let him go in peace."

"You're right, of course, but, oh, God, I'm going to miss that dear sweet man. He has been a part of my life for so many years."

The day the family laid Harrison to rest, a quiet rain was falling. The crowd was small, just a few friends and family, for he had become family to Sadie, her children and grandchildren. All wanted to be at Uncle Harrison's funeral to say goodbye.

While the minister gave the eulogy, Sadie's mind went back to the first time she had ever seen Harrison. She chuckled to herself. Wonder what these folks would think if they knew how we started out.

Goldie felt Sadie's shaking shoulders and wrongly assumed she was crying again until she looked into Sadie's eyes. There she saw a hint of amusement. She's remembering the good times. That's as it should be. She nodded her head at Sadie and went back to listening to the minister say great things about a man he never knew. When the pallbearers lowered the casket into the waiting earth, the rain stopped and a rainbow shone on the horizon.

"God has stopped crying. One of His children is back home," murmured Sadie and made the sign of the cross.

The world seemed empty and cold without Harrison's ready smile. The two women tried to keep themselves busy with Emily and her many friends, but Harrison had become such an integral part of their lives that it was as though a part of them was missing, too.

Miss Jane had left them the year Emily turned eighteen saying, "I've always wanted to go to Spain and now is my chance. I'm booked on a ship leaving next week. I will write, but remember I will be traveling around a lot so the letters will take time to reach you."

Emily left for college and Miss Jane left for Spain. Goldie and Sadie were left in that big house alone, except for a stray dog that whined at the door to be fed.

After making a half-hearted attempt to find the owners, the women accepted the fact that they were now owners of the animal. He trained them well. He barked when he wanted in or out. When he wanted food, he carried his dish to one of them and when he wanted love he climbed into one of their laps, licked a hand, and nodded off to sleep. Dog, for that's what they decided to name him, became an important part of their lives.

The days became an endless search for chores to fill the long hours between rising in the morning and retiring at night.

Sadie began working in the garden with enthusiasm and dedication for the rose bushes that she felt needed her attention. She even joined a group of ladies who had formed a rose club, trying to fill the empty days. At first it seemed to work, but not for long. Soon Sadie started complaining to Goldie, "All those women want to do is talk about their friends and neighbors and we don't get anything done except gossip. When I first joined, they said it was to raise money for the people on the WPA, you know, help them with a few things to get them started. Now all we do is talk about what we want to do and don't accomplish a thing!"

"Well, Sadie, No one says you have to belong to that group, there must be other clubs you can join, if you have a mind to."

Huh, it seems there's no sympathy from her, thought Sadie.

The one bright spot in an otherwise dull day was Emily's letters. Her accounts of school, her friends, and teachers became the focal point of Sadie's day. The women would set the things out for tea and sit by the fire and read and reread the humor filled letters.

Dog took turns sitting by the two chatting women with his head tilting side to side as though trying to understand why they were chuckling when they held those pieces of paper.

Sadie was having difficulty finding constructive projects to wile away the lonely days.

One Sunday morning after suffering through another boring church service, Sadie ran across an article written by the editor of the local paper that stated the Nazis under Adolph Hitler's orders forcibly herded the Jews of Germany and Russia into ghettos. They also were forbidden to own wireless sets according to the underground information of the editor.

When Sadie read this to Goldie, they both had found a cause. They threw themselves into any plan that had to do with aiding the Jewish people in Germany and Poland.

Goldie's mother and grandmother were still in Germany and their letters told of the inhumane treatment their friends and neighbors were receiving.

Goldie's ninety-three year old grandmother wrote that her friend, Ingrid Elks, had been sent to a camp for sub-humans because she was a gypsy. Goldie's mother wrote in the next letter that Mrs. Elks was dead. She had been forced to strip the clothing from her body, put it on a pile that was as high as her head and then march to a ditch that was filled with the remains of most of the elderly in her village and there she was shot. One of the old men lay in that ditch all day pretending he was dead so he could escape and give an account of the murders.

Goldie felt helpless each time she read a letter from her mother. It especially hurt when her mother asked, "How could this happen in these enlightened time? This is 1937, not the middle ages."

Sadie read the newspapers from front to back, always searching for articles that had to do with Hitler's dreadful war.

"If that man gets away with invading his neighbor lands, he won't stop there. I believe he's greedy enough to swallow up the whole world," Sadie predicted."

"Surely the people of Germany won't let him get away with that. They're still hurting from the last fool that got them into war," remarked Goldie. "I wish Mama would've listened to me and came to America to live. It is so much safer here. Her friends are dying or disappearing right and left, but no, she wouldn't do that. She said she couldn't leave her homeland when it's in trouble."

Goldie now had another dilemma to worry about; her mother and Grandmother's letters had stopped. No warning, they just stopped coming. She had to face the terrible assumption that they were either imprisoned or dead. It was an disquieting time for Sadie's closest companion.

As the months went by Emily's letters began to change. Her letters spoke of meetings and clubs forming to preserve the integrity and purity of the white race. At first it was just a couple of small inferences about the Jews owning the world, then it became almost a chant in her letters. Each letter became increasingly vehement about the Jews being less than human, "Why, they don't even believe in Jesus Christ!"

"That's it," shouted Sadie. "I'm going to call that foolish child and give her a piece of my mind. We have been more than patient with all this crap she has been trying to spoon feed us. I want that child home now if that's all she's learning."

When Sadie finally did reach Emily, the girl was totally astounded that her grandmother didn't understand her point of view.

Sadie tried to reason with the stubborn girl, but to no avail. As a last resort Sadie used the best weapon she had in her arsenal. She told Emily how she was being used and manipulated by the same group who had indoctrinated the man who killed her father.

"That man was a Nazi, too. Those people have been here for years trying to undermine the strength of our country and I won't have a granddaughter of mine consorting with such people!"

Emily couldn't believe it. "I will talk to my friends and prove that isn't true; they are a peaceful group and only want to preserve the Aryan race."

Three days later a repentant Emily called home to apologize for being so foolish and gullible.

"My so called good friends explained to me how sometimes enemies of the party must be eliminated, so the party can grow and flourish. How could I have been such a fool?" she cried, "Will you forgive me?"

"Of course, I forgive you! Now, when are you coming home for Christmas vacation? It is beautiful this morning with the snow falling and the sun sparkling on each flake. We don't have a tree yet. We thought we would wait until you were here to help us pick out the tallest and straightest one in the woods. What would you like for Christmas dinner? Turkey, game hens, or do you have any suggestions?"

"Grandmother, would you mind if I brought a friend for the holidays? She doesn't have anywhere to go. Her parents are in Europe on business and won't be home in time for Christmas. Oh, by the way, I heard from Seth and he thought he might drop by for the holidays since he is going to be in town for a little Christmas shopping at Sach's."

"Of course, bring her. We certainly have enough room and Goldie would love to have two healthy appetites to cook for. She's always scolding me about not eating enough. Do you think that's a sign of old age? The scolding I mean," she said with a twinkle in her eye. "And, of course, we all will be pleased to see Seth. My grandson is always welcome here," but she couldn't control the frown that slid across her thoughtful countenance.

Seth arrived on the third of December and Sadie couldn't help but be reminded of John O'Shonessey, her first husband. Seth was the spitting image of his grandfather. He had the same laughing eyes and smile. Sadie's heart skipped a beat just remembering.

Emily and her friend arrived on the fifth in the late afternoon. Snow had fallen for two days and the house and grounds were a winter wonderland.

Jenny, Emily's friend, had never seen snow and was intrigued by the thoughts of building a snowman and having a snowball fight. The three of them spent all day Saturday playing in the snow and driving around in the horse drawn sled that Sadie kept in the barn.

Sunday morning after church the family sat hashing over plans for the day when the radio that had been playing music in the background suddenly announced, "The Japanese have bombed Pearl Harbor!"

"This has to be wrong," Sadie cried. "We aren't at war with the Japanese or anyone else for that matter." The rest of the day was spent listening to the news reports, how many ships were lost, and how many men were assumed dead. Everyone kept asking, "Where are our planes? What happened to our army?"

Winston Churchill delivered a speech denouncing Japan and declaring the bombing act as a crime that will go down in history as an act of infamy.

"That's it," announced Seth, "I'm heading into town to join the army. We can't let those bastards get away with that."

"What about your wife? Doesn't she get a say in this decision?" asked Sadie"

"Oh, that's all over. We agreed to disagree. I'm free as a bird!"

Emily's face beamed and Sadie's heart sank. *No,* she thought, *not again, not that terrible loneliness and heartbreak for Emily.*

The girls agreed with him and made ready to go back to town to see what they could do to help out. They hadn't finished college yet, but both had some training in the medical field. Sadie talked them into staying until after dinner, but as soon as the meal was over they packed up and left.

They were ready to take on the world, full of righteous indignation as only the very young can be.

Sadie later found out that Emily and Seth had spent a week together before they both went off to war. She had mixed emotions about that news but kept her feeling to herself.

Now the letters came from all parts of the world, white envelopes edged with red and blue. Two days a week were set aside for letter writing and the rest of their days were filled with rolling bandages, knitting socks, visiting hospitals and selling war bonds.

Sadie and Goldie began inviting young men in the armed forces home for a home cooked meal and the house came alive again. With the rationing in effect it was a little hard to get foodstuffs, but they always seemed to manage. Sometimes one of the guests would play the Baby Grand that stood in the parlor. Many times the young people would gather around the piano singing. For those few hours the war was forgotten.

That horrible war that was supposed to be over in months, dragged into a year and the end was nowhere in sight.

When a sobbing Katy called saying that Seth had been killed on Guadacanal, Sadie sat for hours just staring off into space. Goldie and James tried getting some help for her, but the life had drained slowly away from her spirit. She suddenly felt very old and tired; all she wanted to do was sleep.

"Thank God they had that week together," she told her picture of Marcus, "they too were cheated, my sweet."

Emily wrote from an island called Okinawa, saying she would be in the states for R&R and she was hoping to see Sadie soon. Sadie smiled as she read the letter and sadly told Goldie, "I hope she gets here while I'm still alive."

James came and talked quietly to his mother for hours trying to ease her grief, but to no avail. Shrugging his shoulders, he went to the kitchen and explained to Goldie that Sadie wanted to rest and needed time to think.

"At her age she's earned a break from this crazy war and she can have it as far as I'm concerned."

Dog seemed to be the only one that understood. He had begun sleeping in Sadie's room in the fall of that year. Her room was always warm and cozy.

Sometimes, her talking in her sleep would awaken Dog. He would lie on the floor tail wagging, listening as though he knew what she was talking about. His ears would twitch and every so often he would emit a low growl.

On this night, feeling extremely chilled, Sadie got up and going to the cedar chest, opened it and began digging until she found the last quilt. Wrapping it around her shoulders she lowered herself into the rocker by the window. Clutching the quilt closer she began to rock, her eyes reflecting her inner peace. Rocking gently, her mind went back to her, long life, the many friends she met along the way and the oh-so-short of a time with Marcus. She smiled as she thought of the love and warmth they had shared.

Dog lay watching, tail barely wagging, waiting to see what she would do next.

Her smile grew wider as she gazed upon the face of her beloved Marcus. She hadn't heard him come into the room. No, wait. He's been gone for many years. How could she have forgotten? He had come for her at last. She rose and took his hand.

Goldie found her sitting slumped in her favorite rocker with a hint of a smile on her serene face.

Dog began to howl a sad lament that went on until Goldie came over and kneeling by the distraught animal released her own despair at losing a friend.

Emily made it home just in time for her grandmother's funeral.

On the way from the gravesite, after a very private funeral, the two men in the hearse were carrying on a conversation about the rich, old gal who had just died.

"Who the hell was she anyway?" asked the younger man.

"Well," answered the driver, "I hear tell she was stinking rich. Made it in the restaurant business a lotta years ago. Owns a newspaper and a whole block in the city. Course, then there's some say she was a famous madam, made her money running a whorehouse. But that's jist rumor. Some folks say she was good to the poor, then there's some say she was a bitch. She's been called a lot of names, but most folks just called her Sadie."

The End

Printed in the United States
35557LVS00005B/1-45

9 781413 731712